REA

ACPL
DISCARDED

P9-EDI-990

FEB 1 0 2004

Walk Like A Natural Man

Walk Like A Natural Man

M. Dion Thompson

Published by BlackWords Press
PO Box 21, Alexandria, VA 22313
info@blackwordsonline.com
www.BlackWordsonline.com

BlackWords Press and the portrayal of
the Fist with the Pencil are trademarks of BlackWords, Inc.

Publisher: Stephanie S. Stanley
Book Design: Do The Write Thing

ISBN 1-888018-27-5
LCCN: 2003107429

All of the characters in this book are fictitious, and any resemblance
to actual persons, living or dead, is purely coincidental.

First Edition:
Printed in the United States of America
1 3 5 7 9 10 8 6 4 2

Publishing Fine Black Literature since 1995

to Mama Jennie

"There is decidedly an opportunity for advancement for Negroes in motion picture. And so, if there are any among you who have definitely decided to gamble with your future, to take some money and some time, along with all your energy and ambition and interest, and throw them on the gaming table, the stakes for which you play will be worth the effort. Therefore, the cry of today is typical of that of yesteryear. 'Go west, young man. Go west.'   —Ted Yates, Harlem Writer's Project, 24 February 1938

"Rejoice, O young man, in thy youth; and let thy heart cheer thee in the days of thy youth, and walk in the ways of thine heart." —Ecclesiastes, Chapter 11, verse 9

ACKNOWLEDGEMENTS

Any book takes time to be born and must be attended to by numerous midwives. In order of no particular importance, I would like to thank John Rechy, who assisted in the beginning; Susan Avery Brown, who passed on before the book's completion, but always kept the faith; Stephanie and Kwame Alexander, for believing in this book; Allegra Bennett, for making it better; Jessie Wilson, for bringing me into this world and sharing her love of language; my dear wife, Jean, who gave up numerous nights with little complaint; my son, Tevin, for smiles and wonder; and to God for countless blessings.

Prologue

SKIP COULD HEAR WILLIE RIDING THROUGH THE DAWN, THE TRUCK horn sounding like scared guinea hens as it busted up another dream about the fantastic life going on in Harlem, Chicago, Hollywood, places filled with sleek limousines and jazz clubs, sharp papas and good looking gals living the moving picture life. He pulled the covers tight around his lean, well-muscled body, rolled over and tried to go back to sleep. But it was no use. Willie had sounded the alarm.

Mornings began with Willie highballing down the newly paved strip of asphalt Roosevelt's PWA boys had slapped on the bottom lands by the Brazos and named Highway 53; began with him pounding the horn as his '32 flatbed Ford raced past the cabins and shotgun shacks along the road, and in those houses there was stirring and grumbling because it seemed too early for Willie to be coming around again.

"Get up, boy. I knows you awake." That was Grandma Sarah, swinging her feet onto the cold, wooden floor, wincing against the arthritic pain shooting through her body as she dressed and put on the old brogans she'd cut holes in to let her feet breathe. She thumped Skip's pallet on her way out. "Ain't no need of tarrying."

She was right. Willie was coming and he wanted to get his crew to Sam Willard's plantation while the cotton was still heavy with dew. The extra weight could add a quarter to everybody's pay. Skip sighed. Best get ready. No time for a tune on the National Steel guitar propped against the foot of his bed. No time to snatch the dog-eared copy of Photoplay magazine from the shelf by his bed and flip through the worn pages until he came to the advertisement for the Ezekiel Washington Colored Actor's School.

"Come to Hollywood and be in the movies," the ad read, the words coming from a handsome, smiling, well-dressed black man standing in front of Paradise Studios. Another quote boldly proclaimed: "If it wasn't for Ezekiel Washington's acting school, I'd be just another cotton picking fool. So, why don't you fill out the form, and I'll see you in Hollywood."

The ad teased Skip with Hollywood dreams and he had taken the bait, mailed his five-dollar registration fee to Los Angeles and waited, even prayed because Grandma Sarah always said God couldn't help you if you didn't call His name. But God hadn't answered, yet. So, Skip put aside his daydreams. Willie was coming. And before too long he'd be in the fields, and the old folks would be singing, "I am bearing the names of many, trying to get home," and somebody might call out a name they wanted carried across Jordan. Up and down the long rows they would go, working hard and fast, fingers pricked and bleeding. However, no one slowed. Saturday was payday.

Walk Like a Natural Man

QUITTING TIME. THE SUN BEGINNING ITS AFTERNOON DECLINE. Skip dropped the heavy cotton sack from his shoulder, glad to be rid of the cutting strap. He stretched his aching back, swallowed hard to work some spit down his dry, dust-caked throat. Streaming sweat stung his eyes and splashed on his lips. He licked it away, tasting salt and dirt. All around him, people dropped the burdens they had dragged up and down the cotton rows. They trudged towards the pay line, an exhausted army worn out by the accumulated fatigue of a week in the fields. Skip figured he'd picked close to one hundred pounds, a good haul for a half-day's work. He'd caught a good rhythm, lost himself in the steady labor. Another five minutes and he would have finished another row. But there was always another day, or someone else.

The line moved quickly, then stopped. People started murmuring and whispering among themselves. Skip leaned out from the line. Up ahead, Billie Dee Josephs pleaded with Sam Willard. The white man's jaws worked viciously on a wad of chewing tobacco. He rolled his eyes, half-listened to his sharecropper, another nigger crying. Two strong, well-muscled young men stood waist-deep in the cotton truck, waiting for the next sack.

"But Mister Willard, sir," said Billie Dee. "I been keeping tabs on my work and I believe you still owes me a dollar."

"Now Billie Dee, you trying to say you're a better mathematician than me?" Willard grinned, leaning on the weighing scale.

"Matma—-?" Confusion furrowed Billie Dee's brow. His mind struggled to understand Willard's big word. He stood a few moments, hanging his head and pawing the ground with his shoes. Then he looked up, defeated. "'Scuse me, Mister Willard. But what do that matmatishin mean?"

"It means who do you think is better at figuring? You, who ain't had but this much schooling?" Willard held his thumb and forefinger close together, leaving barely enough space to pass a needle through. "Or me, who finished high school and got a diploma hanging on the sitting room wall? Besides, I had to make deductions for your sugar and meal. Them boys of yours are growing pretty fast. I declare, they'd probably eat me out of house and home."

Back down the line, Skip felt a bad taste, nauseous and awful, boiling across his tongue. He gulped it down, clenched his fists against the outrage building inside him. Maybe Willard had been fair. Lord knows Billie Dee couldn't add. But Willard could just as easily be cheating Billie Dee and there was nothing the sharecropper or any other colored person in Tunis could do about it. Billie Dee stood silently. He was a lean man, his muscles stringy from too much work and not enough meat. He spat a long stream of reddish-brown tobacco juice into the dirt.

"Guess you right," he mumbled, looking away.

"'Course I am," Willard said. "I'm a fair man, Billie Dee. You know that." He counted out four dollars. "You ought to teach them boys how to really pick cotton, 'stead of playing around." He handed over the money.

Billie Dee stuffed the pay into his pocket, gave Sam Willard a tight-lipped "thank you" before joining his family beside the sway-backed mule his sons had tied to a chinaberry tree. Next to the haggard mule stood Willard's fine gray mare, coat glistening from countless brushings and years of good feed. Billie Dee's two oldest boys jumped on the mule's back and kicked its flanks. Skip swore the animal's back dipped a bit more as it plodded along, laboring under the weight that had bent its spine.

A few minutes later, and it was his turn. The bad taste was still in his mouth, strong and bitter like stomach acid churning up his gullet. He tried to relax, but he couldn't stop thinking about Billie Dee, couldn't put aside the soul-bending uneasiness he always felt around white men, especially the boss man. Willard seemed to tower over him, though they were nearly the same height. His steely blue eyes fixed on Skip. One of the young men jumped out of the cotton truck and set the scales.

"You been half-stepping this week, boy?" Willard asked as Skip hoisted his sack onto the scale's hook.

"Been doing my share," Skip replied, tense.

The worker toyed with the weights and called out Skip's load. "Ninety-five pounds."

Willard raised an eyebrow. "Wish I had more boys like you. Steady workers, instead of nigras like Billie Dee, who put in just enough work, then accuse me of cheating."

"Best be glad there ain't more boys like me," Skip mumbled.

"Why's that?" Willard frowned, noticing the cold tone in Skip's voice.

"'Cause you wouldn't have any boys at all," Skip said, surprising himself. "We'd all be gone, soon's we got the money to take us on away from here. And I done made my mark."

Willard shrugged. "Nigras will be picking cotton until a machine comes along to replace them." He jotted Skip's tally in his notebook. "I figure you got seven dollars coming. Right?" Skip nodded.

"See," Willard smiled. "I ain't no cheat. You want it all in bills?"

"Gimme some change, too," Skip said.

The worker took Skip's sack off the scale and, with an easy motion, tossed it to his buddy in the truck. Willard peeled three two-dollar bills from his wad, dipped into his bulging pants pocket and pulled out a dollar in change. He dropped the money into Skip's upturned palm. Sunlight glinted off the coins, sending small spears of light into the day.

"This sure ain't much," Skip said, testing the weight in his palm. "Not much at all.

"Hell, boy, you want a king's ransom for picking cotton? It's exactly what you earned," Willard said.

Skip tilted his palm. The money fell. The coins dropped quick, the first one making a dull, empty sound that didn't amount to anything. The other coins landed and made a musical clink. A pile of metal formed, reflecting the sun. Then came the bills, falling gently as autumn leaves. Grandma Sarah whispered fiercely in Skip's ear.

"What you doing, child?"

He did not answer. A wild surge of power had a hold of him. He didn't need Sam Willard's cotton-picking money. He'd already saved up thirty-five dollars, and he was going to Hollywood. He lifted up his right foot and brought it down hard, ground his wages into the dirt, as if they were all the years he had lived in Tunis, abiding by the rules, having no say when it came to the white man.

"Say, boy," cried Willard. "That's good American money you're stepping on. If you don't want it, I can damn well use it." He stooped over.

"It's my money," Skip said through clenched teeth. "I'll do with it what I please. Burn it if I get a notion to."

He looked down, laughed to himself as Willard clawed through the dirt. The crazy feeling teased him with dangerous ideas. He wanted to kick the white man over. Willard grabbed one of the bills, looked up at the impassive black faces staring at him and scrambled to his feet, his face flushed and red with anger. His eyebrows coiled across his forehead. Laughter bubbled from Skip's lips. It seemed like forever before Willard raised his right hand. Skip tried to block the coming blow, but Grandma Sarah pinned his wrists behind his back. Willard's hard backhand slammed against his face. The shock of sudden pain brought Skip back to the reality of this Saturday afternoon in a Tunis cotton field. The crisp crack hung in the dense air. Then there were voices: angry, apologetic, defiant.

"Get off my land, nigger. You're fired. Get off my land, I say!"

Grandma Sarah stepped in front of Skip, her hands held up. "He's sorry, Mister Willard. I don't know what's got into him."

Skip pushed her aside. "I ain't sorry," he yelled. "God dammit, I ain't sorry."

"Get your black ass off this plantation, boy."

The feeling fired through Skip again, this time fed by Willard's insult. He raised his fist. He wanted to hurt Willard, smash him and all of Tunis.

"Go on, boy," Willard said. "Go on and hit me, so's I can lay you out right."

Skip's fist trembled in the air, then fell limp to his side. The feeling wasn't strong enough to carry him further across the line and into violence. He took quick, shallow breaths to calm himself, felt a hot, dry anger in his throat as he bent over to pick up his pay. Willard stepped closer, burying the money under his boot.

"I done already told you, get off my land," he said.

Skip stood and looked into Willard's cold, blue eyes. The plantation boss stared him down until he turned and marched off, his pockets empty. No one said anything to him when he took a seat in back of Willie's truck. He sat alone, face burning with shame and anger, chest heaving up and down. His heart pounded like a trip-hammer worked by a madman. He grabbed hold of the bench, rocked back and forth, cursed himself for losing control. Damn this Tunis, he thought, half wishing he'd kept his mouth shut and at the same time struggling to convince himself that he really didn't need the seven dollars, that in the madness of those moments he had done right by himself. He'd already saved enough to make a break. Across from him, John Lee reclined on the truck bed, head resting against his wife's pregnant belly. The big man closed his eyes, slumped his tired shoulders, then turned, surprise and joy on his face.

"Did you feel that?" he said. "The baby kicked me."

"Yes, honey. I felt it," said Emma, bending over to rub the knotted muscles in her man's back, fingers working in the easy, patient manner a woman uses when preparing a lump of dough for baking.

Skip watched, envious. His body ached too, as much from the work as from his run-in with Sam Willard. Outside, he heard Grandma Sarah pleading for his pay, and he hated her for doing so. She should just let it go.

He was still hanging his head when Miss Hattie, Old Man Williams and Grandma Sarah got on the truck. The old folks didn't seem tired. They knew how to pick cotton. Grandma Sarah sometimes said the best thing about growing old was that a body learned how to live. She said young folks were always in a hurry, killing themselves over work, worrying themselves sick about things they couldn't change. Whenever Skip started talking about his big-city plans, she would smile and shake her head, tell him to pray about it and take his time, because time was the only thing he would have plenty of. She sat next to him now, mopping her brow with a handkerchief, calmly untying her Indian braids and letting her white hair hang loose about her shoulders. Skip licked his lips and sucked down some spit. Grandma Sarah dropped four dollars at his feet.

"You done lost a lot over this little bit of money, child."

"It's just a little bit," Skip said, trying to sound unconcerned.

"If it's so little, then how come you got to make such a fuss?" Grandma Sarah untied the handkerchief in which she kept her pay and let the money fall on the floor. "Now, what you think of that?" She turned to Skip, then to Miss Hattie.

"Girl," said Miss Hattie, squinting through her fading eyes. "That ain't nary enough to set this old mind to worrying."

"But that's what I'm talking 'bout," Skip said, pointing to the money. "It ain't enough to do nothing."

"Oh, hush up, Skip," Miss Hattie said. "Be thankful you got money. Plenty folks these days ain't got two nickels to rub together. What you planning on doing anyway, buying New York City?"

"But shouldn't there be more than . . . than just this?"

"More?" Grandma Sarah said. "Child, you done asked the question that's been bothering folks ever since Adam and Eve was kicked out of the garden. Everybody's wanting more, and some of us, like Billie Dee Josephs, could darn well use some more. How you think he feel? His chirrun go to bed hungry every night, wanting more to eat and he ain't got nothing to give them. Onliest thing he got too much of is hard times."

"And that's what's got him behind that whisky bottle," Miss Hattie chimed in. "Worrying and crying 'cause there ain't enough money or food. Everybody's got them wanting more blues, Skip, even Mister Rockefeller, and he got more than all of Lee County."

"And what about Sam Willard?" Skip said. "How come he got to act like he doing us a favor? Hell, we the ones picking his cotton."

"'Cause he's a white man," Grandma Sarah said. "And that's just his natural way."

"Yes, yes, Lord," said Old Man Williams. "That's why you got to live right, study your Bible and let Jesus take you above this mess." He turned to Skip. "Trust in the Lord, son, and lean not upon thine own understanding. There'll be more, bye and bye."

"Bye and bye!" Skip had heard enough. "What about right now," he said, standing. "I don't see no Lord doing any providing around here."

The feeling was back, putting words in his mouth before he could stop them. A couple of traveling bluesmen who'd joined the crew for a half-day's work chuckled and nudged each other. The old folks stared at him with stern, disapproving looks. What was wrong with this boy? Who was he to question their belief in a heaven where no one wanted more? God and Jesus were real, and they were providing for the faithful in Tunis. Couldn't he see that? They didn't answer his question. They just looked at him and shook their heads, and he returned their gaze, his eyes going from face to face, seeing in their harsh expressions the calm, abiding belief in Christianity, in an afterlife in which the last would be first and the faithful and downtrodden who lived right and kept the command-ments would walk down streets of gold, drinking milk and honey long past the end of earth and time. The faith was sacred. No one could ques-tion it. God and Jesus were providing in Tunis. He sat down and looked away.

Willie slammed the truck's door. The engine started. Skip watched the others, wondered who among them worried about wanting more. The Christian soldiers didn't. They had a promise. The bluesmen proba-bly didn't care. They knew there were plenty of women in the world, plenty of money to be made, if not here, then somewhere else down the line. They did not worry. He looked at Emma's belly bulging from nine months of baby. Would her child come to want more than Tunis could offer, or learn to put dreams aside. He watched Grandma Sarah gather up her pay. Did she understand that he could not stay in this world? He had to get out. He moved to the back of the truck.

"You best do some praying," Old Man Williams said, loud enough so everyone could hear.

"Humph," Skip replied. "Praying don't do nothing. That God I'm sup-posed to pray to took my mama and papa."

"Yes, but he gave you your Grandma Sarah."

That stopped Skip. The old man was teaching again, and he was right, didn't matter if it was playing a guitar or quoting scriptures. Old Man Williams was always right. He'd taken to Skip years ago, right after the little boy came to live with Grandma Sarah. He'd made the orphan child laugh when no one else could, taught him how to fish and play old railroad songs, told him stories handed down from slavery times. His life stretched back to the year of Jubilee, when Lincoln's smoked Yankees brought freedom. He was an old Buffalo Soldier. His left ear had been mangled by an Apache bullet. He'd been there on San Juan Hill when a Spanish bullet took Skip's grandfather. His stories had thrilled Skip, con-nected him to the long line of lives lived before he crawled out of his mama's belly and took his first, screaming breath. They filled his head with visions of adventure, patrols on the western desert, and charges through Cuban battlefields. And Old Man Williams, who had gone through his early life with a rifle and his later years with a Bible, had survived it all, cheated death more than once to come home to Tunis and make good on his promise to look after Miss Sarah.

He didn't have to work the fields. He and Miss Hattie had set aside enough money for decent Christian burials, but the work gave them a break from days spent on porch rocking chairs, watching the world age, thinking about the fates of old friends, some of whom had crossed over to glory, while others lay bedridden in dark cabins, waiting for death.

Skip felt the weight of the old man's wisdom on him, and said nothing. Dust swirled up from the truck's tires. Rocks bounced against the metal bottom, sounding like grease popping in a hot skillet. Soon Willie was back on Highway 53. One of the bluesmen jumped out at Willie's juke and returned with a guitar and a case of harmonicas. Grandma Sarah got off at her house.

"You coming?" she asked Skip.

"Naw, I'm-a go on into town, check the mail."

Their eyes met. Willie honked the horn and revved the engine.

"Make up your mind, young daddy," said one of the bluesmen. "We got to get into town while people still got spending money."

Skip waved off the comment, looked into his grandma's worried eyes. "I'll see you this evening."

WILLIE'S TRUCK SKIDDED TO A STOP, TIRES KICKING UP GRAVEL AS he slammed the truck into neutral. He had to talk to Skip. The boy was crazy, raising his hand against a white man. Lucky his grandma was there. The bluesmen jumped out of the truck bed, the guitar player with his instrument slung over his shoulder like a soldier's carbine, the other cradling a satchel of harmonicas. Skip sat alone, wishing he could close his eyes, open them and find himself somewhere else, didn't really matter where, long as it wasn't Tunis, or anyplace like it. The guitar man looked up at him and smiled. He was tall and slender with an angular face and wavy, jet black hair glistening and smelling of sweat and pomade.

"That was some strong stuff you put on the boss man, young daddy." He turned to his stocky, round-faced partner. "Ain't that right, Scrapper?"

"Foolish stuff, I'd say, but he got the makings of a man."

The tight, choking tension that had gripped Skip ever since the argument eased. He relaxed his grip on the bench and let himself slouch. At least somebody thought he'd done good.

"Guess I did shake up Sam Willard," he said. "Cost me a job, though."

"Shoot," said the guitar player. "Plenty places to find money."

"Not around here," Skip said.

"Ain't talkin' 'bout this town, young daddy. I'm talking 'bout this mean old world. Hell, me and old Scrapper been on the road goin' on six years. Steady after that green. We travelling men. Been everywhere. From Maine to the Mobile Bay. Old Mexico. Thought we'd set down here a spell and make a little money," he held out his hand. "Folks call me Delta Slim. That there's Scrapper, best damn harp player this side of the Big Muddy."

"Pleased to meet you," Skip said. "My name's Skip Reynolds."

"Reynolds? You any relation to Blind Joe Reynolds over in Mississippi?" asked Delta Slim.

"Not that I know of. My peoples come from that way after emancipation, though. You a guitar player?"

"I beat this box a little, young daddy. How 'bout yourself?"

"Got me a National Steel I can play like nobody's business."

"Then what you doing staying 'round here picking cotton? Young daddy like you ought to have them leaving blues, ain't that right Scrapper?"

The harp player nodded, took off his glasses and cleaned the lenses with the end of his shirt. "Plenty life and green in this world," he said.

Skip leaned forward, excited. "I been thinking 'bout going to Hollywood. Even got me thirty dollars saved up. I'm gon' join an acting school out there."

Delta Slim nudged his partner and gave him a wry smile. "Told you this young daddy had some stuff. Hollywood."

"Gon' be a certified moving picture man, huh," Scrapper said. "Take over for old Steppin' and Sleep 'N Eats." Scrapper started shuffling and whining like a Hollywood darky. "Yassuh, boss, I gwine work sumdey, but not right now. See, I'm feeling mighty poorly. My feets hurt."

Skip shook his head at the bluesmen's laughter. "I ain't doing none of that coon stuff. I'm gon' do something different, maybe be a gangster like Slim Thompson was in *The Petrified Forest*. Y'all ever seen that picture?"

Before the bluesmen could answer, Willie walked up, smoke churning from his pipe. "Skip," he said, pushing past the bluesmen. "You know I can lose Sam Willard on account of what you done today? Oh yeah, I can hear him now. 'Sorry, Willie-boy, but I cain't have you bringing ornery nigras out here.' And another thing . . ."

"Aw, man, hush," Delta Slim said. "This here young daddy stood up for himself back there. Who you for anyway?"

"Me," Willie said, thrusting his thumb toward his heart.

"Um, um, um," Scrapper said. "Man don't even appreciate a mannish boy trying to make a stand."

Willie threw up his hands, disgusted. "Y'all trying to lead this boy to his death? Y'all been around. You know what can happen. A boy over Somerville way killed a white man not too long ago. Found him hanging from a tree with his face all blacked up with cork. You remember that Murchinson boy, Skip?"

"Yeah, yeah, but I didn't mean you no harm, Willie. Besides, I didn't even hit Willard."

"That don't matter, and you know it," Willie said. "You ain't alone in this mess. Remember that the next time you get a notion to tangle with a white man. Now, get out of my truck. I got another crew to pick up, then I got to talk to Sam Willard 'bout a pickin' machine." Willie turned to the bluesmen. "Be at my juke at eight, ready to play." He limped back to the cab, pulled himself in and slammed the door.

Skip heard the engine grinding into gear. The exhaust pipe coughed thick, black smoke that sent the bluesmen backing away. Willie honked the horn, gunned the engine a couple of times and honked again. Skip leaped out as the truck pulled away.

"Where y'all headed?"

"The best place in this here town for a couple of fine musicianeers to make some money on a Saturday afternoon, young daddy."

"Town square's the best place," Skip said.

"Well, lead on, young daddy," Delta Slim said. "Lead on."

TUNIS HAD CHANGED LITTLE IN THE SEVENTY-TWO YEARS SINCE SAM Willard's grandfather, Colonel Artemis Jehosaphat Willard of the defeated Confederacy, had come seeking seclusion and reaffirmation in what was then an empty land. He built the town, saw to it that the train line between Houston, Dallas and Fort Worth stopped here. Progress brought radio, electric lights and indoor plumbing into the best homes. Jim Crow defined the life of Tunis. Everyone had a place and they stuck to it, or left.

Delta Slim and Scrapper followed Skip through the meandering Saturday afternoon crowd to a square patch of hardy grass bounded by four wooden benches. A bronze statue of Colonel Willard stood guard, the heroic soldier proudly pointing his sword as his war-crazed steed charged into the deadly hell that was Antietam, Brandy Station, The Wilderness. Delta Slim took a seat, spread an old shirt on the ground to catch the coins of passersby, and started tuning his guitar. Overhead, the relentless sun burned bright in the clear, late September sky, throwing the guitar player's shadow across the grass. Scrapper wiped his brow, pulled a harmonica from his satchel and started warming up, first tapping the harp against his palm to loosen the reeds, then sliding it across his lips, producing whoops, the sound of chugging trains and car horns. He looked at Skip.

"You say you can play. But, tell me, can you sing? Can you cry?" Scrapper leaned toward him and made the harp sound like a baby bawling for its mama's tit.

Skip answered with his best blues moan. "Ah-oooh. Peoples I'm lonely and blue. Got traveling on my mind."

"Uh, you might have some talent somewhere in that singing voice, young daddy, but we're out here trying to make some money," Delta Slim said. "Why don't you take a seat and enjoy." He did a tumbling, single-note blues run that ended with him bending a low note in the key of E.

Scrapper raised his eyebrows. "I guess you ready," he said.

Delta Slim nodded and started a rambling, sing-song introduction. "Well, we traveling men, peoples. Do as we please. Playing some of these old blues, trying to put our minds at ease." Then he started singing about that poor boy long ways from home.

"Mister Engineer," he sang. "Let a man ride this line. I say, Mister Engineer, let a poor boy ride this line. He said, `I wouldn't mind it, fella, but you know this train ain't mine.'"

"W-a-a-o-o-w-n. W-a-a-o-o-w-n."

Skip put himself inside the story, made up a second guitar line to follow Delta Slim and Scrapper as their song wound its way through a journey of meeting paydays and catching freights, laying up in a fair brown's arms and slipping out the back door before her man comes. Scrapper's train-whistle harmonica huffed and puffed like a highballing freight on ribbons of steel, danced around the melodies and played off the lyrics as Delta Slim's rich, resonant voice cut through the heavy afternoon heat like a refreshing autumn breeze. Skip tapped his feet and let his troubles go. His mind emptied of everything, except the blues. He watched Delta Slim's fingerings, hoping to steal a lick or two. The bluesman stopped to put his guitar in an open G tuning. The sound was bluer, more sorrowful. He slipped a piece of glass tubing on his baby finger and slid it up past the twelfth fret, producing a piercing, high-pitched wail to accompany Scrapper's crying harmonica. Delta Slim raised his voice to a high-pitched plea as he called out one of Robert Johnson's laments.

"I gotta keep moving. I gotta keep moving, blues falling down like hail, blues falling down like hail. And the day keeps on worrying me, there's a hellhound on my trail, hellhound on my trail."

"Play that blues!" Skip yelled, imagining himself on some old lonesome highway, heading west, a savage hellhound dogging him all the way.

A crowd gathered. Some people gave the musicians a quick glance, then went on about their business. Others stayed for a song, or two. One sad-faced woman, her hair hidden beneath a bright, green and white scarf, broke into a broad smile and sang along to Delta Slim's version of *Stone Pony*.

"Saddle up my pony, saddle up my black mare," she sang, her lilting voice harmonizing with Delta Slim's. "I got to find my rider out in the world somewhere."

She patted her daughter's head, put a nickle in the child's hand and pushed her toward the musicians. "Go'n now, Jessie Lee," she said.

The little girl crept forward, big brown eyes drinking in the world, eyelids fluttering as she dropped the coin and scurried back to hide her face in the flowing cloth of her mama's dress. Delta Slim winked at her and kept on playing, not missing a beat. Scrapper puffed his way through a grunting solo, his hands muffling the sound. He squeezed an almost human cry out of his harp.

"W-a-a-o-o-w-n!"

Time melted away. Finally, Skip stood and got on with the rest of his day. "I'll see y'all at Willie's juke," he said. "And I'm bringing National Steel."

Scrapper nodded, almost losing his glasses during a wicked vibrato. The sweet sound of ringing guitar strings and puffing harmonica followed Skip up Main Street. He strolled along, thinking about what to do. He felt good now, able to look back on the morning's confrontation without getting all tight inside. He'd surprised himself, losing the only job he had. No use trying to beg Sam Willard to take him back on as a cotton picker. Plantation work was behind him. But he needed more money. Tunis didn't have any steady jobs, just day work: an afternoon unloading a shipment at Murphy's Emporium, or stacking cotton bales at the ginning plant. Maybe it was time to leave Tunis, head on out to Hollywood and find Ezekiel Washington. These thoughts and ideas so consumed him that he didn't see the three young white men walking towards him until it was almost too late. They wore matching blue denim pants, red and black plaid shirts, sleeves rolled up past the elbow. He recognized Tommy Ray Jones, a friend from his childhood days before they took their respective places in Tunis. They didn't speak anymore. Tommy Ray looked through him, ice-cold gaze revealing nothing. Skip stepped into the dirt and let them pass. One confrontation was enough.

He walked on to Murphy's Emporium and U.S. Post Office, where Murphy, a stocky, barrel-chested Irishman, was a blur of constant motion, running behind the counter to pound out a sale on the ornate National cash register, hurrying back onto the sales floor to coax a reluctant farmer into buying a handful of nails, climbing a ladder to grab a bolt of cloth for somebody's wife. Murphy stocked just about everything a farmer might need: fifty-pound bags of flour and beans, new plow blades, packs of rough cut chewing tobacco and fine cut for smoking, wooden fire engines painted a brilliant red. He even kept a current copy of the Sears & Roebuck catalogue on hand, so whatever he didn't have could be shipped in. Skip moved quickly through the crowd, passing Elaine Murphy who was busy helping women try on bonnets. He heard snatches of conversation, gossip, even his own name mentioned a couple of times. At the counter where Murphy had put up a red, white and blue sign: United States Post Office, he stopped and flipped through the latest copy of Photoplay, looking over the edge of the page whenever he felt somebody's eyes on him.

"How's the resident anarchist?" Murphy said, loosening his string tie a bit and mopping under his wilting, high collar.

"Huh?" Skip said, putting the magazine down.

Murphy leaned toward him and imitated the voice of a redneck farmer. "I tell yuh, hit don' do a nigra no good to be ehjicaited. The boy ought to be whupped, treatin' American money that-a-way. Must be reading dem damn New Yawk mag'zines Murphy's got."

"How'd you hear 'bout this morning?"

"Look around you, Skip. This is the best place for news. Got anything to post?"

"Naw. Mail come yet?"

"He's running late. Probably be in around suppertime."

"I'm gone then," Skip said, turning and heading for the door.

A crowd of women gathered around bottles of perfume blocked his path. Atomizers showered the air with a fine, delicate spray that tickeled his nose, the scents too sweet and flowery to make him think of romance. Once outside, he took a deep breath, turned the corner of Main Street and looked down Willard Boulevard at the welcoming sight of the Rialto Theater. Sam Willard's father, Robert E. Lee Willard, had built the movie house in 1923, the year he went to Hollywood and came back enchanted. He gave the construction crews pictures torn from magazines and they created for him a box, topped with a Chinese pagoda. An art-deco style sign graced the theater's facade, its curving letters pumped full of neon gas. On Saturday nights, the sign lit up the street in blues, reds and greens flashing on and off, bathing the dirt in iridescent hues, "Rialto Theater" written in shadows on the ground. Bobby Willard even bought palm trees and had them planted alongside the Rialto. The trees never prospered. Their huge, withered leaves hung limp.

Skip hurried on. He didn't want to miss *Imitation of Life*, a three-hankie job saved by the presence of the beautiful, rebellious Fredi Washington. He waited at the ticket booth until the attendant, B. K. Simpson, decided to see what he wanted. She was a frisky, buxom, young white gal who wore cotton shirts with the top three buttons undone. She leaned on the counter, giving Skip an eyeful if he dared look.

"See something you like, boy?"

Skip stared past her, his gaze ending on the back wall of the booth. "Just gimme a ticket, B. K."

"That's Miss Simpson to you," she said, flicking her sandy brown hair over her shoulder, taking Skip's dime and giving him a ticket.

He grabbed the stub and walked to the worn, rickety staircase leading to the colored-only balcony. He stopped at the first step for a moment, his shoulders heavy with the weight of Tunis. Colored folk sat on benches upstairs in the stifling summer heat, while white folks reclined in padded chairs, the air stirred by standing fans. He wanted one of those seats down front, even thought about taking one once, but the cost and a helping of good sense kept him in his place. White folks were crazy. They'd hang a nigger just because he looked at them funny. He continued on into the hot, stuffy darkness, where the thick heat pulsed from the dusty walls. Cigarette smoke floated through the widening beam of light the projector threw on the screen. He unbuttoned his shirt and took a seat way back in Lover's Lane. It was empty now. The couples didn't come to the matinee. They waited for nightfall. He smiled, glad to be in this place where he could escape from the world. It was here that he first came under the spell of moving pictures. They were herky-jerky then, without sound, but he didn't care. They were magic. He cheered Douglas Fairbanks through daring sword fights, crouched low and hid his eyes from Lon Chaney's monsters. In Lover's Lane he discovered the sensual pleasures of a willing girl. There had been sex-play, hot breathing and hungry kisses, sultry Jean Harlow stretched out cat-like on a cushioned sofa, while his fingers played in the soft place between Lilly Hawkins' legs, stroking down under her panties where she was wet and warm to the touch, her shuddering moans making his cock hard, her hands squeezing him, their lips meeting until neither cared about the moving picture or the people around them. All in the past.

Up in the front row a rambunctious gang of school boys punched each other and joked about a bald-headed white man down below. Some cheered as Dizzy Dean came on the newsreel, smiled at the camera and threw the fastball he hoped would carry his Cardinals past the Yankees in the World Series. They didn't pay any mind to the voices that tried to shush them. They just kept on playing, even after the credits for *Imitation of Life* began. The movie always brought a good crowd. Louise Beavers played Delilah, prize cook for Claudette Colbert's Miss Plummer. Their daughters went to the same school because Peola was high yellow and could pass. Miss Plummer built a baking empire, based on the unbeliev-able quality of Delilah's pancakes. She started living the luxuriant life of high-society, while Delilah was content to wear an apron and a smile. But not Peola, played by the tawny-skinned, green-eyed Fredi Washington. She could pass.

"Mama, I want the same things in life other people enjoy," she said, her anguished words coming in sobs as she lay on her bed, hearing the gay sounds of a grand party in the ballroom not thirty feet away. The same things in life.

She ran away from her big, black mama, who stayed, wanting only to serve and have a big funeral with a team of six white horses pulling her coffin. Delilah wanted no part of the financial empire born of her recipe.

"I makes you a present of it," she told Miss Plummer.

Peals of laughter rippled through the balcony. Someone yelled out: "Girl, what's wrong with you? You'd better take that money."

"Hell, yeah," Skip said, his voice anonymous in the dark.

Delilah didn't listen. She refused all offers. She couldn't take the money and run.

"You gonna send me away?" she cried, when Miss Plummer suggested she take part of the company. "How I gon' take care of you if I'se away?"

Sheeit. Mammy was alive and well, then dead, her one dying wish to see Peola, her baby, who returned, repentant and ashamed, but too late. The horse-drawn hearse bearing Delilah moved slowly down a broad Harlem avenue. The scene was filled with hundreds of black folk moaning and wailing their spirituals. White women in the Rialto's front rows started crying. The boys in the balcony snickered and pretended to sniffle. The theater lights came on.

If not for Peola, Skip would have forgotten the movie, labeled it as one more reason why he had to find Ezekiel Washington and knock some sense into Hollywood, but her plea was his. He wanted the same things in life white people enjoy, not just the grand things, but the simple things, too, like a cushioned seat at the Rialto. He got up and walked into the fading daylight.

No customers crowded Murphy's Emporium when he returned. Only Murphy remained, lazily sorting the newly arrived mail.

"Anythin' for me," Skip asked.

Murphy shook his head, reading the names. "Nope." "Nope." "Nope." Skip felt his heart sinking. He had to hear from Ezekiel Washington, needed to know his five dollars hadn't been wasted and that Hollywood waited, palm trees and searchlights, cream-colored limousines and premiere nights, waiting for him. The stack of letters grew smaller. His stomach tightened. Four months and no response.

Murphy kept thumbing through the letters, then stopped. "This might interest you." He held a large envelope at arm's length. "It's from the Ezekiel Washington Colored Actor's School in . . ."

Skip snatched the envelope, fumbled with it, his fingers gone clumsy with excitement. "Gimme something to open it," he said.

Murphy calmly pulled a letter opener from under the counter and handed it over. Skip took a deep breath. This was the moment he had waited for, saved for, even prayed for. It began in late spring, when cotton rows had to be hoed, grew slowly, quietly, fed by desire, desperation and hope.

"Want me to open it?" asked Murphy.

Skip shook his head, slit the envelope and pulled out a crisp, folded sheet of white paper. He scanned the page once, then again. Ezekiel Washington said come on out to Hollywood. The letter almost slid from his fingers. He started to smile, then laughed, the joy consuming every bit of his soul.

"What's so good to you?" asked Murphy.

"My day of Jubilee has come," Skip shouted.

"Day of Jubilee?"

"Yeah. Emancipation! Freedom! I'm gon' to Hollywood, Murphy. I'm . . . gon' . . . be a moving picture star! I can already see my name in lights." He held up his hand as if he was reading a movie house marquee. "Presenting Hollywood's newest sensation, Skip Reynolds."

"What do you know about acting?"

"I ain't got to know nothing, Murphy. Ezekiel Washington is gon' teach me. All I got's to do is show up. Yes, sir. You can color me G-O-N-E, gone!" Skip slapped the counter. "Whoo whee!" he said, feeling flush and rich. "Gimme a box of that Wyler's Bubble Bath. Grandma Sarah loves that stuff, and wrap it up real nice." He rifled Murphy's 78s for the jumpingest tune he could find and settled on "Roll 'Em Pete," a fast boogie-woogie he'd heard some barrelhouse boy play at Willie's Juke Joint. The record featured Joe Turner wailing the blues while Pete Johnson ran it down on the '88.

The town square was deserted when he stepped outside. He stopped at the war remembrance. As a little boy he thought the statue's stone eyes were watching him and that one day horse and rider would spring to life and charge into the sky. He smiled at the childhood memory. Billie Dee Joseph's wagon wobbled toward the highway. The sharecropper spat a stream of tobacco juice and flicked the reins. Skip waved and wished him a good evening.

The houses along the highway didn't look as dismal and falling apart as when Skip had rode into town. He saw life in them now, children spinning tops on the warped porches, women singing and bringing on the night. A train whistle blew near the Brazos, its cry mingling with the keening of Willie Jean Mason, whose husband had been run over by a train. Willie Jean cried everytime a train went by. Skip saw her sitting in her doorway, head bowed into the bowl her hands made to catch her tears. Her once firm, supple body had gone to fat. Loose flesh sagged from her arms, hiding the bend of her elbows. Rings of old, dried sweat showed white around her armpits. Skip figured the state people would come soon enough and take her children, then they'd put her in an asylum where, forever haunted by the train's screaming whistle, she could live out her days wailing her lamentation, the sight of her husband's torn body forever etched on her soul.

Farther up the road, he saw a strange machine approaching. It had six long blades pointing out up front and a cab the driver got to by climbing a ladder. A chute behind the cab emptied into a large, wire-mesh basket. The machine sputtered toward him, its coughing, wheezing engine barely heard above the clanging metal. Willie was in the driver's seat.

"Hey there," he shouted.

"What the hell is this?" Skip walked around the contraption, putting its pieces together in his mind.

Willie shut off the engine, struck a match and dipped the flame into his pipe. "This here's the future, Skip. That's right. This here is progress come to the cotton fields of Tunis, Texas."

"But what is it?"

"It's a cotton pickin' machine. Can out-pick fifty John Lees, and all you need is one man to drive it."

"This thing is gon' put people out of work," Skip said.

"Sho'. But prices is low these days, and Sam Willard say he got to save money every way he can. Wanna see how it works?" Before Skip could reply, Willie climbed down from the cab. "Looky here." He bent as low as his gimp leg allowed and pointed to the blades. "They're adjustable, raise 'em up or down. Back yonder is a vacuum mouth. Sucks cotton into that bin. You see, Skip, it works on the same principle as them vacuum cleaners white folks buy." Willie smiled proudly, as if he had invented the machine. "Yes, sir. This is the future."

"When's this future start?"

"Monday morning. I'm only taking the best pickers. Sam Willard say he don't want no half-steppers. You want to work? I might be able to get you on, if you promise to behave."

"I ain't picking no more cotton, Willie."

"Suit yourself. But let me know if you change your mind. You may be a hard-headed young buck, but you do good work."

Willie struck another match, puffed slowly, then hauled himself up the machine's ladder. Skip watched him turn the ignition key. The machine rattled to life, spat black smoke and shook the way a cartoon jalopy does before falling apart in a heap of gears and loose springs. Willie leaned out from the cab and yelled above the din.

"You know what I like best about this here cotton picking machine, Skip? If it works out, I'll get a raise to drive it!"

Willie worked the gear shift and waved good-bye. Skip shook his head. Now what would Grandma Sarah say about God providing? Seemed like He was up to the same old mess, letting the poor man get poorer, the rich man richer. Willie knew the hard work in the fields meant food, clothing, rent. People would starve without it. Skip pushed away the image of Billie Dee Joseph's children crying to ease the pain in their empty stomachs, empty because a machine had taken their father's place. He hoped the machine would fail. He walked on, thinking about Willie and all his talk about colored folk being together. Lies. If the machine meant a step up, then the crew be damned.

Up ahead, he saw lantern lights glowing and glimpsed Grandma Sarah through the window. She was stoking the stove, getting dinner ready. He fingered the precious gifts and the answered prayer that would carry him to a new world.

BESSIE SMITH'S BLUES SPILLED FROM THE HOUSE, CARRYING ITS sad tale of loneliness into the coming night. "Keeps on raining. Tonight it's raining. Papa, he can't make no time." Skip could hear the pops and scratches as the heavy needle rode across the thick 78. He stopped on the porch, peeked inside and saw Grandma Sarah at work, her lips mouthing Bessie's song. Already he missed her. He pushed the door open, hiding her gift behind his back.

"Where you been, boy?" she said, looking up from a mound of biscuit dough.

"Been buying you a present," he replied, showing her the gift-wrapped box.

"Ooooohhh!" Grandma Sarah smiled, joy lighting up her brown eyes as she wiped her hands on her apron. "Ain't this pretty? Purple and white ribbons." She held the box to her ear and shook it. "Now, I wonder." She set the box on the table and carefully unwrapped it, making sure not to tear the paper that Skip knew she would save for another gift. Watching her, he wondered how she would feel when he told her he'd finally gotten the letter from Ezekiel Washington, that he was leaving her to chase a dream.

"Boy," she said. "I been wanting me another box of Wyler's all summer. It reminds me of spring time." She walked over to him, stood on her tiptoes and tenderly kissed his cheek. "Thank you, son. Now, where you been all afternoon?"

"Town. I spent some time with them musicians, Delta Slim and Scrapper. Seen a picture show and . . ." Now was not the time. He could not destroy her happiness with his good news. "And I stopped by Murphy's. Bought me a copy of `Roll `Em Pete.' Wait'll you hear this."

He took Bessie's blues off the Victrola, dropped the jump tune on the turntable and found a groove for the needle. Pete Johnson stormed into the room, flying fingers pounding out a riff in the piano's upper register, then descending through the middle keys before rolling into a steady, boogie-woogie that propelled the song along as Joe Turner started singing about his gal up on the hill, the one with eyes like diamonds and teeth shining like Klondike gold.

"Roll me, boy. Let us jump for joy. Yeah, man, happy as a baby boy. Well my girl done bought me a brand new choo-choo toy."

The song moved like a `38 Cord Turbo flat out on the highway. Skip danced around the room, hands flailing an imaginary piano, while Grandma Sarah clapped and moved her shoulders from side to side.

"Yeah, man," he said, taking her hand and giving her a twirl.

He wished the song would never end. It kept him from having to tell his secret. He played it twice, all the while looking around for something to do.

"Slow down, Skip," said Grandma Sarah. "You jumping around like a chicken with its head cut off."

He looked up and tried to smile through his confused emotions of joy and sadness all jumbled together and firing off at the same time. How could he leave her? Standing in Murphy's Emporium, he'd thought only of his freedom and the life that waited for him. Now he thought about what leaving really meant: Grandma Sarah, alone in the last of her old age, while he toasted his youth and dreams in Hollywood. So be it, he thought, seeking courage in tired words. Grandma Sarah took the needle off the record and went back to fixing a pan of biscuits. The image of Grandma Sarah baking biscuits in the still of evening settled into Skip's memory, joined itself to a lifetime of others. Sorrow crept into his heart. Leave her?

"What's got into you, Skip?" she said. "You been acting mighty strange lately, like you ain't got a lick of sense. Throwing away money.

Now, I know I raised you better than that." She turned and closed the stove's door. "You hear me talking to you?"

"Yeah, yeah," Skip said, letting her chastise him. "I just get tired sometimes, Grandma Sarah. And if you ask me, it's a damn shame the way Sam Willard treated old Billie Dee. Using them big words. Mathematician. Sheeit."

"Watch your mouth, now, `fore I make you taste some of this here Wyler's."

"Yes, ma'm. But I had to get him today, especially after he come sucking up to me. Guess I just lost myself."

"Humph. What you lost is a job. Would've lost the money too, but for your old grandma."

Skip winced, remembering how she had begged for his pay. "Well, we won't have to worry `bout picking cotton no more. Sam Willard done gone and bought himself a pickin' machine."

"Pickin' machine?"

"Yep." Skip flipped over a pair of pants. "Seen Willie driving it this afternoon. Boy, he was all puffed up, strutting around on his gimp leg like a crippled-up banty rooster. He say Sam Willard ain't gon' need near as many pickers. Say he even gets a raise to drive the damn thing."

"When's all this start?"

"Monday week from now."

Grandma Sarah shook her head. "Um, um, um. And he didn't even have the goodness to tell nobody. Well, we'll see what the Lord has to say. But about this morning, Skip. I understand how you feel about that white man, Lord knows I do, but it ain't just your money to do with as you please. It's our money, or is there something I don't know."

The words stopped Skip. He tried to remember if he'd done anything to give away his secret. "Ain't nothing you don't know," he said.

She saw the lie flash across his face, but decided not to press him on it. "Now, listen to me, Skip," she said, waving her finger in his face like she'd done a thousand times before. "No matter how mad you get, always take the money first. Then you can do whatever you want. But take the money. And if I ever catch you pulling some mess like you done this morning, I'm `gon beat your behind. Yes, I will," she said, giving him the angry look that had made him mind more times than he could remember. "I ain't too old to lay you out, and you ain't too old for that switch." She tried to hold the look, but a smile broke through. "Step aside now. I'm `gon out on the porch. See if I can catch me a breeze. Watch them biscuits so they don't burn."

Take the money. Always take the money. He nodded to himself, thinking about his grandma and her rules. The house grew quiet around him, save for the sounds of night: birds chattering on the boughs of a chinaberry tree; the fire crackling; the rhythmic creaking of Grandma Sarah's rocking chair. He moved slowly, his secret burning inside him like a consumptive fever. He had to tell her, couldn't let her go on talking and acting like he'd always be here. But how? What words were there to hold all he felt, happiness making him dizzy and sorrow growing inside him each time he thought of her? He smelled the biscuits and knew they were done. He set them on top of the stove and walked onto the porch, grabbed his stiff-backed chair and leaned it back against the wall, balancing himself on the rear legs, every now and then stealing a glance at his grandma. A cooling breeze spread around the house, gathering up puffs of dust and dirt. In the distance, two hounds howled across the empty land in a call-and-response.

Grandma Sarah rocked slowly, her gaze lost in the green, rolling land. Across the highway, an abandoned shack stood lonely and desolate, its frame collapsing in upon itself. Skip picked up pebbles and tossed them off the porch. She caught him looking at her, but he turned away before she could read his face. He couldn't look her in the eye. He knew going to Hollywood meant the end of this life of quiet moments shared sitting on the porch listening to the distant howl of unseen hounds; the death of this life for the hope of another.

Grandma Sarah sighed deeply, squinched up her nose and relaxed, her eyes closed. Skip stopped what he was doing and kissed her softly on her forehead. She did not smile.

"What's on your mind, Skip?" she asked, opening her eyes.

"Nothing," he said.

"Come on, now. What's on your mind?"

"I . . . I . . . I got that letter from the acting school."

"What they say?

"Come on out to Hollywood. You want to read it?" He pulled the letter from his pants pocket and thrust it toward her.

She unfolded the sheet of paper and held it up to her squinting eyes.

"I needs me some reading light and my glasses," she said, standing and going inside, leaving Skip tense and alone.

She read slowly, mumbling the words to herself over and over again. A colored actor's school? Who'd ever heard of such a thing? All actors seemed to do was carouse and walk hand in hand with the Devil's painted women. And Skip? She laughed to herself. He couldn't even tell a good lie.

Outside, Skip waited, wondering what Grandma Sarah would say.

"I told you the Lord was listening," she said, returning to the porch. "And He answer in His own time. You gon' out there?"

Skip shrugged. "I guess."

"Well, you sure don't act like you're glad about it. Honest to Pete, it's all you been talking 'bout these last few weeks. Guess we gon' have to start getting you ready. Gon' have to . . ." Her lips started trembling as her words trailed off. Then she spoke again. "When you thinking on leaving?"

"Ain't thought about it much. Letter just came."

"Well, you best start thinking 'bout it. Don't want them folks out there forgetting 'bout you."

"I don't want to leave too soon. I mean . . ." Skip fumbled for the right words. "I mean there's things to do and . . ."

"I hope you ain't worrying 'bout me," Grandma Sarah protested, her face a defiant mask of calm. "I ain't crippled."

"But I am worried 'bout you. Who's gon' take care of you?"

"Me, and I been doing pretty good going on sixty-five years, thank you."

"What you gon' do for money? Willie say Sam Willard ain't gon' be taking no old folks. He say from now on only the best pickers is going."

"I ain't studying what that white man wants," Grandma Sarah said. "If I ain't good enough no more, fine. I can start back to taking in people's washing. Got them hens and the garden, your granddaddy's pension. I'll fare okay. You ought to be worrying 'bout yourself. The way I hear it, actors don't make a steady wage, 'specially colored ones."

"I'm still gon' make sure you're set 'fore I go. I'm gon' see if Willie can get me back on with Sam Willard. He said he could. And if that don't work, I'll get on one of them crews picking cotton on the other side of the Brazos. I'll find something."

Their eyes met. Grandma Sarah smiled bravely, looked away and twitched her nose. "Lordy me. We smell near `bout as bad as the back of Willie's truck. Get on in there and take a bath. I'll wait."

Skip brushed past her, his head down. Inside, he filled a number three washtub with pots of water pumped up from the well and heated on the stove. The sound of water splashing into the tub reminded him of rainstorms when he was a little boy, seeking shelter in his grandmother's love.

❧

A SEVEN-YEAR-OLD BOY LIVES WITH HIS GRANDMA. HIS NAME IS William Henry Reynolds, but people call him Skip because he has a slight limp and when he runs, it is more like skipping. His parents are dead. Memories of the car wreck sleep during the day, but in dreams he remembers the crunching metal, the screams, the slow, slow arcing flight of his body catapulted from his mother's arms.

The little boy stands by the window and stares out at the cotton-boll clouds crowding the gray-black sky. Big raindrops splatter against the pane. It has been raining for four days. Water sloshes under the floorboards. People use boats because the Brazos has overflowed.

The late afternoon grows darker. Flames consume wood set in the fireplace. Charred chunks break into red-hot glowing embers. The logs crackle and pop. Bubbling sap spits and catches fire. Grandma Sarah says she will make him popping corn and tell him a story after dinner. He stays by the window, listening to the falling rain drumming on the roof and walls. It seeps through a crack, plops and plunks into a bucket Grandma Sarah placed beneath the hole. More buckets hang out from the kitchen. Grandma Sarah says rain water is good water.

A jagged flash of light slashes across the sky, touching down beyond the live oaks. He blinks his eyes and the light is gone. He sucks in his breath, waits for the heavy rumbling he knows will come. Thunder explodes in waves of angry sound. The windows rattle. He is thrilled and afraid. Will the house float away? Grandma Sarah says Jesus won't let anything happen to them. He remembers that and then he is not afraid, because he is safe in Grandma Sarah's house, where it is warm and smells of supper. After the meal, she sneaks up behind him and gives him a big hug and a kiss.

"Who's my little man?" she asks.

"I am, Grandma Sarah," he says in a child's high-pitched voice.

"Well, I'm gon' get this popping corn ready," Grandma Sarah says, releasing him and sending him back to the dishes.

Thunder booms and shakes the windows. The flood water rises. He finishes the dishes and goes to warm himself by the fire. His shadow climbs the wall, stretches almost to the ceiling. A covered pot set by the fire echoes with the muffled explosions of bursting corn kernels ricocheting off cast iron. Grandma Sarah bends over a kerosene lamp and, with one breath, turns the flame into a spiral of black smoke. The room surrenders to darkness broken only by the dancing light of burning wood, the sudden blue-white flashes of lightning. The thunder rolls. Grandma Sarah sits next to her grandson and thrusts her hands toward the fire. When there is no more sound of corn popping, she wraps part of her apron around the pot's handle and pulls it from the fire, removes the lid and pours in salt, brushing aside her grandson's darting hands.

"Hold on now, Skip," she says. "Let me salt this corn."

He cannot wait. He is hungry for the steaming white kernels, the tang of salt on his fingers and tongue. Grandma Sarah smiles, content to let her grandson have his way. She puts down the salt bowl and wipes her hand on her apron.

"Okay, now," she says. "I'm gon' tell you a story 'bout freedom. 'Bout a man who wanted it so bad, he had hisself mailed out of slavery."

"Aw grandma," he whines. "Is this one of them fairy tales?"

"Nawsuh. This story is for real. Now, eat this here corn, boy, and listen."

He fills his small fists again and again. Wood chunks fall together in the fireplace. Shadows jerk along the walls, the image of the little boy and his grandma by his side, telling him the story of Henry "Box" Brown, who was a real smart man, so smart he thought of something special and had himself mailed out of slavery.

After she finishes, the little boy splashes his face with cold water, mops it dry, undresses and puts on his nightshirt. Into the steeple of darkness made by his hands folded together, he whispers: "Now I lay me down to sleep. I pray the Lord my soul to keep . . ." No shadow-demons climb the walls tonight. Grandma Sarah has chased them all away. She tucks him into bed and he snuggles deep into the warm cocoon. The sound of the gently falling rain becomes a lullaby singing him to peaceful sleep — plip, plop, plink, plunk; plip, plop, plink, plunk. His eyes grow heavy. The sandman is coming.

"Goodnight, Grandma Sarah," he calls out.

"Goodnight, baby," she says. "Goodnight."

SKIP FRITTERED AWAY HIS LAST AFTERNOON AND WAS PASSING the Williams' place when the old man's familiar voice called out to him.

"Come on over here, boy," he said, sitting on his porch and smoking a hand-rolled cigarette. "Ain't you gon' give me some time 'fore you leave?"

"Wouldn't think of passing you by," Skip said and approached the lean, old man, whose face was a darkened version of Sam Willard's father: the same deep-set eyes and Indian nose. "Where's Miss Hattie?"

"Gon' up the road to set with Emma and that baby. Why don't we step inside, get out of this heat?"

Skip followed Old Man Williams into the dark, musty-smelling cabin, paused just inside the doorway to let his eyes adjust to the darkness that was broken by thin strands of sunlight. Gradually, he saw the familiar surroundings: layers of unfolded Cream of Wheat boxes tacked to the wall to keep out the cold and wind; framed jig-saw puzzles hanging as decorations. The old man did not have an altar to Bessie Smith. His altar was for Jesus. Over the bureau he'd hung a calendar from the Walter J. Pettibone Funeral Home in Houston with a three-quarter profile painting of the fair-skinned, blue-eyed savior. Above this, on a piece of brown wrapping paper, Old Man Williams had written in uneven script: "His blood for the sins of the world."

Skip sat down on the Williams' lumpy sofa, careful as always to keep the lace doilies in place. The old man went into the kitchen and returned with two glasses of sweet tea. He set one before Skip, who nodded and stared at a puzzle of a boatman on the canals of Venice, Italy, remembering childhood days when he and the old man spent long afternoons putting together jigsaw puzzles and he sat listening to stories of the Spanish-American War, Havana, and life on the western plains with the Tenth Colored Cavalry. And there were guitar lessons, the old man patiently nodding as the child struggled to play an old railroad song.

"You been getting ready," the old man said, breaking Skip's reverie.

"Packed before I went on that cotton pick the other side of the Brazos," Skip replied. "Even practiced some of what that acting school book says."

"I don't mean none of that," the old man said, waving off Skip's answer and leaning forward. "I mean is you been getting ready in here," he pointed to his head. "And here," he pointed to his heart.

"Sure, I been getting ready," Skip said, wondering what the old man was trying to say.

"Don't be telling me no tales, boy. I knows you ain't been getting ready. Lessen you been saved in the last five minutes. The Lord is waiting on you, Skip. All you gots to do is open your heart to him. Jesus don't Jim Crow nobody. He take everybody who comes to him, even hard-headed boys like you."

Skip took a mouthful of tea, swished it around and swallowed. "I ain't studying Jesus right now, Old Man Williams. Onliest thing I'm studying is getting out of Tunis and going to Hollywood."

"That's one of the things I wanted to talk to you about," Old Man Williams said. "See, son, there's plenty temptations in this world, especially for a young buck leaving home. Lord, Lord. I can tell you 'bout the temptations, the subtle and sly ways of the Devil. And, seeing as how you fixing to leave, I wanted to give you some advice."

"Can I use it?" Skip asked.

"It can save your life." Old Man Williams nodded, seeing a question in Skip's eyes. "That's right. Now, listen to me, Skip. Don't be wandering where you ain't wanted. Find yourself a place and stick to it."

"Sheeiit," Skip said. "I ain't gon' out to Hollywood so's I can stick to my place. Hell, I can do that right here in Tunis."

"You ain't listening, Skip," said Old Man Williams. "Stop trying to be like white folks."

"Be like white folks! I ain't trying to be like them. I'm trying to be me!"

"Son, you stepping out of your element with this acting mess. Ain't you got no mother wit? Don't you remember that Murchinson boy over Somerville way? That there's a lesson about stepping out of your element. Boy forgot who he was and where he was. Forgot his place."

"Why you bringing up poor Tommy? He's dead and gone. The only lesson he has for me is to get gone. Hell, look what happened to those two little boys who saw him hanging from that tree. They ain't been right since, minds all scrambled up. I heard tell they still cry in their sleep. Tommy did what he had to do," Skip said, staring into Old Man Williams' eyes. "He did what he had to do."

"He stepped out of his element. That's what he did."

"And what was he supposed to do?" Bad enough we got to mind the white man, but to stand aside and let him do whatever he wants to my family. Un unh." Skip shook his head. "I ain't gon' stand for that."

"Would you risk your life?" asked Old Man Williams.

"I wouldn't give 'em the chance to take my life. I'd be gone. I'd kill the man I needed to kill, then I'd pack up everybody and everything and get the hell out of here. That was Tommy's one mistake. He should've lit out after he killed that guy."

"And how far you think he could-a gone with every white man in Lee County looking for him?"

"Hell, I don't know. Don't matter anyway. What you want him to do? Nothing? The white man took his wife!" Skip gulped down a mouthful of tea. "Shit. That's why I'm leaving, get out from under this mess."

"This mess is everywhere, son. Don't think you can escape by running."

"Yeah, but they got a law in some places. And that's where I want to be."

"So be it," said Old Man Williams. "But before you go, let me put it to you the way my pappy laid it down to me. Then, maybe, you'll see what I'm trying to say."

The old man took a long pull on his cigarette and collected his thoughts.

"This story goes back to when I lived on the old Willard Plantation. Every once in awhile my pappy would take me fishing down by the Brazos. Well, sir, we had our lines in one day and pappy got holt of a big catfish, a mean old boy, full of fight. But pappy got him up out the water and let him thrash around, let him feel his life slipping away. Then pappy put him back in the river. That old cat started heading for the bottom, but he couldn't go nowhere. See, we had him hooked. Well, pappy let him swim a couple-three minutes, then winked at me and pulled the cat back out. This time he let him thrash a long time, till the old cat was too tired to live. Pappy looked at me and said, 'That there's a lesson, Georgie boy. Catfish is a lot like a nigger. Cain't no harm come to him long as he's in his mudhole. But let him get caught outside it and he's in a world of trouble.'

"Now, that relates to what I'm trying to say 'bout Tommy Murchinson and you, Skip. Colored folks got to stay in our little mudhole. Cain't go hauling off doing whatever we please the way white folks do. We gots to sit tight. Take what they do to us and be strong."

Skip sighed. "Sit tight, huh? Live my life like that old saying: 'Nigger and a white man playing seven-up. Nigger win the money, scared to pick it up.' Well, I'm picking up my winnings." Skip stood and drained his cup. "You got any other advice?"

Old Man Williams walked slowly to his altar and picked up a new, palm-sized Bible. "Me and Miss Hattie figured you might need this. I marked some scriptures, 23rd Psalm, the Beatitudes, Ecclesiastes 11. Here."

He thrust the book towards Skip, watched him absently flip through the crisp pages. "You leaving tomorrow?"

"Catching that 11:50 with Delta Slim and Scrapper. Ain't no need of staying on any longer. Grandma Sarah's set," Skip said, turning for the door. He wanted to get away from the old man and his tired old story about niggers and catfish. "They taking me up to Fort Worth. Then I'm on my own."

Old Man Williams reached out his hand, hesitated a moment, then touched Skip's shoulder. "I'll walk you outside." As they stepped into the blinding light, the old man shaded his eyes and fanned himself. "I remember the first time I left home. My mama cried. Pappy just said, 'Don't bring no shame on the family.' Seems a man don't really start living till he gets out in the world, gets roughed up a bit and finds out who he is."

Skip felt uneasy and sad for his old friend, who had returned from war to live out his days haunted by an ancient story. He stepped off the porch.

"We had a lot of good times, eh, Old Man Williams? Remember that song we used to sing in Sunday School? How'd it go?" He waited for the old man's creaky, yet melodic singing voice.

"Yield not to temptation, for yielding is sin. Ask the savior to help you . . . Oh, Lordy me, Skip. I almost forgot something." Old Man Williams dug into the chest pocket of his overalls and pulled out a small, hand-made pouch filled with tobacco and a pack of Bull Durham cigarette papers. "I seen you smoking. Figured you could use some homestyle tobacco. It's special stuff. Double-cured it myself." A hint of mischievous pride rang through the old man's voice. "I know some folks say smoking is a sin, but a man's got to have at least one little bitty vice."

Skip took the pouch and held his friend's hand. The pouch meant more to him than the Bible or the story because it came from the young man inside Old Man Williams, the young man who'd joined the Tenth Colored Cavalry and charged up San Juan Hill to save Teddy Roosevelt's Rough Riders. The smoking kit was a gift from one young man to another.

"Thanks," Skip said. "I'll try and stop by before I leave. Cain't promise it though."

"That's all right," Old Man Williams said. "Just remember what I told you. And, son, be careful."

"I'll do that," Skip said, and headed for the highway, turning to wave good-bye to Old Man Williams who, gnarled hands gripping the straps of his overalls, nodded slowly, then went back into the dark, musty-smelling cabin, where sunlight streamed through the cracks in the worn, wooden walls and baked the layers of Cream of Wheat boxes that had been tacked on for insulation.

Skip headed for the Brazos, glad to be alone, glad to be leaving Tunis before he became like Old Man Williams, stuck in the old ways, or like John Lee, saddled by family. He wasn't ready to go home. Visiting the old man brought memories to his mind, each one connected and streaming from the old man who walked him home from Sunday School under the shade trees, told him war stories by the light of a flickering kerosene lamp, and taught him to play guitar. A broad-winged crow circled lazily overhead and settled amongst the leaf-covered branches of a live oak. The late afternoon sun slid slowly towards the horizon. A thousand crickets took up their evening song. The wet, muddy land sucked at his shoes. He heard the 5:09 racing along the tracks, steel wheels on iron rails creating a rolling rhythm: click-clack chung, click-clack chung. The train's whistle blew loud and long as it approached the river crossing. Waaaown. Wa-waaaown.

He smiled, knowing he'd be on that train tomorrow, heading north.

He found a dry spot near the river's edge, kicked off his shoes and squatted, fanning the mosquitoes and gnats swarming around his face. Dragonflies prowled the river bank. Life flourished in the rich, dark soil. The fetid smell of rot and stagnant water hung thick in the air. Splotches of moss floated along the shore.

Skip saw no one. He plucked a stone from the mud and skipped it across the river, concentric rings pushing out wherever the stone hit. He picked up another rock and threw it over the water, watched it arc above the river and fall near the other side. He'd never thrown a stone across the Brazos.

He sloshed his feet in the cool, dirty river, remembered coming here years ago on a Sunday, when the grown church folk had dressed in white and the circuit preacher, a stern man wearing a black suit and string tie, had recited scriptures and told the lost souls that it was time to find the sweet grace, time to be baptized in the spirit and washed clean of sin. The haunting, dirge-like spiritual came to mind.

"Take me to the water. Take me to the water. Take me to the water to be baptized."

He was a little boy that long ago day, scared and confused when he saw the preacher push Grandma Sarah beneath the dark water. He had run from her when she came towards him, her hair matted, sheets of black water streaming from her face and robe. It was not Grandma Sarah he saw, but a nightmare water demon coming to get him. When she caught him, she hugged him close to her wet, soaking body and told him everything was all right. She had seen God.

He wondered if he was near where Old Man Williams' pappy had caught the catfish and told that crazy story. He wondered if it was even true. Maybe Old Man Williams made it up. Wouldn't be the first time. But even if it was true, he didn't think it mattered to him. Sure, he could stay out of some trouble by keeping to his place, his element, as Old Man Williams said, but that didn't mean he wouldn't end up getting cut in a knife fight. And where was his place, anyway? Who defined it? Was it the colored side of Tunis?

He dropped another stone in the river, watched it sink out of sight, then looked around at the trees, the green, rolling fields, the bridge crossing the Brazos. Another thought came to him. Perhaps he could make the world his place. The catfish died because it couldn't live out of water. But he wasn't a catfish. He could learn new ways of living. He could do what Old Man Williams did a long time ago, make the world his home.

Night crept up on him, stealing the light of this last day. Dusk gave way to a full moon, still red from the sun's light, rising slowly, imperceptibly, a huge ball pushing above the horizon. Soon, the red would drain away, leaving the moon a snow-white disc swinging along the starry night. He put on his shoes, picked up another stone and tested its weight. Maybe this was the one, he thought, rubbing his fingers across the rough rock and stepping back.

He cocked his arm and charged towards the river bank, planted his lead foot at the water's edge, reared back and sent the stone flying, his whole body going into the throw like Cool Papa Bell firing a ball in from deep centerfield. He waited for the inevitable splash, but instead heard only a dull thud.

༄

GRANDMA SARAH WAS HEADING FOR THE CHICKEN YARD WHEN HE returned. She had left a batch of boiled potatoes, collard greens, biscuits and peach cobbler on the stove. Nearby sat the cast iron skillet she used for frying chicken and a tub of water. Skip watched from the back porch, knowing it was best to stay out of her way.

The hens and roosters moved cautiously around the yard when she untied the wooden latch to the coop's rickety door. They cocked their heads, spied her with their beady eyes to see if any food was coming.

Grandma Sarah looked for the fat, young Rhode Island Red hatched this spring. Its meat would be tender, with just enough fat to be juicy. Skip saw it cowering in the crowd huddled behind the old, bare-butt rooster. Grandma Sarah saw it too, and picked up a stick she kept handy for sparring with the rooster.

"Get on out the way, you old devil," she said. "I gots killing to do."

She jabbed at the feisty old bird. The hens scrambled into the hen house, while the rooster made his stand, leaping and flapping his wings, making quick, jerking stabs. She poked him away and backed into the hen house. The Red sat up on a far wall. Grandma Sarah crept forward, calling softly.

"Here, chicky. Here, chicky, chicky. Come here now."

For each step she took forward the Red took one back until the bird's tail feathers brushed the corner. Then, the Red leaped over her head, wings furiously beating the air. It landed behind her and ran squawking into the yard. The rooster stood in the doorway, ready for a fight. Grandma Sarah swung the stick again, but the cantankerous old bird advanced, its claws ripping the hem of her dress. She swung again, this time catching the rooster full in the chest. He fell, stunned. Grandma Sarah headed after the Red, cornered it against a fence, then lost it as the frightened hen scurried between her legs and zig-zagged towards the safety of the hen house. Grandma Sarah recovered quick-ly and barred the doorway. The Red wheeled around, headed back for the fence, squawking and flapping its wings. The rooster stood near the hen house door, watching, guarding his covey.

Grandma Sarah walked towards the Red, the stick tight in her fist. All she needed was one good swing to knock the Red cold, then she could get on with the killing. The Red dodged her advance and again tried to reach the hen house. Grandma Sarah swung the stick, caught the Red on the butt and sent it scooting along, but the Red wasn't hurt. It scrambled frantically about the yard, ran until Grandma Sarah stopped and leaned against the chicken-wire fence, her chest heaving, her breaths coming quick and shallow. Skip fought to keep his place by the door. He wanted to tell her to stop. Greens and biscuits were enough.

He watched her push herself off the fence, grab the can of chicken feed, reach inside and scatter a handful on the ground. The Red didn't take the bait. Grandma Sarah went after it again, swinging wildly. The Red tried to slip past, but a lucky swing slammed across its back. Grandma Sarah was on it quick, clutching it between her hands, raising it off the ground and holding it at arm's length. She tucked the struggling bird under her arm. Its pulse raced beneath her fingers. She covered its scared, knowing eyes with her free hand, slipped her hand around its slender neck and turned her wrist until she felt the Red's tiny bones snap.

The broken-necked bird dropped to the ground and started running mindlessly, tripping and falling, colliding against the fence, the hen house wall, wings flapping, an awful croak coming from the head hanging limp to one side. Skip watched the death dance as if for the first time. A trail of blood marked the Red's dying passage through the dusty yard. The hen made one last mad dash, stumbled and collapsed near her feet, its wings brushing the dirt softly, slowly. Then, it was still. Grandma Sarah picked up the dead hen, carried it back toward the house. She grunted when she saw him.

"Been here long?" she said, grabbing a butcher knife and cutting off the bird's head. Blood spilled over her hands. She looked at him, grim-faced. "Make yourself useful, child. Set the table. Mash them potatoes. Do something. But leave me be."

Skip went to the bureau and took out the white, lace tablecloth used only on Easter, Christmas and Thanksgiving. The house seemed warmer than it had ever been, the smells of frying chicken, sugar-drop biscuits, and peach cobbler more tantalizing than ever before. He rinsed his face and hands, and noticed the smell of sweet pastry on the drying towel. When he had finished, he leaned against the wall and watched Grandma Sarah place a batter-covered leg-quarter into the bacon grease sizzling in the skillet.

"Yes, sir," she said. "We in business now. Go'n and sit down, Skip."

He did not move, but froze an image in his mind: Grandma Sarah expertly testing her fried chicken. It was a bit of Tunis to take with him. At last Grandma Sarah pulled the last piece from the skillet, made her gravy and brought the dishes to the table.

"You say grace this time."

"Gracious Lord," he began. "We are truly thankful for . . ." Those weren't the right words. He'd heard them so often they were almost without meaning now. Grandma Sarah raised her head and looked at him. "Got to make this special," he said, grabbing her hand and bowing his head.

"I am thankful for the love I have found here. Thankful for the people who have helped me through the good and the bad. Thankful that we are healthy and not wanting. Thankful for dreams and Ezekiel Washington's acting school, and above all, thankful for Grandma Sarah. Amen."

"Amen." She looked up, her eyes brimming. "Thank you, Skip. Now you carve up that bird, and I'll dish up the rest of this food."

She ate slowly, distractedly, her smiles forced, tight-lipped. Skip forced his food down and never went for a second plate. After dinner, he and Grandma Sarah walked along Highway 53. They passed Willie Jean Mason's house, heard her keening in the still night. Above them, the brilliant full moon bathed the countryside in white light. Skip heard the rustling whisper of leaves, the wind through the trees. A breeze passed around his ears. He collected another memory of Tunis: Emma and John Lee's baby girl howling for her mama's milk. This was his home. The shotgun houses along the highway, the black people living within them, the young and old people who laughed and cried and survived. Grandma Sarah turned her face upward and told Skip to make a wish as a shooting star rocketed across the sky.

When they returned, Grandma Sarah made coffee, and they sat on the porch to have the tasty peach cobbler. Neither of them spoke. Grandma Sarah finished her cobbler, stepped into the house and returned with a package wrapped in the paper from the gift of Wyler's Bubble Bath.

"Got to take something with you," she said, thrusting the box towards Skip. He carefully unwrapped the present, knowing Grandma Sarah would use the paper again. He pulled out a small picture case with two photographs: one of Grandma Sarah as a young woman; the other of his soldier daddy, his mama, and baby Skip sitting before a painted backdrop of palm trees and ocean.

"Them some old ones," Grandma Sarah said. "Something to remember us by."

Skip fingered the pictures and smiled. Grandma Sarah still held hints of the beauty that had turned Sam Reynolds' head so long ago.

She reached into her pocket and took out his father's war medal. "Hold your head down," she said. "This here's a Croix de Guerre. Frenchmen give it to your daddy for his bravery and courage," she said, fingering the cross. "Well, I'm gon' get me some sleep. Leave them dishes alone, hear. I'll get them in the morning." She turned back towards the house and as she passed, Skip felt her touch on his shoulder.

He rolled a smoke from Old Man Williams' cured tobacco, brought a match to it and took a long drag. Beneath the bite of nicotine he noticed a faint taste of alcohol. Old Man Williams and his little, bitty vice. He passed his fingers lightly over the picture case and touched the medal hanging from his neck. Did he really want to lose this life for the dream of Hollywood? Was it worth the chance of failure? He took another pull on the cigarette. Damn this mess! He went inside and walked around, lay on his pallet, tried to sleep. White moonlight slanted through the window and drew a line across the room. He tried to relax, but could not. Occasionally he dozed. Every now and then he looked out the window and marked the moon's passing.

꙰

TAP-TAP-TAP. TAP-TAP-TAP. A KNOCKING ON THE WINDOW. TAP-TAP-TAP.

"I don't know, Slim," Scrapper said. "Maybe this young boy done changed his mind."

"Keep on tapping," replied Delta Slim. "I tell you this young daddy's got some special stuff. He wouldn't back out."

Tap-tap-tap.

Skip's eyes jerked open. It was time! He rolled out of bed, ran to the front door and whipped it open.

"How long y'all been here?" he said, rubbing sleep from his eyes. "Want some breakfast?"

"I was counting on you asking that last question, young daddy," Delta Slim said as he sauntered into the room. "We got a couple of hours 'fore that Fort Worth train comes rolling through. Bit of breakfast would be right nice." He smiled and looked around. "You ready?"

"Been keyed up all night."

Delta Slim nodded. "Told you, Scrapper. This boy's got some stuff."

"You weren't doubting me now, were you Scrapper," Skip said, winking at Delta Slim. Scrapper didn't answer. "Y'all take a seat. I'll get some coffee going." Skip hurried into the kitchen just as Grandma Sarah came through the back door, cradling fresh eggs in her apron.

"Woowee," she said. "They still upset 'bout yesterday. I must-a took the hen house queen. Looky here." She thrust her right arm forward. A ragged, bloody line of torn skin marked where the old rooster had scratched her. "I should've killed that old buzzard a long time ago. Did I hear Delta Slim and Scrapper," she asked, her voice casual, as if this were an ordinary morning.

"They in the living room, waiting on breakfast."

"How y'all doing?" Grandma Sarah called out.

"Pretty fine, Miss Reynolds," said Delta Slim. "Hope you feeling spry this morning."

Grandma Sarah shooed Skip from the stove and started cooking up a skillet of eggs and bacon scraps. The house filled with breakfast smells. Pork grease popped and sizzled. Scrapper stood by the Victrola, his round, wire-rimmed glasses resting on the end of his nose. He fingered a few records, lips moving as he read the titles.

"Ain't you all gon' play me a song?" said Grandma Sarah. "I always likes a little music in the morning."

"Give out with it, man," Delta Slim said. "I'll sing along."

Scrapper chuckled softly, took a seat in one of the dining chairs and pulled a harp from his pocket. He tapped the instrument against his palm to loosen the reeds, took a deep breath and brought the harp to his lips. Grandma Sarah knew the song. Her voice mixed with Delta Slim's in harmony to Scrapper's melody. Skip knew it too, but he didn't sing. He listened. It was a song the slaves sang as they toiled beneath the foreign southern sun. He saw their black, sweat-washed faces, heard them singing to ease the pain and set their hearts on the promise of a better life after death. They leaned upon one another, big men like John Lee, chained together in the dark, stinking holds of slave ships making the Middle Passage; strong men, broken down in old age, their dying wish to be buried facing east, home to Africa. And there were beautiful black women suckling white babies; women becoming lighter and lighter with each passing generation, their hair straightening, their lips and noses losing the fullness of Africa; women strong enough to bring life into the cruelest of worlds and raise it up to carry on. Skip heard the music and knew Tunis would never leave him.

"I'm heading 'way from Egypt, Lord," his elders sang. "Marching to freedom's land. Heading 'way from Egypt, Lord. Gon' make it, yes I am."

Breakfast wasn't Grandma Sarah's best effort. The eggs were over-done, the bacon bits burned.

"Bit nervous," she explained. "You all understand, but come on. I ain't never had nobody walk away from my cooking."

Skip ate quickly, then excused himself to take a last walk outside the house. He stopped at the chicken yard, nodded toward the old, bare-assed rooster, whose meat was so tough the bird wasn't worth killing.

"You old bastard," Skip said. "Tore up my grandma's arm."

The rooster eyed him and ruffled its feathers. Skip remembered the time he'd knocked the bird stone cold. But the rooster recovered. Always did.

"Live long," Skip said.

The rooster puffed out its chest and crowed defiantly. Skip banged on the chicken-wire fence and walked away.

"Y-o-o-u-u, Skip!" He heard his grandma calling. She met him on his way back to the house. "Getting one last look?" she said.

He nodded. "Remember when Johnny Mason got killed on the train tracks?"

"Willie Jean ain't been the same since. Now, I recall when you was first learning to pick cotton. Seemed you was gon' prick your fingers to death. Lord, how you cried." She laughed at the memory of the little boy whose face was streaked with tears.

"Nothing but memories around here," he said.

Grandma Sarah sighed. "Ain't no need of lingering on them, son. Let's get you on that train."

She followed her grandson into the house, closed the door and waited until he had collected his things. Then she took his hands in hers.

"Lord, protect this boy on his journey. Keep him from harm and always in the light of your love. Walk with him, oh Lord. Lead him in the right path, oh Lord, for that will bring him to your glory." She gripped his hands tighter. Her voice wavered. "Dear Lord, bless this day. And I thank you, Lord, for letting me live to see this boy become a man. And, please, Lord, let me live to see him again." She took him in her arms and kissed his cheek. "Let's go."

Skip grabbed his suitcase, slung National Steel over his shoulder and led Grandma Sarah outside. He held the door a moment, then pulled it shut. The bluesmen headed for the bridge crossing and went over their route, nodding as Grandma Sarah fired one question after another.

"After Fort Worth, he gon' catch the Santy Fee to Los Angeleez, right? Do he need a weapon, Slim? I reckon there's plenty of fools riding the rails these days?"

Delta Slim grunted and kept on moving. He stopped at a long, banked curve a short run from the bridge, sat down and patted his guitar case.

"I makes a point of staying away from fast-moving trains," he said. "Tried to catch one once. Tossed my guitar up in the box car, and the damn thing shook right on off. Got crushed. Wasn't no use in riding then. So, if I ain't catching them in a freight yard, I try to catch 'em when they on a curve, or heading for a bridge and going real slow."

The group huddled on the low side of the tracks, each one listening for the train's whistle. Skip heard it first, blowing loud and long. He looked at the bluesmen, eyes wide with fear and excitement. They smiled calmly, their faces telling him: Steady, young daddy. Steady. The train wasn't close enough to make a move, yet. Grandma Sarah shoved a knotted handkerchief into his hands.

"It's a little bit of money," she said.

Skip tried to push it away. He had thirty-five dollars hidden in his suitcase.

"Ain't you learned, yet?" Grandma Sarah said, handing him the pay he'd given her from his last cotton pick.

Skip straightened up to stuff the handkerchief into his pants pocket.

Scrapper glared at him. "Stay low," he commanded. "No need of letting Mister Engineer see us," he said and nudged Skip. "See that green stock car a little ways up from the caboose? That's us."

The steam engine roared towards them, huffing and puffing,

slowing as it made the bridge. It was a screaming, groaning steel monster whose massive weight pushed the wooden ties into the earth. When it had passed, Scrapper stood and started running in a low crouch. Skip saw him disappear into the open stock car. The freight cars rattled past, too fast, Skip thought. He saw himself slipping under the wheels, getting run over like Johnny Mason.

The stock car was almost up on him. Scrapper was in the doorway, arms held out, hands telling him to get the hell on this train. Skip sucked up some courage, tossed his suitcase, bedroll and National Steel on board, then leaped, banging his chest against the stock car's floor. Scrapper pulled him in. Delta Slim threw his guitar case through the doorway and jumped on. The train started picking up speed. Skip leaned out and waved. His journey had begun.

THE NORTHBOUND KATY ROARED THROUGH LEE COUNTY, ROCKING and swaying, its deafening clamor filling the stock car where Delta Slim and Scrapper sat leaning against the rattling, clattering slats. Skip was in the doorway, looking back to Tunis. He wondered if Grandma Sarah was home now, sitting alone in the three-room house . He caught sight of Sam Willard's plantation, his old crew stuffing cotton into the long, dirty sacks trailing behind them. Was that Willie driving the picking machine through a far section of cotton? He waved, hoping someone would see him. The engine blew a long, piercing whistle that shot into the hot after- noon. Kids making mud pies looked up and waved to the train crew and all the other men sitting in the open doorways of boxcars and stock cars.

A square, white-washed building with a wooden cross nailed above its door and a graveyard out back came into view: The Greater True Light Missionary Baptist Church. Skip remembered his last service. The circuit preacher brought down the spirit that day. People talked in tongues and praised His holy name. Sister Wilson got so happy she had to be carried outside to catch her breath. The preacher was on fire all day, leaning from the handmade pulpit, dog-eared Bible held high. His booming voice filled the small church: "And Ecclesiastes said I have seen all the works done under the sun and have found that in much wisdom there is much grief, and that all is vanity and vexation of the spirit."

"Say, young daddy," yelled Delta Slim. "Pull away from that door. We gotta keep out of sight."

Skip scooted along the hay-strewn floor until he was near the bluesmen. He tried to relax. Delta Slim read a crumpled, week-old copy of the *Houston Post*, while Scrapper sat with his eyes closed, his hat pulled down low.

"Wooowee!" Skip said, slapping his thigh and starting to laugh. "Can y'all believe this? I'm really gon' to Hollywood. What else is happening in this world, Delta Slim?"

"Same old stuff, young daddy. Looks like war's coming over there in Europe." He ran his long, thin fingers through his straightened hair, folded the paper and slapped it against his partner's leg. "What you think, Scrapper? War coming?"

Scrapper pushed his hat up over his eyes. "I don't give a good God damn what them white folks do, Slim. Anything happens, I'm too old to draft. They might take this youngun, though."

"Shoot," Skip said. "I ain't studying nothing 'bout no European war. I'm gon' to Hollywood."

Scrapper snorted. "Uncle Sam don't care where your butt is. If he wants you, he's gon' get you, even if you are in some colored acting school."

"The Ezekiel Washington Colored Actor's School," Skip said, correcting him. "I got a letter from 'em."

"Mind if I take a look," asked Scrapper, sitting up and putting on his reading glasses.

"I surely don't," Skip said.

He opened his suitcase, lifted up the stack of clothes and pulled out the precious envelope. Scrapper grabbed it and scanned the note.

"So, Hollywood needs colored actors, huh," he said. "You got any other proof?"

"I don't need no other proof," Skip said, taking back the letter.

"Now, I ain't siding with Scrapper, young daddy," said Delta Slim. "But the onliest thing I seen colored folks doing in moving pictures is singing, dancing and putting on Rastus for the Boss Man. You don't need a school to teach you that."

Skip cleaned a piece of straw and stuck it in his mouth. "Now, I done told y'all I ain't gon' out there to play no head-scratching fool."

Scrapper nudged his buddy. "This here boy's looking to take on the world, Slim."

"Just Hollywood," Skip said. "Y'all gon' see me up on that screen. And I'm gon' be acting like a natural colored man. You'll see."

"And how in hell is all this gon' happen?" asked Scrapper.

"A little luck and that acting school," Skip replied. "They gon' put me in moving pictures, and once I'm in, hey, Skip Reynolds don't mess around."

Scrapper shook his head. "Never mind, boy. I'll check you next year, after you done had a real taste of this world. Way I hear it, that town you're heading for chews up folks." He turned to his partner. "Remember that guy we met up north, Jim Lowe? He said he wouldn't go back to Hollywood if they paid him Clark Gable's money. And he was making good money when he left. Yeah, that Hollywood is a tough town." He pulled his hat down, closed his eyes and leaned back against the slats.

Skip moved to the square of sunlight streaming through the door. To hell with Scrapper, he thought, unbuttoning his shirt and letting the heat bathe his chest. Everything's gon' be fine. He wiped sweat off his brow, wrinkled his nose at the lingering stench of old piss and shit, unwashed cows headed north to the slaughterhouses. He heard a guitar twang behind him, turned and saw Delta Slim leaning over the instrument, listening to the notes. The bluesman did a quick improvisation, then nodded.

"You got any words for me?" Skip asked.

"It's a mean old world, young daddy. And there's gon' be some blues." Delta Slim did a low-down riff on the bass strings. "First time out. Got to be some blues. And you got to watch your step. Know what I mean?" He started strumming a rhythm to match the train's clicking wheels.

"I'm a steady rolling man. I roll both night and day. Said, I'm a steady rolling man, be rolling both night and day. Just looking for some sweet woman to be rolling my way."

The song rolled on through juke joints and makeshift recording studios. Delta Slim sang about a pig meat papa, and a little queen of spades, about going down that big road by himself and playing with Blind Lemon Jefferson on a Chicago sidewalk, both of them sick, broke and hungry, playing for the coins of passersby. Skip moved closer. He wanted to get inside the music and Delta Slim's rambling story. Leaving sadness pushed up in his mind. He forced it back down. Not now. He didn't want to surrender to it now in front of these traveling men. Later, maybe, when he was alone. Delta Slim brought the song to its end, switched the rhythm to a ragtime beat with a nod to Blind Willie McTell.

"So, I'm leaving you, baby, can't stay in your town. Said I'm leaving you, baby, though I loves my fair brown. And I'll be looking for ya, if I'm ever back around."

Delta Slim strummed the guitar one last time and let the final chord fade into the afternoon.

"Yeah, hey," Skip said, clapping his hands.

"Why, thank you, young daddy. I always loved that sound of appreciation. It's right up there with a woman's loving moan. What say we have us a taste?" he said, and pulled a bottle of rye whiskey from his traveling bag.

Warm whiskey. Skip preferred his cool, sipped. But today was special. "I'm following your lead," he said.

"Here, you take the first swallow."

Skip unscrewed the cap and brought the bottle to his lips. He took a mouthful, held it awhile before sucking it down. The amber liquid burned its way into his gut. He tensed a moment, shook his head and whistled. Delta Slim laughed and took a hearty gulp.

"Hoo-wee," he said. "This stuff can sure set the blues to running."

He took another gulp and passed the bottle back to Skip. They kept on drinking, passing the bottle back and forth, watching the countryside roll by. Scrapper started snoring, his belly rising and falling. Delta Slim nudged him, but Scrapper only grunted. The bottle went back to Skip, who took a long swallow and laid back on the stock car's floor, arms held out at his side. Delta Slim took the bottle from his hands and chuckled softly.

"What you laughing at?" Skip asked.

"I keep thinking of this moving picture with you and Bojangles Robinson dancing behind that little ole white gal. What's her name?" Delta Slim waited, a sly smile on his face.

"Shirley Temple. But that's one moving picture you ain't never gon' see."

"Maybe, but I hope you can do a little buck and wing." Delta Slim finished off the last corner of whiskey and threw the bottle out the stock car's door. He crawled to his guitar, picked it up and gently set it back in its case. Then he propped his head on his traveling bag. "Sing me a song, brother rye," he said, stretching out and folding his hands behind his head. "A lullaby, if you please."

Skip scooted back to the doorway. Another bridge was coming, then Waco, and after that, Fort Worth. The first leg was almost over. A hot blast of steam rushed into the air as the engine slowed to make the bridge. Metal screamed against metal. He smelled river rot, saw willows trailing leaves in the muddy water, another hobo running to catch the freight. The whiskey was working on him now, enfolding him in a warm, hazy embrace that stilled his anxious heart. He thought about Hollywood, finding Fredi Washington and doing Peola's story, the other side of "Imitation of Life." Anything could happen out there. He kicked his legs from the doorway, wheeled around and found a slat to lean on. The train's easy rolling rhythm lulled him to sleep. Then a passing shadow startled him. A bird? Something banged inside the stock car. His eyes snapped open in time for him to duck the bedroll that slammed near his head. An intruder rolled across the floor, feet in the air, hair picking up splinters and hay. Blonde hair.

"Good God," he said. "A white gal."

She ended up head over heels, then rolled forward and looked about, scared and frantic. Skip tossed her the bedroll. She caught it and pushed herself back into a corner, all the while reaching inside the bedroll and pulling out a small-caliber pistol.

"You niggers stay away from me," she said. "I ain't afraid of using this."

The train cleared the bridge and sped north. The rattling, clattering clamor returned. Skip nudged Delta Slim, shook Scrapper, who woke in an instant and caught the frightened stranger in a menacing glare.

"Gal, what are you doing in here, trying to get us all killed? Get out," he said.

"Ain't trying no such thing, nigger. I'm just trying to get to Fort Worth. Ain't my fault I jumped in the wrong car."

"Well, it sure in hell ain't ours," Scrapper jerked his thumb in the direction of Skip and Delta Slim.

"That don't settle nothing," she said, still waving her pistol.

"Put that thing down, 'fore you kill somebody," said Scrapper. "Put it down, I said." The girl lowered her pistol. "Now," Scrapper said. "What's your name?"

"Hetta Mae McFarland."

"Well, Miss McFarland, why don't you trot your little tail on out of here so's we can all get where we're going in one piece?"

"I wish to hell I could, but look out there. This train is moving too damned fast."

The freight was highballing now. The landscape whipped past as the locomotives pulled the load on to Fort Worth.

"Shit," Scrapper said, turning to Hetta Mae. "What are you doing here if you can't ride a fast train?"

She flinched at the question, drew her knees up and wrapped her arms around them. She looked fifteen, maybe younger. Her face had a baby softness. Skip saw a slight bulge in her belly. She swayed to the train's motion, lowered her head and stared at the floor. Scrapper moved closer, got down on one knee.

"Well," he said.

Hetta Mae mumbled something.

"Say what?"

"I said I'm going to be with the man what give me this child I'm carrying." She raised her eyes to Scrapper. "He said he loved me."

"Love?" Scrapper spat out the word, stood and dusted the back of his pants. "Ain't there some song says love's gon' get me killed, Slim?" He didn't wait for an answer, just moved to the doorway and stared outside.

The sun was falling from the sky. He looked up and down the train, saw men casually hanging their legs out of their stock cars, relaxing and smoking, talking to unseen companions. He shouted over his shoulder.

"What time is it, Slim?"

"Getting on 'bout five-thirty, I reckon. Fort Worth in an hour, maybe less. What you say?"

"Sooner the better, Slim. Sooner the better." He turned from the doorway and joined Skip and Delta Slim. The three leaned together as Scrapper whispered a plan. 'The way I figure it, we jump out soon's we hit the freight yard. I'll tell her to get off after us. Cain't let nobody see us together. Nobody. Okay?"

He passed the plan on to Hetta Mae, who sat scrunched up in a corner, hugging her bedroll. Skip tried to relax, but could not, here in the coming darkness. The worst things could happen, did happen. He remembered hearing about the Scottsboro boys, nine black boys just like him, one of them a 13-year-old kid, and all of them accused of raping a white girl. Folks said the girl made up the story. But that didn't matter. Those boys were doing hard time. His heart stumbled, unnerved with fear. Prison. Life on a chain gang. What if Hetta Mae said they'd done something to her? They could get the electric chair! Who would believe them? Damn this white gal. She done messed up everything. The 23rd Psalm came to mind, and he started repeating, 'The Lord is my shepherd, the Lord is my shepherd, though I walk through the valley of the shadow of death.' Delta Slim filled a rolling paper with tobacco, pinched it at both ends and tried to make a cigarette. The paper ripped apart. He tried three more times before getting a poorly rolled smoke to his nervously trembling lips. Scrapper was back at the doorway, looking for Fort Worth.

Hetta Mae yanked a comb through her frazzled hair. Skip figured she was getting herself ready for her man. She was almost pretty behind the hard mask she wore. Her cool, blue eyes might have smiled if she were someplace else and everything was different. She tossed her hair back and stared at him.

"What you looking at?"

"Ain't looking at you," he said.

"Best not be."

"Coming up on Fort Worth!" yelled Scrapper.

"Let's get ready to make some fast tracks, young daddy," said Delta Slim.

Skip grabbed his suitcase and bedroll and swung National Steel over his shoulder. "I am ready to leave this mess." He looked at Hetta Mae. "You know the plan?"

"I ain't dumb, nigger."

"Didn't say you was, just looking after my own hide."

The freight slowed as the lead engine rolled through the maze of switches leading into Fort Worth's cinder-strewn yard. Metal jerked against metal, the couplers straining and pulling, the train creaking along. The stench of the sprawling stockyards nearby mixed with the steam and coal smoke from a dozen locomotives. Skip could hear hogs and sheep in their pens, the deep bellowing of long horn steers corralled and waiting for slaughter. Through the open doorways of idle box cars he glimpsed a herd being packed onto a train on the far side of the railyard. Hoboes started jumping from the train as it lumbered toward its terminus. He saw them scrambling and running for safety. Some struggled along on crutches. They wore patched denims and ratty shirts, overalls, ragged suits with the names of expensive clothiers in New York, Dallas, Chicago, or San Francisco still on the inside coat pocket, suits bought in the jazzy days when everybody did the Charleston, quoted Cullen and Hughes and had a high time before Black Monday sent the world crashing down, and the suits, once the toast of a thousand gay evenings slowly made their way down the line from second-hand shop, to rag pile, to a bum's back in the part of Forth Worth the cowboys called "hell's half acre." Skip saw a snot-nosed kid leading a blind man. The boy savagely kicked lumps of coal out of his way and wiped soot from his baby face, while the man tapped a path. "Look out there, pap," Skip heard him say. Wind moaned through the railyard. Scrapper gauged the train's speed and turned to Skip.

"Let's make that move."

"Check and double-check," Skip said, then looked over his shoulder at the scrawny girl still huddled in a far corner. "Bye pregnant mama," he said and jumped, landing hard, but making sure nothing happened to National Steel.

The bluesmen hustled out of the yard, Skip following, turning now and then, watching as Hetta Mae strained to reach a handle on the stock car and swing herself down.

"Come on, young daddy," said Delta Slim. "We ain't got time to be worrying 'bout nobody."

Skip heard a scream as he leaped over a rail, turned and saw Hetta Mae slip from the stock car. Her head snapped back against one of the steel tracks snaking through the yard. She did not move.

"What'll we do?" Skip said.

"Just keep moving," said Delta Slim, eyes scanning the yard for cops. "Just keep moving. Somebody'll take care of her."

"But what if she's hurt, or maybe losing that baby?"

Scrapper stopped. "You a doctor?" Skip shook his head. "Then there ain't a damn thing you can do for her. Where's your mind, boy? Worrying 'bout a white gal." He walked on, too disgusted to say anything else.

Skip trudged after his friends. They were right, but he kept looking over his shoulder, hoping to see Hetta Mae up and walking. Thoughts of Scottsboro clashed with the insane idea that he should help her, even if she was a white gal. He found himself thinking about Sunday school lessons, the Golden Rule and how black folks had to show white folks how to be Christians. He dropped his suitcase.

"I'm gon' take a quick check on her," he said. "See if she's all right."

"You what!" said Delta Slim. "We best keep moving, young daddy. Ain't nothing but trouble back there."

"Let him go, Slim," urged Scrapper. "We done our part. He's on his own now."

"You mean y'all ain't gon' wait for me," Skip said, scared now.

"I know I ain't," said Scrapper, turning and walking on.

Delta Slim pointed to three rusting engines. "I'll be on the other side of them locomotives. Five minutes, young daddy. Then I'm gone, too."

Skip gave him his gear and ran through the yard of empty freight cars, forgotten engines, cabooses waiting to be hooked up for a ride to Abilene or El Paso. His heart beat like a trip hammer. His ears strained to hear every sound. His eyes were on high alert, searching for yard bulls. He hurried to where Hetta Mae lay unconscious, leaned over her and lifted her head. There was no blood, just a wicked bruise along the side of her face. He tried to steady himself. He'd never been this close to a white girl, so close he could feel her breaths upon his hands as he pushed her hair back from the ugly splotch of purple and black that bloomed where she had hit her head on the rail. Should've kept her ankles crossed, he thought, suddenly remembering B. K. Simpson back home, who always looked so inviting in her tight denim shirts unbuttoned just enough so you could see a flash of breast if you dared to look. Yeah, she was something, he thought, then stopped. What the hell was he doing here. He took his hands off Hetta Mae. His blood turned to ice water, and he whispered to himself, "Boy, let's get this Christian charity over with."

He searched her bedroll, found a canteen and poured some water over her face. "Come on now, Hetta Mae. Come on." His breaths came quick and shallow. The yard was quiet, except for the moaning wind. He looked over his shoulder, saw no one, and splashed her again.

Her eyelids fluttered open, confused, then afraid. Her mouth opened, to speak? to scream?

"Sshh," Skip said. "You all right. I seen you fall from the stock car. I came back and helped you." He stood. "Take care of that baby," he said, turned and started running.

"Stop right there, nigger-boy."

The commanding voice seemed to come out of nowhere. Heavy boots crunched the gravel. Skip heard a billy club slapping against an open palm. He turned and saw a strong bull of a man striding towards him, 38-caliber pistol hanging low on the man's hip, worn leather gun belt lined with bullets. Sweat dripped from Skip's underarms. His pulse thundered. He started breathing long and slow to calm himself. *I didn't do nothing,* he thought. *I only helped her. It'll be all right.* The yard cop stopped beside Hetta Mae, who was sitting up now, rubbing the back of her head and gingerly touching the bruise. The cop hitched up his gun belt and tapped the club against his thigh.

"Come on over here, boy," he said.

Skip obeyed. He walked slowly, cursed himself and every Sunday school lesson he'd ever heard. He should've listened to Scrapper. The cop's square face was set in a menacing glare. He looked about forty, his hair thinning, a slight paunch forming around his gut. "Williamson" was sewn on his brown jacket in fancy script. His left jaw bulged from a plug of chewing tobacco. He spat a brown stream into the dirt.

"This don't look good," he said. "Don't look good at all. What you been doing to this child?"

"N-nothing, sir," Skip said. "I seen her fall and I come to see if she was all right. I ain't done nothing to her."

"Looks to me like you done something. Her face is all beat up, and I seen you running. Must've done something." He turned to Hetta Mae. "How 'bout it gal?"

She did not speak, just clutched her bedroll. Her body trembled. Williamson kneeled down and looked into her frightened eyes, his hand rested on her shoulder. "My God, boy, what you hit her with?"

"I didn't hit her, sir. I swear to God. I ain't done nothing." Skip looked at Hetta Mae. "Tell him. Tell him I ain't ..."

Williamson was up in an instant, wheeling around and swinging his billy club, catching Skip full on the thigh. "Shut up. You already done enough to this child," he said. "I'm taking you back to the station, charging you with vagrancy, assault and attempted rape."

"Rape! But I was just trying to . . ."

The billy club slammed into Skip's gut. He crumpled, but Williamson yanked him up and hit him in the face, hard. "Now you know how this gal feels. But that's only the beginning, nigger-boy. That's only the beginning."

Skip clenched his teeth against the pain exploding in his head, the panic growing inside him. He knew Williamson would shoot him down if he ran, if he even raised his hand. He looked at Hetta Mae, his eyes in a silent, desperate plea. He thought he saw her lips move.

"Turn around so's I can put these handcuffs on you," Williamson growled. "And get on your knees." He hit Skip again, this time a vicious blow to the back of the legs. A stream of tobacco juice splashed against the back of Skip's neck and oozed down his spine.

"P-p-please, sir. I ain't done nothing," he said. "I swear. I ain't done nothing."

Williamson grunted as the handcuffs cut into Skip's wrists. "Save it, boy."

Skip wanted to yell for help, but he was on his own, alone in this strange place, with an angry yard cop eager to arrest him for the worst possible crime. Williamson tugged on the cuffs, tried to pull Skip up, but Skip's legs were limp, weak from fear.

"Get up, damn you," Williamson shouted. "You need some coaxing?"

Williamson raised his boot and kicked Skip in the back of the ribs, pitching him forward, face down in the gravel, hands cuffed behind his back. Williamson laughed, raised his foot to deliver another blow, this one aimed at Skip's head. Boom! A gunshot shattered Williamson's concentration. He lost his balance, kicked wildly, missing Skip. He turned around. Hetta Mae was standing, holding her pistol in unsteady hands.

"What the hell's wrong with you, gal?"

"H-he ain't done me no harm."

"Don't be protecting him."

"I am. Let him go."

Williamson spat another stream of ugly tobacco juice. He looked at Hetta Mae and grinned. "A nigger lover, huh. Bet it's his baby you're carrying."

Boom! Another shot. The acrid smell of sulfur hung heavy in the still air.

"Don't be calling me a nigger lover," screamed Hetta Mae. She brought the gun level with Williamson's eyes. " Now take them handcuffs off him."

"Jesus, fucking Christ," Williamson leaned over Skip and whispered, "You been saved, nigger-boy. But you better pray I never see your black ass again." He stood and turned to Hetta Mae. "I guess you two want to be alone."

"Get out of here," she said, her voice firm as she could make it.

"And you go to hell, you bastard-carrying slut."

He turned and walked away, looking over his shoulder every few steps.

Skip lay motionless, exhausted. He struggled to his feet, leaned against the stock car, hands resting on his knees. He tried to take a deep breath, but couldn't get past the pain. He slumped against the car, almost went down. The world swirled and rocked before his eyes. He shook his head and stared at Hetta Mae. Her hard, humorless expression had returned.

"Thanks," he said.

"We're even," she replied. "You done me a favor, otherwise I'd have let him beat you to death. I ain't no nigger lover." She tucked the pistol into her pants, picked up her bedroll and ran out of the yard.

Skip wanted to run, too, but his body would not respond. He heard more footsteps, heavy, drawing near. He stiffened. Williamson? Terror swept over him. His eyes closed. He started to black out. Let it come, he thought.

"Young daddy! What happened, boy? You been shot?"

It was Delta Slim. Skip opened his eyes, tried to smile.

"A. . a . . cop beat me up. That gal stopped him." He fell into Delta Slim's arms.

"Anything broke?"

"Don't think so. But I got hurt bad, Delta Slim. Swear to God I was a dead man. He was gon' arrest me for attempted rape." Skip gasped, then began to cry without shame. He coughed up blood. "Shit."

Delta Slim grasped one of Skip's arms and placed it around his shoulder. "Just lean on me, young daddy. Scrapper found a flophouse that ain't Jim Crowing. Can you make it?"

"Yeah," winced Skip, taking small steps. He limped out of the rail yard, tears blurring his vision. "I was just trying to do good, Delta Slim.

What went wrong?"

"Nothing. You just been baptized into this mean old world."

༺❦༻

THE NEXT MORNING WAS HOT, THE SUN HIGH AND BURNING DOWN on everything. Its heat soothed Skip's aching body. After breakfast at a cheap bacon-and-eggs joint, Delta Slim and Scrapper took him back to the rail yard. Even though his body still hurt from last night's violence, he felt ready to move on. Ezekiel Washington was waiting. He met a short, fierce-looking black hobo and asked him about the westbound trains.

"Calforny," the little man said. "Sure, there's a freight going there. Pulls out half past noon."

Skip thanked him, turned and started walking away, but the hobo's bony, misshapen fingers grabbed his arm. "Spare some change, brother?" The bum scratched his dirty, scraggly beard.

Skip dug in his pockets. "How's two bits?"

"It's a couple of days eating." The little man paused and looked beyond Skip, his gaze wistful and far away. "Calforny," he said, licking his sun-cracked lips. "I hear food falls from trees out there."

Skip slapped the coins into the man's hand, then ran off to join his friends behind a battered old coal car.

"You ready to solo?" asked Scrapper.

"Ready as I ever will be." Skip rubbed his bruised ribs, took out his wallet and counted his money.

"Safest place for green is next to your body," Scrapper said, matter-of-fact. He took off his belt and handed it to Skip. "See here, it's got a hiding place for cash. Take it."

"Thanks, Scrapper," Skip said, tucking his bills into the belt's slot, then slipping the worn strip of leather through the loops of his traveling jeans.

"You're on your own now, young daddy," Delta Slim said.

"Yeah." Skip checked his suitcase, made sure it was secure. "Just me and this mean old world." He stopped and looked at the two bluesmen. "You all think I'll make it?"

"Don't much matter what we think," Delta Slim said. "You the one got to believe."

"Right," Skip nodded. "And I'm gon' be on that moving picture screen. You wait and see."

The bluesmen laughed and agreed. Skip was gon' be a sure enough moving picture star. Delta Slim pulled out a fresh bottle of rye. "A toast to the next sepia king of the moving picture screen," he said, smiling at his rhyme as he twisted off the bottle's cap and took a long swallow.

The bluesman passed the bottle to Skip, who took it and tossed down a last swig, forcing a smile as the whiskey settled into his stomach. He capped it and flipped the bottle to Scrapper. For a moment his gaze rested on these two bluesmen in whom Grandma Sarah had entrusted his safekeeping and in whom he had found guardians to guide him in the time of his baptism. Would he ever see them again? This leaving brought more sadness, the bitter, increasing knowledge that traveling meant sorrow and loss, a continual rending of connections made. But every ending had a beginning, at least that's what Grandma Sarah said. Every ending put you at another door. The noon whistle blew.

"That's you, young daddy," said Delta Slim.

"See this boy off, Slim. I'm gon' find out how we can get to St. Lou'." Scrapper stood and nodded at Skip. "Watch yourself."

Delta Slim and Skip followed the hobo's directions until they found the California-bound Santa Fe on the far side of the rail yard. Delta Slim picked out an empty freight car, looked around for cops, then peeked inside.

"This'll do," he said.

Skip tossed in his suitcase, guitar and bedroll as the lead engine let off a shot of steam. The train lurched forward, couplers pulling together with enough power to crush a man's arm. Three short bursts of steam exploded in the air. Leaving time.

"You got any protection?" Delta Slim asked.

"Just my fists," Skip said.

"Humph. You gon' need more than that. Here." He unhooked a pocket knife from his belt loop.

Skip held it in his hand, felt its weight, rubbed his fingers across the smooth wood. He flicked his wrist and the blade swung out, deadly steel catching his reflection. Here was protection. "Delta Slim?" He hesitated, folding the blade down and putting the knife in his pocket. "Would you write me if I gave you the address?"

"Well, I ain't much of a writing man, young daddy. But, sure, where you gon' be?"

"The Ezekiel Washington Colored Actors' School, Post Office Box 981, Hollywood, California."

"Gotcha."

The train jerked again. Slowly, the long procession of steel and wood began its journey. Skip grabbed Delta Slim's right hand, held it tight, then let go. Each man shrugged and forced a tight smile.

"Get on now, young daddy."

Skip trotted off, jumped into the freight car and landed easy, with little pain. The train picked up speed, the lead engines huffing and puffing, gathering speed for the long run to the coast. As Skip leaned from the doorway, he heard Delta Slim yell above the growing noise:

"Stay alive, young daddy. God dammit, stay alive."

T HE SOUTHERN PACIFIC FREIGHT RUMBLED OUT OF WEST TEXAS, leaving behind the old haunts of Billy The Kid, Wyatt Earp and Deadwood Dick, the boom and bust frontier towns, the villages named by homesick immigrants, the land where oil derricks plumbed a liquid mother lode— Abilene, Pecos, Sweetwater, Odessa— land that had been spared the wild dust storms that roared through the panhandle, smothering farms and blotting out the sun. In the streets of Amarillo people fell to their knees and begged forgiveness, seeing in those terrible, gigantic, wind-blown clouds signs of the Apocalypse. Later, after the storms passed, survivors loaded creaking jalopies with whatever they could scavenge and joined the trek west.

Skip stared in wonder at the scrub brush and cactus. The entire land-scape was painted in browns and reds. Tunis, land of memory and lush, green fields lay two days behind him. He fingered his money belt, remembering a portly harmonica player who, after all was said and done, cared about him. Delta Slim's parting words came to mind. "Stay alive, young daddy." Hell, yeah. Got to. He took off his shirt and waved it from the stock car's door like a victory flag.

"Look out world!" he yelled. "Skip Reynolds is on his way!"

A young white man in the next car leaned out. "How far you going?" he yelled, eyes smiling behind wire-rimmed glasses.

Skip ignored him. He'd had enough of being friendly to white folks.

The young stranger called out again. "My name's Joe Bob Winslow, from Oklahoma way. How `bout you?"

"Ain't none of your business who I am or where I'm from," he said, and retreated into his stock car. He opened his suitcase and pulled out the letter from Ezekiel Washington:

"Dear Actor:

The Ezekiel Washington Colored Actors' School is the place for you to make a start in Hollywood. Our staff members have appeared on stage, in traveling shows and, of course, in moving pictures. You've probably seen them in The Green Pastures, So Red The Rose and many more too numerous to list here. They are all eager to pass on their knowledge and tips of the trade.

Also, we often have surprise visits from such well-known stars as Miss Louise Beavers, Mr. Clarence Muse, even Steppin' Fetchit himself. Now is an especially fine time for the colored actor in Hollywood. Movie makers know the power of our creations. They hunger for our humor and grace. Just yesterday, a famous director asked me when I'd have another group of graduates. He needs colored actors!

You, too, can become part of this century's most fascinating industry. I urge you to read the enclosed booklet and, when you're ready, catch the first thing west.

Hollywood awaits!

Cordially yours,

Ezekiel Washington, Esq."

Skip reread the letter. His eyes lingered over the famous names. Phrases tickled his imagination—"Now is an especially fine time . . . a famous director . . . needs colored actors . . . catch the first thing west . . . Hollywood awaits!" Hollywood. He closed his eyes, saw the glamorous town all lit up with neon, the leaves of slender palm trees swaying in a cool Pacific Ocean breeze, rustling like the skirts of Hawaiian hula girls. Movie stars were everywhere. He saw himself six months from now, a slick dandy in a blue, double-breasted suit, a gold watch chain hanging from his vest pocket. He was going to straighten his hair, part it on the left side. Nobody back home would recognize him. He slapped his dusty denim pants and swore to buy big-city trousers the first chance he got.

The train rolled on through the coming night. He rolled a cigarette

from Old Man Williams' pouch and smoked in the doorway. The powerful locomotives strained up the Continental Divide. He listened, his mind
considering the ingenuity to forge those intricate machines up ahead, the
gears, pilot wheels, drive wheels, trailing trucks, hammering pistons and
fire doors; the skill to connect them all in mechanical perfection and,
with lumps of coal, make those mighty four-eight-fours link cities to
towns, farms to markets, himself to Hollywood. Far off a car's headlights
pierced the dusk. The evening cooled. He put on a jacket, went back to
the doorway and relaxed, the cigarette burning slowly down. He leaned
his head out.

"Great night," yelled Joe Bob Winslow.

Skip waved, glad for the conversation. "It's not too bad. Where
`bouts you headed?"

"Cal'fornia. Some place called the Imperial Valley. I'm gonna join my
peoples, but I want to see that Pacific Ocean first."

"What for?"

"Ain't never seen an ocean, `cept in them moving pictures. I want to
do like them rich folk do, lay in the sun and have a bathing beauty bring
me anything I please. And I want her to look like Jean Harlow." Joe Bob
laughed and made an hour-glass shape with his hands.

"You take Harlow and I'll take Fredi Washington," Skip yelled back.

"Where you headed?"

"Hollywood. I'm gon' join an acting school out there and see if I can
get in moving pictures."

"Naw. Hollywood? I wouldn't think there's enough work out there for
colored."

"Shows how much you don't know," Skip said. "They got acting
schools out there and everything. You look for me up on that screen in a
year or two."

"Hmm. Say, where you from?"

"Tunis, a little old town down Houston way. I used to pick cotton."

"I done my share of that," Joe Bob said. "Now, I'm gon' out to
Cal'fornia to pick peaches. But I ain't long for that, no sir. I'm just gon'
help the folks a little, then find me a bathing beauty and . . . Oh Jesus!"
Joe Bob pointed towards a freight car falling over a ways behind the locomotives. "Sweet Jesus! Grab hold of something, buddy!"

An awful shaking rattled through the train. Desperate screams rent the air as cars derailed. A violent motion jerked Skip's car off the tracks. He slid backward, splinters driving into his shoulders, arms, legs. His head banged against a far wall. Then all was dark.

⬥

SKIP IS A CUTE, ROUND-CHEEKED, LITTLE BROWN BOY WITH A PRETTY mommy and a soldier daddy who wears a uniform full of shiny medals and red, blue and green ribbons. Grown folks visit, each one wanting to see the three-year-old boy, who is trotted out to be hugged and kissed, bounced on laps. Smiling ladies with long, delicate fingers smelling of perfume pinch his soft cheeks. "Gimme some sugar," they say. Big men drop shiny coins into his pudgy palms. They gaze into his eyes and nod, satisfied.

"That boy's the spitting image of you, Bill," they say. "The spitting image."

One bright, sunny afternoon the soldier daddy sits brooding and quiet in his big chair. He does not smile, does not offer to bounce his little man on his knee. He is too busy drinking. The soldier daddy never talks when he drinks. He just puts on his uniform and sits and pours and drinks and pours. Skip is afraid of him. He takes his toys and plays in a corner of the living room, far from the soldier daddy's seething anger. The pretty mommy bustles about, looking for things to do. She knows the soldier daddy is hurting deep inside where her love cannot reach. He still wears his uniform, even though the Armistice was five years ago.

"We were there first." The soldier daddy grumbles, his bitter voice breaking the tense silence. "Bloodied and all. The 369th, colored troops, first Americans to reach the Rhine River." He lurches to parade rest, sways on alcohol-weakened legs. "I damn near lost my life over there. *Over there.*"

But he does not sing the war song. He grabs the bottle and swings it toward his lips. His Adam's apple rides up and down his throat. Brown liquid disappears with each swallow. He shoots a glare past the pretty mommy, stares at the room, sees second-hand couches, chairs, a bureau from his slave grandfather's master.

"Let's go to Grandma Sarah's," he says. "I want to see my mama."

"Not today, Bill. You cain't drive now." The pretty mommy's voice is full of a fear she cannot hide.

"The hell I cain't. You scared?" With a gait rolling like a ship on a stormy sea, he walks over to Skip and breathes the stink of alcohol into his little man's face. "You want to see Grandma Sarah? My little William Henry wants to see his Grandma Sarah, don't he?"

He lifts the little boy toward the ceiling, dips him from side to side, up and down like a merry-go-round. Skip giggles and laughs, giddy from the strange, almost sickening feeling of his stomach floating up inside him. The soldier daddy wheels him around the room, faster and faster. The pretty mommy watches, helpless, her hands reaching out for her child.

The spring day is filled with the sweet scents of roses, magnolia, mint and honeysuckle blooming beneath an egg-yolk yellow sun shining in the clear, china-blue sky. Frightened and tense, the mother and child sit quiet in a Model-T racing down the highway. The soldier daddy is driving, one strong hand gripping the steering wheel, the other tilting a bottle to his sucking lips. A green and white striped scarf around his neck whips and snaps in the wind like a regimental pennant. He flashes a full-toothed smile at his little man, his spitting image. Skip presses close to his pretty mommy, breathes deep her comforting smell and tries to hide in her soft body. She pats his head and tells the soldier daddy not to drive so fast, tells him to remember the time they went to Grandma Sarah's house, the time he swerved the car from one side of the road to the other just so he could play chicken with the oncoming cars. He grunts and takes another drink, tries to drive straight, but cannot. The car drifts toward collision with an advancing truck. Skip's fingers grab handfuls of his pretty mommy's blouse. Her sheltering arms cover him. The soldier daddy laughs and steers back on the right side of the road as the truck whizzes past, its horn honking, its driver leaning out, yelling curses torn by the wind.

The bottle empties, is flung high behind the speeding car. The Model-T continues to swerve. Its right front wheel catches in a rut running alongside the highway. The soldier daddy does not slow down. He tries to turn back on the road. Skip feels the car begin to flip over. The pretty mommy holds him tight as they catapult across the green fields. She screams until they crash against the hard ground. He hears her gasp, hears bones breaking. Then, silence.

He wakes up later, struggles from under her cold body. Is she sleeping? He nudges her.

"Mommy. Mommy. Wake up mommy."

The soldier daddy hangs upside down in the overturned car, his body frozen in a grotesque contortion. A thin streak of blood trickles from his ear. Sightless eyes stare at his spitting image, a dazed little boy who crawls toward the car, twisted broken leg leaving a small furrow in the grass.

"Daddy. Daddy."

He pushes the body. Blood gushes from the soldier daddy's mouth. He pushes the body again and again, hands wet and sticky from his father's blood. The horrible, lopsided creak of wheels slowly turning on a bent axle fills the air. A wounded cry spills from his mouth, takes the form of the first words he ever spoke: "Mommy! Daddy! Mommy! Daddy!" It builds into a wordless wail rising into the clear, china-blue sky, where the egg-yolk yellow sun burns down to the horizon.

Big white men in dark blue uniforms with silver, five-pointed stars on their chests find him crying amid the wreckage.

"What is your name, little boy?" they ask. "What is your name?"

He cannot remember.

❧

"HEY, BUDDY. YOU ALL RIGHT? SAY, ARE YOU ALL RIGHT?" A VOICE, concerned and friendly, reached into the blackness into which Skip had fallen. Someone pushed him. "Say, buddy. Come on, now."

Skip's eyes fluttered open. Joe Bob Winslow's sunken-cheeked, bony white face stared down at him, deep-set eyes squinting in the darkness. He sat up. The old wound throbbed in his left leg. Gingerly he tapped the newly formed knot on the back of his head, then slowly pulled a long splinter from his arm.

"We best get moving `fore they arrest us and put us to work on this train," said Joe Bob. "Here, let me help you."

Joe Bob Winslow grabbed Skip's suitcase and together they crawled out of the upended freight car, Skip cradling National Steel. There was a fresh crack along the guitar's resonator cone. Here and there glowed the orange flames of lanterns swinging on the hands of crewmen inspecting the wreck. Derailed cars lay on their sides like toys scattered by an angry child. Skip shook his head, trying to bring into sharp focus the surreal, dreamlike scene. Joe Bob Winslow fiddled with his glasses, which had been bent in the wreck and now sat crookedly on his face.

"I heard you crying, so I stopped," he said. "Boy, you sure was carrying on in there. Screaming and hollering."

"Hollering?"

"Hell yeah. Like you was wrassling the Death Angel. Say, can you play that guitar? I gave it a try once, wanted to be like Jimmy Rogers. Yodel-eee-ooo. You know any Jimmy Rogers?"

Skip shook his head. Numb and without words, he trudged toward the highway that ran not too far from the train tracks. Joe Bob Winslow picked up the pace. The stranger's stride was easy and loose-legged. Was he a friend, a thief? Skip felt his belt for the slight bulge of money. It was still there. All around, men fled the wreck. Some limped along, or leaned against friends. Everyone made for the highway.

The night grew cold. Joe Bob Winslow kept up a rambling monologue that sounded muffled, as if heard from under water. Cars and trucks raced out of the highway's darkness, then whooshed past, red taillights growing smaller and smaller. Each time one came near, Joe Bob Winslow stuck out his thumb and smiled. Finally, a pick-up truck stopped. Five refugees from the wreck huddled in the truck's bed.

"'Bout time." Joe Bob Winslow ran to the cab, talked to the driver and came back grinning. "They heading west. Come on."

A beefy-faced man poked his head out from the passenger's window. "We ain't got but room enough for one," he said.

"Aw, hell," yelled Joe Bob Winslow. "There's plenty room back here. You can squeeze in another."

"Room for one," the passenger said. You riding or not?"

Skip nodded toward the truck. "Go'n and take it."

Joe Bob Winslow shrugged, mumbled that he was sorry about leaving Skip this way. "I'm riding," he yelled to the passenger, and tossed his bedroll in back. He turned to Skip. "See you in Cal'fornia!"

Damn, shit. Skip stayed by the highway, hoping to catch a ride, but nobody stopped. He walked along the roadside until the moon began its gradual slide toward dawn and sleep whispered—Enough, maybe tomorrow. He felt like a shipwrecked sailor who, washed up on a deserted isle, stares with heartbreaking sadness at the vast ocean separating him from the land he had known.

He turned from the highway, bent over and unrolled his bedding near some scrub brush. The face of the passenger in the pick-up came back to him. The guy looked like a white boy he'd beat up a long time ago, a mean, sour-faced kid, who'd taunted him, told him he really wasn't an American because only his palms were white. The rest of him was nigger, and niggers weren't Americans. He laughed to himself. That boy went home crying. He tapped a cigarette from the pack of Chesterfields he'd bought in Fort Worth because he wanted to save Old Man Williams' gift and because the castles on the package made him feel royal. That was yesterday. A good day. Today? No use worrying `bout it, he thought, drawing on the Chesterfield. He pulled Delta Slim's knife from the suitcase, put it beside him and stretched out. A deep sigh escaped on a long stream of smoke. He crushed out the cigarette and closed his eyes, leaving his worries to tomorrow.

SKIP STOOD BY THE ROADSIDE ALL MORNING, STICKING OUT HIS thumb and wearing his best, harmless colored boy smile. But no one stopped. A couple of times drivers pulled over, waited for him to get close, then sped off, their passengers leaning out the window and waving bye-bye. Out by the railroad tracks work crews wrestled with the wreckage. The knot on his head sent a dull, throbbing pain through his brain. What the hell was going on? The trip was supposed to be easy: a couple-three days' ride then—presto!—Los Angeles. Instead, here he was, stuck in the middle of nowhere, his body banged up and nobody to lend a hand. Damn, shit. He looked across the road. What if he crossed, stuck out his thumb and caught a ride in the first car heading east? How long could he ride in that car? An hour? A day? The idea wasn't worth considering. There were only two options: keep trying to hitch a ride, or start walking. He picked up his gear and headed west.

The heat was inescapable. The sun beat down on him. After a couple of hours he longed for a drink of water, or the good sense to have packed a canteen The asphalt softened and grew sticky under his shoes. Cars whizzed by, but he did not try to flag a ride. He just put one weary foot in front of the other, and sang every song he knew. The day grew hotter. Sweat began to pour off of him. He licked his lips, glad for the taste of something wet on his tongue. Another hour passed. How far to the next town? A '34 Plymouth two-door raced past him, then screeched to a halt about a quarter-mile up the road. Skip ignored the insistent honking. I know the game. Twice a fool, three times a damn fool. The driver kept on honking. Skip fought the urge to quicken his pace. He heard the Plymouth shifting gears. See, he told himself. But the car did not drive off. It backed up, slowly, swerving a bit until it stopped beside him. The driver leaned across the passenger seat and smiled.

"What's shaking, colored brother?"

Skip's heart sent up a prayer of thanksgiving. The driver was black. He was short, maybe a year or two older, and built like a welterweight fighter—all muscle. A sweat-soaked tee-shirt stuck to his coal-black skin. Friendly, brown eyes looked out from his round face.

"Where 'bouts you headed," he said, a toothpick bouncing between his teeth.

"Hollywood," Skip said. "Going even if I have to walk."

"Ain't no need of that, colored brother. I'm going your way, going to Los Angeleez. Come on, let's ride."

Skip tossed his stuff in the back seat, laid National Steel on top and had barely sat down before the Plymouth's perfectly tuned six-cylinder engine powered into first. Its tires screamed a trail of smoking, black rubber as it fishtailed down the highway. The driver smiled, shifted to second, then third, all the while drumming his hands on the steering wheel to the wild beat of a jumping swing band blaring from the radio.

"My name's Marcus Aurelius Jones," he yelled above the music. "Folks call me Pee Wee." He stuck out his hand.

"Pleased to meet you," Skip said. "Damn pleased to meet you." He pointed to the radio. "Who's playing?"

"Ain't you hip, colored brother? That's Count Basie and his Kansas City Seven. Forget about Ellington, Goodman, Chick Webb. The Count is swing."

He leaned over and turned the volume knob to the limit. The band swung into a double-time tune, the beat racing faster than the Plymouth's singing wheels. Pee Wee sang along with the frantic, opening riff, "Clap hands, here comes Charlie. Clap hands, here comes Charlie. Clap hands, here comes Charlie now." Lester Young's deep-throated sax soared above the horn section, rapid notes climbing up the scale, plunging down, firing along in a frenetic jazz style that was all blues. Skip could barely hear the Count's deft piano licks chasing Young, or Walter Page's bass line keeping the bottom tight. He couldn't miss Joe Jones' crashing drum solo. It filled a brief break before calling the band back for the final swinging chorus.

"Man," yelled Pee Wee. "Them cats can fly!"

Skip nodded. The song moved like "Roll 'Em Pete." He wanted to hear it again, but the radio man switched gears, gave the air over to Louis Armstrong, whose golden horn swung as precise and easy as a rocking chair on a sunny, summer day. Skip tapped his hand on the passenger door, marveled at his luck, his beautiful, fantastic luck. He turned to Pee Wee.

"Thanks for picking me up," he said.

"Shoot. Cain't leave a colored brother out here. Probably die before white folks give him a ride. Been walking long?"

"All day. I was on that train got wrecked back yonder. Spent last night sleeping by the highway, woke up and tried to flag a ride. No luck, least until you."

"Damn, colored brother. You're lucky I was passing this way. I was visiting my sister down near Silver City. She's in a family way, if you know what I mean." Pee Wee made the shape of a womb. "Yeah, I'm gon' be an uncle. She wanted me to stay on another day, but I figured I'd best be getting on. Lucky for you I did. You say you're trying to get to Hollywood?"

"Yeah. You know anything about it? What it's like?"

Pee Wee pulled an almost broken Camel from the crushed pack on the dashboard. "Hollywood ain't shit to me," he said, leaning over as Skip struck a match.

"Why's that?"

"Anything they got on the westside I can get on Central Avenue, and don't have to put up with no white folks' attitudes."

"What about them moving picture studios? You ever been in one of them?"

"Nope, and don't care to. They ain't making nothing for me." Pee Wee fiddled with the radio dial. Static crowded out the swing station. "What you care about Hollywood anyway?"

"I'm gon' out there to be an actor."

"An actor? Shoot, you must be jiving, colored brother."

"Jiving?"

"Yeah, you know, running a line on me, telling a tale, taking me for a fool."

"Naw, none of that stuff. See, I figger they ain't making pictures for us 'cause they aint' enough good colored actors out there."

"Humph. You sure you ain't sunstroke?" Pee Wee checked the rearview mirror for cops, then gave the Plymouth more speed. The car began to shake as the speedometer swung past seventy and neared eighty.

Skip tensed, the nightmare memory rising up again. "Ain't we going a bit fast?"

"Shoot, this ain't nothing compared to the world record set last month up in Utah. A guy drove a car three hundred fifty-seven miles an hour. Can you believe that? Three hundred and fifty-seven miles an hour! I read the story twice, just to be sure. I'd love to see that engine." He winked at Skip. "I know plenty of speed records. Ask me one. Go 'head. Ask me."

"How about airplanes. What's the fastest one of them flew?"

"An RAF pilot got a Hawker Hurricane up to four hundred eight point seven miles an hour not too long ago." Pee Wee took one hand off the steering wheel and flew it around the car. "Zoom. Zoom. Zoom. Four hundred miles an hour! As the gals say, colored brother. That sends me." Pee Wee playfully rolled his eyes and landed his hand back on the steering wheel.

"Well, since we ain't riding in no airplane, you mind slowing down a bit," Skip said. "I hear the police don't like speeding."

Hours later, Pee Wee pulled into a roadside gas station and café. A huge neon sign near the road flashed 'Eats' on and off in big, red letters. Pee Wee parked next to a gas pump, yawned and stretched.

"Man, me and the Plymy are on E. How 'bout you, colored brother?"

"My stomach's been talking to me for the last hour," Skip replied. "What you want? I'm buying."

"Good man, colored brother. Good man." Pee Wee smiled, swung open his door and stepped out. He leaned back inside. "These folks don't mind us buying their food, but they sure as hell mind us sitting inside and eating. Make mine a hamburger steak, heavy on the onions, and an orange soda."

"Gotcha," Skip said, opening his door and heading for the café, feeling light and carefree, his gut growling in anticipation.

A dusty Ford with California license plates drove onto the lot. I'm getting close, he thought. Hollywood by tomorrow. He clapped his hands and put some rhythm in his stride. He felt good, the best since he'd waved good-bye to Delta Slim. No more detours. No more riding freights. Just him and Marcus Aurelius "Pee Wee" Jones highballing down the highway. An overburdened jalopy piled high with mattresses and a chifforobe rolled slowly to a stop. A little boy sat high up on the mountain of belongings and strained to read a page of Sunday comics by the light of the flashing neon. Inside the cab a sunken-cheeked young woman sucked on a cigarette while a baby girl pawed her thin, sallow face. They reminded Skip of Joe Bob Winslow's story about the dust storms that drove his family off the land and onto the intinerant caravans that followed the crops in the green valleys of California.

He moved on to the café's take-out counter. The inviting smell of onions, hamburger steaks and ham sizzling on the grill set his stomach to tossing and grumbling. A dumpy, stringy-haired waitress caught his eye, waited a few moments, then waddled over.

"All we got is burgers," she said.

"I had my heart set on a fried ham sandwich," said Skip. "Swear to God I can hear that one on the grill calling my name."

"He's already got a home, and he's the last one. Burgers is all we got."

"Make it two, heavy on the onions and a couple of orange sodas."

She scribbled furiously on her pad, ripped off a sheet and held it up to the screen. "You mind paying now." It was more a command than a question.

Skip leaned on the narrow counter and gave the waitress a hard look. He wanted to say something smart, like maybe he was figuring he'd pay the next time he passed through, or how he'd bet her a week's pay the icebox was filled with sliced ham. But he let it pass.

"Guess I don't have a choice, do I?"

"Nope. All travelers got to pay first. Nothing personal."

Skip put a dollar on the counter. The waitress lifted the screen, snatched the bill and muttered a "thank you" and walked over to the grill. She returned with a grease-soaked paper bag. "There you go," she said, reaching in her apron and slapping thirty cents next to the bag. "No need to count it. I ain't no cheat."

"That's good," Skip said, grabbing his meal and the change. "Be bad for business." The screen slammed shut behind him.

"Damn," he said when he got back to the car. "That waitress was one mean bitch."

"She be's like that sometimes," Pee Wee said, reaching for the bag. "Gimme my burger."

Skip doled out the sandwiches and sodas. Pee Wee pulled over to the lot, stopped and tuned in to a station playing the "Negro Music Hour." Boogie-woogie blues came on over the air waves. Skip asked Pee Wee to turn up the volume as he wolfed down his burger, filling both cheeks with meat and bread, washing it all down with soda.

"You really want to be an actor?" asked Pee Wee. "I mean, if you're gonna stake out something hard, why not go for Roosevelt's job? At least you'd get to call the shots. But acting?" He shook his head.

"I want to do stories about us, stuff to make you want to see a moving picture." Skip swallowed the last bite of his sandwich and took a swig of soda. "Don't see why white folks got to have all the fun doing stories. I want to put folks like you and me up on that screen. I'm tired of old Sleep 'N Eats and mammy."

"What about them colored westerns and those Harlem detective stories? They ain't so bad."

"Yeah, but I want to go big-time."

"You talking big dreams, colored brother. But I guess you already know that."

"Lord knows I do. Folks back home thought I'd lost my mind. Hell, the way I see it, you don't know if you can do something lessen you try."

"Amen to that." Pee Wee drained off the last of his soda, waited for Skip to finish, then carried the bottles back to the counter. "It'll be a sad day when they stop giving money for empties," he said, standing by the passenger window. "Want to drive? I could use a break."

"I cain't. Ain't no cars back home. Just mules, horses, wagons."

"Damn, colored brother. That's too country for me," Pee Wee said, stretching and patting his chest. "Guess I better get me a cup of coffee for the road."

He returned with two cups of coffee that he gulped down before firing up the Plymouth and easing back onto the highway. The car leaped through the gears, hit third and started to cruise like that famous Hawker Hurricane over in England. One of Blind Boy Fuller's ragtime tunes came over the radio, the rhythm pushed along and accented by Bull City Red's nimble, thimbled fingers scratching fast on a washboard. Skip tapped the dashboard in time with the familiar music, then climbed into the back seat and grabbed National Steel. Pee Wee adjusted his rearview mirror.

"You fixing to play that thing?"

Skip nodded, pushed his bedroll out of the way to give himself some room and found Fuller's key by the second verse. He loved the Carolina boy's rags, especially because Fuller played the same model as National. Pee Wee started drumming along on the steering wheel, and when the song stopped, he turned off the radio and told Skip to keep on playing. Rags and hokum songs rolled out of Skip's fingers for half an hour before he finished, singing "Yellow Rose of Texas."

"God damn, colored brother," said Pee Wee. "You played the hell out of that thing. How'd you learn to do all that?"

"An old soldier back home got me started. Built me a cigar-box guitar when I was in short pants. I been playing some kind of guitar ever since. It's in my blood."

"I got motor oil in mine. Ain't nothing I don't know 'bout cars. Come on back up here and let me toast you," he said, leaning over as Skip climbed back into the front seat. When Skip had settled in, he reached up under the dashboard and pulled out a rolled cigarette. "You smoke reefers?"

"I smokes some," Skip said.

"You got to be careful with this stuff. But we should be alright. Cops don't work this stretch of highway," said Pee Wee, striking a wooden match with his thumbnail and sucking deep. The pungent, marijuana smell filled the car. "Roll down your window, colored brother," he said, and passed the smoke.

Skip took a few quick puffs, then gave the reefer back to Pee Wee. He brought a match to his Chesterfield. The still, black night pressed them together. Pee Wee coughed, took a final puff and snuffed out the smoke with his thumb and forefinger.

"You're all right, Reynolds," he said as he slipped the reefer back under the dashboard. "Man, you should've seen your face when I stopped, looked like you'd seen God and Lena Horne all rolled into one. Talk about your lucky day!"

"Yeah, I was one happy fool. I can still see this white boy who played a trick on me. Stopped then pulled off. I can still see him leaning out his window, laughing and waving bye-bye. I made up my mind right then and there that I was getting to Hollywood, even if I had to walk."

"You sure looked like it when I came up on you. I said to myself, 'Who is this crazy Negro walking across the desert in the middle of the day?' So I stopped." He slapped Skip on the back and started laughing, the reefer taking over. "Wooo hooo! I'd sure love to hear 'Clap Hands Here Comes Charlie' right now. That song moves." He took his hands off the steering wheel and drummed on the dashboard. "Whoo, Lord. You're all right, Reynolds," he shouted. "Damn, all right. Must come from good people."

"The best from the Lone Star state," Skip said, a little high and giddy. "My pappy crossed the Rhine and put a bayonet in the Germans' behind. And my grandpappy saved Teddy Roosevelt on San Juan Hill. So, you know I'm ready to wrestle the world. How 'bout you? You got folks?"

A curtain of sadness fell across Pee Wee's face. "They're okay, long as I don't stick to 'em. Them people drive a nigger crazy, if he let 'em. So, I don't. My sister's the only one I carry in my heart." He sighed and didn't speak anymore.

The engine's smooth hum filled the silence. The world slept. Stars shone in mysterious patterns against the deep, eternal sky. Skip looked out onto the desert night and wondered how anyone could see the shapes of dogs, archers, bears and scorpions in those distant twinklings of light. Pee Wee said nothing. Talking about family seemed to have cast a spell over him. He stared straight ahead. The Plymouth's wheels ate up Route 66, the towns flashing by, Winona, Flagstaff, Kingman. The odometer kept turning, the miles adding up.

"Getting close, colored brother," said Pee Wee, stifling a yawn. "Pass me one of your Chesterfields. I need a smoke. We'll be coming up on the Cajon Pass not too long from now. That's a tricky little stretch."

Skip tapped out a cigarette. He wanted to stay awake to see his first California sunrise, but the weight of the long day pressed his eyelids shut. His head dropped forward, then snapped back, his eyes wide open for a moment before he started nodding again.

"Pack it in," Pee Wee said. "Ain't nothing to see."

Skip thought he'd only slept a few minutes when blaring car horns and the heavy, rumbling clatter of streetcars on old tracks ripped his eyes open. The Plymouth was caught in a sea of cars creeping along a wide avenue lined with massive steel and concrete buildings, skyscrapers that dwarfed anything he'd ever seen before. People packed the sidewalks. He turned around, saw a range of mountains in the distance, then looked at Pee Wee, an unspoken question on his lips. Could it be?

"Hometown," said Pee Wee. "El Peblo de Nuwaystraw Sinyoura la Raina de Los Angeleez do porcincula."

"Say what?"

"The City of the Angels, Skip. Los Angeles. You done made it to the coast!"

"Woo wee!" Skip said and started clapping his hands. "Los Angeleez! What did you call it?"

"I was just giving you the Spanish name."

"You speak Spanish?"

"Poquito, which means just enough to start a conversation with one of them fine sinyouritas I might introduce you to, if you stick."

"Oh, I'm gon' stick. You can bet on that."

"Well, there's plenty Mexicans around here. Chinese, too, though I ain't too hip to them, yet. This ain't no black and white, horse-and-buggy town like that Tunis of yours. This here's a Technicolor city. Where you want off?"

"Anywhere, long's I can get to Hollywood, a cheap hotel and," he reached into the backseat, fumbled through his suitcase and pulled out the envelope from Ezekiel Washington, "and 5512 Central Avenue."

"Central Avenue! Boy, I'll be glad to see that old strip of black top." Pee Wee pulled over to the curb, put his Plymy in neutral and turned to Skip. "The Plaza Arms at Manchester and Central is a good place, and cheap. That address is up the street from there. To get to Hollywood, just take the No. 3 red car over on Hill Street. You'll know when you get there."

"Okay." Skip stepped out, grabbed his suitcase and slung National Steel over his shoulder. He leaned on the open window and smiled at Pee Wee. "I'd still be walking that highway if you hadn't stopped."

"Shoot. You might have made the ride in a Cadillac." Pee Wee laughed and asked for a Chesterfield.

Skip tapped out two, passed one to his friend and lit the other. "Yeah, but the company wouldn't have been as good. Thanks, Pee Wee."

"Sure thing. Listen, check me out sometime. I work at the filling station on Central and Vernon. I'll show you the black side of town."

"You got a date."

"Make it Thursday night," said Pee Wee, holding out his hand. "Skin me."

Skip slapped the open palm, grasped Pee Wee's hand for a moment before letting go. The Plymouth eased into the flow of traffic, blended with the cars, trucks and trolleys crowding the street, turned a corner and disappeared.

Los Angeles! He shook his head and tried to take in the overwhelming rush of new sights and sounds. Across the street stood the Sunlight Drug Co., a three-story box with a gold and blue mosaic sunrise over its doorway, and a polished brass eagle in flight crowning its flag pole. Three blocks down, fire-engine red streetcars rumbled in and out of the Pacific Electric depot, their wheels grinding and screeching along rails set in the middle of the traffic-clogged street. A river of strangers jostled him as he stood on the sidewalk, giddy and lost. People brushed past him, window-shopped, greeted friends, slipped through glass doorways and into the immense office buildings lining the street. Faces whipped by like a scene from a newsreel in fast motion. There were more people on this street than in all of Tunis. And on the next street there were even more people, maybe more than in Lee County. He began to move along, wondering where to go, what to do. He could check into the Plaza Arms, find Ezekiel Washington's school, catch a No. 3 red car and ride to Hollywood. He smiled. That's what he would do.

He strolled through a park in the next block. Lush tropical plants grew in manicured gardens, their brilliant orange, red and violet flowers improbably bright. Skip approached a dazzling cluster of Bird of Paradise just to feel the velvety soft leaves and the delicate blossoms. Around him shoe-shine boys chatted up passersby out on a mid-morning walk. A big-bellied man and a hunchback stood nose to chest, arguing.

"Socialism! That's what it is. PWA. WPA. CCC. All that alphabet soup stuff of Roosevelt's is just a front for them dad burn Bolsheviks who are trying to give this country over to the Russians." The fat man shouted in a voice as big and loud as a hog caller's, crooked his thumbs around his suspenders and chewed viciously on a cigar stub.

The hunchback, standing barely five-feet tall, fired back. "The hell it is. All for one and one for all, I say. Who needs your capitalists taking all the dough. Look at the mess they got us in. People are starving!"

"Who's starving?"

"Open your eyes, man. Okies are pouring into the state everyday, and folks are going on the dole by the dozens."

"Well, that's just the law of nature. Survival of the fittest." The hog caller spat out bits of chewed tobacco leaf. "I make a living wage. Don't see why everybody else can't. This country doesn't need no communist hand-outs." He saw Skip passing nearby and called to him. "Ain't that right, colored boy?"

Skip ignored the question. No sense getting involved in a fight between white folks. Best to play simple-minded and keep on moving. "I wasn't studying y'all's conversation," he drawled. "But any of you gentlemen know where I can catch me one of them streetcars to Hollywood?"

"Hollywood!" The hunchback threw up his hands and mocked him. "'Ain't studying y'all's conversation'. Brother, we're talking about the important issues of the day!" He walked over to Skip, one arm hanging limp, a crooked finger jabbing the air. "Brother, are you awake?"

Skip looked down on the little man's beat-up, pock-marked face. The guy looked like he'd lost plenty of fights. "I just wants to get to Hollywood. Can you help me?"

The hunchback turned to the hog caller. "Unbelievable. A somnambulist looking for dreamland." He turned back to Skip. "You can catch a streetcar to Hollywood in that yellow safety zone in the street. But I pity you, brother. The Negro has the most to gain from our program." The hunchback dismissed him with a wave of his good hand.

The argument picked up as Skip headed for the streetcar stop, glad to be rid of the white men and their talk about programs and capitalism, yet hating having to put on the darky. He didn't give a damn about their two-bit argument. But Tunis was still with him. He couldn't shed all those years in one day. Those rules were deep down in him, guiding him and protecting him.

Cars and trucks roared past the unprotected safety zone. What if a driver lost control, he thought? Where could he run? He waited, anxious and uneasy, searching the street for a break in the traffic. He crossed just as a huge red car with gold bands wrapping around its front lumbered up to the stop. A pole reached from its roof and grabbed the electric wire that fed its hungry engine. He stepped aboard, holding National Steel above his head. He pulled seven cents out of his pocket, dropped the coins in the fare box and looked for a seat in the rear. Grandma Sarah had told him that's where colored folk were supposed to sit, at least that's the way it was in Houston, and she didn't figure Los Angeles would be any different. White folks is white folks. He looked down the long aisle. People were sitting everywhere. Whites were in the back and in the front, colored folk too. The only empty seats were near the motorman.

"No standing," the man said, as the streetcar jerked forward. "Find a seat, buddy."

Skip moved cautiously down the narrow aisle. An immense black man sitting near the front watched his dilemma with an amused, devilish smile, then pointed to an empty bit of his seat.

"You must be a southern boy," he laughed as Skip sat down.

"I got it writ on my face," Skip said, stuffing his suitcase beneath the seat and cradling National Steel in his arms.

"It's just the way you act, like a scared rabbit looking for his Jim Crow hiding place. Well, old Jim keeps a low profile out here, but don't let that fool you. He's around. Just doesn't slap you in the face all the time."

"You from the south?" said Skip.

"Aren't we all?" The guy looked Skip over, twitched his nose at the stink of freight cars, railyards and sweat built up from a few days on the road. "New in town?"

"Just got in this morning. This the train to Hollywood?"

"It is. But come now, surely you haven't come halfway across the continent to walk those celluloid streets and, perhaps, catch a glimpse of some modern-day icon. Or have you?" He leaned close to Skip and studied him as if he was a curious, new form of life.

Skip leaned back. "I came out here to be an actor," he said, defiant. He wanted to set this guy straight.

The fat man arched his eyebrows. "Then why on earth are you here? All the serious acting is done in New York. Any fool can tell you that.

Hollywood only makes cartoons, and money. But I guess you're here to make some changes, right?" He gave Skip a sly wink.

"Well, I . . . ." Confused and caught off-guard, Skip stumbled over his words. "I'm gon' try."

"Excellent. Our people must try new and adventurous ways, and we are already well-suited for acting. We do it all the time. Dunbar said it best. Do you know his poem, *'We Wear The Mask*?'" The man frowned, seeing a blank look come over Skip's face. "My God, what backwater school house did you crawl out of not to have heard of Dunbar?"

"I didn't have too much time for schooling, what with picking cotton and all."

"Ah, a salt of the earth type. Well, no matter. Go to the public library and look him up. You can read, can't you?"

"Listen, just 'cause I ain't heard of this Dunbar guy don't mean I'm dumb. Who is he anyway?"

"A poet and writer, gone to his own literary Valhalla."

They rode on in silence. Skip looked out the window at Bunker Hill's collection of dreary apartments and rooming houses. He shook his head, wondering how many people were crammed into those little boxes. The man sitting next to him pulled a cord running along the top of the passenger window and heaved his body up, pushing Skip into the aisle.

"Excuse me," he said. "Time to go to work."

They were the same height, though the stranger was a good one hundred pounds heavier. Rolls of fat spread out from his chest to flop over his belt. His worn, gray slacks were stretched across his wide butt. He grabbed his suit coat and a small valise, then gave Skip a friendly clap on the shoulder.

"Success to you, my friend. You're on a grand adventure. It might even turn out to be profitable. After all, you already wear a mask. Why not get paid for it?" He turned, waddled to the rear door and stepped lightly into the noonday crowd.

Skip slid next to the window, pulled his gear up onto his seat and stretched out as the streetcar labored up Hill Street, passing Third Street, where a small cable car descended a short line of track while another ascended. People clustered at each end, preferring the short ride to and from Grand Street to the long walk up a steep flight of concrete steps. He touched his reflection in the glass. What did the man mean about wearing a mask? Clowns were the only people who wore masks. Everybody else just carried the face they had. Not so, according to the stranger. He said colored folk were always acting. Skip remembered putting on the darky in the park. Was that acting? He shrugged off the thought, jerked the window open and breathed deeply the cool breeze brushing past his face.

The streetcar turned west on Sunset Boulevard, clattered along the border of Elysian Park's one hundred acres of forested hills, stopping every two or three blocks. Courtyard apartments with barrel-tiled roofs and names plucked from the city's dream of itself lined the boulevard: El Cielo, La Francaise, Shangri-La, painted in turquoise, pink, and pastel blue, each identical to the other. A honey-blonde in a canary yellow Packard that had stopped next to the streetcar looked up at Skip and blew him a coquettish kiss off her bright red lips. He looked away, startled. Was the girl crazy? Didn't she know the risk, or was there any risk. He stared down at the Packard. Everybody inside the car was laughing and pointing at him. The girl blew him another long kiss. He shook his head as the Packard drove off and the streetcar made a slow, wide turn onto Hollywood Boulevard. Skip jumped out of his seat. Hollywood! He looked for studios, but instead saw the same procession of courtyard apartments and storefronts. He slumped back down in his seat, disappointed, until he saw, high on a mountainside, HOLLYWOODLAND, in huge white letters.

"Let me off," he yelled, reaching up and frantically pulling the cord. "Hey, conductor. Let me off."

He grabbed his stuff and waited in the stairwell, heart racing. The streetcar rumbled to a stop, and he stepped off at the corner of Hollywood Boulevard and Highland Avenue, the heart of his promised land. He made it to the sidewalk in time to be nearly run over by a gang of middle-aged white women. Their leader stood half a block down, waving and pointing to the Rexall Drug Store. Clark Gable was inside, she yelled.

He moved on along Hollywood Boulevard. He wasn't a Gable fan. Outside the oriental façade of Grauman's Chinese Theater, he bent over and placed his hand inside a palm print of Wallace Beery that had been set into a square of concrete sidewalk. It was almost a perfect fit. He imagined himself stepping out of a Cadillac limousine, walking up the carpet while huge searchlights swung their beams across the night sky and flashbulbs exploded. He looked dashing in a black tuxedo and top hat, which he dipped to the screaming women straining to touch him. But none of them had a chance because Fredi Washington was on his arm.

Blocks passed under his feet. He went down Gower, turned on Melrose and soon found himself standing across from Paradise Studios. He couldn't believe his luck. He rifled through his suitcase, pulled out the worn copy of Ezekiel Washington's ad and held it up. The guy in the ad had stood right here! The company's slogan whispered seductively: "If it's Paradise, you know it's right." Skip carefully folded the ad, tucked it back into his suitcase and slowly approached the entrance. A uniformed guard let him get near enough to almost touch the gate, then called out.

"Say, colored boy. You got a pass?"

"I'm here to see Mister Jones," Skip said, matter-of-factly. "Got to deliver this guitar." He swung National Steel off his shoulder and walked up to the gate.

"Not so fast there, buddy." The guard stepped out of his shack and flipped through the pages of a clipboard. "Funny, I don't see nothing here about any deliveries this time of day." He looked at Skip. "Who'd you say it was for?"

"Mister Jones. He just called. It won't be on that list."

"I just bet it won't. Now listen, colored boy. I wasn't born yesterday. I can spot a sneak a mile off. That's why I'm on the gate. Now, you got a pass or not?"

Skip fumbled through his pockets, patted himself down while the guard waited, a smug, self-satisfied look on his face.

"Don't tell me, you can't find it, right? Just like I suspected. You got to work harder than that to try and slip something past old Bobby Mumford. Yes, sir. See, I got a sixth sense about sneaks." He tossed the clipboard back into the shack. "Maybe you should've had Mister Jones pin that note on your shirt, colored boy."

"I'm not a boy," Skip said, remembering his vow. No sense giving up any pride now that the game was played out.

"Oh? Well, excuse me, Mister Negro." The guard folded his hands across his chest and stood with his legs shoulder-length apart. "Now, what do you want?"

"I want to talk to somebody about getting in moving pictures. Whadda-ya say?"

"Hell, boy, you and nearly everybody else in this g-damn city wants to get in and talk to somebody. So, I'm telling you just like I tell them. Get a pass."

The guard returned to his shack. Skip muttered a curse beneath his breath as he walked away, stopping every few minutes to look over his shoulder at the beautiful entrance with its three arches and slender palm trees swaying slightly in the gentle breeze. He made up his mind to get a pass from Ezekiel Washington, first thing Monday. He rode back downtown to catch a streetcar headed for Central Avenue.

The city's hub glowed from dozens of streetlights and neon signs lining every block. A kaleidoscope of pulsing green, red and white bulbs bathed Broadway. The street looked like something seen only in a dream, a fantasy of color and shadow, its sidewalk barely passable. Stone gargoyles set high above the Million Dollar's towering marquee surveyed the multitude that moved below, their gaze fierce and frightening. People lined up in front of the chrome ticket booth for the evening show of Frank Capra's latest, *You Can't Take It With You* and a B-picture called *Girls on Probation.* Skip moved to the edge of the sidewalk and studied the crowd. People seemed lost in their own worlds. Black folk and white folk jockeyed for position, bumped into each other and walked on, sometimes without even apologizing. That didn't seem possible. But it kept happening. There would be a collision, then, maybe, a few words muttered between passersby. Skip watched the scene, fighting within himself to break out of his old ways and join the mass of hurrying, pre-occupied humanity, throw himself into its midst and feel the crush and bump of strangers. He'd already sat in the front of a streetcar. He'd told a white man not to call him "boy." Now there was the challenge of Broadway. He picked out a white man plowing a path through the crowd. The guy was immersed in a newspaper and seemed to pay no attention to the world around him. He caromed off of people without ever looking up. Skip gauged the man's movement, then sucked up some courage and like a kid shouting "Geronimo!" plunged forward. The white man bounced off of him, lost his balance and recovered.

"Excuse me, sir," Skip said. "I . . .I . . .I didn't see you." He waited for the inevitable insult.

"Huh?" the guy said. "Yeah, yeah, sure buddy," then walked on, eyes scanning his newspaper.

Skip stood, slack-jawed, like he'd been slapped upside the head. The realization of what he had done and what had happened settled over him. Suddenly he wanted to grab someone and tell them the news. It was true, god dammit! Every place wasn't like Tunis. The world was a wonder of hope and possibility. Down the street, a hoarse newspaper boy yelled out the day's headlines.

"Yanks clobber Dizzy Dean! DiMaggio socks a homer!" The kid caught Skip's eye and stuck out an evening edition. "Paper, mister?"

The kid called me "mister," Skip thought, smiling and liking the sound of the word. He almost wanted to walk around the block and buy another paper, just to hear the newspaper boy call him "mister." He pulled a nickel out of his pocket and grabbed the copy of the *Los Angeles Examiner*. He liked the paper's slogan: "The Newspaper For People Who Think." Hell, yeah. He was going to be a thinking man. He walked all the way to Ninth Street, turned and headed back up Broadway, savoring the freedom. He tired at First Street. The suitcase and National Steel felt heavier than a cotton sack on his best days. From the crest of Broadway he could see the festive lights of Chinatown. Behind him, a block east on Spring Street, stood the Los Angeles Times building. The newspaper's name glowed in powder blue neon. A clock read nine-thirty. Sparks from streetcar wires rained down along the city's wide avenues, reminding him of Fourth of July fireworks. Two radio towers on top of another building reached their antennas up into the black sky. K-R-K-D flashed off and on. The air was alive with voices, baseball and music. A passing breeze fluttered the pages of the newspaper crooked in his arm, pages that were filled with tales of F.D.R.'s campaign against conservative Democrats, dispatches from war zones, and all the myriad stories and reports of a day in this city's life, a day in which Skip Reynolds arrived to chase his dream. He smiled to himself, satisfied. Time to find the Plaza Arms.

SOMETHING WAS WRONG. SKIP WAS HALFWAY INTO DOWNTOWN and there was no sign of Ezekiel Washington's school. He pulled the letter from his pocket, checked the address against those lining Central Avenue. The streetcar crossed Vernon at the 4400 block of Central. The letter said the school was at 5512 Central Avenue. Damn! He'd missed it. He hadn't seen anything that looked like a school, just drab one and two-story storefronts. Maybe somebody hit the wrong key when they typed the address. Maybe it was supposed to be 4512. He rode three more blocks, this time marking each address, his head turning from side to side. The trolley reached the 4400 block. Still there was no acting school. He grabbed the cord running above the windows, pushed past a woman snoring next to him and got off at the next stop. The first few drops of the storm pushing down from the north stung the back of his neck. He stopped at 4512 Central Avenue. It was a drug store. He marched on, confident now. The letter was right. He should've paid attention, instead of daydreaming. The rain started to pick up, and he turned up his collar, cursed himself for not having an umbrella.

An uneasy feeling shook him when he arrived at 5512 Central Avenue. It was a vacant. He checked the letter again, read the promising words, pressed his head against the windowpane, eyes straining to see past the streaks of gray paint. He could barely make out broken, upended chairs, discarded booklets, a dusty floor littered with crumpled papers, a fading, water-soaked calendar from 1937. A wrecked desk tilted forward on its bad leg. A black telephone lay on its side in an open drawer, the mouthpiece dangling to the floor. He grabbed the locked doorknob, knocked several times. No one answered. He stepped into the growing storm, yelled up at the second-story window.

"Mr. Washington? Mr. Ezekiel Washington! You up there!"

Only the thunder responded. Maybe I'm early, he thought. Sure, that's it. Early. Damndest thing though, school without a sign. Beat-up building with nobody in it. He turned around and looked for a warm place to wait out the storm. The smoky aroma of sweet Texas bar-b-que escaped from a restaurant across the street. A sign hung above the doorway: Two citified pigs in tuxedo and evening dress doing the Lindy Hop, the words "Henry's Dancing Bar-B-Que" surrounding them. He ran for the door, stopped as soon as he entered. Moving picture posters covered the walls: "Imitation of Life," "The Green Pastures," publicity stills of Clarence Muse and Hattie McDaniel, Slim Thompson with a shotgun from a scene in "The Petrified Forest." Had Ezekiel Washington moved here? No. This was a restaurant, with a counter and a dining room, a jukebox in the corner. A tall, handsome black man, his hair flecked with gray, leaned from the back room.

"Too early for food," he said in a deep baritone.

"I ain't hungry," Skip said, shaking off the rain and walking to the counter. "You got any coffee?"

"First pot of the day," the man replied, wrapping a white apron below his bulging stomach and pouring Skip a steaming cup.

He then went about his business, took chairs off tables, stacked dishes, arranged silverware. Every few minutes he checked on a slab of pork ribs cooking in the oven. A short woman with a body just this side of fat stomped into the room, wet shoes squeaking across the linoleum.

"Lord a-mercy," she said, pulling off her coat. "I don't know what I was thinking 'bout this morning, running out the house without my umber-rella. Just look at me. Lord, Lord, Lord. Hope I don't catch the pneumonia." She looked around the cafe. "Where's that clean-up man?"

"Probably sleeping off last night's drunk," the cook said as he tossed the woman a towel. "Get some of that rain out your hair, Di."

"Thank you, Henry," she said. "Don't want to catch me one of them head colds. Brr." She shook herself, gave her hair a vigorous rubbing with the towel. "I must look a sight," she said, passing Skip. "Morning, sugar."

Skip mumbled a greeting, warmed his hands on the cup of coffee and waited, tense. Where was Ezekiel Washington? He walked to the door, looked across the street, hoping to glimpse something, anything going on inside 5512 Central Avenue. An hour passed, then another. He'd look away from the clock for what seemed ten minutes, raise his eyes and see that barely a minute had passed. He filled his gut with coffee, asked for an ashtray and started filling it with cigarette butts. An occasional customer blew in from the storm for a hot rib sandwich, or a cup of coffee, but it was a slow day. Skip held his place at the counter, his nerves jangling and fraying a little more with each puff, with each gulp of coffee he sent sliding into his empty stomach. The cook and the waitress idled about, watched him out of the corners of their eyes. Finally, the cook spoke.

"Looks like you been stood up, buddy. How 'bout a sandwich? Might make you feel better?"

Skip shook his head and pointed for another refill. "You know anything 'bout that acting school over yonder?"

"Acting school?"

"Yeah. The Ezekiel Washington Colored Actors School. They was supposed to have a acting class starting up in that building across the street. I got a letter right here says so."

He pulled the letter from its envelope and handed it to the cook. Outside, rain hissed in the troubled air. The cook read the letter slowly, hid his face behind the sheet of paper. Skip heard him chuckle.

"Looks like old Zeke's done it again," the cook said, giving Skip the letter. "You an actor?"

"I want to be," Skip said, stuffing the letter back in its envelope. He stopped. "Say, what are you talking 'bout? Looks like old Zeke's done it again?"

The cook leaned on the counter and smiled broadly. "Now, don't get me wrong, son. A colored actors school is a fine idea, but Zeke's not the one to do it. Not by a long shot. And no one's been in that place across the street for, oh, I guess going on a year now."

Skip felt a nervous twitch disturb the corner of his right eye. His stomach convulsed. The last gulp of sweet coffee fought its way back up his throat. He struggled to keep it down, gripped the counter and turned away, head shaking, breaths coming in short, choking gasps. The cook put a steadying hand on his shoulder.

"You all right, buddy?"

"Yeah," Skip said, feeling a cold sweat breaking out on his brow. He stared at the grounds in his empty coffee cup. "Yeah, I'm all right."

He swallowed hard, tasted coffee and bile, looked up at the cook, then past him to three framed photographs on top of the dish cabinet. The cook was in each one, as a gangster with a Tommy-gun; a cowboy, wielding twin six-shooters; Uncle Tom gazing mournfully. Skip nodded to himself. It all made sense now. This guy was Ezekiel Washington, and he was putting him on, playing some kind of crazy acting game. That had to be it. Why else would he have all this moving picture stuff and be right across the street. Maybe the address was supposed to be 5513 Central Avenue. His eyes locked on the cook.

"Look," he said. "I may be from the country, but I ain't dumb."

"How's that," the cook said, giving him a look that said what the hell are you talking about.

"How's that? Hah!" Skip slapped the counter, stood and walked back and forth. "How's that, he says. Skip Reynolds ain't no fool now. I know what's going on. You're here telling me there ain't no acting school, and you got moving picture posters all over the place, even got pictures of yourself, Mister Ezekiel Washington."

The cook looked Skip straight in the eye. "Listen to me, son," he said, his voice calm and measured. "There is no acting school. Understand? No school."

No school? Skip shook his head. How could that be? He had a letter, and it said come on out to Hollywood. Now is an especially good time for colored actors. Another class is starting. He looked at the empty building across the street. No school there. No school anywhere? He willed his mouth into action, heard a voice he did not recognize as his.

"B-but . . . Aren't you Ezekiel Washington?"

"My name's Henry Lewis," the cook said, jerking his thumb toward the framed pictures on the cabinet. "I was an actor, once upon a time. Now, I'm a full-time chef. Why, I make the best . . . ."

Skip turned and ran for the door, knocking an armful of plates out of the waitress' hands on his way out. Big city noises, as grating and unnerving as fingernails scratching across a chalkboard, clawed through his brain. Stinging sheets of rain lashed his face. Water soaked through his clothes as he crossed the broad avenue and grabbed the doorknob of 5512 Central Avenue. He pulled angrily, turned it back and forth, hoping it would open. A bolt of crackling lightning, alive with electricity, slashed across the gray, cloud leaden sky. A vicious clap of thunder followed. The cook's words stormed through his mind: "There is no school."

He heard himself mumbling and talking to himself: I've got to get out of here. He stumbled back toward Manchester, tripped over the railroad tracks leading to the Goodyear factory and fell face down in a puddle of black water. People hurried past him, everyone rushing to get out of the raging storm. He pulled himself up, struggled on until he reached the Plaza Arms.

No one saw him lurch into the lobby. He dragged himself up the carpeted stairs, stopped outside his door and fumbled for his key. The door slamming shut behind him was loud as thunder. He peeled off his wet clothes and dropped on the bed. Old springs wailed beneath the sudden weight of him climbing in and burying himself beneath the covers. All that hoping and traveling for nothing. Nothing. He started laughing, a wild, crazy laugh. Old Man Williams' story circled, twirled and echoed in his mind.

"A nigger is a . . . is a lot like a . . . is a lot like a catfish! Let him get caught outside his mudhole, and he's in a world of trouble."

"*I* GOT TO CROSS THAT RIVER OF A JORDAN."

Evening. A man sings in the shower down the hall, his voice wavering like a badly warped record. "I got to cross that river of a Jordan. I got to cross it by myself."

Hours become days marked by the man singing in the shower. Always the same song.

"Ain't nobody here can work it out for me. I got to cross it by myself."

Skip opened his eyes. The pulsing colors of the neon light outside his window flashed cross the room's bare walls. He lay on his back for a few minutes, then tossed the covers back, swung his legs onto the cold floor and sat up. A pile of clothes, dry now, lay in a wrinkled heap. The window was open, its thin curtain blowing inward, furling and unfurling slowly, like the battle-scarred flag of a defeated army. He went to his suitcase, pulled out some clothes and got dressed. What to do? His stomach screamed to be fed. Was it Sunday I last ate? Monday? He looked out the window, heard a tired, clanging bell as the last streetcar pulled into the layover depot. He rolled a cigarette from Old Man Williams' pouch, lit it and tossed the flame into the cool night. He took a long pull on the cigarette, enjoying the smoke. It tasted like home. His stomach growled again. Time to eat.

He walked north on Central, past darkened, closed-up shops and drug stores until he found a small cafe at 70th Street that had just enough room for a counter, seven seats, a grill and a tiny utility room in the back. A single, low watt bulb gave off a subdued light. He took a seat and read a handwritten notice taped next to the menu. "No Credit or Sad Songs. Cash Only." He shrugged his shoulders. He had plenty of cash. On the other side of the menu there was a framed, yellowing newspaper story and photograph of Joe Louis taking the heavyweight title from James J. Braddock. That was a good fight, the Brown Bomber bringing the title back home where it belonged. Willie threw a special party at the juke joint that night. Free drinks! The cook, a gentle looking black man with an easy smile, peeked out from the utility room, saw Skip waiting and came forward, wiping his hands on his grease-stained apron.

"What'll it be?"

"Couple-a hamburger steaks," Skip said and nodded towards the coffee pot. "How old's that coffee?"

"It's a fresh pot," the cook said, and slapped two small steaks on the grill. "Have some?"

"Yeah."

He poured a steaming cup and placed it in front of Skip along with a knife and fork. Skip took the first gulp black to jolt his senses. Then he added cream and sugar. The beefy, greasy smell of sizzling steaks made saliva squirt in his mouth. He tasted it, tart and acidic. His stomach churned again, growled with anticipation.

"Ain't seen you around before. New in town?" The cook casually flipped the steaks and covered them with sliced onions.

"Came in Saturday out of east Texas." Skip said between sips of sweet coffee.

"I hope it ain't work that brings you to Los Angeles, 'cause jobs is tighter'n a mule's ass in fly season." The cook placed the steaks on a plate and slid it over to Skip.

"Looking to be an actor," Skip said, wolfing down one of the steaks, savoring the spicy taste as hunks of delicious meat worked down his throat and into his empty gut. "You know anything 'bout Hollywood?"

The cook rolled his eyes and draped his apron across the counter. "How could I not know about Hollywood? I got this niece who gets all twisted every time them ofays put out the call for a few black faces."

Skip finished the first steak and washed the last bite down with a gulp of coffee. "Maybe you can help me."

"How's that?" The cook poured himself a cup of coffee and gave Skip a refill.

"I gotta know how to connect with Hollywood."

"Fraid I can't help you, brother. All I know I get from this niece of mine."

"And what does she say?"

"Well," the cook sipped his coffee. "She gets the low-down from three places.

"One is Cornelius Pinker. He's a columnist in *The Eagle*, pretending to be Mister Read All About It, the colored man's Walter Winchell. She also gets acting books from the library. And, she sometimes goes to these late-night get togethers for colored actors over at the . . . the . . ." The cook snapped his fingers several times. "Damn, I can't recall the name of that place. I don't go for none of that imagination business, myself. Gimme something real, like The Bomber knocking out another ofay." He smiled and nodded towards the newspaper clipping. "I won money on that one. Bet a white boy. I tell you, son, the easiest money you'll ever make is finding a white man who'll bet against Joe Louis."

"Amen," Skip said, and they toasted The Bomber. He finished off the second steak and pushed his empty cup forward. "How 'bout another refill?"

"Sure thing." The cook smiled and poured as a burly, white cop entered.

The guy was dressed in menacing black, billy club held in a relaxed grip, pistol hanging low on his right hip. "Couple-a regulars and a java to travel, Bill," he said.

"Yes sir," the cook said, putting on an ingratiating smile. "Streets quiet tonight, Officer Farrell? And you want those medium rare, right?"

The cop nodded and took a seat near the door. Skip pulled out his pack of Chesterfields, lit one and thought about going to the library and finding out what Cornelius Pinker had to say. He felt better now, his belly full, his mind relaxed. The cop's steaks sizzled on the grill. Damn he thought, drinking down another gulp of coffee, that food was good. The cook flipped the steaks over, let them cook a few minutes more before putting them between slices of bread, wrapping them and stuffing them into a paper bag. He poured the cop a cup of coffee and delivered the meal.

"On the house," he said.

The cop nodded, waved good-bye and went back to his patrol car. The cook turned to Skip. "Never did like serving them ofay cops," he said. "But it's best to be on their good side. Never know when you might need them."

Skip took a last gulp of coffee and crushed out his cigarette. He dug fifty cents out of his pocket and slapped it on the counter. "I'll let you know how things turn out," he said, standing and heading for the door.

"Do that," the cook said. "And do me a favor. Flip that sign on your way out. It's closing time."

Skip hit the night, feeling good. He was back in the world, and moving on.

He woke up late the next morning, took a hot shower, dressed and caught the number three into downtown. He relaxed in the soft, red seat and, for the first time saw that Central Avenue seemed on a collision course with City Hall. The building was easy to spot. Set off from the business district, it was the city's only skyscraper, rising twenty-eight stories into the sky. The streetcar headed straight for the white, pyramid-topped building. Then the avenue curved and hit the stretch where Skip had gone looking for the Ezekiel Washington Colored Actors School. He looked for the building, hoping to see it open, inviting him to come inside. Where was Ezekiel Washington? Maybe he'd gotten a role in a moving picture and couldn't act and teach at the same time. Maybe he'd taken a whole class of actors with him, including the dandy in the *Photoplay* advertisement. Maybe. Skip stared at the school until the streetcar hit a turn and moved on to downtown. He slumped in his seat. No use worrying about maybes and what might have beens, best to worry about the business of getting on in this city.

Downtown was in its full workday bustle when the streetcar pulled into the Pacific Electric terminal. People came and went. Some stood by a bar, their legs propped on the railing, cold glasses of beer in their hands, others flipped through magazines displayed on racks outside the terminal's drug store. Crowds gathered at street corners, businessmen with briefcases clutched in their hands, heading off to appointments; secretaries in tight gray skirts and white blouses, high heels clicking on the pavement as they hurried along on errands. Traffic cops stood in the intersections, giving signals with their whistles and hands. Poor boys wandered along, lost, cigarettes jammed in their mouths, some talking to themselves. Skip looked at the black and white faces around him, wishing to see someone he knew, someone who would smile and call his name. He turned on Sixth Street and headed for Hill Street, cut across Perishing Square and turned east on Fifth Street. Chauffeur driven Cadillac limousines stood idle in front of the Biltmore Hotel. A black doorman, dressed in a dark blue suit with gold buttons, spats, top hat and white gloves, waved. Skip paused long enough to ask if the public library was near. The doorman said it was on the next block. He crested the south end of Bunker Hill, saw a three-story building topped by a blue pyramid and a painted flaming sun. The library? He hurried down the hill to Hope Street and stopped at the main entrance. Never had he seen anything so beautiful. The concrete walkway was half a block long, lined on both sides by evergreen trees, that looked better than any he'd ever seen at Christmas time. A three-tiered reflecting pool graced the middle of the walkway, the water catching the reflection of sun, blue sky, the trees and the library's entrance.

Inside, the library was cool and quiet. Ceiling fans turned slowly. An arrow pointed his way to the second floor. His footsteps echoed. He stopped in the magnificent rotunda, again overwhelmed. A huge globe hung from the apex on long brass chains. Murals of Los Angeles history covered each wall: Spanish conquistadors pointing to the Pacific Ocean, priests offering the Bible to the Indians, William Mulholland bringing water and life to the desert basin. Skip studied the paintings.

"Do you need something?" Plump fingers tapped his shoulders.

He turned and saw a stern-looking white woman, built like a fullback, staring at him. She wore her steel-gray hair pulled back in a tight bun. Her severe, cold blue eyes demanded an answer.

"Yeah, I . . ."

"Sshh." She frowned and brought her index finger to pursed lips.

Skip lowered his voice. "You all got any books on acting?"

"Acting?"

"I'm gon' be an actor," Skip said.

"Oh really," She looked him up and down. "Acting books are in the east wing, but you must have a library card to check them out. We've lost too many books to . . ." She paused and eyed him again, suspicion in her eyes. "Transients." She held the "s" and frowned with distaste, wheeled around and tip-toed away, her heels never touching the floor.

The east wing. Hundreds of books, more than Skip had ever seen in one place. Black folks and white folks sat at tables, hunched over open volumes, their lips moving softly as their eyes scanned the pages. He lost himself in the maze of aisles, walked down one, then another, reading titles, searched for books on acting, but found none. He forced himself back into the lobby, steeling himself as he approached the librarian. She sat behind the information counter, looking superior and all-knowing.

"Yes?" she hissed.

"I didn't find any acting books, ma'am," Skip said, hoping his helpless tone appealed to her conceit.

"All our books are arranged in precise order," she said. "Acting is in the east wing." She sighed heavily. "You must not be acquainted with the Dewey Decimal System. Didn't your home library use standard library procedures?"

"Ma'am," Skip said, already tired of the librarian's condescending tone. "Are you gon' help me out or not? I mean, you are sitting at the information booth and I come for some information."

"Here." She pulled a pre-printed card out of a file and handed it to Skip.

He stared at the card, still confused. All he saw were words and numbers, nothing on acting.

She leaned forward and looked at Skip. "Are you having any trouble?"

"Nothing I cain't handle." He walked away, scanning the card until he found his destination: Acting.

This time the number code didn't scare him. He searched the aisles until he came to the 700 section, comfortable now that the library's mystery was solved. He found the right shelves and read the titles: *Acting Made Easy; Your Career in Hollywood; You Ought To Be In Pictures! The Actor's Craft.* Too many choices, he thought, before taking down the book with simplest title: *Acting Made Easy.* He carried the treasured volume to a heavy table and took a seat across from an old white woman who sat reading through a magnifying glass. He pored over the pages, trying to decipher the meaning of phrases like don't mimic the character; be the character; voice is mood. He looked for a dictionary, read the definition of mimic and scratched his head. It didn't make sense. How could you be someone if you didn't copy them? He read on, his interest wan-ing, his mind wandering, calling up scenes from moving pictures. Did Edward G. Robinson have to sit in a library and read a book? How much book learning did it take before he could slump against a wall, put his hand to his bullet-riddled chest and say: "Mother of Mercy! Is this the end of Ricco?" He took down a copy of *Hollywood Calls*. It was more to his liking, lots of pictures of movie stars and a whole chapter on people who'd stood in front of studio gates for parts as extras and ended up with talking roles. Hell, that was the way to go, he figured. Just go on out there and wait for Lady Luck to tap you on the shoulder and lead you into the Promised Land. The book didn't say anything about colored actors. None of the books did. He remembered the cook whose niece talked about meetings and tidbits from Mister Read All About It. Damn! Where was Ezekiel Washington? He slouched in his seat and thumbed through the pages, resenting the lucky break of those smiling white faces, those nobodies who got to be somebodies. White folks got it easy in everything, he thought, closing the book and leaving it for the librarian.

The streetcars heading down Central were packed. Skip got off at 71st Street and walked the rest of the way home. A warm Santa Ana wind blew lightly, carrying with it a faint dusty smell of the vast Mojave Desert beyond the towering, rugged San Bernardino Mountains. He rounded Manchester, swung open the front door of the Plaza Arms and headed up to his room. After a quick shower, he laid on his bed and smoked a cigarette. Bits of excited conversations floated up from the street. The streetcar bells sounded like music. All of Central Avenue was heading for a good time, while he lay in a rented room and smoked cigarettes, like he was too old to have fun. Damn, shit. Damn shit! He sat up. Today was his birthday. He was 19. He ought to be out celebrating. He looked out the window. Neon lights flashed above bars and nightclubs, people hurried into a night of pleasure. He had to join them. His suit was wrinkled and dirty from Monday's disaster and, judging from the way men dressed out here, definitely out of style. He crushed out a half-smoked cigarette, put on his second-best pair of slacks and a light, cotton shirt. The last thing he wanted was to be holed up in this lonely room on his birthday. Outside, a car door slammed and a few moments later someone knocked on his door.

"Skip Reynolds. You in there, colored brother?"

He swung open the door. "Pee Wee!"

"Told you I was gon' check up on you." Pee Wee hurried into the room, jaws working fast on a stick of gum. "What's shaking? Feel like stepping out?"

"Hell, yeah. It's my birthday. I was just getting dressed."

"You call that dressed?" Pee Wee walked to the middle of the room, did a flashy turn to show off his dark gray double-breasted suit, then touched his heavily pomaded hair, and ran his hands down his sides. He snapped his fingers. "This is what you call dressed."

"Sheeit, Pee Wee. I ain't got nothing to touch that suit of yours."

"Well, we just gon' have to get you some style, colored brother."

Skip smiled and admired his friend. "I guess you gon' have them, what y'all call 'em, them Kitchen Mechanics waiting in line."

"That's the idea, Skip. Line 'em up and I'll take my pick. How you been?"

"Shoot." Skip lit another cigarette and sat down. "You wanna hear a sad story?"

"Save it, birthday boy. We gon' ball tonight. All night. I know this tea pad that's gon' be swinging. And the girls are gon' be there. Buddy, I'm getting hard just thinking 'bout 'em," Pee Wee winked. "You with me?"

"Uh, yeah, Pee Wee. I'm, " Skip paused, trying to remember a bit of hipster's jive he'd heard on the streetcar. "I'm in your groove."

"Well, awrighty-o! I'm gon' warm up the Plymy," Pee Wee said and headed for the door. He stopped in front of the mirror, turned around and smiled. "Ain't I one sharp papa?" He didn't wait for an answer.

Skip took some polish out of his suitcase, did a quick shine on his shoes and strutted over to the mirror. He didn't see the best-dressed man, but the one he saw didn't look bad, looked pretty damn good in fact, lean and well-muscled. He backed up and tried to glide like he'd seen guys do on the avenue. Sheeit! He walked like a country boy making his way through high cotton. He tried again, but stopped midway across the room. Pee Wee was honking the Plymy's horn.

He rushed downstairs and stopped as soon as he got outside the Plaza Arms. The Plymy looked beautiful. Sitting beneath the soft glow of a street lamp, its wickedly powerful engine purring softly like a jungle cat waiting to spring into high gear, the black car shone from Pee Wee's careful waxing. Skip slid into the soft passenger's seat and slammed the door.

"Where we going?" he said.

"Fortieth and San Pedro," Pee Wee said, putting the Plymy in gear and pulling away from the curb. "Guy I know is throwing a party. We gon' on a midnight ramble, my brother."

"Midnight ramble?"

"Yeah, Skip. You gon' see the sun rise tomorrow morning."

Pee Wee headed west on Manchester. Traffic was light. Most people were already at their first stop of the evening. The clubs were in full swing. Music and gay laughter spilled from open doorways. Kitchen Mechanics on a one-day pass from their housekeeping jobs on the west-side strolled the boulevard. Some were cool and pretty, knowing they looked good in their skirts and blouses, legs looking firm as their high heels clicked along the pavement, others were no more than giggling, excited school gals, high on being back home. The Plymy pulled up at a stoplight and Skip smiled at a couple of pretties waiting for the light to change. They were too busy talking to notice him.

"Broke his heart!" one said. "Girl, you ought to be shamed, good as that man was."

Pee Wee honked his horn and leaned across Skip. "You gals want a ride?"

They waved him off and started walking soon as the light changed.

"Damn," Pee Wee said, driving slowly past the girls. "I wouldn't mind strapping on that yellow gal. I bet I could turn her dampers down." He picked up speed and gave the girls a good-bye toot on the horn.

Skip turned to his partner. "How you been?" he said, lighting a ciga-rette.

"Everything's hanging on the awreet side for me. Nothing's up in the speed world, though."

"Hard times for record breakers, huh, "Skip said.

"Yeah, but the month's just beginning. Now, September was a month for records. Man a racing plane hit 289.19 miles an hour September fifth. That boy was flying! Lots of records last month. I tell you, Skip, I'd sure like to get in one of them airplanes."

Pee Wee turned north on San Pedro, drove through an industrial dis-trict of factories and warehouses. The dark, pot-holed streets were quiet. Packing trucks waited for tomorrow's deliveries, idle stock cars rested at rail heads. The area stank of old grease and oil dumped on the asphalt or poured into open 55-gallon drums. Stale water collected in pools. The Plymy rumbled over a set of railroad tracks cutting across Vernon as Pee Wee fiddled with the radio dial.

"How you like Los Angeles?" he asked.

Skip started to reply, but stopped. He didn't know what to make of this fantastic city. Certainly it was big, bigger than any place he'd ever been before. And more crowded. People were everywhere, crammed into apartment buildings and houses. There was never any peace and quiet.

"Hell, man," he said, deciding to play it safe. "I just got here."

"You been here near 'bout a week," Pee Wee said. "You must have some idea.

"What about the moving picture business. You faring okay with that?"

"You want the truth?" Skip said, puffing long and slow on his cigarette."

"Always."

Skip took one last puff and crushed the cigarette out in the ashtray. "Pee Wee," he said. "This town kicked the hell out of me Monday. You remember that acting school I was all hot about?"

"The one over on Central?"

"It was on Central. Damn place ain't even around no more. They done closed up."

"So, what you gon' do?"

"Guess I'm gon' keep on pushing. You know, cross that Jordan River," Skip said. "I didn't come all this way to turn tail at the first sign of trouble. Just got to come up with a new plan."

"Damn straight," Pee Wee said, turning left on Fortieth and straining to read the house numbers.

Skip slouched in his seat and rested. "How's your family?"

"Had to bail old pops out of the jail house this morning. Damn whiskey head couldn't find his way home last night and got picked up for loitering." Pee Wee shrugged. "They doing all right. Here," he said, pulling two reefers out of his coat pocket and passing them to Skip. "Hold these for me. I don't know 'bout where you come from, but the stuff is illegal out here."

"Illegal?" Skip touched the two slender reefers he'd put in his pocket. "You mean I could go to jail for holding these?"

"Damn straight," Pee Wee said, then noticed Skip's worried, troubled expression. "Aw don't worry none. I ain't gon' let nothing happen to you."

"Then how come you want me to hold them?"

"Cause I'd smoke them before we hit the door. I figure they're safe with you." Pee Wee smiled.

"Oh," Skip said, wanting to believe his friend.

"Come on, Skip. Put a smile on your face. We gon' ball tonight, and might even stumble across some girlfriends. You into that, ain't you?"

Skip nodded.

"Well, skin me brother." Pee Wee held out his hand and Skip slapped it. "Now, let me school you a bit. If you aiming to be a sharp papa in the city, you call them reefers tea sticks, and if you smoke 'em, well, that makes you a viper. And the place you go to smoke them is called a tea pad. You got that?"

"Check," Skip said. 'Viper.' 'Tea stick.' 'Tea pad.' Kitchen mechanic. Guess I'll be jiving in no time."

"I'll shake that country out of you." Pee Wee scanned the street for addresses, then pulled up in front of a large apartment building. "Here's the place."

Skip heard muted music and voices coming from an open window high up in the building, saw The Grandview written in gold lettering on the front door's glass. He rolled up the window and stepped into the warm night. Pee Wee clicked the driver's door shut, walked around and tapped a kiss on the Plymy's hood.

"We want the sixth floor," he said.

The plush carpeting in the entry hall cushioned their foot steps as they walked beneath twin crystal chandeliers. Pee Wee led the way. In the elevator he patted his hair and checked his reflection in the polished brass panels. Skip copied his moves, hoping he'd make out all right with these city folk.

"How come you always pulling me out of some mess?" he asked.

"Somebody's got to look after the country boy," Pee Wee said as the elevator glided to a soft stop. "Let's hit it."

Pee Wee walked straight to apartment 610, pushed the doorbell and waited. Muffled applause sounded behind the door, became louder when someone opened the door a crack and peeked outside. Skip saw part of a man's face, a slice of a dimly lit room.

"Y'all got a reason to be," the man whispered.

"We awreet, man. Couple-a colored brothers on a midnight ramble. Jack Thompson told me to come over." Pee Wee shifted his weight, looked up and down the hall like an alley cat looking for a place to hide. "Loosen up, brother. We being kind of conspicuous out here. And I know you don't want none of your neighbors calling the cops."

"You say Jack Thompson told you to come?" the man asked.

Pee Wee turned to Skip. "Now ain't that just what I said?"

The man hesitated, whispered over his shoulder to someone before letting Skip and Pee Wee inside. "Party's in back," he said, brightening. "And they jamming in there. Got a brother playing an electric guitar."

An electric guitar? Impossible. It sounded like a twangy, high-pitched saxophone. It gave off a strange, fluid sound. Skip pushed by Pee Wee and headed for the music, his curiosity driving him through the crowd in the smoky front room until he found the band. A lanky trumpet player in dark glasses leaned against one wall, waiting to solo. The bass man thumped along, while the drummer kept the beat on a kit covered with towels to muffle the sound. A cool-cat white boy stood near the guitar player, popping his fingers in time, nodding his head back and forth. Skip squeezed in beside him.

The guitar player's quicksilver fingers ran up and down the neck of his Gibson ES-150, stopping here and there for a bluesy arpeggio, or a piece of the melody. He was incredible, producing dazzling steams of sound, shattering everything Skip had ever thought about playing guitar. He'd heard plenty of guitar players in Tunis, but none of them could play like this guy. His style was an intricate, complex mixture of blues, jazz and swing. Yet he made it seem so easy, sitting in his chair, eyes closed behind wire-rimmed glasses, fingers bopping along, throwing in stunning, fiery flourishes, octaves, complex chords. Skip leaned forward, tried to wrap his mind around the singular brilliance of this flawless performance. But he could not. The guy was light years ahead of him. Where he was a finger picking country bluesman, content to get hot with a little ragtime ditty, this guy possessed a boundless imagination. His playing went places Skip had never dreamed of going. And he was young. They might be the same age. Damn, shit. Who was he? Skip had to know. It was not enough to stand here, thrilled beyond words. He had to talk to this guitar playing fool, learn how he made that guitar sing like a horn. He looked around to see if anyone else realized what was happening. Only the white boy seemed to understand. His eyes were wide open now, lit by a burning excitement. He half-shouted, mumbled: "Go man, go! Oh God!" He turned to Skip, breathless, his face flushed with delight as if he'd had a revelation. "Did you hear that?"

Skip shook his head, heard the guitar player wail through a wonderfully inventive riff, and lost himself. "This guy is too much," he screamed and, without thinking, held out his hand.

The white boy slapped skin with him and pointed to the guitar player. "Listen," he said. "The gods are speaking."

Skip stared at his hand. It still tingled from the joyous slap of a white boy who, just like him, was getting his top blown by a jazz playing brother with an electric guitar. All around him black folk and white folk mingled easily, walked about, argued, joked, laughed, even danced. He saw Pee Wee approaching, a broad smile on his face.

"Didn't I tell you this place was jumping?" Pee Wee said.

"Yeah, but you didn't say how much it'd be jumping," Skip cried. "It's jumping like Jesse Owens! You got to listen to this brother, Pee Wee. He's the greatest guitar player on earth."

"Yeah, yeah," Pee Wee said. "He's hot. You taking care of my reefers?"

"Got 'em right here," skip said, tapping his shirt pocket. "Say, can I really go to jail for having these, what you all call 'em, tea sticks?"

Pee Wee nodded. "A mean judge could send you to The Rock, and I do mean Alcatraz. But you ain't got to worry about that here. This place is strictly undercover, like a speakeasy in the twenties. You dig me?"

"Yeah, uh, like a steam shovel."

Pee Wee arched his eyebrows. "Not bad country boy."

"Yeah, I'm getting holt to this town." Skip looked around and whispered another question. "What happened to Jim Crow?"

"He ain't allowed in here, puts a damper on the festivities. Come on, let's see what old Jack has laid out to drink."

Skip waited a moment. The band was starting up again. He hesitated, then followed Pee Wee back to the front room and over to a tall, light skinned man whose thick, dusty blond hair was styled in classy waves. His expertly tailored gray suit hugged his body. A cigarette dangled elegantly between his manicured fingers. A dreamy-eyed blonde stood next to him, her low-cut, floor-length dress showing off her curves and the smooth white skin above her breasts. Damn, shit, Skip thought, this place cain't be for real, a black man and a white woman standing side by side like it ain't nobody's business. Again he asked if the place was safe.

"Will you stop it," Pee Wee snapped, then lowered his voice as they approached Jack Thompson. "Now, I done told you this place is under-cover. Hell, you in the city now, Skip. Let go of that country shit."

Thompson smiled at Pee Wee and extended his hand. "Marcus, glad you could make it." He turned to the blonde. "Linda, here's the fellow I've told you about. Best mechanic in the City of the Angels." Pee Wee smiled, turning to Skip.

"This here's the pride of the Lone Star State," Pee Wee said. "Jonathan Elliot Thompson, meet William Henry Reynolds."

"Ah," Thompson said. "You must be the movie star Marcus told me about."

"Well, I ain't no star yet," Skip said, shaking hands and noticing a disapproving look come over Thompson's face when he said "ain't."

"Only a matter of time, hmm?" Thompson winked and spoke to Pee Wee. "Marcus, why don't you and your friend stroll over to the bar and help yourselves. Everything's on me. And give a listen to the guitar play-er. He's phenomenal." Thompson put an arm around the blonde and gave her a slight push as they walked away.

Pee Wee watched them, envy in his eyes. "That guy is ultimate class. And check out that ofay chickie hanging on his arm? Now, I ain't fool enough to go chasing white gals, but I wouldn't mind popping a pretty like Jack's, just to see what the tail is like."

"Tail is tail," Skip muttered. "Besides, I never did go much for niggers putting on airs and acting like they shit don't stink."

"Aw, lay off the brother, Skip. He's just using what God gave him. Shit, I would. C'mon, let's check out the bar."

Skip followed Pee Wee to another room with a "Bar" sign written on a sheet of paper hanging above the doorway. "Where's that guy get the money for all of this?"

"Damn if I know," Pee Wee said. "I heard tell he's mixed in the crim-inal side of life, prostitutes, the numbers, something. I think his papa's the money man and Jack's just along for the ride. But it's got to be crim-inal. Any other nigger with cash is too busy trying to be some God damned upstanding example for white folks." Pee Wee swung open the door to reveal a small, dimly lit room with four tables and a bar. "See what I mean? First-class all the way."

Pee Wee ordered a pint of Old Grand Dad and two shot glasses.

"Happy Birthday," he said, tapping his glass against Skip's. "What number are you up to?"

"Nineteen."

"Shoot, you're younger than me."

Pee Wee refilled the glasses. Skip felt the alcohol burning into his gut, flowing into his blood, his head. He looked around the dark room, smiled and finished off the shot. Ain't smart to drink without eating, he thought. Two drinks and I'm already slow. He turned a heavy-lidded gaze to Pee Wee.

"How come that guy calls you Marcus?"

"Jack don't like nicknames. Says they're . . ." Pee Wee paused, trying to recall Thompson's description. "He says they're 'plebeian,' street talk, and he don't want no part of it. So he calls me Marcus Aurelius Jones, and I call him Jonathan Elliot Thompson. Strange, huh. But he's awreet with me. And the way he talks, just like them rich white folks in the moving pictures. Guess that's how come he got them ofay gals eating out his hand. He's forbidden fruit wrapped in a high-yellow package." Pee Wee shook his head, looked around and poured another round. "How you like Los Angeleez now?"

"It's settling on me pretty good, what with Old Grand Dad and this midnight ramble." Skip sipped his drink and rocked his head.

The guitar player was starting a slow blues. Conversations stopped in mid-sentence as people listened to the strange, liquid sound of the electric guitar. Skip stood, swayed on drunken legs before gaining his balance. He knocked off the last bit of whiskey in his glass.

"I'm gon' to the music."

The white boy next to the band nodded his head in four-four time, as if agreeing with the music's sad story. The bass man, tall and lanky, with a cigarette dangling loosely from his lips, stood behind the seated guitar player, his long brown fingers working strings thick as rope. Skip felt the bass notes throb in his chest. The drummer's brushes swished across the snare in soft circles of sound, every fourth beat on the cymbal. As he lit a cigarette, he closed his eyes, and let himself be carried away by the blues, slow as the evening sun going down, bringing the lonesome night and tales of sorrow, passion and unrequited love, a heart done wrong, but soothed by the music flowing like a healing salve. The trumpet player came in with a muted solo, his horn almost intelligible, talking up and down the scale, the notes sliding into the night, with here and there a quote from St. James Infirmary: "Let her go. Let her go, and may God bless her, wherever she may be." Then back to the basic melody, the musicians walking the blues. No one spoke when the band finished. The room was quiet, everyone wrapped in the song's afterglow. The applause came slowly, interspersed by voices saying: "Yeah…That's it…Tell it to me again." But the band left the blues behind in favor of an upbeat, Tin Pan Alley tune made for dancing and flashy solos. Skip puffed his cigarette, listened as female voices, slightly drunk, picked up on the song's lyrics and started singing: "I'm just wild about Harry and he's just wild about me."

"Man, would you dig this scene." That was Pee Wee, standing close by weaving slightly, the near empty bottle of Old Grand Dad held loosely in his hands. He nudged Skip, who opened his eyes and saw Pee Wee offering the bottle. Skip shook his head.

"You sure?" Pee Wee said before draining off the last swallows. "Woo wee!" Pee Wee sucked in a mouthful of air, shook his head and capped the empty bottle. "Enough of that," he said. "Where's that reefer?"

"Coming up," Skip drawled, pulling one of the cigarettes from his shirt pocket, sticking it in his mouth and lighting it.

He took a couple of long draws and let the smoke carry him even higher, before passing the reefer to Pee Wee. Out of the corner of his eye, he saw the guitar player smile and point to him. Skip nodded. He'd make sure the player was around for the next one. The band picked up the beat, swinging furiously now. The two singers popped their fingers, pumped their legs in time, and scatted in counterpoint to the building crescendo of dueling solos. When it was over, the musicians laughed, exhausted, while the girls called for alcohol to wet their throats. The applause came quick this time. The guitar player, his face bathed in sweat, leaned back and slid his fingers down, then up his guitar's neck, producing a sound that said: "Thank you." From the front room Skip heard a record playing and the thump of dancing feet as Billie Holiday's voice sang out. Pee Wee took a final puff on the reefer, smiled at Skip and pointed to one of the singers, a dark-skinned girl with big, brown eyes and a firm body that seemed about to burst from her tight dress.

"There's my gal," Pee Wee said, and was gone.

Skip stayed against the wall, the reefer tight between his fingers, trailing pungent smoke.

"Say, now, don't let that good stuff burn away," the guitar player called out.

Skip handed him the reefer, glad for the chance to talk. "That was the best damn playing I done heard in a long time, and the first time I ever heard an electric guitar."

"Thank you," the guitar player said, drawing long and slow on the reefer. "This electricity stuff is pretty new. I'm still learning how to control it. You play?"

"I'm a bluesman. Got me a National Steel."

"Everything comes from the blues," the guy said. "But jazz is my thing, and that Gibson over there is my queen."

"You from round here?"

"Just passing through," the guitar player said. "I'm coming down from North Dakota, heading home to Oklahoma City. Sure will be glad to see that old patch of land. You a city boy?" He handed Skip back the last bit of reefer.

"I'm a Texas man," Skip replied, taking a Texas-sized pull and snuffing out the reefer. He struggled to hold the smoke. "I come out here to get in the movies," he said, relaxing and breathing easy.

"Guess that makes us a couple of wayward sons."

"You got that straight," Skip said. "Say, where'd you learn to play like that?"

The guitar player shrugged. "Just messing around. Guy back home name of Eddie Durham put me on to electricity. He was in the Count's band. And I listened to Lester Young. You know him? I want to sound like a horn blowing wild."

Skip nodded. "What about all them notes? Where'd you learn that?"

"Oh, that's just scales and stuff, experimenting. Here, let me show you." He took a slip of paper and a pencil from his pocket and quickly diagrammed two guitar necks up to the twelfth fret, then filled them with dots. "Okay," he said. "Major scales in C and E. You being a bluesboy, you probably know these. Practice 'em until your fingers drop off, then run 'em some more. Play 'em with songs on the radio. You might give the blues a whole new way to go."

"Thanks," Skip said, folding up the sheet. "By the way, what's your name, colored brother?"

"Oh, I'm Charlie. Charlie Christian."

"I'm Skip Reynolds."

"Pleased to meet you, Skip," Charlie said, then headed off to the bar. "Got to wet my whistle before the next set."

Damn, shit, Skip thought as the young musician joined his band mates. That brother can play.

From the front room he heard more Billie Holiday, laughter and the shuffling of dancing feet. The party was going strong. He gathered his senses and tried to pull himself from against the wall. It wasn't easy. The reefer and Old Grand Dad had a strong hold of him, and the place they had him in was soft and deep as a fine feather bed. He lay back against the wall, listening to the music, watching the black and white faces passing before him, feeling disembodied, his eyes a camera on the world, while his mind floated away on a Billie Holiday serenade, her words phrased like a horn player blowing a smooth solo, the syllables dancing out long and slow; rising up and down the scale, finding places between the notes.

"Ah cigaahrette that hoolds the lipstick's traaces. An a-i-r-line tickket to r-o-m-a-antic pla-a-ces. Still my heart has wings. These foolish things remind me of you."

Skip tried again, this time succeeding and finding himself off the wall, swaying on unsteady legs. He waited for the rocking to stop, then headed into the front room, checking his stride, trying not to walk like a country boy on a stroll through the cotton fields, but like a city man, a slick papa on a midnight ramble.

He looked for Pee Wee but didn't see him amidst the couples dancing slowly, their bodies pressed close together, hands feeling up and down backs and hips, nor did he find him on the sofas, where other couples embraced, lips drinking in long kisses, and he wasn't among those who sat in clusters, smoking, drinking, laughing. Skip shrugged, licked his dry lips and headed for the kitchen and a drink of water to soak his reefer-dried mouth. On the way he passed a pretty, brown-skinned girl who wore a gardenia in her hair, Billie Holiday style. She was dancing with a sorry-looking guy who leaned heavily into her and tried to dry-fuck her on the dance floor. She caught Skip's eye and gave him a weary, tired smile. He looked her up and down, winked and pressed on to the kitchen, thinking maybe he'd give her a try if she ever pried herself away. He liked the way she was built, short and stocky, with a little roll of fat around the middle, cushion for pushing.

The trumpet player and the white boy who'd sat next to the band, nodding his head in time, engaged in a fierce, loud argument.

"Harry James the best trumpet player! Ain't that just like a white boy to come on Central Avenue talking that Harry James shit," the trumpet player cried, before turning to Skip who stood nearby, filling a glass from the faucet. "Hold me back, colored brother, before I knock some sense into this ofay."

"Don't go calling names now," the white boy said, flustered. "I swear, you colored guys are so damn hot-headed. You asked me who I thought was the best, and I told you. Harry James."

"Aw, hell," the trumpet player said, putting his hand to his head in mock disappointment. "I guess there's only one way to show you." He brought his horn to his lips and blew the virtuosic opening phase of Louis Armstrong's masterpiece, "West End Blues." The notes ran up the scale in military precision, higher and higher, before sliding back down, twisting around and around, tumbling and ending in a full, yet softly blown final blue note. The trumpet player brought his horn back down, smiled and waited.

"Blow my top, man!" the white boy said. "What was that?"

"That was Pops!" the trumpet player said.

The white boy shook his head. "Pops?"

The trumpet player turned to Skip. "I'm depending on you, colored brother. Tell him who Pops is. Please, school this boy."

Skip shifted nervously. He didn't know who Pops was, and he didn't want to disappoint, but he didn't want to put the white boy down. They'd shared Charlie Christian's music. He decided to play it cool. "Pops." he said, mimicking the voice of a dandy he'd met on the street car, "is the best damn trumpet player on God's green earth."

"You got it colored brother," the trumpet player said, holding his free hand, palm up, letting Skip give him five before he turned to the white boy. "Louis Armstrong is the best. Why, he could blow Harry James to kingdom come."

The white boy smiled sheepishly and hung his head. "Old Harry never played nothing like you just did. What was that anyway?"

"West End Blues," the trumpet player said, proudly. "I been trying to get it right all year. Here, lemme do it again."

He brought the horn back to his lips and started to blow. Skip heard the guitar player picking up on the trumpet's intro and tracking it note for note. God damn! The horn player heard it too and ran off to find his jamming buddy, the white boy following close behind. Skip filled another glass of water and watched them go, as Pee Wee pushed his way into the kitchen.

"There you are! Come here. I got somebody for you to meet," Pee Wee said, grabbing Skip and putting his arm around him. "My gal has a girlfriend and she's lonely for some good company. You digging me? The gal needs to groove with a down home boy, somebody who could smooth out her rough spots. I figured you could help her out."

"You mean wear her out," Skip laughed, clapping his buddy on the back. "Now, take me to this needy child."

He felt joyously alive in the swinging whirlwind of this night. He could feel himself grinning from ear to ear, feel himself on the verge of laughing at nothing in particular, just glad to be here. Pee Wee steered him toward a pair of girls sitting at the edge of a sofa. One was the tall singer Pee Wee had chased down, the other was the girl he'd seen dancing with the sorry drunk. His eyes locked on her.

"Well," Pee Wee said. "Here's the fella I was telling y'all about. Skip Reynolds, meet Bessie Lee Watkins, the pearl of Central Avenue, and Virginia Lynn Daniels, who has fled the confines of the westside for a little fling in old darktown." Pee Wee waited for everyone to exchange greetings, then took Bessie Lee by the arm. "We gon' cut a little rug, children. See y'all around."

For a moment, with Pee Wee gone, Skip felt stranded, suddenly shy and tongue-tied, but the feeling quickly passed.

"I seen you dancing," he said.

"Thank God that's passed," Virginia said. "Some men, Lord have mercy. First they can't hold their liquor, then they think you want them in your drawers just 'cause you let 'em hold you close on the dance floor."

"Yeah, I seen him working on you," Skip said, deciding right then and there to wait until Virginia gave him the "go" sign. "You one of them Kitchen Mechanics?"

"Yes, sir. I work in this mansion in the Hollywood Hills. A big old place, but I ain't long for that. Un uh," she shook her head. "The boss man's been getting that look in his eye. You know the one I'm talking 'bout? He wants him a taste of brown sugar, but I ain't studying him." She turned to Skip. "Pee Wee said you're an actor."

"I ain't acting yet, but I'm gon' be," Skip said. "I been in town a week. Come out of east Texas."

He casually lit a cigarette and told his story, embellished it, cast himself as a world-wise tough who tangled with a yard bull in a Fort Worth freight yard. "Knocked him stone cold," he said.

He was fearless, hitchhiking his way across the country with a switchblade on his hip, bound for the City of Angeles and a chance to make his stake in Hollywood.

"My, my, my," Virginia sighed. "With all you done you should-a rescued me, 'stead of walking on by."

"I didn't know you wanted to be saved." Skip said, rolling the cigarette between his fingers.

"Couldn't you see it in my eyes," she said, before throwing herself across his lap and putting a hand to her forehead like some swooning Hollywood heroine. "I was trapped and needed a prince from the east to rescue me." She laughed and looked up into Skip's eyes, held his gaze a moment.

He shrugged, confused. Was this girl playing with him? Before he could make a move, Virginia sat up, still smiling. Somebody had put on a jumping tune, Pops singing "Swing that Music." The big band roared at break-neck speed. Virginia started bouncing up and down.

"Can you do the Lindy?"

"I can try," Skip replied and let her lead him onto the dance floor.

She was a good teacher, patient and understanding, but Skip couldn't figure out the acrobatic moves. He felt clumsy and self-conscious, lead feet shuffling along, out of time. The catfish was outside his element again. He preferred the slow songs, where they could hold onto each other, press close and reveal bits of themselves. Virginia said she was born in Los Angeles and raised on Central Avenue. She was thinking about becoming a teacher, just to pass the time until she found a good man with a job. Then she was going to get married and make babies, lots of babies. She'd never picked cotton and wouldn't know a boll if she saw one. Skip laughed when she said that. It was true, she replied, smiling eyes shining. He caressed her small, soft hands, tenderly kissed each fingertip. She pulled him close when he told her about his parents, nuzzled him and said, "Oh, baby. I'm so sorry." He was about to go for her lips when he felt someone tapping his shoulder. It was Pee Wee, hugging Bessie Lee and smiling like a mischievous little boy who knows he's breaking up something important. He shrugged his shoulders when Skip and Virginia cut their eyes at him.

"Me and Bessie planning on leaving this scene. I didn't know if y'all had a way home," he explained. "Ain't no streetcars this time of night. I didn't want to leave y'all stranded."

"Guess it's time to fold up the tents," Skip said, disappointed.

"Now, I didn't say that," Pee Wee said. "It's just time to move on to a," he paused for a moment, "a more intimate setting. Namely my place. 'Course, I could take y'all home."

Skip felt Virginia squeeze his hand. She wasn't thinking about leaving. Besides, they were just getting to know each other, and there was still a kiss to be had.

"Y'all go on," Skip said. "We'll fare okay."

They built the tentative bridge of early friendship. Skip learned the basic Lindy steps, forgot himself in the exultant delirium of this night, released his spirit and, in a moment of spontaneous perfection, twirled Virginia, brought her close, dipped her, then leaned over as if to kiss her, held her gaze for what seemed an eternity before pulling her back up and continuing to dance. He was 19, celebrating life on a Midnight Ramble with a girl who was happy to be with him. In the background, the best guitar player he'd ever heard blazed through one radiant solo after another until dawn paled the sky and it was time to go home, time to hail a Black and White cab for Virginia, pay her fare to the westside, seal their night with a kiss, exquisite, wonderful, satisfying, the press of her lips lingering on his as the liquid sound of an electric guitar sang through his mind and the sun rose, glorious on a new day.

MONEY, OR AS PEE WEE LIKED TO SAY, DINERO. BUT WHATEVER you called it—jack, moolah, cash, mean green, dough, scratch—everything came back to that do-re-mi, that M-O-N-E-Y. There was no getting over, under or around it. It made the world go around and right now Skip was standing still on a Central Avenue street corner, jingling the little bit of change in his pocket, thinking about how he needed to get hold of some cash to keep the landlady at bay and his stomach full. He'd been in Los Angeles more than a month, spent money up and down the avenue, his bankroll getting smaller and smaller. The money problem hit him hard last Monday when Mrs. Harrelson, the landlady, asked if he planned on paying his two weeks' overdue rent anytime soon. He told her he would, but he didn't say when. So, she told him he'd better come up with the rent money quick, or she'd have to put him out. She wasn't running a flop house. Now it was Friday, and he didn't even have enough to make a token payment, just 75 cents in his pocket and two dollars in his wallet. The rest had gone to movies and streetcar rides, three meals a day, shaves and haircuts, here and there a bottle of Old Grand Dad to share with Pee Wee. He'd been working on some new songs picked off the radio, melody lines mostly, but he figured he might find a bench in Pershing Square and play for tips. The bluesboys back home did it all the time.

He scratched his scruffy four-day beard and crossed the street, looking for a cheap diversion to take his mind off his troubles. Overhead, an
airplane dropped low in the sky, heading for a landing at Inglewood
Airport. Sunlight glinting off the plane's wings transformed the craft into
a silver, still-winged bird in flight effortless as a gliding eagle's. He lit a
cigarette and watched the plane until it dipped below the line of rooftops
on Central Avenue. What to do? Rootless and unemployed, he walked the
barely familiar avenue, a stranger in a city teeming with thousands of
people, but only one person would do him a favor. He walked the avenue
until the Friday night party people started filling the sidewalks, their cars
crowding the streetcars running up and down the avenue. A long line of
couples stood outside the Lincoln, buying tickets for the evening showing of *The Duke is Tops* with Lena Horne. Skip watched their happy faces,
wanting to be with them, but feeling apart, near broke and adrift. He
thought about catching a red car and riding the two or three miles to the
Plaza Arms, but decided against it. Determined to walk all the way, he
marched down Central Avenue, making good time, but losing his resolve
with each passing red car. City life was getting to him. Back home, he'd
think nothing of walking two or three miles to get somewhere, but here,
with streetcars to take him all over town for seven cents, walking just
didn't make sense. Twenty blocks into his journey, his feet started hurting and his stomach cried for a meal. He jingled the coins in his pocket,
hating having to keep tabs on every penny. He had to make change. He
stopped at a Rex-All drug store, went to the newspaper rack and pulled
out copies of *The Sentinel* and *The Examiner*, figuring he'd double his
chances of finding a job by reading the want ads in the black and white
newspapers. Back out on the street, he ran to the safety island and waited for the next car. It came rumbling down Central Avenue, sparks flying
off its electric wires. A gang of laughing, sharply dressed young men got
off when the car pulled up in front of him. They were going to the Club
Alabam. They were going to ball tonight, find a midnight ramble when
the club closed. Skip remembered his midnight ramble. Those days are
gon' come again, he thought, boarding the car and settling into a seat for
the ride back to the Plaza Arms.

He was glad Mrs. Harrelson wasn't at the front desk. The last thing
he wanted to do was start poor mouthing about how he didn't have the
weeks' rent, but, if she just gave him another week, he'd start paying

again. Relieved, he walked the three flights to his room, passing the man who always sang in the shower. The guy wore a ratty, silk smoking jacket over a dirty shirt and pair of slacks. He smiled broadly and whispered as Skip passed by.

"You got a surprise coming, buddy," he said. "Hope you got peoples close by."

Skip shrugged, dismissing the man as he pulled out his key. He stopped outside his door, startled. Someone was inside. Mrs. Harrelson? He thought about running away, but where. Everything he owned was in the room. He lit another cigarette, puffed hard and fast, working himself into a cool, mean mood. He wasn't going to take any mess from whoever was in there, even Mrs. Harrelson. He opened the door. There she was, wearing a high-fashion pink dress that in Tunis would have been some woman's Sunday best but in Los Angeles was just something to wear to work. Skip watched her rifle through his suitcase, saw her pause now and again to inspect his possessions. The picture case caught her attention.

"Um, um, um," she said, shaking her head. "The low down dog was a pretty baby."

Skip pushed hard against the door. It banged against the wall. "You trying to rob me?"

"Ain't doing no such thing, Mr. Reynolds," Mrs. Harrelson said in her best nothing-but-business voice. "I'm just checking to see if there's anything here you might be able to pawn and put towards your rent. You know you're overdue, and I got bills that won't wait."

"I told you I'd pay."

"When? You told me that Monday and here it is Friday and I ain't seen not one red cent."

"I know, I know. But I'm looking for work." Skip held up the newspapers. "I done already found some places to look into tomorrow. Gimme another week."

Mrs. Harrelson started shaking her head. "Can't do that, Mr. Reynolds. Be setting a bad example. Next thing you know, everybody'll be sliding, come poor mouthing to me, talking 'bout how they gon' get me some rent money next week. Friday come and they just another week deeper in the hole. No sir, Mr. Reynolds. I told you about this Monday. You had plenty of time."

Skip walked over to the rickety table and crushed his cigarette out in an ashtray.

"How come you treating me so bad, Mrs. Harrelson?"

"Treating you bad! Boy, I done already let you slide going on three weeks now. That ain't no way to run a business."

"But that don't mean you got to turn me out. Back home colored folks stick together, ain't all the time kicking people when they're down. Even the boss man won't throw a 'cropper out just 'cause he misses his mark."

"Well, honey, this ain't back home," Mrs. Harrelson said, putting one hand on her wide hips, moving her head side to side in rhythm with her words, while her free hand jerked back and forth, pointing at Skip. "This is the big city. You got to pay to stay in this town. The Plaza Arms ain't no relief station. You want that, find yourself a Hooverville somewhere or join the WPA." She picked up National Steel and headed for the door.

"Where you going with that?"

"This here's ransom." Mrs. Harrelson said, turning and staring him down. "Long's I got it, I know you'll come up with that rent money."

She pressed on. Skip grabbed her by the arm, spun her around.

"You ain't taking my guitar," he yelled.

"Turn me loose, nigger," Mrs. Harrelson said, trying to free herself from Skip's grasp.

He tightened his grip, reached for National Steel.

"Give me that guitar," he said through clenched teeth, wrenching Mrs. Harrelson's arm behind her back, pulling it up until she bent over and surrendered. He snatched his guitar from her and pushed her away. "This is mine," he screamed, shaking. "Mine! And nobody is gon' take it."

He laid the guitar across his bed, cursed Mrs. Harrelson and this city, where everything came down to the God damned dollar, this city where even colored folk were happy to kick a brother just because he was on hard times. Mrs. Harrelson backed away from him. She rubbed her sore arm and stared, fear and anger in her eyes. Skip heard his heart beating like an out-of-control trip hammer. He sat on the bed, lit another cigarette and tried to calm himself. Mrs. Harrelson broke the silence.

"You can't sleep here no more, Mr. Reynolds."

"Fine." Skip started packing his suitcase.

"Ain't no need of doing that."

"What," he stopped, the cigarette dangling from his lips.

"Everything stays. Now, you got your guitar, but everything else stays until you are paid up in full. Now, come on," she said, waiting only a moment. "Get out of here before I call the police."

Skip heaved himself up off the sagging mattress, realizing he'd messed up and played the landlady the wrong way. He looked absently around the room, saw the picture case on the nightstand. He snatched it quick, walked past Mrs. Harrelson and into the hallway, dragging his feet, avoiding her eyes. Begging would do no good.

"Give me your key," she said, locking the door with her master key. Skip handed it to her, his eyes studying the shape of her black pumps, the paisley pattern of the rug beneath her feet. "I hate to do this, Mr. Reynolds, but I can't keep letting you slide. It sets a bad example." She pocketed his key. "See me when you get some money. Your stuff'll be here." She walked away, still rubbing her sore arm.

He leaned against the locked door and puffed sadly on his cigarette. Damn, shit. His mind scrambled for a place to spend the night. Pee Wee? He was already in deep with Pee Wee, maybe too deep to ask for another favor. Still, he didn't want to sleep outside. People got murdered in this city all the time. The crimes were in every newspaper. He imagined a headline in *The Sentinel:* "City proves too tough for country boy. Body found in Pershing Square." He took another puff, thought about two-bit flop houses, roaches crawling over his face, dirty men mumbling in their sleep, lice infested blankets. He pounded the door, kicked it with the heel of his shoe, turned and headed for the stairs. Down the hall a door opened. The shower man stepped out, still smiling broadly, an empty cigarette holder in his mouth.

"Looks like they done picked poor Robin clean," he said. "Yes sir, feathers all on the floor."

Skip took a last puff on the cigarette and crushed it out on a door knob, happy to see the embers burn tiny holes in the rug. "Guess this damn catfish is caught out of his mudhole again," he said to himself.

"How's that?" the man said, approaching.

"Nothing," Skip said, absently. "Just something an old man once told me."

"Where you from boy?"

"Tunis, Texas."

The guy tightened the belt on his smoking jacket. "Looks like old country's got some serious problems. Yes, yes, serious problems indeed."

"Yeah, and standing here ain't doing me no good." Skip headed for the stairs.

"Hold it there, brother," the guy said. "Hold on now."

Skip kept on walking.

"Come here, boy, and quit being so hard headed." The guy frowned, then relaxed. "Come on, daddy-o. I ain't gon' fool you. I'm gon' school you. I got something that's gon' bust your conk, though I see you don't wear one. But anyway, what I got is gon' ease your gloom and have you spending the night in that room." He pointed to Skip's locked apartment. "Are you hip to my jive. I mean, do you dig me daddy-o?"

"What you know?" Skip said, eased by the playful banter.

"I know 'bout something that's gon' bring pleasure to your life. You ain't sleeping outside tonight. Now, that old biddy might think she's slick, but she ain't hip to all my tricks and I, if I may introduce myself, am Phineas T. Weatherby, part-time preacher and hoodoo man, seer of the future and traveler to distant lands. Gimme your palm, boy. I feel like reading."

Skip almost gave the stranger his hand before pulling back. "Get to the point, man. I got to find a place to sleep,"

Weatherby rolled his eyes. "Daddy-o! You ain't listening." He pulled a polished piece of metal from his pocket and waved it as if it were a magic wand.

"I ain't got time for this," Skip said, turning to walk away.

Weatherby reached out, grabbed Skip by the shoulder and spun him around. "Boy I do believe you in need of some serious schooling. Observe." He went to Skip's apartment, worked the piece of metal between the doorjamb and the door. The lock clicked open. He bowed graciously. "Entre monsieur, and make it quick." He closed the door behind them and whispered. "Now, what do you think?"

"I think I like it," Skip smiled, walking over to his suitcase and starting to pack. "How long's it gon' take before Mrs. Harrelson gets wise to this scheme?"

"Not long. She's got a nose like a Mississippi bloodhound. You can probably stay till Monday, cleaning day. This ploy is merely to buy time, to prevent your lowering yourself to accepting such undesirable alternatives as sleeping on park benches, or in some flea-bitten flop house." Weatherby settled into a chair and elegantly crossed his legs, the cigarette holder held loosely between his stubby fingers.

Skip lit another cigarette.

"Ixnay on the okesmay," Weatherby whispered.

"Huh?" Skip said, sucking down the first puff.

"Nix the smokes, daddy-o. You got to play it cool, baby. Like Q.T. Hush.

"Harrelson could have you arrested for trespassing. And don't be packing them clothes. You don't want to leave any clue that you been here, just in case Harrelson comes through before Monday."

Skip stopped packing and snuffed out the cigarette. He paced around the room, feeling strange to be back inside after fighting Mrs. Harrelson. He stopped at the window, his mind trying to put together a plan. Weatherby looked over his shoulder and sighed.

"Ah, the night, time of mystery, time of dreams, a time when things can be better than they seem. An evening of joy can erase a day of sorrow, don't you agree?"

Skip grunted, pulled a stick of gum from his pocket and started chewing, his jaws working fiercely while his mind scrambled for a way out of this mess.

"Have you any evening plans?" Weatherby said.

"Shit," Skip said, tiring of Weatherby's high-toned way of talking. "Have I got any evening plans. What, do I look like, some damn Rockefeller? Have I got any evening plans," he said derisively, mocking Weatherby. He turned from the window. "Yeah, I got evening plans. I'm gon' visit one Marcus Aurelius Jones and see 'bout getting me some employment, lessen you know where I can get a job."

"Job!" Weatherby rocked back as if he'd been hit. He waved his hand and shook his head. "God hasn't made the job that is worth my time. I prefer to live by my wits and," he reached inside a pocket of his smoking jacket and produced a small bottle filled with a dark, reddish brown liquid, "by this." He held the bottle up, smiling at Skip's curious expression. "This, my callow, young friend is Eternity's Breath. A marvelous elixir I have sold from coast to coast. Guaranteed to cure any number of common ills. It has been known to grow hair on many a bald pate and to have fired desire in the glands of frigid women and men whose mojos done broke. It is a veritable fountain of youth. In this I have combined the knowledge of ancient alchemists and down-home conjurers. This, my friend, along with a monthly check from my dear sweet mother, has allowed me to live a life free of the worries of those sorry Babbits who waste their lives in the service of others." Weatherby unscrewed the cap and took a long swallow, his Adam's Apple working up and down. He sighed with pleasure. "Ahh. If Juan Ponce de Leon had but known of this secret formula, he'd be walking Central Avenue this very day. Instead, his bones lie lost in the mud and mire of Florida's Everglades. Have some?" He offered Skip the bottle.

"No thanks, but that was some spiel. Swear to God you'd make a killing in Tunis."

"Thank you," Weatherby said, capping the bottle and stowing it away in his pocket. "I'll put your hometown on the itinerary of my next journey."

Skip's stomach growled loud enough for Weatherby to raise an eyebrow.

"The maw cries for sustenance. Feed me, yells the insatiable beast. God dammit, feed me!" Weatherby stood and walked around the room, waving his arms, shoving them towards his mouth as if he were shoveling food. "It is only by death that life is sustained. A wonderful paradox, don't you think?"

"Whatever you say," Skip said, heading for the door. "Since I ain't got no Eternity's Breath to peddle, I'm off to see about a job. Mind if I keep this little thing of yours?"

"I have several," Weatherby said. "However, a token of your appreciation for my timely services would be much appreciated."

"Huh?"

"Money, boy," and he put a hand on his hips. "Like the old biddy said: 'You got to pay to stay in this town."

Skip laughed at Weatherby's high-pitched impersonation of Mrs. Harrelson. He brought 48 cents out of his pocket. "How much?"

"Two bits and that's bargain. Why, I've known ne'er-do-wells to pay a dollar for this handy tool which, I've been told, is highly regarded in the burglary trade." Weatherby accepted a quarter and headed for the door. "Allow me." He peeked into the doorway.

"The coast is clear."

Skip joined Phineas in the carpeted hallway and pulled the door shut. The latch clicked behind them. He tested the knob, made sure it was locked then slide the piece of metal between the door and the latch. With a slight push, the door swung open.

"I'll be God damned," he said, closing the door again. "I don't see why you mess with that Eternity's Breath stuff, Phineas. You'd make a fortune with this thing."

"The elixir is my bread and butter. It can be sold anywhere, while this small scrap is best used in big cities teeming with hard luck stories such as yours. Diversify and thrive, that is my motto."

"Well, awreet, pops," Skip said, heading for the stairs. "See you in a few."

Weatherby followed Skip down the hall, then pulling him aside. "Ixnay on them stairs." He pointed to the fire escape. "There is your means of egress."

Skip nodded, did an about-face, and sneaked down the fire escape, jumping the final feet to the ground. He walked out of the alley and onto Central Avenue. He made his way to Bill's cafe at 70th, exchanged a few greetings and broke one of his two remaining dollars down for a two bit pork chop dinner and a cup of coffee. He decided against burning another nickel for a piece of pie. Maybe tomorrow, if he found a job he'd celebrate with dessert. But tonight he was strictly meat and potatoes. Between cups of coffee, he dialed Pee Wee's number and listened to the phone ring. Nobody home, and why should he be home. The night was still young. He finished eating and headed back into the night, letting his feet carry him up Central Avenue in the general direction of Pee Wee's apartment. He felt homesick for familiar faces and places, his chair on Grandma Sarah's porch. The seat accepted the shape of his body whenever he sat down and tilted it back and waved at whoever passed by: Willie, Billie Dee Josephs, John Lee. People here were always dying here: shot, stabbed, found beaten to death in any alley, no identification found on the body, no way of telling who it was, just John Doe, age and address unknown. Nobody told him how hard it was going to be. Old Man Williams told him to stay in his place, but that was the old man talking. Skip wondered what the young man inside of Old Man Williams would have said, the young man who'd seen death in Cuba and spent drunken nights whoring in Havana, who'd seen a good piece of the world and yet, when his soldering was done, had come back to Tunis, put away his uniform and taken up the Bible, become a soldier in the army of the Lord. Old Man Williams had let his wisdom, not his youth speak. Up the street a neon sign flashed off and on: Fall On Inn. It looked cheap, a hole in the wall where the drinks wouldn't burn up too much of his cash. He fell on into the dark cool bar, surprised to find it nearly empty on a Friday night. But there was no band and not even a juke box to spin a tune or two. The place was strictly for drinking. A couple of old guys, their bellies distended from too much beer, sat near one end, while a drunk sat midway down the bar, face down in a glass. Skip took an empty seat, slapped a quarter on the bar and ordered a glass of Rainier Ale. He figured he could nurse the beer longer than he could a glass of liquor. Halfway through the bottle, he went to the phone booth in back and dialed Pee Wee's number. Again the phone rang and rang, rang fifteen times before Pee Wee came on the line.

"Lo."

Skip smiled at the sound of his friend's voice. "Damn, man. Where you been?"

"Been chasing tail I couldn't get. How 'bout you?"

"Struggling. You busy? I was thinking 'bout stopping by."

"How 'bout tomorrow, Skip. I'm wore out."

Skip frowned, but pressed on. "It's gotta be tonight. I'm in a jam, Pee Wee. I figured you could help me out."

Pee Wee was silent. Static hissed over the wires. Skip made out faint voices in conversation on his line. The bartender banged on the booth and pointed to the door. Closing time.

Skip waved him off. On the other end Pee Wee sighed heavily.

"Get your butt over here and make it quick. I'm five minutes from calling it a night."

The line clicked dead. Skip hit the Fall On Inn's front door and ran up Central, turning left on Fortieth, going three blocks before he slowed down and started looking for the court apartments where Pee Wee lived. He found them silent and dark, except for the rear left apartment, where a desk lamp glowed low, warm light and a radio played softly. He rapped lightly on the door. Pee Wee, shirtless and wearing boxer shorts, peered around a curtain.

"I'm all ears," he said, letting Skip in and laying down on his sofa.

"Got a smoke?" Skip said, settling into a chair.

"What, you bumming now?"

"I'm taking whatever I can get. You got a smoke?"

Pee Wee tossed him the pack of Camels on the coffee table.

"I need a job," Skip said, lighting the cigarette and taking a deep puff.

"You know anything 'bout engines," Pee Wee replied. "We got a guy over there don't know a carburetor from a distributor. Damn fool could put us out of business if we don't get rid of him."

Skip shook his head. "How 'bout something easy. You know, like being the friendly service man. Pump the gas, wash the windows?"

"Thought you was gon' be a moving picture man," Pee Wee said, lighting himself a Camel and blowing lazy smoke rings.

"Right now I got to get hold of some cash money. That damn heifer that runs the Plaza Arms locked me out."

"You looked anywhere?"

"I'm starting tomorrow."

"Shit. The way you talking you should'a started last week. Way I look at, living is like driving a car. You never let that gas gauge get on E and you never get down to your last dollar. 'Course, that don't help you now." Pee Wee paused, flicked ash off his cigarette. "I could loan you a couple-a bucks, something to tide you over."

Skip leaned back and mulled over the idea of taking Pee Wee's money. Grandma Sarah always said to take money, but that was only when it was money due you. She didn't mean for him to take charity. But, a couple of bucks, maybe even a fiver, would do real nice right now. It wouldn't pay the rent, but it would keep him in meals. He leaned forward and took a long drag on his cigarette, then rolled the smoke between his fingers, gave Pee Wee a tight smile. The money was his for the taking.

"You sure you don't know anyplace I can get a job?"

"Not at this hour of night. I might by this time tomorrow, though. You want the loan?"

"Lemme look first," Skip said, hoping he wouldn't have to come back asking if the offer was still good. "Town as big as this Los Angeleez ought to have something for a hard working boy."

"Suit yourself." Pee Wee stretched out on the couch, crushed out his cigarette. Skip settled back in the chair, feeling comfortable. He felt like talking.

"You ever heard of a Phineas T. Weatherby? Man who goes around selling this . . ."

"Marvelous elixir known to have filched many an ignorant fool out of a day's wages," Pee Wee turned over on the sofa. "Yeah, I know the crook."

"Crook!" Skip said, surprised.

"The man's a damn parasite, Skip. Got a college degree and won't do an honest day's work. Why, he tried to sell my daddy some land in the Mojave Desert. Said Victorville was gonna be the next oasis. Shit, I wouldn't trust him as far as I can throw him, and he's a heavy man."

"He's a big boy all right, but he pulled me out of a tight spot this evening." Skip took the piece of metal from his pocket and tossed it towards Pee Wee. "He gimme this. It gets me in my room pretty as you please."

Pee Wee turned the piece of metal over in his hands. "How much he charge for this?"

"Two bits."

"Must be that country charm of yours, 'cause I've seen him selling this junk for a dollar, and seen people buying it too. 'Course, he don't tell nobody he makes it out of tin cans. That would be like taking money out of his pocket, and Weatherby don't go for that. No sir. He's a sly one, Skip. Watch him." Pee Wee flipped the piece of metal back across the room, sent it banging against a wall.

"Hey," Skip cried, scrambling for his treasure. "Careful with that, Pee Wee. This the only thing keeping me out of Pershing Square."

"Pershing Square, my ass. You'd be sleeping on this sofa if you'd have come to me earlier. Can't let my little country boy sleep out in the cold. Anyway, don't get too close to Weatherby. He's a snake if there ever was one. I've heard tell that when he was baby, he stole his mama's necklace while he was sucking her titty. Yes, sir, you gotta watch him." Pee Wee reached over his head and grabbed his alarm clock. "Three thirty." He slumped back on the sofa and groaned. "I gotta meet the boss man in five hours. Get on out of here, Skip, and let me sleep."

Skip pulled himself out of the sagging chair and walked to the door. "When should I come by the station?"

"Downside of sunshine, 'bout six."

"Okay," Skip said, opening the door. "Thanks for the help, Pee Wee."

"Man, will you quit thanking me all the time. I ain't done nothing special. You'd do the same for me if I was a stranger in your hometown and I was in a pinch, right?"

"You know it."

"There you go." Pee Wee stood and headed for his bedroom. "See you tomorrow. Door locks by pushing the button on the knob. Goodnight."

Skip stepped into the night, and softly pulled the door shut behind him. Walking back to the Plaza Arms tired but refreshed, he sent a prayer to Lady Luck: double-sixes, please.

~

HE HIT THE STREETS EARLY THE NEXT MORNING, STOPPED AT JOE'S Cafe for a cup of coffee and a sweet roll, bent over his newspapers and started circling want ads of places on the avenue. Dish washer, stock boy, clean-up man, it didn't matter so long as he could start today and start putting some of that mean green in his pockets. The tiny newspaper print blurred in front of his tired eyes as he gulped hot coffee, listening to the tantalizing sound of bacon strips on the grills, smelling the heavy, break-fast aroma of smoked pork, beef steak and eggs. His mouth watered, his gut quivered and rumbled. Three seats down the counter, a guy in a busi-ness suit raised an eyebrow and stared at him before stuffing a forkful of sausage and eggs down his throat. Skip looked away, pulled a cigarette out of his crumpled pack. The smoke eased his appetite, gave him time to think about the day ahead. He didn't feel like going around town putting on the good face, telling lies about how much he wanted to do whatever the boss man wanted. And he didn't feel like walking. He felt like some out of gas jalopy on empty, coasting. But he knew he'd have to walk, just like the time on that empty stretch of New Mexico highway. He jammed the last bit of sweet roll into his mouth, licked the sugar from his fingers and washed it all down with the final gulp of coffee.

The morning sun seemed unusually bright and warm for early November as he strolled Central Avenue, the want ads folded in his back pocket. He spent two hours going from store to store, scratching out cir-cled addresses, accepting rejection: 'Naw, you should have come yester-day . . . You mean that ad is still in the paper! . . . You got any experience mopping floors? . . . We just hired a guy.' Lies, Skip thought. All of it nothing but lies to keep a black boy down. He trudged on through the quiet heat of high noon, stopping to buy a soda and sit in the shade before pressing on, stopping again to stare in a store front window and finding a scruffy, unshaven young man staring back at him. Was that him? The guy looked like a hobo just off a freight. He had forgotten one of Grandma Sarah's old adages: Never go looking for a job looking like you need a job. Shoot, he thought, staring at his reflection, even I wouldn't hire you. He turned away and watched the passerby, men slipping into dark bars for a cool beer, women making their Sunday shopping rounds, kids on their way to the matinee, all of them living in the world, while he sought entry into the rhythm of working life. He pulled out his newspaper and ran his fingers up and down the columns until he found the only unscratched ad. The Rex-All drug store at 32nd and Central needed a clean-up man. He headed back up the street, stopping on the way at a gas station where he slipped into the bathroom and washed his face, cooling himself with the soap and water. He checked the mirror, saw the scruffy guy, looking a bit cleaner now, staring back at him, smiling. He strutted into the store and asked a cashier for the manager. She pointed out a small man near the back, poring over an inventory sheet.

"This here paper says you need a man to keep the place clean," Skip said.

"Go away," the man replied without looking up from his sheet. "You are a young man. A man who will work only long enough to make a few pay checks, then you will leave and I will have to hire someone else. I'm looking for a married man, someone with responsibilities."

"What makes you think I ain't married," Skip said.

The man looked up and laughed. "Hah, a handsome young man like you. Only ugly fools like me marry young. Besides," the store manager took off his glasses and cleaned them with a handkerchief. "You don't want to mop floors for a living, do you?"

"I ain't looking to make a living out of it. I just need some work."

"Do you have references, do you have people who will say: Yes, this is a good man. Give him a job. Do you have that?"

Skip shook his head. "Mister, all I got is my word, ain't that enough?"

"Go away, young man, I'm busy."

"Just give me a try," Skip said, pleading. "I'll stick. Swear to God I'll stick."

"No, no, no" the manager said. "Married men only."

Skip wanted to grab the man and shake some sense into him, but instead he turned and marched out of the store, staring hard at the picture of a pretty strawberry blonde painted on a soda ad, the girl smiling like she didn't have a care in the world, telling him to drink Royal Crown Cola and please, oh please, come back soon. Not in this life. Skip slammed the door behind him, cursed the day and Lady Luck's bad roll of the dice.

❧

PEE WEE SAT AT THE COUNTER OF HENRY'S DANCING BAR-B-QUE, sucking on a rib bone he kept dipping into the pool of tangy, sweet sauce on his plate, savoring Henry's fine concoction and thinking about Skip, the country boy who just couldn't seem to get right with Los Angeleez. He dipped the meatless bone back into the sauce and checked his watch. Fifteen minutes and the dinner hour would be over. Behind him, at a table in the middle of the cafe, Diana feasted on a plate piled high with bar-b-que pork ribs and a side order of white bread. Henry, a dish towel thrown over his shoulder, leaned against a dish cabinet, waiting for Pee Wee to finish so he could collect the plate. He cleared his throat.

"Don't you have a job, Pee Wee?"

"You know it, but I got a few minutes," he dragged a finger along the greasy counter and wiped his hands on a napkin as Henry came from behind the counter and hung the closed sign on the front door. "How come you closing so early, Henry?"

"My dish washing man got a W.P.A. job last week, Pee Wee," Henry said, annoyed. "Third man I done lost since summer. Don't see why these young boys won't stick. Can't be the wages. I'm paying ten dollars a week, plus meals."

Pee Wee pushed his plate away, downed the last of his orange soda and lit a cigarette. "So, what you gon' do about it?"

"Look for another man, I guess. But this go round I'm taking my own sweet time about it. Maybe conduct some interviews. Find somebody who'll stick."

"Hmm," Pee Wee said, puffing his cigarette and seeing an opportunity. "Well, sir I know I ain't got no sayso in the matter, but the way I sees it, taking your own sweet time could be bad for business. Why just the other night, a couple of rich white ladies pulled into the station, I could tell they was rich 'cause they was wearing furs, mink probably, and driving one of them fine Cadillacs. Anyway, they pulled into the station and I overheard them talking 'bout how they'd come all the way from Beverly Hills to eat at this fabulous place they'd heard about, place called Henry's Dancing Bar-B-Que, and damned if the place was closed. I believe one of them said she was highly disappointed. Seems she was really looking forward to a down home colored meal." Pee Wee paused and studied his cigarette. "Them rich folks is good customers, Henry. Treat 'em right and they carry your name across town. And they don't mind spreading a little cash around. Hell, they tipped me two dollars and I didn't do nothing 'cept wash the windows, check the oil, fill the tank, and tell 'em a decent place to eat."

Henry shrugged, making his way back behind the counter, picking up Pee Wee's plate carrying it to the kitchen. "Couple-a white ladies aren't going to break me, Pee Wee. Business is just fine."

Diana dropped a rib bone on her plate and yelled across the room: "Ain't no need of telling tales, Henry. You done already asked me to take a reduction in pay."

Pee Wee wheeled around on his stool. "Girl, you must be jiving." he said.

"Nawsuh, Pee Wee. Just the other day Henry come walking up to me asking 'bout do I mind taking a small reduction 'cause we done hit on some hard times. And he running hisself ragged behind the counter, cooking, washing, taking orders."

"Don't you pay Diana no mind, Pee Wee," Henry said as he washed the plate. "She's been a little ornery lately."

"Aw, Henry," Pee Wee said. "I don't need Diana to tell me what a blind man could see. Your dishwashing man's gone, you're closing early and rich white ladies are spending their good money some place else. Shoot, man, you in as bad a fix as this friend of mine. Swear to God, y'all ought to make a connection so's you could talk about how hard times is."

"You got a friend?" Henry raised his eyebrows.

"I got plenty of friends and the guy I'm telling you 'bout just happens to be an expert dishwasher and clean up man, available for immediate employment."

"Nothing shaking here, Pee Wee. Like I told you, I'm going to take my own sweet time about this." Henry called across the room. "Shake a leg there, Di. Finish them ribs so I can wash that plate and go home." Henry leaned across the counter and looked back at the clock on the wall. "What kind of dinner hour are you on, Pee Wee?"

"A long one, but don't you be worrying 'bout me. You got problems, Henry. Business is down, Diana and her family probably cutting back, eating less so's you can take your sweet time. Man, you need help."

"Not from you, Pee Wee. Hell, I'd be a fool to trust one of your friends. The last one I hired stayed long enough to make one payday and tried to make off with a day's receipts to boot. You remember him, don't you?"

Pee Wee dismissed the memory with a wave of his hand. "Forget that sorry ass nigger, Henry. He wasn't no friend of mine, just an acquaintance. The guy I'm telling you 'bout now is strictly on the up and up. He's a hard working, honest Texas boy. Ain't that where you from? He's looking for a little help from his people. I'd swear to all of this on a stack of Bibles." Pee Wee said, raising his right hand. "Fact, I'm ready to swear to it right now if you got a Bible handy."

"Since when did you and the Bible become such close friends?" Henry said, carrying a stack of drip-dried plates in from the kitchen and setting them in the cupboard.

"Tell old Texas to keep looking. I don't need any help."

"Can't do that, Henry. He's in a bind. Why don't you give him a chance, unless you're prejudiced."

Henry crossed his arms. "Prejudiced?"

"That's what I said. Dictionary says it means holding a bad opinion of someone you don't even know. White folks do it to us all the time, and it's a damn shame to see it on this side of town." Pee Wee shook his head, picked up his cap and trudged towards the door, stopping to give Henry his last words on the matter. "Guess I'll have to tell this real good friend of mine Jim Crow ain't hiring."

"Hold on now," Diana said, standing up and walking towards the counter. "I done heard enough. Why you being so hard-headed, Henry. All of Pee Wee's friends can't be as bad as the one you hired."

Pee Wee nodded, making sure to keep the defeated look on his face. Henry's eyes moved back and forth from Diana to Pee Wee. He sighed and uncrossed his arms.

"You say this guy's honest?"

"Why I don't believe he's told a lie in his life and he's the finest dish-washer this side of the Mississippi. Plus—"

"Cut it, Pee Wee. Can the nigger wash dishes and mop floors?"

"Shoot, ain't you been listening to me, Henry? You think I'm trying to put one over on you?"

"I wouldn't doubt it. Tell your friend to stop by Monday morning around nine. We'll see if he's all you say. No promises though."

"Don't need one," Pee Wee said, smiling. "You will not be disap-pointed." He slapped his cap on and tilted it at a rakish angle. "Well, back to the grease pit."

As the door closed, Diana turned to Henry and laughed. "The way that boy talks, he ought to be in sales."

"Or politics," Henry said, scooping up Diana's bone littered plate.

❧

"NO LOITERING." PEE WEE'S BOSS MAN SHOOED SKIP AWAY FROM the office wall, where he'd been sipping a soda. "You got your pop. Now, move on."

"I'm waiting on Pee wee," Skip said.

"Well wait somewhere else. This is a business." The boss man pulled a greasy rag from his back pocket and wiped his oil-stained hands. He glared at Skip, his beady eyes narrowing, his bushy eyebrows coiling across his furrowed forehead.

"All right, all right," Skip pushed himself off the wall and headed for the corner.

"Don't want to be getting in the way of no business."

He walked over to the giant, red Pegasus sign that turned around and round above the filling station's corner. He ran the day's hunt over in his mind, wondered if a shave would have changed anything. Probably not. The fish just weren't biting. If Pee Wee didn't come through, he'd try again Monday, had to, because by then Mrs. Harrelson would be onto him and he'd be on the street. Damn shit. He watched the late afternoon traffic, took another long pull on the soda, his jaws sucking down the carbonated sugar water. A car horn tooted three times and Pee Wee pulled into the filling station, waving as he parked the Plymy by the garage. He jumped out and hustled towards Skip, a carburetor in his hands. A blue Chevrolet pulled up to the gas pumps and Pee Wee went back to work, pumping gas, wiping windows and checking the Chevy's oil, all the while listening to the pump's bell chimes ringing up every dime's worth of gas. Skip left Pegasus and walked casually towards his friend, trying not to draw the boss man's attention.

"Any luck?' he said.

"Maybe." Pee Wee looked at the boss man, smiled and gave him the okay sign.

"What you mean, maybe?" Skip said, finishing the soda and jamming the empty bottle into his back pocket.

"Just what I said." Pee Wee wiped off the Chevy's dip-stick, slid it back in its holder and slammed the hood. "Bout a quart low," he called to the driver. "And dirty as hell. Take fifteen minutes to change it."

The driver shook his head. Skip followed Pee Wee to the gas pump, bumped into him as he did a quick turn pulling the hose from the Chevy's gas tank.

"Take a walk, Skip," Pee Wee said, anger slashing through his voice. "I got to be on my job."

"But did you have any luck? You said maybe."

"Be at Henry's Dancing Bar-B-Que Monday morning," Pee Wee said over his shoulder as he made the driver's change from a pouch he pulled out of his pocket. "I told Henry you were an expert dishwasher." Pee Wee patted the Chevy's side and waved as the car pulled away.

"Dishwasher?" Skip said, dogging Pee Wee back to the garage.

"Yeah, dishwasher. You got a problem with that?" Pee Wee wheeled around and stopped. "Listen, Skip, if you're too good for washing dishes, say so. I got better things to do with my dinner hour than spend it talking you up to folks."

"Naw, I ain't too good for washing dishes, Pee wee," Skip said. "It's just. Aw, hell. Nothing. Thanks. What's the address?"

The boss man leaned out of the office and yelled. "Look alive there, Pee Wee. I told Mr. Jones we'd have that carburetor replaced by closing time. Tell your buddy to shove off."

Pee Wee picked up the new carburetor, leaned under the waiting car's hood and whispered. "Daddy-o, the boss man is about to blow his top. Henry's is at 5513 Central Avenue. Take your best shot. Now get, 'fore that old coot comes over here."

"Awreet, daddy-o. Let me beat these feets on the street. I'll give you a report come Monday."

Skip headed down Central, feeling the boss man's hard stare at his back, pushing him down the avenue. On the way home he window-shopped, looked in store windows at radios, suits and shoes. All he need-ed was a job, and he was going to get one. If not the one Pee Wee found, then another. Somebody was going to hire him. In a week or two he'd be back in the money, spreading cash around, getting a shave and a haircut, maybe even calling Virginia and seeing if she wanted to midnight ramble. He thought about surprising Mrs. Harrelson with a week's rent in advance. That would wipe the nose-in-the-air, saditty smile off her face. He stopped, frowned. The hell with her. He was going to pay up and move out. Let her put the screws to somebody else.

He ducked into the alley behind the Plaza Arms, sneaked into the back door and cautiously made his way to the third floor, peeking around corners and down hallways, constantly on the lookout for Mrs. Harrelson. She was nowhere to be seen. He made the third floor easy, tiptoed down the hall to his apartment, slipped the piece of metal between the door jam and lock and let himself in. Everything was as he remembered, a mess. He opened a window, laid back on the bed and kicked off his shoes, thought about having a smoke to relax, but Phineas had warned him about smoking in the room, said Mrs. Harrelson had a nose like a Mississippi bloodhound. Bull shit, he thought. He'd made it up here and hadn't seen her. He looked around the room, grabbed a shirt and jammed it up by the door, just to be safe. Then he rolled a fat ciga-rette from Old Man Williams' tobacco.

The smoke hit him like a soothing down home memory. He was halfway through it when someone knocked on the door. He froze and held his breath, afraid to let anymore smoke into the room. Damn! His legs started itching, but he didn't want to scratch, didn't want to move and make the old bedsprings squeak, letting whoever was on the other side of the door know someone was in here when nobody was supposed to be here. He waited for the dreaded sound of Mrs. Harrelson's voice, her keys rattling in the lock, the tumblers turning, the door opening. He waited and heard nothing. Then a voice, ominous yet playful.

"Fe fi where's the fan, I smell the smoke of a foolish man."

He relaxed and blew out a lungful of smoke. It was Phineas. He jumped off the bed, kicked the shirt out of the way and opened the door. Phineas stepped inside quickly, waving his hands to clear the lingering smoke.

"Bad habits can lead to one's downfall," he said, strolling over to a chair and setting his rolly-polly body down.

"Well, my young friend, your devil-may-care courtship with disaster must mean the city's angels have taken you under their wing."

"W-e-l-l," Skip threw back his head, took a long pull on his cigarette and blew smoke rings. "I got a job," he said, a song in his voice.

"Wonderful. Is your employment imminent?"

"Huh?"

"When do you start?"

"Oh, Monday morning. Yes, sir, I got a date with a man and a pay-check."

"Ah, yes, the paycheck, ball and chain of the working man, but no matter. Good news has arrived and we must celebrate."

"Uh, you forgetting, Phineas. I ain't got but fifty cents between me and the bread line."

Weatherby waved his hand dismissively. "Money isn't the key to a celebration. Don't you have any mother wit? Don't you know anything 'bout getting on in this city, 'bout using the available resources?" He watched Skip's expression go blank. He shook his head, feigning sadness and disbelief. "I'm afraid we are declining as a resourceful people. If you in any way exemplify the younger generation, then . . . Be that as it may, we must celebrate your good fortune with, shall we say, a steak dinner, or maybe pork chops, something from down home." He started laughing and singing an old country rag: "I heard the voice of a pork chop say come on to me and rest."

He slapped his thighs and stood. "I shall retire to my abode for a change of attire and you, my friend, should do the same. You look awful. I'll announce my return with a bit of Beethoven, the Fifth Symphony. Do you know it."

Skip shook his head.

"My God!" Phineas said. "Is there no culture in that crossroads you call home? Don't answer that. Here's the signal. Da-da-da DAH. You got it? Three sharp knocks and boom. I shall return in fifteen minutes. Open the door for no one and please, Skip, try to control your urge to smoke."

When the opening of Beethoven's Fifth Symphony sounded on the door, he let Phineas in, hoping the huckster would approve of his wrinkled brown suit.

"A fine improvement," Phineas said, standing near the door. "And don't you feel better?"

"A little, but I'll feel better with a full stomach."

"Then let's scoot on over to Clifton's Cafeteria, a downtown eatery where the good proprietor has seen fit to help those of us who find ourselves in dire straits."

Phineas led the way down the back stairs, acting as the point man checking the hallways leading from every landing, then motioning for Skip to follow. They eased into the alley, Phineas walking lightly, careful not to soil the cuffs of his pants in the muck and filth. Mangy stray cats, sneak thieves feasting on garbage can delicacies, stopped in the midst of their meals and eyed the passing pair suspiciously, their bodies poised to spring away on padded feet if Phineas and Skip made any sudden moves. Halfway down the alley, Skip heard a woman singing and wondered if it was Mrs. Harrelson. He started to turn around, but Phineas grabbed him by the arm and pulled him along.

"Remember what happened to Lot's wife," he said.

A carpeted staircase led up to Clifton's formal dining room on the second floor. Women in evening dresses and men in tuxedos sat beneath a mirrored ceiling ornamented by hanging plants and chandeliers. Skip drew in his breath, smelled steak and beef stew, potatoes and pork chops, sweet pastry from a bakery somewhere beyond the dining rooms. Elegantly dressed waiters carried platters to the second floor. Tired, haggard looking young men and women sat at a counter along one wall of the first floor, their hungry faces bent over steaming plates piled high with food. He hurried towards an empty seat and grabbed a menu, his eyes scanning the restaurant's fare. Phineas joined him and frowned, told him to mind his manners and hide his desperation. Bad enough that their sustenance depended on another man's charity. Skip barely heard him as he looked for the heaviest meal: steak and mashed potatoes with two vegetables. His stomach rumbled in anticipation.

"Somebody must be hungry," said a blonde waitress, standing before the pair, a pencil behind her ear and a pad in her hand. "Evening Professor," she smiled at Phineas. "Who's the kid?"

"A young man of ample dreams but without financial means," Phineas replied. "Have you a special tonight?"

"Steak dinner, potatoes, two vegetables and, seeing as how old Mr. Clifton is feeling especially generous, dessert." She turned to Skip. "Interested?"

"Hell yeah, and how 'bout a cup of coffee."

The waitress turned to Phineas. "Professor?"

"I'll have the same, with tea, please, and thank you, my dear, from the bottom of my empty gut."

Skip tore into his meal, smiling through bulging cheeks and a mouthful of coffee. He quickly finished one serving, then boldly asked for another, this time with an order of biscuits to mop up the gravy. The meat, potatoes, bread, collard greens and peas rode over his tongue and down his throat, leaving his mouth alive with the riot of tastes, the salt, pepper, grilled onions, butter, all of it mixed with the juices pouring from his mouth and the sweet creamy coffee he gulped down. A sugary slice of peach pie, topped with cinnamon, gave the meal a perfect ending. He leaned back in the seat and patted his gut, feeling the food's energy course through his body.

Phineas, who had eaten slowly, delicately working his knife and fork around the plate, finished with a flourish, waving his napkin and daubing the corners of his mouth.

"You look like Elmer's contended cow," he smiled.

"Yeah, buddy, I'm 'bout to burst wide open. You sure this is all free?"

"Foolish questions do not deserve answers," Phineas said, turning to watch the diners on the second floor, his eyes in an envious gaze.

The waitress' return cut short Phineas' daydreaming. "Well, Professor, shall I order a wheel chair for your friend?"

Phineas turned around and smiled. "That may be necessary, my dear. I believe he has been crippled by his own appetite." He sipped his tea, his cheerful smile giving way to a grave, serious expression that drew his eyebrows together. "One day, my dear, times will get better and when they do, I shall repay the proprietor for his generosity during my time of need. And you," he grasped her hand. "You shall dine at the finest Beverly Hills restaurant, courtesy of Phineas T. Weatherby."

The waitress laughed and headed down the counter, calling over her shoulder. "I'll hold you to that, Professor, and I'll tell Mr. Clifton to start keeping a tab."

"I'm not joking," Phineas yelled to her. "Mother just wrote to say a check is in the mail."

⁕

PHINEAS' ROOM WAS A RAT'S NEST. STACKS OF BOOKS LINED THE floor, climbed waist-high up the walls, teetered, supported half-empty bottles of scotch, dirty glasses, newspaper clippings. A table-top Victrola sat on a desk beside a leaning tower of records. Bottles of clear Karo syrup, boxes of Aunt Hester's Yeast Tablets, a pickle jar of grain alcohol, measuring spoons, food coloring, and clear eight-ounce bottles with Eternity's Breath labels pasted on them crowded one corner. Skip picked his way through scattered piles of clothes heaped on the floor.

"Just kick 'em out of the way," Phineas said, sweeping an armload of shirts and underwear off a chair, looking around a moment before adding them to a pile of pants. He bowed. "Your throne is ready, sire."

He plopped down on his bed, folded an overcoat under his head and pointed to the chair. "Sit."

Skip dropped into the seat, let the heavy meal settle in his stomach. "You read all these books?"

"Indeed I have. I was at Morehouse, you know. Degreed and all, chemistry, the classics. I read the *Aeneid* in Latin. There's brain food in those pages, Skip. Just as the body requires sustenance, so too the mind. This," he reached behind his head for a copy of Darwin's *Descent of Man*, "is what separates us from the apes. I don't suppose you've ever heard of Darwin, have you? Imagine, a dispassionate, scientific analysis of our slow, slow fall from the trees to where we stand now, proudly on two feet, *homo erectus*. Yet, we haven't come so very far, really. Some folks don't believe Darwin. They prefer the old Hebrew fable. Jehovah and his lump of clay."

"Guess you ain't a church man," Skip said, striking a match and tasting an after-dinner Chesterfield.

Phineas sat up, a serious look in his eyes. "Skip, I'll go to church when we're on equal footing with the white man. Till then, I'm sleeping in Sundays. How 'bout you?"

Skip shook his head. "I ain't got time for God. I mean, look around. We got churches everywhere, folks praying and carrying on, and we're still getting our butts kicked. Naw, they ain't holding a place for me in the Amen corner."

"Yes, it is a sad commentary on our plight. Just what did we do to be so black and blue? What on earth did we do? I've thought about it and, swear to God, I can't figure it out."

"The Christian soldiers say it's all part of God's plan. This here's a test, see if you can make it to them pearly gates without messing up. Everything's just fine in heaven. No Jim Crow. No back-biting. Just milk and honey, streets paved with gold. Least that's what they say."

"Ah yes," Phineas said. "The blessed rock faith. My daddy preached many a sermon on that. Be a damn shame if the joke was on him and all the faithful. Be a damn shame. But, I'm afraid this," he pointed around the room, "is all there is. But enough of that. Next thing you know, we'll start brooding and worrying." He opened the window, kicked a pile of shirts against the door, then rifled his desk drawer. He turned and smiled, a fat reefer dangling between his fingers. "Aperitif, monsieur?'

HIS EYELIDS SNAPPED OPEN EARLY MONDAY MORNING, HIS PEACE-FUL sleep shattered by the first streetcar clanging and rumbling up Central Avenue and Mrs. Harrelson singing in the hallway, banging the mop and bucket she pushed as she cleaned out the empty rooms. Skip jumped out of bed, fully dressed. He slapped on his shoes, grabbed his suitcase, guitar and bedroll, then crept to the door. He peeked outside, saw Mrs. Harrelson stepping into the room down the hall. He waited until she'd pushed the mop and bucket inside, then opened his door wide and walked quietly towards the back stairs.

"You low down thief!"

Mrs. Harrelson! He turned around, waved good-bye and broke into a run.

"You come back here, Mr. Reynolds," she yelled, brandishing a broom and chasing after him as he bounded down the stairs, two and three at a time. "Help. Somebody help me! I'm being robbed!"

Skip was laughing out loud by the time he hit the first floor landing. He turned around and watched as Mrs. Harrelson waddled down the steps, her fierce gaze set on his laughing face. He blew her a kiss. She cocked her arm and sent the broom held in her hand zipping down the stairs. Skip ducked, but the broom hit the banister, flipped wildly and clipped him on the forehead.

"Hah," she yelled. "You yellow dog thief. That's the least bit of hurt you'll get from me. Wait till I catch you."

"Not in this life," Skip said, jumping the last four steps.

He rushed into the alley, pulled down trash cans to block the door, and kept on running. A few houses down, he turned again and saw Mrs. Harrelson come stumbling into the alley, holding the broom like a warrior's spear. She caught sight of him, jerked her broom spear menacingly and continued the chase.

"I've got you now, you low life country boy. Can't take me for a fool."

Skip watched her approach, her stumpy legs pumping fast and hard. He waited until she was almost at him, then he kicked another trash can in her path, backed up a few steps, turned and raced down the alley. A stray cat yowled. Mrs. Harrelson cursed, kicking cans out of her way. Somebody threw open a window and yelled.

"What the hell's going on down there?"

"I'm being robbed," Mrs. Harrelson said, pointing down the alley. "That man owes me fourteen dollars! Come back here, Mr. Reynolds."

Skip didn't stop running until he was eight blocks up Central Avenue, and the Goodyear Tire and Rubber plant was coming into view. He slowed his pace, looked over his shoulder and saw no one following him. He dropped his suitcase and bedroll, bent over, took a deep breath, glad to have made good his escape, but worried that Mrs. Harrelson might go to the police and put an arrest warrant out on him. Wouldn't that be some shit. Locked up over fourteen dollars. Damn. He stood and tenderly touched the knot forming on his forehead. The old biddy had got him good, left him a hickey the size of a quarter, sore and painful to the touch. He pulled out a cigarette and puffed slowly in the quiet morning. The work day was just beginning. Red cars rumbled north every 15 minutes filled with passengers bound for downtown and the west side. Traffic thickened, slowly. "Open" signs started to appear in the shop windows. Across the street from the Dancing Bar-B-Que he saw that 5512

Central Avenue was still vacant. He looked for a gap in the traffic, then hurried to the storefront and peered through the soaped-up windows.

There were no signs of the acting school, only an empty bucket. He peered through the soaped up windows, strained to see signs of the acting school. There were none, only an empty bucket and a mop pushed in one corner, the faded outlines of a puddle on the linoleum floor.

He shrugged, disappointed but not broken. Today was a new beginning, another chance. He turned and saw someone moving inside the Dancing Bar-B-Que.

Henry Lewis opened the door before he knocked. "You Pee Wee's pal?"

"You got it," Skip said, smiling nervously as he stood just inside the door, waiting for direction.

"Take a seat," Henry said over his shoulder. "I'll be with you directly."

The place was as Skip remembered, chairs resting on the tables, the familiar smoky sweet smell of barbecue heavy in the room. It had worked its way into the walls, become part of the restaurant the same way the smell of sweat was part of Willie's truck. He propped his arms on a table, took a deep breath and imagined the sauce, poured over a rack of ribs set on a plate laid out just for him. He watched Henry fiddle behind the counter, saw the publicity photos up on the wall and wondered why Henry was cooking ribs instead of acting. Henry looked across the room, caught Skip's gaze and stared.

"Didn't you come in here about a month ago looking for Zeke Washington's acting school?"

Skip nodded and looked down at the table. "I was pretty tore up that day."

"No lie. What did you say your name was," Henry said.

"William Henry Reynolds. People call me Skip."

"Hmmm, I like that middle name of yours, but I guess Skip is okay." Henry held out his hand, gave Skip a firm shake and sat down. "Now tell me, Skip, why should I take you on? I mean, after all, Pee Wee hasn't sent the best guys over here. Fact is, the last so-called friend he sent me turned out to be a thief."

"You ain't got to worry 'bout me stealing," Skip said firmly, hoping Henry and Mrs. Harrelson would never cross paths. "I don't go for that. I'm here 'cause I need a job."

"So. Plenty people out of work. Men with families to support, guys probably more deserving than you, a young buck without a care in the world."

"I can give you three good reasons why I'm the best man for the job," said Skip. "One, I'm young, which means I can work long and hard. Two, I ain't got no family to run home to. Nothing to distract me. And three, I'm healthy, so you know I'm gon' be here." He pounded his middle finger on the table. "Right here."

Henry nodded. "I need a man who's going to stick, not somebody who's just around to make a couple of paydays."

"I'll stick like white on rice," Skip replied.

He looked at the older man and smiled a bit, but Henry only frowned. Silence filled the room. He stood and looked down at Skip.

"Okay, you got this one day to prove to me you're the man. The cleaning stuff's in the supply room back of the kitchen. We open in one hour." Henry walked away and went back to work.

Skip kept to his seat, studied the room and the job ahead. It seemed easy enough. Mop the floors, take down the chairs and arrange them around the tables, keep the sink full of sudsy water. A schoolboy could do it. But what about tonight. Even with a job, he had no money and no place to stay. Maybe, if everything worked out right, he'd ask Henry for an advance, the way croppers did back home. A week's pay was all he needed. He leaned back in his chair, then stood and grabbed his gear. All he had to do was work, take hold of the job and turn it every which way but loose. He headed into the supply area, passing Henry who labored over a slab of ribs, his cleaver slamming into the cutting board, his hands deftly pushing the meat aside.

The morning went smoothly, the hour before the eleven o'clock opening passing in the easy rhythm of preparation. Henry's directions were simple: clear the tables and counters of dishes as soon as the diners paid their tab and left; keep the dishwasher hot and the sink as near empty as possible. Skip took his position in the kitchen and lit a cigarette. It was gon' be easy as pie.

High noon. Diners jammed the Dancing Bar-B-Que, filled the tables and the counter, while others stood waiting, craning their necks and looking for an empty seat. Diana hustled about, taking orders, ferrying plates of ribs balanced two and three at a time in her strong hands, maneuvering her wide hips through the obstacle course of tables. Henry was a blur behind the counter, where ham fried and hamburger steaks sizzled on the griddle, the meat spitting hot, stinging grease on his bare arms. He pulled pans of ribs out of the oven and doled out orders on clean white plates he slid to diners waiting at the counter. Once in a while he paused to wipe away the sweat pouring across his brow, then he went back to work, telling Diana to pick up an order, yelling at Skip to bus the dirty dishes, cursing to himself and smiling at the customers, never once overwhelmed. Skip tried to keep up, but became lost in the rush of things to do: washing dishes, bussing tables, clearing the counter, filling and emptying the sink. Pee Wee came through the door, flashed a smile, a wink and the okay sign, then left before Skip could say anything. The dishes were coming too fast. He leaned over a sink full of them, poured in Palmolive soap powder, turned the hot water on full blast, then bolted into the dining area to make a sweep of the tables and the counter. He returned to find the sink overflowing, the floor slippery. Soap suds crept down the sink's sides and crept onto the floor, moving slowly towards the wall, as unstoppable as water from a broken dam. He grabbed a mop, slopped it across the floor to soak up some of the water, then jammed his hands deep into the sink's scalding hot water. His hands burned as he fished around for plates, saucers and glasses that he scrubbed quickly and rinsed in soothing cold water. Diana stepped in for a breather and watched him work. She picked up a freshly washed plate and held it loosely between her hands as if it were a filthy dishrag.

"You dipping or scrubbing?" She asked. "Onliest thing different about this here plate is that it's wet." She dropped it back in the sink. "We can't be serving Henry's good bar-b-que on dirty dishes."

Henry's voice boomed from the counter. "Move your hams, Di! Table by the window just filled up!"

The waitress whipped a pad from her apron pocket, pulled the pencil from behind her ear, wheeled around and strode back into the dining room, ready. Skip unplugged the sink, let some of the hot water out, then turned on the cold water until the dishwater was warm enough so he could work without pain. He took the rejected plate and washed it slowly, held it up for his own inspection, then repeated the process again and again; dishes, plates, saucers, cups, each one dipped, scrubbed and inspected.

The restaurant emptied by mid-afternoon, leaving Henry, Diana and Skip spent but glad to have weathered the rush without disaster. Henry brought a platter of ribs, a loaf of bread, a pitcher of water and three sodas from the red and white Coca-Cola machine by the front door to a cleared table. He and Diana sat down to the meal while Skip stood off to the side, his belly rumbling, hungry eyes watching Diana drown her plate of ribs in rich, red sauce. Henry saw him staring, kicked a chair from the table and dipped a slice of bread into the sauce.

"Sit down and eat, boy. 'Cause if you don't come quick, Diana will lay all these ribs to rest."

"Tell the truth, Henry," Diana said, patting her broad hips with one hand and dipping a rib bone with the other. "Lord knows you make the best ribs in town, done ruined my girlish figure. I'm about to bust out of this girdle right now."

"Since when did you start being so concerned about your figure?" Henry replied.

"Since you brought this fine young man in here," Diana said, flashing Skip a sly, friendly smile. "Can't have him thinking I live to eat. There's other things a woman needs, you know."

"I thought the Deacon was taking care of all of that," Henry said. "Your youngest is twelve years old."

"That don't mean I ain't been doing nothing with my good thing." She smiled at Skip again.

He forced a nervous grin. Mess with another man's woman? No thanks. Besides, Diana was too old for him. He ate quietly, feeling outside the circle of camaraderie and easy banter flowing between Henry and Diana. They wandered off to the kitchen when they finished. Skip heard their muffled voices, their laughter. He trained to catch a bit of what was being said. Were they talking about him? Had to be. He imagined Diana turning the one dirty plate into an entire stack of dishes that needed to be washed twice because she couldn't stand to have Henry's good ribs served on dirty dishes. Damn, Skip thought. Can't nobody expect a man to do everything right the first day on the job. If it wasn't for that g-damn flood and Diana coming in to inspect that plate, he'd have been perfect. Shit. He lit a cigarette and sipped his soda, scrambling in his mind for a place to spend the night. At least he'd ate his fill. Diana came towards him, pulling her arms through her sweater.

"See you around, sugar," she said, then leaned close to him and whispered. "G'on talk to the man. He in there playing possum, waiting on you."

Damn, shit. Skip crushed out the butt end of his cigarette, rinsed his mouth with a swallow of soda, then carried his dirty plate into the kitchen. Henry busied himself with the stock shelves, his back to Skip.

"How long were you going to wait?' He asked as he counted loaves of bread.

"Till you called." Skip slid his plate into the sink and washed slowly.

"And what if I never did," Henry turned around. "What if I just went about my business, closed up shop and left. What would you do, boy?"

"I don't know. I . . ." He felt stupid and confused. What was Henry getting at. "I guess I'd have stopped you."

"You guess! Damn, boy, I ain't the Lord. Don't wait on me. Swear to God you country boys are too damn polite. You have to take the initiative, confront the issue, else you'll end up on the sidelines, wondering and watching instead of being in the thick of the action, finding out for yourself. You follow me?"

"Sure, but you're the boss. I figured you're the one to tell me."

"Tell you what?"

"If I got the job or not."

"Oh, you got the job alright," Henry said, his stern expression pushed away by a smile. "You got it as long as you don't mess up. Okay?"

The weight that had nagged at Skip's spirit like a heavy cotton sack hauled down an endless row vanished.

"Well, don't just stand there smiling, Skip. Let's get this place ready for tomorrow," Henry said, slapping him on the shoulder and heading out to clean the grill.

Yeah, get this place ready. Skip threw himself into the work. He bussed the dining room and counter one last time, collected dishes and washed them with an easy, relaxed motion, all the while whistling and singing to himself an old tune that bubbled up in his mind and carried him away with it's happy story.

"We're in the money. The skies are sunny. Let's lend it, spend it, send it rolling along."

Henry took care of the counter, scrubbed down the grill, polished the metal cabinets and stacked the dishes Skip washed, every once in a while casting a satisfied glance towards his new worker. Skip caught Henry staring, but kept his mind on his work, hoping his new boss marked the care he took in doing his job. Henry finished before him and was busy counting the day's receipts when Skip joined him at the counter. Skip studied Henry's full face, saw kindness in the soft smile, the gentle, yet studious way he went about counting the day's earnings. He compared this face, with its furrowed brow and deep-set eyes, hair turning to gray, with that of the young man smiling in the photos hung on the wall behind the counter.

"What're them pictures for?" he asked.

"Memories from the past," Henry said, counting out ones, twos and change. "I am a restaurant owner, come around again to live the simple, albeit not totally untroubled life of a restauranteur on Central Avenue."

"An actor! I came out here to be an actor, and I'm still gon' be one, even if that g-damn Ezekiel Washington done flown the coop."

"Don't see why you came out here," Henry said. "Hollywood can break your heart."

"I want to do us right," Skip said, ignoring Henry's comment "I want to put an end to all that clowning they make us do. Why back home, I read this magazine story said there's need for people like me. Said Hollywood is looking for a new kind of colored actor."

"Hmmm. You don't believe everything you read, do you?" Henry said, carrying the cash behind the counter. "Besides, what do you know about Hollywood?"

"I know they're doing us wrong," Skip said.

"Well, good luck," Henry said, coming from behind the counter and heading for the door. He surveyed his business one last time, put up the "Closed" sign and opened the door. "Leaving time, Skip. Let's go."

Skip stared hard into the counter, as if there he could find the courage to ask Henry about getting an advance on his pay. He heard Henry approaching, then felt his presence at his back.

"What's on your mind?" Henry asked.

"I need some money," Skip replied, turning around to face Henry.

"Payday's the end of the week. Saturday."

"I need something now, lessen you know a free place to sleep."

"Can't say as I do," Henry said, leaning on the counter. "Let me get this straight. You're broke and don't have a place to stay, right?" Skip nodded, lighting a cigarette to stay calm. Henry sighed deeply. "Pee Wee didn't say anything about this. I figured all you needed was a job."

Henry put his hand on his chin and thought a moment. "You want to make a deal?"

"No deals," Skip said. "Just cash money. Hell, back home the boss man always gives his cropper some to get the year going. All I need is a five spot."

"You haven't heard the deal yet," Henry said. "Come on."

He led Skip through the kitchen, up the back stairs to a locked room. He pulled a ring of keys from his pocket, tried several in the lock before one clicked the latch open. He pushed the stubborn door and punched a light button. A dozen roaches scurried for safety. Dusty cobwebs stirred lightly in the sudden rush of air. Skip looked over Henry's shoulder. The room was cluttered with empty boxes of restaurant supplies, crumpled cans of Airways Coffee, broken-down furniture. Henry stomped across the room, killing a roach that ran, too late for cover. He opened a back window and sneezed.

"That ought to help some," he said, letting in an evening breeze. He wiped his finger along the dusty windowsill. "Well, what do you think?"

"Bout what?" Skip said from the doorway.

"The room. Might not look much now, but with some imagination and elbow grease, it could be a fine place. Can't beat the location. Hell, I bet you won't find a better place in all Los Angeles, and right in the heart of Central Avenue." Henry tugged on the yellowed, frayed window shade, that rolled up quickly, the paper clattering and slapping against the glass.

Skip stepped into the room. "You want me to stay here?' He looked around. 'It'd take me days to get this place right. Look at this chair?" He gave it a shove and watched it collapse in a heap of rotted, worn-eaten wood. "See."

Henry shook his head. "You want to be in moving pictures, right?"

"So."

"This here's part of my deal. I may not act anymore, but I still keep in touch. I could help you out. Plus there's a room, free eats downstairs and a job. Any right thinking man would jump at it in these days and times."

Skip stared at the yellowed walls, a huge brown-rimmed water stain in the ceiling. Grandma Sarah always told him never to let on how much you need something, or people'll make you beg. "I ain't no charity case," he said.

"I can see that," Henry said, sitting on the windowsill. "You're one of those tough country boys, too proud for charity, ready to sleep in Pershing Square, instead of some place warm and safe. Yes sir, I can see you'll make your own way in this world." Henry laughed to himself. "Tough country boy who wouldn't know a good thing if it kicked him from here to Hollywood and Vine."

"Why you want to help me?" Skip said. "I mean, you even said there's probably people more deserving then me, men with families and such."

"Let's say I'm a sucker for a sucker."

"Say what?" Skip fired an angry look at Henry, who waved his hand and chuckled.

"Just playing, Skip. But the way I see it, you wanted to be in moving pictures so bad, you fell for old Zeke's scheme about a colored actor's school. That makes you a sucker, a starry-eyed, dyed in the wool, sucker. But that's water under the bridge. Now, what about the deal?"

Skip kicked some boxes from against the wall and leaned back. He had no place to go, and Henry wasn't giving up any money. He held out his right hand. "Deal."

"Okay, then" Henry gave him a fast shake, unhooked the room key from his ring. "Be ready by nine." He headed for the door.

"When you gon' tell me 'bout acting?"

"We'll get to that soon enough. Right now, you best worry about keeping this job and this roof over your head."

"Well, thank you, Mr. Henry."

"Think before you say that," Henry said from the doorway. "Moving pictures are the only place where everything works out fine. I got an old army cot in here somewhere, but no clean sheets."

"I got a bedroll," Skip said.

"Well, then, you're all set," he said, stomping on a roach making its way across the floor.

"Damn. Don't let these boys bother you. It's the rats that are the mean ones."

"Rats?"

"Hell, yeah, big as well-fed alley cats and twice as mean. They'll come in that window, nibble at your toes and give you a good night kiss." Henry smiled broadly, turned and headed down the stairs. "See you tomorrow," he called out and started whistling a Count Basie blues.

THE AGENTS ARE COMING! CENTRAL AVENUE BUZZED WITH THE news running like wild electricity between friends and strangers, sparking imaginations, turning idle conversations into fanciful visions of bright lights and cameras, neighborhood faces on the moving picture screen. *Gone with the Wind* had finally started production and Selznick needed plenty of black folk to work Miss Scarlett's beloved Tara. *The California Eagle* and *The Sentinel* both said every Negro man, woman, or child hungry for a chance to be in moving pictures would be a fool not to be at the Lincoln Theater tonight. A columnist for The *Hollywood Reporter* called the audition "the biggest raid on dark town since *The Green Pastures*."

"The tom-tom beat of feet rushing down the avenue will surely sound like drums along the Congo," he wrote.

Skip poked his head out of the Dancing Bar-B-Que's kitchen and surveyed the crowd. Two folks sat at a table, talking and drinking coffee. Three guys lingered at the counter, dawdling over plates of ribs. Ten minutes' work, he thought, checking the clock hanging above the counter. It was three-thirty. He had to be at the Lincoln by six. He was ready, had spent hours rehearsing his own gangster-style death scene in between fantasies about being discovered and whisked away to Hollywood and the high life on Sugar Hill, dreams of himself leaning back in a hot, sudsy bath, a glass of champagne in his hands, his smile beaming into the cameras as he told yet another reporter about the bad old days scuffling around Los Angeles, washing dishes. He shook his head and grabbed a dirty plate, hoped the agents wouldn't ask him to sing, tap dance, do the Eagle Rock or a little Buck-and-Wing. He wanted to die on stage.

Putting the plate aside, he dried his hands and grabbed yesterday's *Hollywood Reporter* from the storage shelf. Front-page headlines screamed the latest news. "H'Wood Doing Record Business!" "Selznick Searches for Miss Scarlett!" "Tracy Set For Stanley And Livingston!" He flipped to Gabby Winston's column and read the latest tidbit.

"Breaking into Hollywood these days is harder than making a break from the Rock and I do mean Alcatraz."

Humph, Skip thought. Cain't be that hard. Seemed every time he turned around some blonde or brunette from Anytown, U.S.A. was being discovered waitressing at Musso and Frank's and being turned into an overnight sensation with a new name and her face all over the newspapers. Plenty folk got into Hollywood. Everyday.

"Got an empty table," Henry yelled from the dining room.

Skip tossed the newspaper aside and grabbed an empty dish tray. "Make way for the cleanup man!"

An hour and half later, long after Diana had left, he swung chairs up on the tables and asked Henry about the audition. Henry laughed.

"Audition! Hah." He counted up the day's receipts and chuckled to himself.

"Selznick's boys aren't holding an audition tonight. This is just an old-fashioned cattle call."

"What's that?" Skip said, a chair in each hand.

"Come one, come all," Henry replied. "You'll have two or three hundred of Central Avenue's most star-struck souls walking across the stage, while Selznick's boys pick out the ones they think look authentic."

"Sheeit," Skip said, his spirits sinking a bit as he set the last chair in place and went to get his mop bucket. "We all look authentic."

"Not in Hollywood's eyes," Henry said, licking his pencil. "Some of us are too light. Some don't have what the Hollywood boys like to call classic African features." He looked up and gave Skip a studious, disapproving gaze. "Take you, for instance. I don't know if your nose is broad enough for you to play an undiluted African. And your skin tone. Looks like I see some Indian there." Henry turned back to the ledger, smiling and looking out the corner of his eyes as Skip self-consciously fingered his nose and looked at his hands. "I don't see why you're so worked up about this thing in the first place. I thought you wanted to be an actor."

"Got to start somewhere," Skip said, pushing his mop across the floor. "Don't figure none of them Hollywood boys are gon' be stopping by for a plate of ribs anytime soon. So, I got's to go where they at."

"Well," Henry closed the ledger and tip-toed around where Skip had mopped. "You might want to pass on the audition and stick around here tonight."

"Why's that?"

"I'm having some real actors over. They're meeting to talk about what's going on in Hollywood. Interested?"

"Hell yeah, but . . ." Skip stopped and leaned on his mop. "They gon' be doing anything besides talking? I mean, this audition seems like the place to be." He worked the mop around the counter stools. "Swear to God, Henry, I hear it calling my name. Shoot, I just might be the authentic Negro Mr. Selznick is looking for."

"Suit yourself," Henry said, pulling his coat off the rack and handing for the door. "Maybe I'll see you later?"

"Maybe."

"All right, but I want this place clean, okay?"

"You ain't got to worry 'bout that, Henry. When I get finished, you'll be able to eat off this g-damn floor."

Later, stretched out on his cot and smoking a Chesterfield, Skip weighed his options. He remembered Joe at the cafe down Central talking about how his niece always went to the meetings, but nothing ever came of it. She wasn't in moving pictures. He imagined himself sitting with a bunch of gray heads, listening to them tell old war stories, watching them wring their hands about how bad things were. He didn't need anybody to tell him times were hard. He knew that, and he didn't feel like talking about it. The audition was the place to be. Maybe Ezekiel Washington . . . he couldn't get Washington out of his head. He was hooked, but Washington hadn't reeled him in, just left him swimming around in Los Angeles with the nagging hook in his mouth, waiting for someone to pull him off of Central Avenue and onto Hollywood's star-lined streets.

Below his window a gang of kids played tag in the alley. They were living the life, he thought. Kings and queens of the family hill, running with their friends, their toughest decision being how to keep from being It. He leaned back on the cot and spied the alarm clock on the windowsill. Five-thirty. Moving time.

A red car rumbled up Central Avenue as he stepped outside the Dancing Bar-B-Que. He caught it on the dead run, grabbed hold of the stair rail and swung up on the bottom step. He dropped in seven cents, checked his walk as he strolled down the aisle. He was moving like a cool city boy. Behind him, two hipsters talked about the audition. They were going for the hell of it, said maybe they'd get picked to work Tara, and that meant some long money could be coming their way - ten bucks every God damn day. Skip turned around, keeping his excitement down.

"Y'all ever been to one of these things?"

"Daddy-o," said a big, light-skinned guy with sad, drooping gray eyes and movie star looks. "We're plugged into all the Central Avenue happenings. Don't nothing get past me and my running buddy. Ain't that right, Tommy?"

"You got it," said Tommy, a slender brother with conked hair. "And you can skin me on that."

Skip watched the two friends slap palms before asking, "What are we supposed to do?"

"Nothing," said the light-skinned brother. "This is one of them don't call us, we'll call you routines. Me and Tommy are just passing the time till the clubs open. Besides, there's gonna be plenty of gals flitting about the Lincoln tonight."

"Time to pick and choose," Tommy said, a playful light flickering in his eyes.

"Everything's gon' be copasetic." He looked out the window and nudged his partner. "This is us."

Skip followed the pair off the streetcar, but lost them in the crowd milling in front of the Lincoln Theatre. Billie Holiday look-a-likes strolled through the festive crowd, laughing and popping chewing gum. Hip daddies fought for position against the walls, leaned back in elegantly studied poses, their hats pulled low, their cigarettes dangling loosely as they watched the girls go by in brightly colored, hip-hugging dresses. Old Black Joe and his family, all decked up in slavery-time rags, stood off to one side: Big fat mama with an Aunt Jemima headrag; Topsy with pick-aninny curls; a Stymie stand-in wearing a Laurel and Hardy bowler; and Old Joe with his pipe, cane and straw hat. Skip could feel the excitement and anticipation pulsing through the crowd. Anything could happen. Ten bucks a day! A couple weeks of that kind of money would put him on easy street for a good, long while. He pulled out a Chesterfield, tapped it against his thumbnail to pack down the tobacco, then struck a match, all the while trying to look as cool as the hipsters leaning against the walls. He was halfway through the smoke when a skinny white man came out of the theater and yelled through a megaphone.

"All right, folks. It's show time."

The crowd surged for the doors. Skip flicked his still-burning cigarette into the street and joined the logjam. A Louis Armstrong record played over the sound system, happy Pops with his deep, gravelly voice and sweet, swinging horn. Trails of cigarette smoke curled into the air. All around, people talked about scheming for tickets to the Joe Louis fight, parties to come, how fat the wife was getting, how the one-time good man was always tired now, or how sweet papa had turned cold and mean all of a sudden, just like that, when all the poor girl had done was flirt a little last Sunday with the church deacon, a harmless old fool. Nobody talked about Hollywood, Selznick, or *Gone with the Wind*. But it was all Skip could think about. This was his night. He could feel it. Forget about Henry and his actor's meeting. He was going to be discovered. He leaned back and crossed his arms behind his head. Yeah, buddy, this was surely gon' be copasetic.

The theater's lights dimmed. The white man who'd held the megaphone walked across the stage, calling for a spotlight and raising one hand to catch the microphone sliding silently down from the rafters. Voices hushed. All eyes locked on the man standing alone in the circle of light.

"Okay," he said. "When I call out the letter that begins your last name, assemble at the east end of the stage, fill out a name card, and walk across, one by one. And please, no showboating. This isn't an audition."

Skip frowned. That's not what the newspaper said.

The white man continued. "We'll contact the people we want to see again." He looked down on the front row, where several white men sat, notepads on their laps. One of them nodded. "Let's have the first group."

Andersons, Browns and Chesters left their seats, formed a line and walked across the stage. Each one stopped in the spotlight, called out his or her name and walked off. Skip fought off his disappointment. He wasn't going to get to do this death scene! The emcee worked through the alphabet, dispensing with Douglass, Edwards, King and McArthur. Slowly, the theater emptied. Skip made his way to the aisle, paced back and forth, anxiously waiting for the Rs, wishing he was an Adams and could have been in the first group, or that just this one time the people in charge had started from his end of the alphabet. He thanked God he wasn't a Wilson or a Young. He was nearing the balcony door when he heard his group called. He hurried for the stage. The sad-eyed brother from the streetcar waited in line and combed his thick, wavy black hair.

"Hey, good brother," he said, forcing a smile.

"Hey now," Skip replied, "Ain't this something? Man, this is my night. I can feel it in my bones."

"You must be jiving. This ain't no way to get into Hollywood. You need an agent for that. Ain't nothing happening here. Shoot, I ain't even scored with none of them Billie Holidays."

"Aw, man, what you down in the dumps for? You might get discovered tonight."

The guy waved off Skip's comment. "I already been discovered. Stick around and I'll buy you a drink. You look like you could use some schooling."

"Humph," Skip said. "I done been to school, but I'll take you up on that drink."

He coolly whipped out his pack of Chesterfields and offered one. The big guy shook his head. Skip lit the cigarette tucked between his lips and struck a pose, taking a long, slow drag and letting the smoke stream from his nose. He tried to work off his nervous energy by tapping his foot to the beat of Satchmo's band swinging through "Ain't Misbehavin'." As he neared the end of the stage, his insides started twisting and turning, like a rubber band coiling around upon itself until it bunched up into one huge knot. When he found himself at the head of the line, staring across the empty stage, his mind went blank. His body froze. The emcee poked his head around the curtains.

"Come on, boy. You're holding up the show."

Skip tried to move, but couldn't. Across the stage, the big buy smiled and made the motion of raising a drink to his lips. Skip sent a message to his legs. Move, God dammit! He couldn't believe it. Here was his big chance, and he was paralyzed. Come on! Move. He stumbled forward, the burning cigarette still in his hands. The spotlight blinded him. He closed his eyes tight, opened them and closed them again, hoping they'd adjust to the bright light. Beyond the glare, the agents waited, pens held expectantly over their pads. Skip sent an order firing through his brain. Speak. Please, speak. Nothing. He licked his lips, swallowed hard, his mouth suddenly dry. He tried again. He barely heard his voice.

A harsh voice roared: "Louder, please."

Another voice, impatient, followed. "Hey, boy, you got a name?"

Skip clenched his fists, squinted and stared around the light. He saw the balcony, the near-empty rows on the first floor and, in the front row, several bored-looking white men grinning and pointing at him. He leaned forward, picked one out and yelled.

"Yeah, I got a name. Skip Reynolds! William Henry "Skip" Reynolds!"

Later, across the street at Ted's Bar, Skip nursed a whiskey on the rocks and tried to remember if any of the agents had written down his name. He only remembered the blinding light, the grinning faces. The guy from the streetcar, who'd introduced himself as Harold Q. "Harry-O" Osborne, raised his glass and took a cool swallow.

"What you thinking 'bout," Harry-O said, swirling his drink.

"This g-damn Los Angeleez." Skip finished off his whisky and motioned for the bartender to bring another round. "Seems tonight was not my night, not by a long shot."

Harry-O clapped him on the shoulder. "Toughen up, baby. You can't let that mess back at the Lincoln get you down. Look at me, I didn't even find a gal, but I ain't blue. Shoot, if you want to break into moving pictures, you got to have a hide tough as railroad iron." He pushed aside his old drink and pulled the fresh one close. "I don't give them cattle calls a second thought. Either I make it, or I don't. There's always another one coming."

"Oh yeah," Skip said, trying to rouse his dying spirit. "How many you been to?"

"Enough so's I don't keep track anymore." Harry-O drained off half his whisky and sucked through his teeth after the drink went down. "I don't feel any pain. Matter of fact, I don't see why I even mess with these things. I get more calls to play Indians than I do to play black folk." Harry-O's voice took on a bitter, almost self-pitying tone. "I'm not what the white boys call, 'authentic'."

Skip shook his head, remembering Henry's words. He swirled his drink, leaned forward and sought a reason to keep going to cattle calls. "You ever had any luck with these things? You ever made it up on the screen?"

"Nope, but I have been on the screen." Harry-O crunched an ice cube, put on a stone-face expression and raised his right hand. "How, white man. Me want wampum, smoke 'em peace pipe. Westerns," he said. "'Course now, I did say a few words in *The Green Pastures*."

Skip rocked back in his seat. He was talking to someone who'd actually been in a moving picture he'd seen. *"The Green Pastures"*! How much money did you make? You got an agent? How'd you get in? Hell, what are you doing at the Lincoln if you done already been in moving pictures?"

Harry-O frowned, his brow wrinkling. "Damn, Skip, I'm not a star. I made a little money. I have a guy who says he's my agent, but like I said, it's tough when you don't look authentic. To tell the truth, I've about had enough of Hollywood. I'm thinking about heading for the east coast."

"You're leaving Hollywood?"

"Soon's I get enough money together, I'm Harlem bound." Harry-O raised his glass in a mock toast. "Hail the home of the New Negro!" He drained his glass. "Harlem folks are setting up a Negro theater. They're going to do Shakespeare."

"Shakespeare?"

"Hell yeah," Harry-O said, excited now. "And I'm pretty good at it. You can have all that Hollywood, dime-a-dozen B'wana Boy, Chester Coon, Rastus with a cotton sack and a smile stuff. I'm going to join the Talented Tenth and do some real acting." He puffed out his chest and surveyed the crowd. His voice turned deep and serious. "You taught me language, and my profit on it is, I know how to curse. A red plague rid you for learning me your language!" Harry-O smiled proudly. "Shakespeare. That's the kind of stuff I want to do."

"Man," Skip said. "Don't nobody want to hear that old-time sounding stuff. Moving pictures is where you gotta be." He countered with a line from *The Petrified Forest*, "Ain't you heard about the big liberation?"

"Yeah, I heard, but where is old Slim Thompson now?"

"Hell if I know, but the way I see it, you make a moving picture and millions of people are gon' see you. Do that Shakespeare stuff and what you gon' get, a hundred people, maybe a thousand? Anyway you look at it, it surely ain't gon' be as many as seen you in *The Green Pastures*, and I'll swear to that on a stack of Bibles."

"Shoot. I'd rather a hundred people see me doing something good, than a hundred million see me acting a fool. I don't want to be famous. I just want to act. What do you want, to be big as B'rer Rabbit Molasses?"

"I want to be big as I can get, and I don't mind being rich and famous to boot. Don't see why I cain't have one of them fancy lim'sines like old Steppin' Fetchit has." Skip paused and lit a cigarette. "'Course, I ain't planning on doing his kind of stuff. I'm gon' do us right, you'll see."

"Maybe I will," Harry-O said, standing. "But let me give you some advice, Skip. Wash all that dreamy-eyed kid stuff out of your head. And forget about being some kind of overnight sensation. That's for white folks. Ain't no such thing as an overnight sensation for us. See you around." Harry-O headed for the door, stopped and turned around, remembering something else. "Don't forget to leave the bartender a tip, about two bits, I'd say."

Skip finished his whisky and called for one more, enjoying the smooth, alcohol high. He was glad he didn't have Harry-O's problem Being brown wasn't so bad after all. And, he wasn't about to wash his dreams out of his head. Kid stuff? Those dreams were all he had, spot lights shining so bright they blotted out everything except the fantastic vision of his name in lights, Skip Reynolds, dusky prince of the silver screen. No shuffling coon. Just a man, like damn near every white boy in moving pictures. A man. A regular Joe. Nothing wrong with that. Why couldn't Hollywood see what had to be plain as day: Every black man wasn't like Steppin' Fetchit? Fact is, he couldn't remember one who was.

He sucked down a mouthful of whisky and leaned back, thinking maybe he'd make out better next time. Newspapers said another cattle call was coming, this time for *Stanley and Livingston*. They'll need plenty of natives for that. He closed his eyes and saw himself running through a Hollywood jungle, shaking a spear and jabbering some nonsense. Harry-O said you needed an agent. Nothing happened with those cattle calls. If only Ezekiel Washington hadn't disappeared. He took a last, bracing swallow of whiskey, paid the tab and slapped an extra quarter on the table.

$$\infty$$

HENRY WAS STILL AT THE DANCING-BAR-B-QUE WHEN HE WALKED IN. "Well, the pride of Texas returns," he said, looking up from a glass of soda. "How'd it go?"

"It went," Skip said, straddling a chair and resting his drunken head on his folded arms. "How was the meeting?"

"Couldn't have been better," Henry smiled. "Hattie McDaniel showed up, said she's behind us one hundred percent."

Skip groaned, disappointment hitting him again. "Damn. Maybe I should've stayed here tonight."

"I don't know about that," Henry said. "Folks didn't do nothing except talk. But some things are going to be happening, good things."

"Like what?"

"Folks are getting tired of letting Hollywood have its way every time, letting them tell lies on us. People are getting ready to do something about it."

"Humph," Skip reached for another cigarette, then decided against it. "They gon' be doing anything 'bout getting folks in moving pictures, or is they just gon' be talking?"

"Don't know which way the wind will blow. What's your interest, anyway? I thought you were planning on making the Lincoln's cattle calls your path to success."

Skip raised his head. "Right now I don't know if the Lincoln and them g-damn cattle calls is the right path. They gon' have another one soon, but I don't know. What do you think?"

"I think you're biting off more than you can chew. Hollywood's not the kind of place where you can show up one day and change everything. What you're talking about, putting real black folk in Hollywood's moving pictures, is going to take time. It's going to take little steps, like what we talked about at the meeting. Giant steps won't do. Hollywood isn't ready for that."

"But what about . . .?" Skip stopped. The letter from Ezekiel

Washington had said Hollywood's directors were looking for a new kind of colored actor, but Washington wasn't around. "I read a story where a man in Harlem said there was a chance in Hollywood."

Henry grunted. "I'll bet a fat man that Harlem boy never set foot in Hollywood. Have you ever heard of Bert Williams?"

"Who's he?"

Henry shook his head. "You want to be an actor and you haven't heard of Bert Williams!" Henry turned and pointed to a picture of a well-dressed, smiling man above the counter. "That's Bert Williams. The best vaudevillian who ever lived. A true pioneer. You like Red Skeleton?"

"Sure."

"Eddie Cantor?"

"Yeah, yeah," Skip said, wondering where Henry was headed.

"They learned from Bert Williams. Stole might be a better word. He was a master showman, even did a command performance for the Queen of England. I saw him once in San Francisco. He did his raggedy coon bit, but he was nothing like that at all, Skip. He was an educated man, studied at Stanford University. But like you and everybody else who went to that cattle call tonight, he was trapped. There was only so much white folks were going to let him do. He once said, and I quote him directly. 'I have never been able to discover that there was anything disgraceful in being a colored person. But I have found it to be inconvenient'." Henry sneered and looked disgusted. "Inconvenient."

"Well," Skip said. "He know what he was talking about. What happened to him?"

"Inconvenience broke him. You see, Skip, Hollywood has a little box for us, and everything's fine, long as we stay in that box. But I didn't know that when I first came out here. I was like you, all starry-eyed and ready to go. I came up through the old minstrel shows. This was twenty, twenty-five years ago. I was with Wallace's Sunflower Coons. Crazy times." Henry smiled at memories of the old days. "Here we were, colored folks doing shows in blackface, traveling, carousing. I tell you, Skip. I had me a time.

"We came through Hollywood about 1920. Town wasn't much then, bunch of fields and farms. Anyway, the whole troupe got into a moving picture, and I got hooked right then and there. Just seeing myself on the screen made me feel good. When that picture ended, I stayed around to meet up with a man name of Dennis Holloway. He wanted to be the Oscar Micheaux of the west coast. Them pictures on the wall? I was with Holloway then. Thought I was big stuff, making moving pictures and wearing silk. Didn't last long, though. After two, three years Holloway and Eagle Pictures went belly-up. Couldn't get the financing. Couldn't get the bookings. Couldn't get the same quality as Hollywood.

"But I hung on, did some bit parts, stage stuff, played Brutus Jones in a local production of *The Emperor Jones.* Come the year of nineteen and twenty-six, I heard Paramount was getting ready to do *Uncle Tom's Cabin.* I tried for the part. Didn't get it, and I thank God for that twist of fate." He looked at Skip. "You must think I'm a fool for saying that?"

"I don't know, Henry. Seems to me you'd be kicking yourself for missing that one. *Uncle Tom's Cabin.* Shoot. That could've made you a star."

"Made me a star!" Henry slammed his fist on the table. "Made me a star? Hell." He stood up and started pacing, mumbling angrily. "A star?" He stopped at the far end of the counter, stared hard at Skip and started talking again, the words firing from his mouth. "Listen to me now, Skip. This is history talking. I'm glad I didn't get that part. That's right. Glad. That was probably the best thing that ever happened to me. That role brought about the demise of two great Negro actors."

"Demise?" Skip said.

"Look it up," Henry snapped, agitated and impatient. He sat down, then got back up. "Charles Gilpin, who played in the original *Emperor Jones* in New York, was the first man to get Uncle Tom. Now, there's two stories about what happened to him. One had it that he and the director fought over the part. Seems Gilpin wanted old Tom to be more of a man, but the director liked the boy just the way he was. The other story is that Gilpin was an alcoholic and couldn't do the role. But that's white folks talking. If he could do Brutus Jones on the Broadway stage, then you know darn well he could do Uncle Tom in Hollywood. Anyway, the end result is that they sent Gilpin packing, minus his thousand-dollar-a-week salary.

"Then James B. Lowe got the part, played it too. He tried arguing like Gilpin, but Lowe had sense enough to back down when he saw Tom was going to be Uncle Tom, no matter what he thought. After that, Lowe never played another role in this town. Hollywood doesn't have time for aggravating Negroes. They just want to keep us in our place. Try stepping out and they scoot you right on out the door.

"Now, I was on the sidelines while all this was happening, but I was watching. And it became clear to me that if two talented colored actors could get messed around for trying to change things, then what chance did I, a small-time player, have of doing anything beyond what was in that little box. Life's too short to spend it banging your head against doors that won't open. I took my savings, got some people I knew to loan me a little money, and opened up this place. My soul is at peace."

"But that was years ago, Henry," Skip said. "Things are different now."

"Are they? Why don't you come to the next meeting and find out for yourself."

A GREASY PLATE SLID OFF SKIP'S FINGERS AND SETTLED IN THE hot, sudsy water. His hands swam idly in the sink, as his mind surrendered to the rhythm of a chore Grandma Sarah taught him long before he picked his first ball of cotton. He could almost feel her standing beside him, her hands on his, showing him how to make a plate squeaky clean. He wondered how she and the rest of the home folks were. He hadn't written since his first days here. He didn't want anyone back home to know the colored actor's school had turned out to be a city slicker's trick. The only stories he wanted to send home were good ones.

Phineas had plucked her letter to him from a trash can behind the Plaza Arms. It wished him well, told him to pray. God would make a way. He told her so. Everybody in Tunis was doing fine, even Willie, who had to eat his words when the picking machine didn't work out. Sam Willard called everybody back, paid extra to get his cotton picked on time. John Lee's baby, Anna, was the cutest she'd seen since Skip. Everything was fine, but the house was too quiet. Didn't seem to be a way to fill the silence. She didn't mind though because sometimes on the porch at sundown with dusk coming on and the sky all purple and red, she swore she could hear his voice whispering on the breeze. One day she caught herself humming the first song Old Man Williams taught him on the guitar: "Will Fox said to the fireman, bring me a little more gin." Did he remember that?

He fished another plate out of the sink and in doing so, dredged up the memory of a little wide-eyed boy playing a cigar-box guitar for his grandma. He rubbed his thumb and forefinger across the plate, smiled to himself and nodded. It was squeaky clean.

Out in the cafe, Diana treated herself to a Coca-Cola and fanned herself with a menu. She'd had a bona fide payday. Nearly two dollars in tips were spread out on the table before her. Henry brought an armload of pots and pans into the kitchen, then went back to cleaning his grill. Skip put the new arrivals aside to soak. No use trying to scrub off the seared-on scraps of meat and bar-b-que sauce now. There was plenty of time to get to it before morning. He pulled three clean saucers from the sink and set them in the drainer. Sweat dripped off his nose. Wisps of steam rose to his face. Bubble islands scudded along a thin, red-rimmed film of grease, broke up and took new shapes each time he plunged his hands into the water.

He was tired, drained, worn out by another long workday, almost ready to turn in and call it an early night. But some actors were coming. Henry even said Ezekiel Washington might show. Ezekiel Washington! Skip didn't know if he would shake the man's hand or punch him in the nose. He decided it was best not to fret too much about it. No sense in getting all excited like a gambler who sees his horse take the lead in the home stretch, only to lose by a nose at the wire. Grandma Sarah always said worrying and fretting didn't get a body nothing 'cept lines on the forehead. And he didn't feel like looking old. He took the last cup out of the sink, pulled the plug and looked into the cafe where Henry gave the grill a final scrubbing as Diana headed out the door, waving good-bye. A few moments later, the door swung open.

"I should've told Diana to lock that door." Henry said, not looking up from his work. "Nothing happening here, buddy. Come back tomorrow."

"Aw, c'mon, Henry." It was Pee Wee. "That ain't no way to treat a loyal customer."

"I'm not feeding anybody now, Pee Wee," Henry said, checking his cold, clean oven.

"Fine with me," Pee Wee said, sauntering over to the counter and taking a seat, tipping his hat back on his head. "I already ate. How's my boy working out?"

"Fine."

"Told you he would. He's the best damn dishwasher this side of the Mississippi and . . ."

"Listen, Pee wee, I don't have time to listen to you run your mouth. I got to get this place ready for tonight. Why don't you get on back in the kitchen and see if you can put a fire under Skip's behind?"

"Sure thing. I can see where I ain't wanted." Pee Wee spun around on the stool. "But you shouldn't work so hard, Henry. It'll give you high blood pressure, and I'd hate to see you blow up behind that."

Skip dried his hands on his apron and slapped skin with Pee Wee. "What's shaking, daddy-o?"

"You know the score, good brother. Hipping, hopping and staying alive. What's Henry in such a fuss over? Didn't even say hello."

"The actors meeting," Skip said, taking off his apron. "And you know how Henry gets when he's rushed. Swear to God, he's worse than a fussy old church lady."

"Ain't that the truth," Pee Wee said.

"Anyway, he's got to finish up, go home and get dressed, then come back in time to relax and play Mr. Host. So, you know his feathers are ruffled." Skip laughed and pushed his mop bucket into the cafe. "What time does that store close?"

"Relax," Pee Wee said. "We got plenty of time. Don't want you taking after Henry." He lit a cigarette and followed Skip.

Henry pushed past them, grabbed his coat off the rack and headed for the door. "See you at seven?"

"You got it," Skip said, pushing the mop across a far corner of the cafe.

"All right, then. Come on, Pee Wee," Henry said, moving Pee Wee along like a mother hen after her chicks. "We can't be holding up Hollywood's next bronze Apollo."

"Where you gon' be," Skip called to his friend.

"Out front in the Plymy, and hurry up. R.C.'s closes in half an hour."

"Dammit, Pee Wee! I thought you said we had plenty of time."

"We do, long's you hurry up." Pee Wee smiled at Skip and casually flicked ash on a dirty part of the floor.

God damn that Pee Wee! Skip hurried through his mopping, missing spots here and there, but careful to give the heavy traffic areas a good going over. He worked his way back to the kitchen, kicking the mop bucket behind him. He finished in record time, took the back steps by twos. The old, wooden boards groaned beneath him. He rushed into his room, took off his dirty work clothes and tossed them towards the pile at the foot of his cot. He grabbed a favorite pair of faded jeans, hopped around the room putting them on, then took a flannel shirt off the hook on the door, and slipped on his shoes. There, he was ready.

He checked the dining room. Everything was in place. Plates, saucers and bowls were stacked side by side in the polished chrome case above the grill, which Henry had scrubbed and rinsed. The chairs were in their end of the day position: upside down on the tables. He smiled, satisfied. He liked working here, liked the easy work and free food; Diana's playful, sassy hands-on-hips way of telling him to bring her some clean plates quick, before she called on Joe Louis to come and knock some sense into him; gruff Henry, barking his orders and frowning to keep from smiling. The dancing Bar-B-Que was his home and its work, his anchor. He looked around one more time, then stepped into the fading light of another day.

Pee Wee gunned the Plymy's idling engine, leaned across the passenger's side and pushed the door open. "Let's ride," he said.

"Where's this place at," Skip asked, switching the radio from a newscast about the Spanish Civil War ending because the rebels had surrounded Barcelona. He fiddled with the dial until he found a swing station.

"R.C.'s is over by the baseball stadium, " said Pee Wee.

"Can we make it in time? You know, I gots some important people to meet."

"Shoot," Pee Wee replied. "You could meet Rockefeller after a stop at R.C.'s."

Pee Wee turned west on Vernon and headed towards Wrigley Stadium, home of the Los Angeles Seraphs, a Triple-A ballclub in the Pacific Coast League. Beer and cigarette ads trumpeted the virtues of alcohol and tobacco from billboards rising high above the grandstands at 42nd Place and Avalon. "Drink Rainer Beer . . . New Vigor and Strength In Every drop."

"You got them baseball tickets," Skip asked between puffs on a Chesterfield and failed attempts at blowing smoke rings.

"Right off first base," Pee Wee said as he steered through the thick, end of the work day traffic. "I sure hope old Satch brings his fastball so's he can mow down some white boys."

Three blocks from the stadium, Pee Wee took a right turn and stopped in the middle of the block. Mannequins in double-breasted suits stood in R.C.'s display windows, along with a life-sized cardboard picture of George Raft looking gangster dangerous and cool, his slim frame caressed by a black pin-striped suit.

"I want that," Skip said, jumping out of the Plymy. "That suit is me."

"Yeah, well wanting and getting is two different things," Pee Wee said. "That suit Raft is wearing ain't store bought. That baby is custom made. You got to be toting some heavy change for that."

R.C.'s was cool and quiet inside. A couple of sharp dressed ladies stood around. Skip figured they were waiting for their men.

"This is one of the best places in town," Pee Wee whispered. "The price is always right and the help can't be beat. Check out Erline over there."

Pee Wee smiled and nodded as one of the women walked towards them, smoothing her tight-fitting dress, stepping light in black high heels.

"A saleswoman?" Skip said, frowning.

"Why not," Pee Wee said. "Who knows better how to dress a man than a good looking woman? And Erline is always looking good." He turned to the saleswoman. "How you doing, baby?"

"Better now," she said, flashing a friendly smile. "You all looking or buying?"

"Buying," Skip said, all business. "I need a pair of pants and a shirt, maybe a tie."

"Sounds like you need a suit," Erline said, stepping over to a rack and sizing up Skip. "How about this one?" She pulled a dark blue pin-striped number and held it up. "Twenty dollars, and it'll fit as good as those in the windows. Here, try it on."

Skip shook his head. "Ain't got twenty bucks. Got just enough to buy what I came for: shirt, pants, maybe a tie." He looked around the store, saw shirts hanging on one wall, pants on another. "How much are those," he said, pointing to the slacks.

"Three dollars a piece," Erline sighed, her smile vanishing.

"Bet I can get a shirt for a buck."

"You can get two," Erline walked back behind the counter.

"But you won't be a sharp looking young daddy," Pee Wee said.

Skip fingered a pair of slacks and thought about Delta Slim. The bluesman had called him young daddy. He ran Pee Wee's phrase over in his mind. Sharp looking young daddy. That's what he wanted to be. Maybe next time. He grabbed a pair of black slacks, found a white shirt and picked out a black-and-white polka dot tie. "Guess this'll do," he said, walking back to the cash register, eyes lingering over the suit rack. No use getting all worked up 'bout something you can't have. He laid the clothes on the counter.

"You know," Erline said, searching for a fountain pen. "You don't have to buy a suit just because you try it on."

"Give it a shot, Skip," Pee Wee said. "See how good you can look."

"Well," Skip hesitated. "Guess it won't hurt, and I always wondered how I'd look in one of them fine suits."

Erline perked up and stepped from behind the counter, the lively stride back in her step, the friendly smile warming her face. She pointed to a row of curtains. "Dressing rooms are over there. I'll hold this other stuff for you."

She winked at Pee Wee, who flashed her the okay sign. Skip walked over to the suit rack, flipped through until he found a pin-striped, double-breasted black one like Raft's. He slung the suit over his shoulder and headed for the dressing room. Inside he undressed quickly, then reached for the suit, feeling the coat's thick weave and the silvery smooth inner lining. The pants felt good. The coat felt even better. It had padded shoulders and tapered in at the waist. He stepped out.

"Now you're cooking with gas," Pee Wee said, "and looking as good as George Raft."

"Think so," Skip said, and stepped in front of one of R.C.'s full-length mirrors. Oh Lord. He was one sharp looking young daddy. He struck a casual pose and smiled, profiled, back, front, three-quarters looking over his shoulder. He looked good from every angle.

"Don't wear that suit on a Thursday night," Pee Wee said. "You'll have some Kitchen Mechanic wanting to overhaul your engine."

"Well, sir," Skip said, still posing. He started singing. "Pee Wee, my engine's done got rusty, and it will not run at all. You hear me, daddy-o? It will not run at all. I think I needs me a Kitchen Mechanic to give me an overhaul."

"Sing the blues, down home style," Erline said.

Pee Wee held out his hand. "Skin me, good brother. Skin me."

Skip slapped his friend's palm and turned to Erline. "How much is this one?"

"Twenty-five dollars. But you don't have to pay all of it right now."

"How's that?"

"Credit, honey," Erline said. "We have thirty-, sixty-, and ninety-days plans. With a little down payment, you could wear that suit out the door."

"Credit?"

"Sure, Skip," Pee Wee cut in. "I use it all the time. Ain't that right, Erline?"

The saleswoman nodded. "Pee Wee's one of R.C.'s best customers."

Skip shook his head and started pulling off the coat. "I don't think I'm gon' go that way. Cash and carry, that's my policy. Y'all talkin' 'bout that stuff that puts a 'cropper in a hole he can't get out of. No, buddy, that ain't for me."

"Now, hold on, honey," Erline said, walking over to him and patting down the shoulders, arms and waist. "You cut a mean figure."

Skip tried not to smile at his reflection, but he looked too good, just like he knew he would in a fine suit. "How's this credit thing work?" he said, striking another pose.

"Depends on how much you put down." Erline said. "Seven dollars is the minimum for that suit. With the sixty-day plan, you'll pay about two-fifty a week. You are working, aren't you?"

"He's in the restaurant business," Pee Wee called out.

"Oh, really," Erline said. "Which one?"

"It's called the . . ."

Pee Wee cut him off. "It's one of Central Avenue's finer establishments. You can't get a seat there at noon. The joint is packed. Why, just the other day . . ."

"Dammit, Pee wee. Will you let me tell the woman?"

Pee Wee stepped back, hands held up "Sure thing, good brother. Just trying to help."

Skip turned to Erline. "I wash dishes at the Dancing Bar-B-Que."

"Best ribs in town," Erline said. "Henry Lewis might be a little tight with his money, but I know he pays a living wage."

"And what if I lose my job," Skip said. "That sixty-day plan still in effect?"

"We can make arrangements," Erline said. "R.C. don't like to take his clothes off a man's back. Shoot, honey, you're a walking advertisement."

"I know you don't want my help, Skip," Pee Wee said. "But any man who can walk away from looking good as you do now must be born to lose and wear rags till he's six feet under. Then he'll get to wear a suit."

"But what if I lose my job, Pee Wee? What'll happen then?"

"Aw, Henry ain't gon' fire you unless you give him reason to," Pee Wee said. "All you have to do is put a little money aside each week and before you know it, the suit'll be paid for. Hell, half the stuff I wear ain't even paid off. Ain't that right, Erline?"

She nodded. "But you pay steady."

"See. Now what's the matter good brother? You scared of rolling the dice?"

"Hell, naw," Skip snapped. "I come halfway 'cross the country, didn't I? Riding freights and hitch-hiking. I ain't afraid of rolling no dice."

He marched back into the dressing room, shut the curtain and slumped against the wall. Damn, shit. He undressed slowly, thinking about credit, losing his job and the finest suit he'd ever worn. He could save up until he had twenty-five dollars, but he wanted the suit now. He took two fives out of his money belt. One bought slacks, a shirt and a tie. Two bought a suit. He put on his jeans, jammed the bills in his pocket, buttoned his shirt and headed for the counter, the suit folded over his arms.

"Write me up," he said.

Pee Wee patted him on the shoulder. "That's a fine suit, good brother, I ain't got nothing can touch it."

"You still want this other stuff," Erline said.

"Just the shirt and tie," Skip said, laying the suit across the counter and pulling the fives from his pocket.

Erline pushed a receipt towards him. "Sign here and you're all set."

He grabbed a pen and held it above the pad for a moment, already seeing himself turning heads on the avenue, then signed his name with a flourish, the "s" in Reynolds trailing off in a cascade of loops and swirls.

The actors were deep in conversation when Pee Wee dropped him off.

He stopped outside the Dancing Bar-B-Que's door, swelling with pride, wondering if his entrance would stop the show. He opened the door, stepped inside and saw a dozen people sitting around a group of tables Henry had pulled together. He felt a twinge of disappointment. Nobody famous was here. He did recognize Helen Lipscomb, a stately black woman he'd seen in the *Eagle*. The paper said she gave up acting to fight Hollywood's producers and directors. She wanted better roles for colored actors. Tonight, she controlled the meeting. Her dark eyes flashed behind her glasses, moved from face to face. Her smooth, yet firm voice spoke carefully chosen words. She nodded slightly as Skip slipped quietly into an empty seat next to a fat, bald-headed man whose black head was as polished and smooth as an 8-ball. The fat man chomped on a two-fingers thick cigar he worked back and forth across his mouth. Skip watched him cautiously, eyes locked on the ash hanging precariously from the cigar. It extended a half-inch and had already started to droop. He scooted his seat a safe distance away from the fat man, settled in and surveyed the crowd. Was Ezekiel Washington here? Henry caught his gaze, pointed to the suit and rubbed his thumb and forefinger together. Expensive? Skip shook his head and smiled. He was already a walking advertisement. He crossed his arms on the table and looked at the woman in control, noticed her high cheekbones, the soft sweep of her gray-streaked black hair. How could such a beautiful woman convince anyone she was a maid. You couldn't dress her down enough. Her voice hardened. People started moving nervously in their seats.

"We can't let Selznick put 'nigger' in *Gone with the Wind*," she said. "Are there any suggestions on what we should do?"

The fat man rolled his cigar around in his mouth, drummed his sausage fingers on the table and waited for someone to speak. The moments crept by. He took the cigar out of his mouth, flicked the now inch-long ash into a tray.

"Don't see what you're getting so upset about, Helen," he said. "I hear nigger everyday, and damn near every time it's from black folks. Besides, a lot of our people are making good money on this picture. No need of jeopardizing their good thing just because some of us don't like the sound of a word."

Henry shook his head. "Helen's not talking about some two-bit B-movie, Zeke. The whole country's going to see this picture, and we ought to do whatever we can to make sure it's right."

"That's right," a little bespectacled guy across from Skip chimed in. "And we don't have to worry about jeopardizing anybody's piece of the action. Selznick can't make the picture without us. I don't know about the rest of you all, but I'm with Henry and Helen on this."

"I still don't see what all the fuss is about," the fat man said, relighting his cigar. "Freedman, freed nigger. It's all the same. I doubt if anyone'll even hear it."

"Oh, yes they will," Helen said. "There's not a colored person in this country whose ears don't perk up at the sound of that word."

The fat man countered. "That don't mean they're ready to go to war over it."

"Jesus, Zeke. Time hasn't changed you at all," Henry said. "I bet you'd say it's okay to wear black face."

Zeke! Henry had only used that name with one person. Could it be? The fat man looked up at the ceiling and blew smoke rings.

"If it means getting a decent paycheck, why not. Blacking up don't bother Ezekiel Washington one bit." He turned to Skip. "How about you, young man? What do you think?"

Skip leaned back in his seat, the stink of the fat man's breath and the nauseating cloud of cigar smoke crawling over his face. It was him! He gulped hard, stared into Ezekiel Washington's bulging, round eyes, his mind scrambling for an answer and a way to match his fantasy image to the fat, bald-headed man sitting next to him. Washington was supposed to be a sharp dresser. He'd read somewhere that Washington once walked a black panther on Central Avenue and drove a pink Cadillac. The fancy signature on the letter suggested a man of class, not this broad-faced man with fleshy lips and rolls of fat bunching up at the back of his neck, this tub of lard whose gut stretched his suit vest till buttons near 'bout popped. This man barely dressed better than Phineas. Skip looked around the table. Everyone was watching him, waiting for his answer. He felt like he was on a high wire. Washington leaned closer. Skip eyed the cigar and scooted back farther in his chair.

"I'm talking to you, young man," Washington said. "What do you think?"

"Me," Skip heard his voice squeak out an octave higher than normal. "Well . . . I . . ." He cleared his throat. "I don't go for putting on black face, but nigger. Well, it ain't like nobody's never heard the word before."

There. He had answered, but one glance around the table told him he was wrong. Everyone was frowning, except Washington. Helen took off her glasses and set them beside her coffee cup.

"Young man," she said. "You are missing the point. The question is not whether we've heard the word, but whether it is accurate in the picture's historical context. And it is not. In the script, Scarlett O'Hara says free niggers. The term should be freedmen. Men, young man, not niggers."

Skip started to say something, but stopped when Helen held up her hand.

"This young man shows the best reason for fighting the inclusion of this disgusting word, which he seems to think is just another word." She gave Skip a severe look. "Just because everybody's heard it doesn't make it okay."

"Yes, m'am," Skip said, feeling as if he'd been scolded by a schoolteacher.

"Now, now, Helen," Washington put his fat paw on Skip's shoulder. "No need to beat up on the boy. He was just speaking his mind."

"I'm beginning to wonder if he even has a mind," Henry said. "Siding with you after what you've done to him."

"How's that?" Washington leaned forward.

Skip cut his eyes at Henry and shook his head, just a little, enough to tell him to keep his mouth shut.

"How's that?" Washington said again. "Why, I've never seen this young man before in my life." He turned to Skip. "Have I done something to you?"

"No," Skip said. Now was not the time to tear into Washington.

"There," Washington said, "The young man was just exercising his right of free speech, which I believe is still in the Constitution."

"Aw, hell," Henry got up from the table and went to the counter.

The guy across from Skip spoke. "You know, Helen, we could picket the studio. Call the newspaper."

"Now you're talking," another woman said.

"Selznick won't go for that kind of publicity," said another man.

Helen smiled. "And he'll probably do whatever he can to make us stop. We might be on to something."

Washington waved his cigar. "This is preposterous. You all can't stop Hollywood with a few pickets."

"We're not trying to stop Hollywood, Mr. Washington," Helen said. "Just win a little battle."

"Well, you can fight it without me." Washington stabbed his cigar out and headed for the door.

Skip watched him go, wisps of cigar smoke drifting towards the ceiling. He fanned the air around him, stood and walked toward the door. Henry stopped him on his way out.

"Meeting's not over yet," he said.

"I got business with that man," Skip said, working himself up.

"Well, you'd better hurry up and catch him."

Skip stepped outside, looked up and down the street, but saw no one. He heard a streetcar's bell ringing in the next block. Would Ezekiel Washington ride streetcars? Hell, with that suit he wore, he might be walking. Skip moved to the curb, listened for footsteps or an idling engine. Nothing, only the whispering wind and the streetcar's bell growing faint as the sparks dancing along the electric wire dimmed in the distance. He ran up the block, turned and ran back down to the corner. Where was Washington? Dammit! He should've gotten up as soon as Washington made a move, instead of sitting in the dancing Bar-B-Que, trying to be nice and polite, pretending he gave a good God damn about what Miss Scarlett said. Damn, shit. Washington took his money!

Across the street he saw the address Washington had sent him to. Remembering that day made him ball his fists and clench his teeth. A car passed by, heading north. He watched it closely, his spirits rising until he saw a woman behind the wheel. He searched the street, desperate. Half a block down, a car's headlights switched on. An engine started. Washington! He ran down the middle of the street, waving his arms, hoping to stop the car before it drove off. So what if it wasn't Washington. Better to make a fool of himself with a stranger than do nothing and let Washington escape. An old, faded pink Cadillac pulled from the curb, its engine wheezing. He stopped and stood his ground. The horn beeped as the car approached, nearer and nearer, the headlamps fixing him in twin beams of white light. It bumped him. A man leaned from the driver's window, yelled and shook his fists.

"What the hell's wrong with you, boy?"

It was him. Skip furrowed his brow and marched over to the driver's side.

"I want my money back," he said.

"I beg your pardon," Washington blew a cloud of cigar smoke in his face.

"My money. I sent you five dollars for the Ezekiel Washington Colored Actors School, but there ain't no school. So, I want my money back."

"I'm afraid I don't know what you're talking about. I don't have an actor's school. Now, if you will please get the hell out of my way. I've business to tend to."

"I ain't moving," Skip said. "You sent me a letter saying I should come out here and join your colored actors' school. I got it right here." He pulled the worn, creased sheet of paper from his inside coat pocket and shoved it in Washington's face. "See. There's your signature."

Washington glanced at the letter, shook his head and clucked his tongue. "Came all the way out here, did you," he said, giving Skip the letter. "Well, that school never did get off the ground. I had high hopes for it. But, c'est la vie. Such is life."

"But, what about my money?"

"I sent you a booklet, didn't I?"

"Yeah, but you said you had an acting school. You said you were going to put me in moving pictures."

"I'm more of an agent now," Washington said. "I don't have time to teach people." He tried to dismiss Skip, but the young man pressed on.

"Where I come from, Mister Washington, a man's word is his bond. But, I guess it ain't like that out here. Folks say anything they damn well please."

Washington grunted and shifted in his seat. He shut off his engine. "What did you think of that meeting?"

"I don't know, Mister Washington. It was my first one."

"Well, you know enough to side with someone who's on the inside," Washington said.

"Those folks back there can't help you. They'll have you walking a picket line and, the next thing you know, you'll be on the out, blackballed. Nobody in Hollywood will hire you. Remember Gilpin and Lowe, that's my motto. Do what you got to do and take the money. The man lives on the inside, in the heart," Washington tapped his chest. "Not on the screen. Look at old Steppin'. He's a millionaire two, three times over."

"Yeah, but I don't see why he has to keep playing the white man's nigger," Skip said. "Now, how 'bout my five dollars?"

"Are you still trying to get into moving pictures?"

Skip nodded. "Ain't had no luck, though. I was counting on you. And when I couldn't find you, well. Hollywood ain't the easiest place to get hold of."

Washington nodded. "How true." He turned the ignition. "Well, it was nice meeting you." He shifted the Cadillac into first.

"Wait a minute," Skip said. "You owe me. You're an agent. What about them new colored actors folks in Hollywood want?"

"I know. I know, young man. But times are tough. Things have changed since I wrote you."

"A man's word is his bond, Mister Washington," Skip said.

Zeke flicked some ash out the window and puffed silently. "The Dutch Masters sure do put out a fine cigar. Yes, a fine cigar. Tell you what young man. Perhaps I can square things with you. Come down to my office tomorrow morning. Do you know where the Bradbury Building is?"

"I can find it. But is this on the level?" He nodded towards 5512 Central Avenue. "There's the last place you sent me."

Washington shook his head. "Young man, whatever has happened was an unfortunate circumstance. However, this offer is, as you young boys say: On the level. I'll see you tomorrow at ten sharp. Now, get out of my way."

Skip backed up and watched Washington drive off. Two blocks up, the car turned a corner and disappeared. He jumped up, twirled around and swaggered back to the Dancing Bar-B-Que, feeling ten feet tall.

"Find him?" Henry asked as Skip strode into the empty cafe.

"Indeed I did," Skip said, sitting down and slapping his hands on the counter. "I'm meeting him tomorrow." He looked around. "How'd the meeting go?"

"What do you care," Henry said, rearranging tables.

"Just asking," Skip replied, leaning back on the stool, then spinning around. "Washington better do right by me."

"You know the old saying, Skip. Once burned, twice a fool. Be careful."

"Don't you worry about me, Henry. I've been burned enough."

HE WAS UP EARLY THE NEXT MORNING, FEELING EXCITED AND ALIVE, ready for Washington to make good on last night's promise. He wished he had a number ten washtub to bathe in, or a shower like the one at the Plaza Arms. Dipping and scrubbing was a half-assed way to get clean. Pee Wee called it taking a whore bath: once under the arms and twice between the legs. Today, he wanted to be squeaky clean, good enough to pass Grandma Sarah's toughest Sunday morning inspection. He ran the water until it was stinging hot, soaped and scrubbed hard, drained the sink, refilled it soon as the water turned a dull, soapy gray. Not until he could rinse his washcloth and see the bottom of the face bowl did he declare himself squeaky clean.

He dressed slowly, luxuriating in the rich feel of his new clothes. Standing in front of his mirror, he fell in love with the suit all over again. The pleated baggy pants fit snug in the hips. The white pinstripes raced down a black field to the cuffs that hit the top of his dull shoes at just the right spot. He put on a white shirt, chose the new polka dot tie and tossed the fine, double-breasted jacket over his shoulder. Outside his window church bells tolled eighty-thirty. Ninety minutes to show time. He hustled down stairs and got the cafe ready. The last thing he wanted was to come back late and find Henry upset because he'd been with Ezekiel Washington when it was the Dancing Bar-B-Que that was keeping him in rent, food and fine clothes. Didn't want to hear that. So he took care of his job, did what he could and headed downtown.

The Pacific Electric depot was nearly empty as the morning's last riders waited for their transfers. A midmorning lull fell over the city. Cars moved without hurry, even stopping at corners before the lights turned red. Skip walked proudly down the sidewalk, his stride loose and easy, his spirit riding high, the suit making him feel a cut above anybody who wasn't turned out their best. On days like this, with the sun shinning and the distant mountains rising majestically against a powder blue sky, he believed everything people said about Los Angeles being some kind of paradise; mid-winter and the sun was warm. Down the street, a blonde-haired pug-faced shoeshine boy headed his way. The kid struggled along, walking in rhythm to the box that hung low from his shoulder, banging against his hip with every other step. He wore a Yankees baseball cap turned backwards. A half-smoked cigarette dangled from his lips.

"Say," Skip said, stopping the boy. "Where's the Bradbury Building?"

"Couple blocks up," the kid said, all the while studying Skip's shoes. "But you can't get in there with them shoes you're wearing. The Bradbury's a class joint. You gotta have shined shoes to get in there." The kid eased the box off his shoulder and lit his cigarette, flinging the match away with a movement as smooth and studied as a Hollywood gangster's. "Yes, sir, with shoes like that, they'd have the police on you lickety-split, figure you was trying to impersonate somebody important."

Skip looked down at his dull, black shoes. He hadn't shined them in the three months he'd been in Los Angeles. "You trying to hustle me?"

"Just trying to make an honest living." The kid smiled. "How 'bout if I shine 'em up? It's a shame to put that fine suit you're wearing with a pair of beat-up shoes."

"Ain't got time for a shine. Now, where's that Bradbury Building," Skip said, moving off.

"Aw, c'mon." The kid slung the box back on his shoulder and trailed Skip. "You got time for a shine. Besides, you'd be helping a juvenile delinquent stay out of the reform school. Whadda-ya say?"

"What time is it," Skip said, trying to shake the kid and get on with his business.

"Let's see." The kid pawed through his box, shook three pocket watches and held them to his ear, frowned, put them back, found a ticking one and read the time. "Nine-thirty."

"Can you do your job and get me to the Bradbury Building before ten?"

"With time to spare."

"Well, go to it," Skip said. Maybe the kid was right. A shine would put the finishing touch to his look.

The kid looked around and pointed to a parked Chevy. "Step into my office," he said.

"Sheeit," Skip said. "I ain't putting this fine suit up against no dirty Chevrolet." He started walking, but the kid ran around in front of him.

"Hold on now, daddy-o." The kid pulled a gray rag from his box and wiped a corner of the Chevy's fender, hood and grill. "I'd be a fool to ask a slick papa like you to dirty his suit so's I can shine his shoes." He spot-checked his work, buffed a couple of spots. "There. Now take a seat and relax."

Skip leaned over the Chevy, brushed away some dust and ran his fingers over the spot once, twice. He turned around, looked up and down the street, then leaned back, hoping the car's owner wouldn't come out of some store, see him and start yelling for the police. The kid kneeled down, grabbed one of Skip's shoes and propped it on his box. He hummed and whistled as he daubed the shoe with polish, brushed the toe and sides, his eyes scanning the street.

"How come you ain't in school," Skip said.

"Schooling don't put food in nobody's mouth," he said. "Gimme the other shoe."

"I hear tell it does in the long run."

"Yeah, well I'm worrying 'bout the short run right now. Me and mama are the only ones in the house making money."

"But can't you find someplace else to do business, say a shoeshine stand somewhere, 'stead of propping your customers up against somebody's car?"

"Hell," the kid said, popping his rag as he worked. "Me and a bunch of other fellas had a good thing going over in Pershing Square, even had our own bench till the cops came and run us out. Said folks was complaining 'bout us causing a disturbance. Shoot, we wasn't doing nothing 'cept making folks look better. Don't see how that's any kind of crime. You?" The kid stood up, pointed to Skip's shoes and smiled at his handiwork. "Looking pretty good there, daddy-o. Swear to God, they're the best shined shoes you'll see today. That'll be ten cents, and I don't mind a tip."

Skip fished a dime and a nickel from his pocket and flipped the coins towards the kid. "Think fast."

"Right on top of you, daddy-o," the kid said, catching the coins in one quick sweep of his hand.

"So where's the Bradbury Building?"

"Middle of the next block. You can't miss it. The name's on the front."

Skip headed off, turned and asked the time. The kid rifled through his box, found the ticking pocket watch and called out, "Nine forty-five. Say, you need a watch? I got plenty of 'em. They're from Switzerland!"

Skip shook his head and hurried along, walking fast now, but feeling even better, stealing glances at the tops of his shiny black shoes. The mid-morning crowd of businessmen, secretaries, and delivery boys making their rounds flowed past him as he passed the Broadway Arcade with its twin rows of shops, its covered walkway cutting through to Los Angeles Street. Across Broadway stood Grand Central Market, a huge open warehouse filled with vegetables and meat stalls, bakeries that made the block smell of fresh-baked loaves and sugar-sweet pastries. He searched the building fronts. The kid said the Bradbury was a classy place, but there was nothing classy on this block, only nondescript brick and concrete stores, unassuming office towers standing shoulder to shoulder. Damn, shit. Hustled again. At the corner of Third and Broadway, he stopped in front of a pale, rust-colored building with Bradbury written in stone above the doorway. Was this it? He stepped inside. The kid was right. It was like something seen in a dream, full of air and light, dark burnished wood, cool marble steps mounting higher and higher, four floors rising to a spectacular skylight. This must be where Washington spent his money, he thought, because the fat man certainly didn't spend it on clothes.

From behind the banks of closed doors he heard the muffled sound of typewriters and telephones, voices murmuring in conversation. His shoes clicked across the tan tiles interspersed by smaller brown tiles set at each corner. His fingers glided along the smooth banisters, stopped to feel the elaborate wrought-iron shapes of filigree and ornamental shields. He found the directory, studied the names until he saw Ezekiel Washington Enterprises, Suite 230. A cage elevator carried him up, slid softly to a silent stop on the third floor. As soon as he opened the door, a nattily dressed midget with spats and a derby stepped inside. The little man snapped open a fresh copy of the *Racing Ledger*, studied it for a moment, then tugged at Skip's sleeve.

"You a betting man, 'cause if you are, I can make you some money." He slapped the paper. "I see a sure thing right here. Yes, sir, the daily double at Santa Anita. Two bucks'll get you twenty. You a betting man?"

Skip shook his head. He wasn't about to trust a midget.

"Sorry to hear that, brother."

Skip stepped out of the elevator and went looking for Ezekiel Washington. Down the hall, a garishly made up redhead stormed out of the Footlight Agency, turned and screamed through the open door.

"I wouldn't lie on his casting couch if it was the last bed on earth!"

She slung the purse over her shoulder and marched past him, her chewing gum popping and cracking, her sickenly sweet perfume filling the hall. A flustered looking man, his suspenders loose and flapping around his knees, yelled after her.

"To hell with you, too." He caught Skip staring at him, slipped his suspenders back on his shoulders and hitched up his pants. "What the hell are you looking at," he said.

The agency's door slammed shut, and Skip moved on. What kind of place was this? He stopped outside Suite 230, patted down his tie, tugged at his suit and said a prayer before rapping three times on the thick glass window pane. The door swung open.

"Good morning, Mister Reynolds. Won't you step in?"

One of the prettiest women he had ever seen stood holding the door. She was tall and slim, with slight hips. She wore a simple blue dress. Shining black hair caressed her face. Skip drank in her full smile, the flash of light in her soft, almond-shaped eyes. Move over Fredi Washington!

"Mister Reynolds," she said again, showing a slight gap in her front teeth. "Won't you come in?"

Skip walked past her, catching the delicate fragrance of her perfume. She smelled like a field of roses. He stood waiting for an order, his mind more on the girl than Ezekiel Washington, the beautiful girl who quietly closed the door, tip-toed to her desk and settled into her seat. She motioned him to one of two empty chairs and went back to typing a letter. Skip tried to relax, but found himself on the edge of his seat, rubbing his hands together and looking around the spare room. Framed pictures of advertisements for Esquire Lightening Creme, Mother Helen's Spiritual Advice, Uncle Ned's Dream Book and the Ezekiel Washington Colored Actors School covered the walls. He frowned at the school ad and put his mind back on the girl at the typewriter. He smiled every time she looked his way. Broadway's noise floated in through an open window. A church bell rang out ten times. Skip stood and smoothed his suit.

"Time to meet the man," he said.

"I'm afraid Zeke's busy right now, Mister Reynolds. He'll buzz me when he's ready."

Fine. More time to sit here and stare at this pretty girl.

"Are you one of Zeke's friends?" she asked, looking up from her page.

"Naw. I'm in the restaurant business. Helping out in one of Central Avenue's finer establishments," Skip smiled. "It's just little something to hold me till I make it in Hollywood.

The girl raised her eyebrows and laughed to herself. "That a Texas drawl I hear?"

Skip nodded. "I'm from Tunis, a little town . . ."

"Bout ninety miles out of Houston. Trains don't even stop there as I hear tell."

Skip brightened and leaned forward. "Where you from to know 'bout Tunis?"

"Somerville," she said.

"Somerville! I did some work in the railroad tie plant over there. I don't remembering seeing you. Hell, I'd remember seeing you."

The girl smiled and primped her hair. "My family left there a long time ago. I barely remember the town. Have you been out here a long time?"

"Going on four months." He pointed to the ad. "Whatever happened to that?"

The girl followed his eyes. "The acting school? Discontinued, I believe. It was just one of Zeke's schemes," she said and pointed to the other ads. "He does a little bit of everything."

Just then Washington's gruff voice barked through an intercom on the girl's desk. "Is that boy out there?"

"He's sitting here waiting on you, Mister Washington," she said.

"Well, send him in."

Skip stood and tugged at his suit again. "What's your name, Texas gal?"

"Sapphire," she said. "Sapphire Louise Davis."

"Pretty name for a pretty gal," Skip said as he walked towards Washington's office. "Say, maybe we can get together sometime, cut a little rug. Now, I know where to find you."

"Maybe," Sapphire said and busied herself with some papers on her desk.

The nauseating stench of cigars slapped Skip in the face the moment he opened Washington's door. It was everywhere, in the walls, deep in the rug, in every breath he took. He coughed and looked at Washington sitting behind a huge, polished mahogany desk set on a platform. The fat man leaned back in his chair and casually rolled a stogie between his fingers. He didn't smile, just sat there on his throne, like a low-rent potentate. Skip eyed the framed, autographed pictures on the walls, smiling photos of Steppin' Fetchit, Louise Beavers, Clarence Muse and others, all of them giving testimonials about their great friend Ezekiel Washington, who now sat august and proud behind his raised desk.

"What the hell makes you think you can act?" he snarled.

The question caught Skip off guard. "Well, uh, I don't know. I like moving pictures. It don't look too hard to me."

"Have you ever acted before, done any road shows, vaudeville, theater? Anything?"

Skip shook his head. "You promised to teach me."

Washington waved his hands as if he were dismissing a bad idea. "Sit down."

Moments passed, Skip fidgeting, his eyes darting around the room as Washington stared him down. Finally, Skip took a deep breath and broke the silence.

"You told me last night you could help me."

"That I did," Washington said, leaning over to tap his cigar on an ashtray. "And I am."

"How's that?'

"Just look, you've already gotten farther than every other darky in chocolate town who wastes his time running to them cattle calls at the Lincoln. You're sitting here in a downtown office, talking to an agent. You're getting more than your five dollars' worth."

"Humph," Skip shrugged. "But this ain't near what you promised, Mister Washington. You said to come on out to Hollywood and you'd put me in moving pictures. Didn't say nothing 'bout sitting here talking."

"Things change." Washington stood, stepped down and walked around the room, waving his cigar as he talked. "Life is change, Mister Reynolds. Mind if I call you Skip? Well, Skip, the best laid plans can come to naught, or they can change, like a river, starting out in one direction and turn in another. Look at these people," he pointed to the photographs. "Every one of them has seen changes in their lives. Why, old Steppin' used to be nothing but a horse groom." Washington stopped, jammed his cigar in a corner of his mouth. "You've come across a change, Skip. A plan has come to nothing. But there can be victory in defeat. The Phoenix does rise from its own ashes."

Skip frowned. What the hell was Washington getting at with all his talk about change, a Phoenix and Steppin' Fetchit? The fat man leaned over his desk and punched the intercom.

"Miss Davis? Bring in that Paradise script," he turned to Skip. "Something you might be interested in."

A moment later, Sapphire stepped in, handed Washington a bound sheaf of papers and gave Skip a wink on her way out. He watched her go, smiling at the sway of her round hips swinging from side to side.

"Pretty, isn't she," Washington said, stepping back up on the platform and sitting down. He tossed Skip the papers. "Take a look at this. It's from Paradise Studios. They're doing a low-budget *Gone with the Wind*."

Skip flipped through the pages, pretending to study the words. "What's this got to do with me?"

"You came out here to get in moving pictures, didn't you? Well, you're looking at the raw product, boy. A script. You want a piece of the action, don't you?"

"Sure, but . . ." Skip kept flipping through the pages.

"I know this isn't how you had it planned in your dreams, Skip. But that's a funny thing about dreams. They disappear as soon as you open your eyes. Now," Washington opened a desk drawer and took out a sheet of paper. He unscrewed his fountain pen and held it towards Skip. "Sign here and I'll have you on Paradise Studio's lot next week."

"What's this?" Skip scooted his chair forward.

"It's a contract," Washington said, leaning back to relight his cigar. "All the actors have 'em. Bogart. Flynn. Muse. Everybody."

"What happens if I sign?"

"Then you agree to let me be your agent. I put you in moving pictures and get a percentage of whatever you make. It's all boiler-plate stuff. Nothing for you to worry about. Hell, most folks don't even read it." He pushed the pen and paper towards Skip. "Just sign on the dotted line, boy."

"What kind of percentage you getting," Skip asked.

"Fifty."

Skip pushed the paper away. "I may be from the country, but I ain't no fool. You're asking me to give you half of what I make, and I'm doing all the work. What if I don't sign?"

Washington stood, shook his head and started chomping on his cigar. "You don't know the first thing about moving pictures, do you? You think you can do it all by yourself. Just walk up to Selznick and say: 'I want to be in moving pictures.' He won't listen to you, but he'll listen to me. See, I got connections," he leaned back and barked into the intercom. "Miss Davis, get me Paradise Studios. Kurt Marshall. Richmond five, two-five, three-five." Washington turned back to Skip. "Without me, you'll be running from cattle call to cattle call. With me, you'll be in Paradise Studios next week. Now, what do you say?"

Skip didn't know what to say. Paradise Studios! Next week! He picked up the contract and tried to decipher the dense language, his brow wrinkling as he read: "Party of the first part . . . blah blah blah . . . Party of the second part . . . et cetera et cetera . . . Agrees to the aforementioned stipulation . . . herewith and forthwith . . ." He shook his head, gazed at the pictures on the wall. Those people trusted Washington. Why shouldn't he? Sapphire's voice came in over the intercom.

"Mister Marshall's not in, Zeke."

"Fine," barked Washington. "Try him later." He tapped the contract and looked at Skip.

"Are you going to sign or waste my time?"

Skip grabbed the pen and signed.

"You're in moving pictures," Washington said, taking the contract and stuffing it back in his desk. Be at Paradise Studios next Thursday. Seven p.m., sharp. Ask for Kurt Marshall. I'll call ahead so you won't have any problem getting in. And don't come on C.P. time."

Skip looked up, wondering what had just happened. Washington said he was in. Just like that! He stood and smiled for the first time.

"Seven p.m., sharp. I'll be there, Mister Washington. Yes sir, you can count on that." He reached across the desk and shook Washington's hand.

"Call me Zeke," Washington said, stepping around his desk and putting a friendly hand on Skip's shoulder. "After all, we're partners now."

"Am I getting a role?"

"That's a lot to ask your first time out, Skip. Let's say you're having an audition, but I'll see that you get something." He pushed Skip towards the door. "You'd better get a move on. The Dancing Bar-B-Que opens in fifteen minutes."

"Fifteen minutes! I'm gon'." Skip ran for the door, stopped and turned around. "Thanks Mister Washington, uh, Zeke. Thank you!"

Then he was gone, backing out of the office, lingering just long enough to catch Sapphire's eye, before taking the stairs fast as he could, running down Broadway and catching a red car bound for Central Avenue.

Outside the Dancing Bar-B-Que, a hungry crowd waited. Inside Henry and Diana tried to keep pace with the orders that flowed nonstop. Dirty dishes piled up in the sink. Diana grabbed the last clean set of plates, while Henry wiped his sweaty brow and slid three plates of ribs down the counter, each one stopping in front of a ready customer. He yelled as soon as he saw Skip.

"Where the hell you been?"

"Downtown," Skip said. "I told you."

"Well, you best get your tail in that kitchen before I put up a 'Help Wanted' sign."

Diana caught him on his way to the back stairs. "You still working here?"

"Is Roosevelt president?'

"Yeah, and he's doing a damn sight better job than you is right now. I got people's lined up waiting and nary a clean dish in the place."

"I'm on it. I'm on it," Skip said, brushing her off and heading upstairs. He tossed off his suit, jumped into a pair of work pants, changed shoes and ran back down to the kitchen, pulling a tee shirt over his head.

He looked in the cafe. Work had stopped. Everybody was waiting on him. Nothing to it. He turned on the water grabbed a handful of soap powder and tossed it into the sink. Steam started rising. He flashed Henry the thumbs up sign, plunged his arms in elbow deep and fished out the first freshly washed plate of the day.

"THINK SATCH CAN HOLD 'EM, BUSTER?" SKIP LEANED DOWN and smiled at the two-year-old boy sitting on his lap. He was a cute kid, with big playful, almond-shaped eyes just like his mama. Sapphire leaned over and kissed her baby boy, who had not cried once since she gave him to Skip.

"Come on, Buster. Cheer for Satchel Paige," she said and tousled the fine baby hair that fell in loose curls from her son's head.

The entire rightfield side of Wrigley Stadium let out a cheer as the lanky right-hander and his team of Negro Leaguers took the field for the bottom of the ninth inning. Anybody on the avenue who could get a ticket was here. Pee Wee was supposed to be in the seat next to Skip, but his boss wouldn't let him off for the game. So, he gave Skip the tickets, told him to call somebody and have a good time. Skip called on Lady Luck and dialed Sapphire at Zeke's office. He couldn't believe his luck when she said, "Yes." She loved baseball. Then she told him about Buster. They were a package. She wasn't coming without her child. She said it as if it was a test, and he knew there was only one response.

He took another slug of Rainer. "I don't know, Buster. Don't seem like Satch brought his heat today."

Paige had been struggling all day. The fastball wasn't popping into the catcher's mitt the way it did a few years ago when Satch went 31 and

4 with the Pittsburgh Crawfords. Even the hesitation pitch didn't seem to fool anybody. The Scuffling Cats, a collection of major leaguers and minor league hopefuls on a winter tour, had been hitting Paige hard, especially the last two innings. Line drives ripped through the infield, long flies rocketed to the warning track. Cool Papa made a spectacular catch at the centerfield wall that had everybody, black and white, whooping and hollering. Now the Cats were up for one last chance at breaking the 4-4 tie and taking the win. The Sentinel's sportswriter had warned the avenue not to expect too much. The guy said Satch had gone soft pitching in Mexico, said maybe Satch's career was coming to an end. Even Sapphire knew better than to believe that. Still, she nervously rolled up her score sheet and tapped her lap as Joe DiMaggio stepped up to the plate with the grace and confidence that had made the Yankee fielder the terror of American League pitchers.

"C'mon, DiMag," a voice called out from the leftfield side where the white folks sat. "Hit that nigger's ball outta here so's we can go home."

A spirited black voice fired back. "Not today, leftfield. He ain't hitting nothing today."

The ballfield quieted as nine-thousand pairs of eyes focused on the duel between Paige and the Cats. The pitcher read Josh Gibson's signals and had a two-and-o count on DiMaggio who caught the third fastball late and fouled out. A sigh of relief went up along the rightfield stands.

"Show you right, honey," said a big woman sitting in the next row. Then she stood and yelled loud enough for everyone in the stadium to hear. "How you like that, leftfield?" She sat down and looked over her shoulder at Skip, Buster and Sapphire. "Damn peckerwoods ain't got a thing to say now."

Sapphire frowned at the woman's cursing. But she was happy for the out. "Downhill from here," she said.

"Yeah," Skip said. "This next guy, Thompson, he ain't nothing but a Triple-A rookie. Easy pickings."

A big, muscular farm boy strode up to the plate, the fat end of the bat hidden within his huge fist. He dug his cleats into the dirt at home plate, took a few practice swings and waited, his bat flicking back and forth like a war club. Paige took a deep breath, kicked up his left leg and came across at top speed. Thompson didn't have a chance. Strike one! Another fastball smacked into the catcher's mitt.

"Ste-e-erike two!" the umpire bellowed.

"Hot damn!" Skip yelled, forgetting to watch his language. "Buster, we're rolling now. All we need is one more pitch."

Paige stepped off the mound and shook his arms. Quitting time. He shook off Gibson's sign, nodded when he saw what he wanted, the fastball, hard, high and strong, blazing toward the outside corner. But it dipped and strayed toward the middle of the plate. Thompson timed his swing perfectly, caught the ball full on the meat of his bat. Skip knew it was gone the moment he heard the crack.

"Buster, there goes the old ball game," he said.

"Oh, shoot," said Sapphire, watching as the ball sailed higher and higher.

Cool Papa tossed his glove in the air. The homer cleared the deepest part of centerfield and landed in the street outside the ballpark. A raucous cheer went up all along leftfield, and then there was swearing and cursing and bad-mouthing on both sides as young Thompson jogged around the diamond, clapping and waving his arms, jumping into the crowd of teammates waiting at home plate. The players from both teams congratulated each other, their camaraderie lost on the fans who still fired insults back and forth.

"Guess we played Thompson a little too cheap," Skip said to Sapphire.

"Oh, that old farm boy just got lucky." She turned and scooped up Buster from Skip's lap. "Come to mommy, little man. Thank you so much, Skip. I had so much fun, and Buster did too. He's glowing!"

The little boy bounced up and down, saying, "Home run! Home run!"

Skip tapped out a Chesterfield and slouched back in his seat, making sure to blow the smoke away from Buster. "He's going to grow up to be a great baseball fan." He grabbed one of Buster's tiny fingers and looked the baby in the eye. "And guess what, Buster? You can say you saw Satchel Paige and Joe DiMaggio when they were kings."

"But don't mention that Satchel Paige lost the game," laughed Sapphire, nuzzling her baby and kissing him again. "I can't remember the last time Buster sat with somebody and didn't fuss. You must have something special Mister Reynolds."

"Must be my country charm," Skip replied and winked at Sapphire. "It worked on you, didn't it?"

"Enough to get me out of the house." She gave him a coy smile, then wrinkled her nose at the sour smell of spilled beer, the rank odor of stale sweat and cigarette smoke. "Let's get out of here."

She pushed into the crowd heading for the turnstiles, her son on her hip. Skip followed close behind, wishing he could put a friendly arm around her waist and walk beside her, but knowing it was too early for such a move. He was just glad to be with her, even if she did have a baby. The boy gave him a safe way of talking to her without having to struggle with awkward silences and the clumsy conversation that comes with discovering another. He reached out and shook the little boy's pudgy hand. Thank God for Buster.

The rightfield crowd moved slowly, their faces carrying a sad look of defeat. They dreaded the bets they'd have to pay off, the boasts they'd have to take back. Folks grumbled and muttered amongst themselves, reassured each other that Thompson's homer was the damndest thing they'd ever seen. The boy couldn't do that again in life!

Outside the stadium, Sapphire stopped and hiked Buster up on her shoulder. "I think this little man has had enough excitement for one afternoon," she said, running her fingers through his curls as he began to doze.

"Yeah, you best get that boy on home," Skip said, wondering how to say "good-bye" and whether he'd have another chance with Sapphire. "Thanks for coming out." His words stumbled a moment, his heart uncertain. "Are you ever available after sundown?"

"Maybe," she said, giving him the coy smile again as she rocked Buster. "Why don't you call me? Good luck on your audition. Now, let me get this sleepy-head on home."

Skip watched her until she had boarded a Red car, then waved as it pulled off, catching her parting smile. His heart rejoiced. He had passed the test. Next time, Buster was staying home.

He looked up at the clock on Wrigley Stadium. It read five-thirty, plenty of time to get to Paradise Studios. Ezekiel Washington told him to be there no later than seven. Skip didn't know what kind of audition Washington was sending him to, but it had to be more than a Lincoln Theater cattle call. Washington was an agent. He caught a downtown streetcar, transferred to one heading for Santa Monica and got off a block past the grand, pink pastel entrance of Paradise Studios. Skip hoped

Bobby Mumford was working the gate so he could have the satisfaction of walking right in, and Mumford could do nothing to stop him. Near the gates, a gang of tourists marked the day's comings and goings. A couple of people stepped toward him as he approached, squinting, wondering if he was Steppin' Fetchit, or maybe Willie Sleep 'N' Eats Best. Certainly not Gable. But what the hell. An autograph was an autograph. One man cautiously pulled an autograph book from his back pocket and held it out. He stopped after a few steps, disappointment draining the unctuous smile from his face.

Skip walked on. He saw a skinny, slump-shouldered man, sitting inside the guard station, eating a ham sandwich and reading a copy of Undercover Detective. It was Bobby Munford. The guard jerked open the station window, picked up a clipboard and rifled through the pages until he found what he was looking for. "What's your name, boy?"

"William Henry Reynolds, and I'm here to . . ."

"Can it. I can read." He shoved the clipboard toward Skip. "Sign here."

He grabbed the pen and thought about his first day in Lost Angeles. "Last time I was here, you sent me away," he said, signing his name in his most elegant script, the final 's' tailing off in a cascade of curlicues. "Now, I'm signing in. How you like that?"

Mumford shrugged. "Don't bother me none. Lots of folks get in once. Some twice. But pigs will fly before some country nigger like you becomes a regular. Now move on."

He picked up his detective magazine and went back to reading. Skip headed on into Paradise Studios, walking slowly at first, then breaking into a fast run. He leaped every few steps, laughed loudly, throwing up his arms and wishing he would turn cartwheels. He was in! God dammit! He was in! The studio beckoned with unknown adventures. An evening breeze danced with him as he passed fairy tale scenes of King Arthur's Castle and green, lush forests painted on huge boards held up by stilts; sauntered along beside him as he strolled past a stretch of one-sided wooden buildings in the style of the old West. He stopped in front of the Long Branch Saloon, hearing in his mind jerky ragtime strains and drunken cowboy voices. He held his hands away from his hips, gunslinger style, turned like Tom Mix on the fast draw and fired off a couple of rounds. A couple of desperadoes fell. A pretty girl, frightened but now without fear because her hero had made the town safe again, hugged him. He felt her hands and a soft kiss. Sapphire. He smiled bravely, casually blew the smoke away from his forefingers, holstered his hands back in his pockets and walked on into the sunset, affecting a slightly bowlegged stride.

Each step took him deeper into this land of sound stages and moveable scenery, this land that knew no boundaries except those of imagination, this factory that churned out fantasies for the silver screens of the Rialtos, Bijous, Metropolitans, and Orpheums lining the Main Streets, Broadways, Lincoln and Central avenues of countless American cities and towns, each theater a magical place where you could forget everyday life and lose yourself in the dreams playing in the dark. He walked on, stalking lions through painted scenes of African jungles; chasing gangsters beneath fake big city skylines; heading west on a desolate stretch of desert highway to no where. A brand new 1939 Dodge, cut off just in front of the windshield, caught his attention. The machine sat on four springs where the wheels should have been. What was it doing here? What was it supposed to do? He checked it from the front and the behind, stood and scratched his head: He couldn't figure it out. He plunged deeper into the studio's labyrinth, his mind wandering to the day when he'd be back home, sitting in the Rialto Theater with some gal knocked out by his oh-so-fine city ways, and he'd hold her close and kiss-talk in her ear about how Hollywood really wasn't so tough, how he used to pick cotton, just up the road mind you, until he got a notion to make a name in Hollywood. Now he was back, just passing through really, giving the homefolks a chance to celebrate his good fortune and see the moving picture he was in, the one they were showing especially for him, the one with his big scenes, the next scene in fact. You couldn't miss him. He smiled to himself. That's how it was going to be.

The street dead-ended and he realized he didn't even know how to get back to the front gate. He turned and retraced his path, but it was no good. He hadn't paid any attention on the way in. Now he was lost, and it was getting late. Had Marshall left? Washington told him to be there on time, not C.P. time. His heart picked up speed. Anxiety tossed him along the empty street. He started running again, scared now, cursing himself for not asking direction, for being so damned puffed up about being here, when he really wasn't in here, just going to an audition where nothing was promised. He ran halfway down blocks, looking for something famil-iar; the jungle, the chopped up sedan, the saloon. He found none of them. A lost little boy inside him started to cry, but he kept the boy in. He had to control himself. Think. He stopped, his chest heaving. Up the street he saw someone standing stock still. He yelled, but the stranger didn't seem to hear him. He yelled again, started running, waving his arms. The guy must be deaf, he thought, a deaf Indian.

"Man, what's wrong with you," he yelled from a distance of half a block. "Didn't you hear me call . . ." He caught his breath and stepped back. Goddamn! A wooden cigar store Indian stared straight ahead.

A nervous laugh spilled from Skip's lips. He ran again, not knowing where he was going, just running, down one street, turning up another, passing the collective junk of Hollywood. Up ahead he saw headlights. The sedan! He ran towards the lights, wondering who had turned them on, figuring that once he got to the sedan, he could find his way back. He didn't notice the headlights were moving until it was nearly too late. A truck's tires screamed against the asphalt. A driver leaned out the win-dow.

"Hey, Mac. You trying to kill yourself."

Skip staggered toward the truck, his mind struggling to fine words. "I . . . I . . ."

"Say, buddy," the driver said, concerned. "You been hitting the bot-tle? Swear to God you look like the D.T.'s been running you ragged."

"No . . . No . . . I," he fought to get his mind straight. "I'm looking for a Mister Kurt Marshall's office. I cain't find it. Do you know where it is?"

The driver pushed his hat back and leaned on his steering wheel. "Can't say as I do. Who's this Marshall anyway?"

"A director. I need to see him for an audition. He's making a moving picture."

"You sure you was suppose to meet him tonight? It's kind-a late."

"Yes, tonight. At seven. Do you know where he is?"

"Hell, partner. I ain't never heard of him, but you might try over in them bungalows back of Stage Nine. They got some sure-fired night owls over there. Keep walking till you get to the next block, where the haunt-ed house is. Turn left there. You'll see the lights burning."

"Thanks," Skip said, calming down.

"No problem," the driver leaned out his window and studied Skip's face. "You sure you're all right?" Skip nodded. "Okay," the driver said, shifting into first. "See you around."

The truck wobbled off, its cargo of boom microphones, cameras and spot lights rattling in the night. Skip followed the driver's directions until he saw a solitary light burning in a row of dark offices. As he drew near, he heard black voices laughing and talking jive. The voices stopped when he knocked. An older black man, his hair gone to white, opened the door.

"You must be number four," he said, stepping aside. "Come in and sit down. Marshall ain't here yet."

Skip nodded around the spare room. Must not be a big-time Hollywood director, he thought, not with this falling-apart furniture. One of the guys, middle-aged and thickening at the waist, sat on a ratty couch, legs propped on a rickety coffee table. A handsome, light-skinned young brother relaxed in an old armchair. He looked familiar, but Skip couldn't place his face. The young brother smiled knowingly at the two older guys as Skip plopped down on a frayed, beat-up easy chair.

"Shit!"

Skip shot out of the chair. A steel spring had ripped through the seat cushion and bit him on the behind. He checked his pants for a tear, while the other guys tried to keep from laughing.

"Should've told you about that chair," the young brother said.

"Damn right," Skip said, moving to the wall.

He pulled out his pack of Chesterfields, offered it around. The older men shook their heads, but the high-yellow brother grabbed the pack and tapped out a smoke.

"Didn't I see you at that Lincoln cattle call," he said, flicking open his silver lighter, casually bringing the flame to his cigarette, then holding it for Skip. "You said you were going to be as big as B'rer Rabbit Molasses."

Skip rifled through his memory. It was Harry-O. "Thought you were Harlem bound?"

"I am, but I heard about this and figured I'd see if I could make a little traveling money before I moved on." He blew out a stream of smoke. "Man, I haven't done any Hollywood work in months."

"You know why, don't you," the white-haired man said grimly. "You ain't the most African looking nigger on Central Avenue."

"That doesn't mean I can't blacken up a bit and play one," Harry-O fired back.

"Boy, all the grease paint in the world wouldn't help you. You got to be born with this," the old man patted his dark brown skin. "You cain't buy it in a store. 'Bout the onliest thing you good for is the Son of Peola, and I don't suspect white folks'll be doing that anytime soon."

"White folks." Harry-O spat out the words. "Bad enough they only see us one kind of way, but they got to see us as all being the same color, too."

The middle-aged guy broke in. "Bet you didn't hear 'bout that Tarzan picture they did a couple months back, did you?"

"What Tarzan picture?"

"See what I mean?" The guy looked around the room. "Hear they had half of Central Avenue running through the jungle, all of us set to sacrifice the lovely white maiden to the hungry god of almighty blackness, then Weismuller got to swing in on his vine and spoil all the fun. All of this going on while our light-skinned brother here pines for a chance to act."

"And how 'bout that Roman one," the old man said. "I made good money on that. Always room in them pictures for a few Ethiopian guards, or slaves." He turned to Harry-O. "Bet your agent man didn't send you on that one?"

Harry-O shook his head. "Ethiopia did not spread forth her wings for me that time."

"This Son of Ham bears a double curse," the middle-aged man said. "He is black, but the white man does not see him that way. To him, our Son of Peola is some sort of curious entity, a mistake in the biological chain."

"Wasn't no mistake," Harry-O said. "Some dumb fuck ofay popped my mama and made tracks. So here I is." He stood and bowed. "America's tragic mulatto." Harry-O slumped back on the sofa and let out a pained laugh. "But that's all right," he said. "I got a good feeling about this moving picture. I mean, it wouldn't be right for old master not to have at least one little not-so-darky child. Hell, them guys was always sneaking down to the cabins for a piece."

Silence filled the room. Skip thought about the Tarzan picture with its black folks running through a Hollywood jungle. He was glad he'd missed that one. Bad enough to play a slave, but an African native. Not in this life. He didn't even know if he could make his eyes bug out. He looked at the two older guys and imagined them standing at attention in Roman costumes, spears in hand. Then he stole a glance at Harry-O, silently sitting, a thick shock of dusty blond hair falling across his forehead. The Son of Peola. He laughed to himself, trying hard to see Fredi Washington as anybody's mama.

Outside the door, tired footsteps approached, heavy and measured. The doorknob rattled. A disheveled white man in a rumbled brown suit lurched into the room. With his scraggly beard and blood-shot eyes, he looked like he'd just come off a three-day binge and had spent the entire time in the suit he wore. He tightened his lips in what Skip figured was supposed to be a smile. The others in the room did the same, but Skip couldn't stop frowning. Was this Kurt Marshall? The director? Probably not. An assistant at best. The white man nodded to Skip and Harry-O, gave a smile to the two older guys.

"How ya doing Dave, Tom."

"Can't complain, Mister Marshall," the old man said. "What you got for us today?"

"The Ghost of Dixie," Marshall said, passing out scripts. "Once again, we venture into cliche, and as always, a few good-natured darkies are needed."

"Oohh, I jess loves this parts," the white-haired guy said in an absurdly high-pitched voice. "Do we gets to sing and dance and pat our feet on de lebby?"

"No, but it can be arranged," Marshall said, moving towards the inner office. "I'll be waiting."

One by one the others went in, while Skip read the script, searching for clues and trying to still his pumping leg. It was a crazy scene. Big Tom, the plantation's boss slave, was telling his little missy how the Yankees was coming and there was gon' be trouble and everybody was leaving. Skip shook his head. Hell yeah everybody was leaving. The freedom train was coming. But Big Tom wasn't getting on. He promised little missy he'd stay and protect her. Damn, Skip thought, remembering Delilah in "Imitiation of Life." Nobody 'cept white folks believe this. He read through the scene again and again, thought about how he'd play Big Tom, how he'd make it convincing. The older guys were in and out of Marshall's office in minutes. Harry-O took a little longer, but when he came out, his smile lit up the room.

"Don't keep the man waiting, Texas," he said. "Get on in there."

"You get a part?" Skip said, looking up from the script.

"Shoot, my brother, this fast-talking boy don't let any chance slip by. Good ole' massa's gonna have at least one high-yellow child. See you on the set."

The door slammed behind him and Skip heard Harry-O's whistle fading off.

"Number four," Marshall yelled.

Skip waited a moment, sucked up his courage, slapped the script against his thigh and walked into Marshall's office. Gray clouds of cigarette smoke floated throughout the shuttered room. A fresh cigarette rested in a full ashtray, burning steady. Marshall sat behind a littered desk, his back to the door. Skip stared at the bald spot poking above the high-backed chair, the cigarette burns on the desk, the dark, burned circles on the rug, the papers and coffee cups strewn on the floors and shelves. A half-eaten plate of steak sat on a ratty chair, the meat gone gray and stiff, the grease and gravy congealed like old gelatin. Skip cleared his throat and waited. Marshall wheeled around, rubbed his tired eyes and picked up his cigarette.

"You the one Zeke sent over?" Skip nodded; Marshall shook his head. "That man must have an endless supply. Take it from the top," he said, turning around to face the blank wall.

Skip watched the cigarette smoke steaming up like the frail wisps from a winter chimney. He started talking. "Missy Lee! Missy Lee! They's Yankees coming up the road and they got them mean scalawags with 'em." He stopped. Big Tom sounded like some tail-swishing punk.

"Relax," Marshall said from behind his chair. "Try it again. With feeling, if that's possible."

Skip tried to imagine life on some South Carolina plantation. How would a loyal slave act and sound when he had a chance for freedom? But the Yankees were not his liberators. They were evil men bent on driving him away from his beloved Missy Lee. They wanted to destroy his life. Once more, with feeling.

"Missy Lee! Missy Lee," he pleaded, his voice deep and slow, but edged with fear. "They's Yankees coming up the road and they got them mean scalawags with 'em, burning everything."

"What are you going to do, Big Tom?" Marshall asked from behind his chair, his voice sounding flat and tired. "Are you going to leave us like the rest did?"

Skip saw the words, but his mouth wouldn't work. The script was all wrong. Big Tom wouldn't stick by this gal and her papa. He'd probably help the Yankees burn the place down, help himself to the food stock, even the score any way he could. The script said no such thing. Big Tom was a good nigger, the kind white folks liked to see. He'd stay and die to save his little missy. Skip dropped to one knee and pretended to look into a little girl's frightened eyes.

"Big Tom ain't gon' leave you little missy," he said, "I'se gon' stay right here."

Marshall chuckled and turned around, raised an eyebrow. This boy couldn't act his way out of a wet, paper bag. The scene continued, Skip calling out Big Tom's part, Marshall deadpan, reading the part of Missy Lee. Bit by bit, Skip felt himself getting comfortable with Big Tom's character. He liked the end. Big Tom caught a bullet in the chest. He grabbed a coat rack, slumped against it, imagining it to be the columned post of an ante-bellum mansion. He staggered across the room.

"Run Missy Lee! Run!" He said, his voice weak and dying, his mind on Edward G. Robinson in "Little Caesar."

Then he fell, crawled toward Marshall's desk, groped for it, but collapsed before he could reach it. So this is Hollywood, he thought, lying on the floor, holding his breath against the stink of old dust, cigarette smoke, spilled coffee and God knows what else.

Marshall stood and leaned across his desk, smiling as he looked down on Skip's prostrate body. "Haven't done much acting, have you?"

Skip rolled over and looked up. "Not really."

"It shows," Marshall said, lighting another cigarette. "Get up off that rug. It hasn't been cleaned in months, maybe years."

"How'd I do?" Skip said, standing and brushing lint from his mouth.

"Terrible. Guess you had a little problem with the script's believability, huh?"

"No sir, I just . . ."

Marshall waved off the reply. "No need to lie about it. I mean, truthfully, you didn't buy that slop, a man choosing to stay and help the very people who'd kept him a slave, people who might've even sold his children?"

Confusion stole Skip's words. Marshall looked like he wanted to know the truth, but that couldn't be. Why should he care what some colored boy off the avenue thought about his picture. Best to just lie. White folks usually couldn't tell the difference anyway.

"I don't know what Big Tom would do, Mister Marshall. Maybe he liked being a slave," he said, seeing a curious smile go across Marshall's face. "Or maybe he was afraid of freedom."

Marshall nodded. "Maybe. But it really doesn't matter. After all, we're not here in search of truth. Entertainment. That's what we do. Make people laugh, forget about life for awhile."

He stared hard at Skip, his deep-set eyes looking even more tired and blood-shot. He crushed out his cigarette, slumped back into his chair and rubbed his eyes. Skip watched, surprised to see a white man acting like just another guy worn out and tired.

"Did I get the part?" he asked.

Marshall shook his head. "No, no, no." He looked up and saw disappointment on Skip's face. "Zeke didn't promise you a speaking part, did he?" Skip shook his head. "Well, then, don't worry about it. There's always room for one more darkie. Interested?"

"If you mean getting in on this moving picture, sure."

"You're in," Marshall said, spinning around in his chair, then handing Skip a pass. "Be at sound stage six around ten Monday morning. Makeup and all that." He waved off Skip's smile. "Don't get too happy about it. It's just scene work, crowds. You might even end up on the cutting room floor."

"Oh, I ain't worried 'bout that, Mister Marshall. I just want to get in, get myself known. Then, I'll really start something."

Marshall tried to smile, but could only manage the tightened lips he'd shown when he walked through the door. "You need a lift? I'm heading downtown."

"That's all right. I feel like walking."

"Then I'll see you Monday."

Skip hustled out of the office and into Paradise Studios' wonderland, leaping and dancing beneath a blue-black sky, splashed with stars and the pale light of a half-moon. Search light beam swung crazily overhead. He headed for their source, thinking he'd kill some time before heading back to Central Avenue for a real celebration with Pee Wee and whoever else might show up at the tea pad. He was glad at the way things turned out, proud that he had stood up to Zeke and forced him to make good on his word. He liked the satisfaction of getting his way. It was a feeling he could get used to real quick.

Hollywood Boulevard was crowded and alive. People made their way in and out of clubs and restaurants. Taxis pulled up to the curbs. Down the boulevard four search lights were grouped in front of Grauman's Chinese Theater. He joined an excited crowd bunched up around the theater's entrance, stood on tip toe and craned his neck to see the red carpet leading from the theater's front door to the end of the sidewalk. A radio announcer yelled into his microphone. Photographers' flash bulbs went off like fire works, the men popping bulbs out of their cameras and swiftly reloading, to catch the well-dressed folks who stepped out of limousines and walked up the carpet, stopping for a word or two with the radio men, or a wave to the anxious crowd that pressed forward, countless arms extended with autograph books clutched in hands, beseeching the famous for a signature and a bit of scribble, "best regards," "love you madly." An electricity born of adoration pulsed through the crowd, gaining strength as it flowed from those at the rear to those in the front row, where it became a thing alive, transforming grown folks into wide-eyed begging children, delighted to be within arm's reach of their icons. Skip inched forward, drawn by the near desperate clamor. The radio announcer spoke in a rapid-fire staccato.

"It's amazing, ladies and gentlemen," he said. "Simply amazing. One of the biggest crowds Hollywood has ever seen. And what a night! Beautiful, simply beautiful. Stars everywhere! The search lights like fingers pointing to here, Grauman's Chinese Theater in the heart, the very heart of Hollywood. Just listen to the crowd!"

He leaned the microphone towards a row of people behind him, smiled and nodded. A dozen frenzied voices let loose. "People are going wild," he yelled, pulling back the microphone. "And here comes the stars."

A stagecoach, pulled by six black horses, stopped in front of the theater. The Ringo Kid, resplendent in black, with polished silver spurs and pearl-handled pistols stepped off the coach, followed by Doc. They helped off the leading lady, her blonde hair flowing loose beneath a bonnet, a flowery parasol in her hand. A barrage of flashbulbs exploded and the air carried the pungent smell of sulfur. The crowd howled as the Ringo Kid did a fast draw and fired a couple of blanks above their heads. Two P.R. men ran along both sides of the entrance, passing out 8x10 autographed glossy photographs of the Kid. Hands stretched forward. Strained for the pictures passed among them like holy wafers. Hardly a picture passed into the crowd complete. Most were shredded as two, three, four people fought over the prized treasures. The radio announcer dragged his microphone toward the entrance for a quick word with the Kid, then raced back down the sidewalk, talking constantly into the microphone, every now and then leaning it towards the crowd.

"If only all of you could be here," he said, "then you could see that this is truly the greatest place on earth!"

Skip turned away, enough of being a spectator. He fought his way back through the crowd and headed for the streetcars that would carry him back to the celebration on Central Avenue. It was Kitchen Mechanic's Night!

"Hey, movie star," a female voice called out behind him.

He didn't turn around, figuring some fan was trying to catch her heart throb's attention. He hurried to the waiting zone as a half-empty Red car rumbled to a stop.

"Hey movie star!"

Again the voice, faintly familiar, this time accompanied by a sharp staccato of high heels. He looked over his shoulder and felt his heart flutter. It was Sapphire. "Hold that streetcar!"

Sapphire ran up beside him, paused to catch her breath, then stepped on. Skip gallantly stepped aside and caught a whiff of roses as she passed. She'd changed clothes since the baseball game and now wore a blue pastel dress, snug at the waist, with a matching hat. Skip watched her take a seat near the middle of the streetcar. He playfully pretended to look for somewhere else to sit, before stopping beside her.

"Is this seat taken?"

"It is now," she said, sliding toward the window in one smooth, graceful motion, gathering her dress and patting the empty space beside her.

Skip plopped down, his spirit struggling to contain the double-barreled joy surging through him. He was in a moving picture and Sapphire was at his side.

"I must be living right," he said. "What brings you out this way?"

"That premiere," she said. "Had to pay my respects. Zeke got Charlie Johnson a role in the picture, a speaking role, mind you. You should have seen him working the crowd. Made sure the *Sentinel* reporter got everything, especially pictures of him and Charlie. I was on my way home, then I saw this nice young man getting on the streetcar."

She looked at him, her clear brown eyes demure and steady, searching his. Skip held her gaze for a moment, feeling a blush come over him. He inched closer to her, felt the tingle of her thighs against his as he casually raised his arm and rested it on the back of their seat. Sapphire straightened up and shoved her purse between them, scooting him back to his side of the bench seat.

"Thank you again for the baseball game, Skip. Buster loved it. He must've said 'home run' fifty times on the way home," said Sapphire. "I'm glad he didn't scare you off. I've been pretty much on the shelf since he came along."

Skip tossed her concern aside. "He was great to have along. Smart, too. Picked right up on the game."

She smiled. "He had a good teacher."

Skip nodded, embarrassed, the compliment catching him off guard. "Yeah, well, I guess. Besides, somebody had to step up to the plate so's he could see old Satch, and get you out of the house." They laughed for a moment, Skip poking her shoulder when he said "you." "Don't his papa come around?"

"That man's about as out of the picture as a man can be." She replied. "I bump into him every now and then on the avenue. But I don't let him visit. Drinks too much. He scared Buster half to death the last time, swung the boy all around the room, tossed him up in the air like he was a football. He always was a little rough. You don't have to worry about him. It's just me and Buster." She said the last bit with a touch of defiance in her voice, as if wanting the world to know that the only man with a claim to her happened to be two years old. "I'm not thinking about that man. Now, tell me about your audition."

"It went great!" Skip said, taking his arm from around the seat and turning to face Sapphire. "I got a part in a moving picture at Paradise Studios. It ain't much, but it's a start."

"Oh, that's wonderful. I'm glad Zeke kept his promise. He's such an operator," Sapphire said.

"Yeah, but he did right by me. 'Course, I had to set him straight first, what with him taking my five dollars and all. But I'm on my way now. Straight to the top," he said, launching his hand towards the ceiling. "Whoosh! Look out Errol Flynn!" He laughed a bit, letting his nervousness drain off. He pulled out a cigarette, lit it and blew out a stream of smoke, saw Sapphire frown and wished he hadn't. But he kept on, his free hand looking for a place to rest.

"Kind-a early to be going home," he said.

Sapphire sighed. "Buster keeps me on a short leash. Besides, I have to work tomorrow."

"So do I," Skip said. "But there's a party tonight a couple blocks off the avenue. Friend of mine said they'll really be kicking the gong around, and Pee Wee knows what he's talking 'bout. They won't get started till late. You hungry?" He looked at her, hoping she'd say 'yes.' "Maybe we could get something to eat and go over there afterwards. I mean, you don't have any plans, do you?"

Sapphire shook her head. "No, no plans. But Buster needs his goodnight kiss." She gave Skip a look that said, 'try again.'

"Then how about let's get a bite to eat?"

"Are you asking me out, Mister Reynolds," Sapphire said, playfully formal.

"Yeah," Skip said, sitting up straight, like a gentlemen in a high-society moving picture. "Yeah, that's what I'm doing. I'm asking you, Miss Sapphire Louise Davis, if you would like to dine with me."

"Do you have a car?"

"Just a Red Car," he said and pointed around him. "But it has plenty of room and a chauffeur." He waited.

"Well," Sapphire said. "It'll be an early evening, but, yes, Skip, I'd love to go to dinner. How about Chinese?"

He nodded. Whatever you say, baby. Whatever you say. They rode into downtown, switched cars at Broadway and headed for Chinatown, where Sapphire said you could get the best food, cheap, and nobody messed with you. Skip relaxed, figuring he'd have Sapphire on his arm in no time. Pagoda-topped buildings, their fronts covered by strange designs and bits of English, lined streets splashed with the glow of red, blue, green and yellow neon. Through cafe windows he saw cooks sweating over steaming vats, while others deftly worked large spoons around huge, half-moon shaped pots. He leaned across Sapphire. She elbowed him in the ribs, not hard, but enough to push him back so she could reach up and pull the signal cord. At the next stop, Skip stood and let her out, all the while fighting an aching desire to slip an arm around her slim waist. He kept his distance, bided his time as he walked beside her, hands in his pockets. She led him to Mr. Lee's Restaurant, where she ordered Schezuan beef, Schezuan vegetables and two bowls of steamed white rice. Skip looked around for butter and sugar, searched the tables for knives and forks. All he saw were two pairs of sticks. Sapphire smiled at him, spread heaping spoonfuls of rice on their plates, then the beef strips swimming in a rich, brown gravy and finally, the vegetables in a clear, lightly spiced sauce. She picked up her sticks and rubbed them together like a woodsman starting a fire. Skip watched, nervous and unsure, his eyes going from his full plate to the sticks resting by his hand.

"Don't these people use forks?" he whispered.

Sapphire shook her head and swallowed. "Chopsticks," she said, clicking her sticks together.

She picked up his chopsticks, grabbed his hand and placed the sticks gently between his forefinger and middle finger.

"Push up with your two fingers," she said.

Skip strained to keep the sticks in place, but they kept falling out, no matter how hard he tried to grip them. His frustration growing with each failed attempt. A creeping sense of embarrassment came over him. Here he could ride freight trains halfway across the country and walk onto a sound stage at Paradise Studios, but he couldn't feed himself in Chinatown. Sapphire looked at him and pouted.

"Guess you need a fork." she said, turning in her seat and calling a waiter to their table.

Skip pushed the useless sticks aside and ate with his head down. He didn't look up until his flush of shame subsided.

"That's all right, Skip," said Sapphire. "Nobody gets it on the first try. I should've thought of that, but the food here is so-o-o good."

"It's different," he said, inspecting a Shitaki mushroom and a snow pea impaled on his fork. "Ain't no heft to it all. Just rice and gravy, and these things. A 'cropper couldn't live off of this. Guess that's why there ain't no Chinese folk in Tunis," he paused to shovel a couple of mouth-fuls. "Why'd you pick this place? Plenty of rib joints on the avenue give you your money's worth, one in particular."

"I wanted to take you someplace different, expand your horizons a little," replied Sapphire. Too many folks spend all their time on the avenue, going to the same old places, eating the same old food. I like a little adventure. Look around you, Skip. We're in a different world, and it's just a streetcar ride away," Sapphire motioned to the darkened room filled with Chinese faces. "And nobody cares who we are. I found this restaurant with Buster. He's my little traveling buddy. We ride all over town, Santa Monica, San Pedro, Pasadena. One day I said, 'Buster. Let's go to Chinatown and eat Chop Suey.'" She looked up from her plate and smiled. "You can appreciate a little adventure, can't you, Skip."

He stabbed another mushroom and held it high. "Here's to adven-ture."

Riding back down Central Avenue, Sapphire told Skip her dreams about going to a teacher's college and getting a steady job, maybe find-ing someone who could be a father to Buster.

"He's going to need a man to show him the way," she said. "Not now, of course. But someday."

"You're looking pretty far down the road there, Sapphire," said Skip. "Seems to me you just need somebody to sit with him so you can have a good time every once in awhile." He smiled and tried the arm around the back of the seat routine again, but Sapphire didn't give in.

"I know all about having a good time, believe me. How do you think I got Buster," she said, shaking her head. "His father is something else. I saw him once on the streetcar heading downtown. He was cuddling up with another girl. I called him out, shamed him in front of everybody, told that girl she'd better watch out because he was no good, and I had a baby by him to prove it. That wiped the smile off his face," she said, laughing a bit at the memory. "I've had plenty of good times, Skip. But right now I need a little more than that."

Skip took his arm from around the seat. As much as he wanted Sapphire, he knew he wasn't ready for what she was talking about. He'd only just started having his fun. Shoot, he thought. No daddy duty for me. He stole a glimpse at Sapphire sitting beside him, her posture per-fect, her body a respectable three or four inches from his. They hadn't gone deep into the district when she raised her hand and pulled the cord.

"Walk me home," she said, her voice mixing equal parts invitation, expectation and command, letting Skip know that this was the right and proper thing to do. "A gentleman always walks a lady to her door."

They stepped off together and she crooked her left arm around his right arm for a brief stroll on the avenue. Then they turned onto a quiet, tidy street where most of the homes were already dark, even though it was barely nine o'clock. Down in the district the nightclubs were just filling up and the Thursday night crowd was getting ready to ball, but there were no signs of such fun on Sapphire's street. Here people shunned the raucous good time, or had exchanged it for a steady, gray time of hard work and a striver's sensibility.

"Well, here we are," Sapphire said, leading Skip down a driveway to a quaint, cottage set behind a modest house. "Come in and say 'goodnight' to Buster. I know he'd love to see you again."

An older man peeked through the curtain and waved as soon as she knocked on the door. "He just fell asleep," he whispered.

Sapphire squeezed through the door and motioned for Skip to follow. He watched her tiptoe to a little boy sleeping on the sofa. She bent down and picked him up, smothering his face with gentle kisses.

"Is mama's boy asleep?" she cooed. "Just a sleepy, sleepy little boy. Look who's here." She turned him toward Skip. "Mister Baseball."

Skip reached over and tenderly touched Buster's pudgy, baby-soft fingers. "Hey, Little B. You look worn out."

The little boy closed his eyes and went back to sleep. Sapphire gently laid him back on the sofa, tucked a comforter around him and motioned Skip to the door. Outside, they stood close together, facing each other, Skip searching Sapphire's eyes for a signal of what to do. He smelled her perfume and wanted to caress her soft, brown face and seal the night with a kiss on her full lips.

"I had a wonderful time, Skip," Sapphire said. "Really I did."

"Yeah, it was nice," he replied. "Don't know if I'll ever get the hang of them chopsticks, though."

"Oh, I wouldn't worry about that," Sapphire said. "I'll just bet you can handle anything you put your mind to. After all, you did get a job at Paradise Studios."

"Yeah, well," he ran his fingers through his hair. "I guess our night's over."

Sapphire nodded. "I hope we can go out again, on a Saturday when I can stay out a little later. Or maybe you could come by one Sunday morning and take me and Buster to church."

Church? He almost felt ashamed of all the wolfish thoughts he'd had about her, almost. He decided not to answer her last suggestion. Down the street he heard someone stepping on a stick, their footsteps drawing near. "Guess I'd better be going," he said, waited to see what she would do.

She stepped up to him and kissed him on the cheek. "Goodnight, Skip," she whispered, squeezing his hand before turning back to the cottage.

He watched her disappear inside, heard her tender voice full of maternal love for Buster. The thought of that little boy disturbed his vision of Sapphire's slim brown body naked and hot against him. She was Buster's mama. She wasn't some fast gal. She might have been, but now she wanted a steady fellow who would take her to church. Whatever wild nights she might have had were long gone. The faint fragrance of her perfume lingered on his cheek, the delicate scent slowly fading, melting away, leaving only the thrill of her lips. He knew he would see her again, and not just at the Bradbury. He wanted to walk her down Central Avenue in broad daylight so everybody could see her with him, wanted to lavish her with attention and gifts, treat her like a lady who, in time, and only if he was a gentleman, might one day let him kiss her full on the lips, and in that instant, with her pressed close against him, with her body in his embrace, his heart would sing. Sapphire. But he'd have to be careful, else he might end up wearing a ring and apron strings. He laughed at the idea and pulled his mind from her. There was a party going on down around Manchester, a viper's den full of jazz and laughter and everybody getting high and happy on the dance floor. He lit a Chesterfield and hurried over to Central Avenue, enjoying the smoke on the way, the thrill of having conquered Paradise Studios and built the beginnings of a bridge to Sapphire's heart. He caught a Red Car on the dead run, leaned out from the stairwell for a moment or two just to catch the joyous sights and sounds of the avenue heating up on Kitchen Mechanic's Night.

BOOM! BOOM! BOOM! SKIP HEARD BANGING COMING FROM FAR OFF. He ignored the sound, rolling over in his bed, grabbed his pillow and held it tight over his head. The noise softened, slightly, but it still intruded. Boom! Boom! Boom! Henry stood outside the door, pounding loudly against the wood, wondering if his $7-a-week man was in and cursing the day he'd given up the room's key. He put his ear to the door and listened. Nothing. No sound of bedsprings or snoring, a radio left on all night. He rattled the locked door knob, shook the door back and forth and knocked again. Boom! Boom! Boom!

"Skip. You in there? Damn," he muttered. "Either this boy ain't here or he sleeps like a dead man." He called again. "Skip. Come on, now. Work's waiting."

Silence. Then bedsprings creaked. Feet shuffled toward the door. Henry stepped back and waited. The lock clicked open. The doorknob turned and the door swung back into the room. Skip, leaned towards him, a wan, wasted look on his face. He tried to focus on the boss man and willed his mouth into action, tried to say something, but his body wasn't ready. He licked a thick phlegm from his teeth, felt his overgrown tongue moving slowly between his jaws. Finally, words came.

"Uh, hi, Henry. Guess I didn't hear you knocking. What time it?"

"Time for you to get to work," Henry said, stepping inside.

Skip dragged himself to the bathroom rinsed his mouth and splashed cold water on his face. He grumbled and mumbled, the icy water clearing his head. Thank God there wasn't a mirror over the sink. He didn't feel like looking at himself, at least not yet with the scotch whisky still working on him and the dull pounding going on in his brain, the pain beating just behind his eyes. He turned on the faucet again and drank deeply, trying to quench his thirst and wash away the stale taste of cigarettes and alcohol. Water. His body cried for it. He sighed and headed for his bed, still moving slowly. It was the only way to mute the banging in his brain and soothe the line of pain cutting through his forehead. He wished he could take his head off, set it aside and come back to it when the pain was gone. He flopped on his bed and laid back down, one hand clutching the pillow to his face, the other dangling over the side.

"Man," Henry said, "You look like last night put you damn near on the cooling board. Got you so drunk you forgot to change."

"Change?" Skip pushed the pillow aside, leaned up on his elbows and took a good, long look at himself. He was still wearing his oh-so-fine suite from R.C.'s. He frowned at the wrinkles and creases, checked his jacket and pants for spots. Finding none, he breathed a sigh of relief. "Good Lord, Henry, I had me a time last night. Whew! I cain't even remember half of it, not even how I got home. And my head," he fell back on his bead and grabbed the cool pillow. "Feels like I got a plow mule walking through my brain."

"Well you better put him out to pasture," Henry said. "We open in half an hour." Henry looked around the still-barren room. "Only thing wrong with Kitchen Mechanic's night is that it comes on a Thursday. Man's still got a day's work to do, and I believe yours started about a half-hour ago. I'll see you downstairs."

"O-ooo-kay."

The word seeped out in one long dying sigh, barely heard through the pillow close to Skip's face. He listened to Henry's footsteps descending the stairs, one by one, fading, the sound coming faintly, then ending as he lay on his bed, feeling disconnected from his flesh and bones, his soul drawn to a small place in the back of his head, behind the throbbing and the pain. He felt his chest rising and falling as his lungs worked. He sent a message to his fingers so far away. His fists opened and closed. He smiled and closed his eyes, marveled at how his body worked. He remembered a magazine picture of the human body and how behind the clothes and the skin, it was all bones and muscles, a network of nerve endings winding around, over and along a pipeline of blood vessels centered at his heart. Deep in the back of his mind, where it was safe and quiet, he heard the morning. A garbage truck ground through the alley and, for a moment, the plowmule in his brain took a few heavy steps, then rested. The truck was gone. Then kids started playing in the alley, little kids, too young for school, playing and running, happy laughter ringing in the air. Other sounds appeared. From the avenue: cars, a streetcar's bell announcing the nearest stop. From the windowsill the bubbling coo of pigeons, a rustling of feathers, the gentle rush of air pushed by wings flapping. From below, in the Dancing Bar-B-Que, chairs slamming down on the floor, Henry at work. Work! He tossed the pillow aside and squinted against the faint light coming through the drawn shades. He sent a message to his legs. Time to move. They didn't respond. He felt himself sinking into his bed, his eyelids, heavy and fatigued, closing, slowly bringing comforting darkness. He sent another message. Emergency. Time to move. His body responded. *Nawsuh. I'm gon' stay right here in this bed and get me some rest. I been working all night and the day before.*

Skip sighed. I know. I know. But we got some serious work to do. *You saying last night wasn't serious work. These feets still hurting.*

It was fun work but it don't pay no bills, won't keep you fed. So, come on, now, let's get moving.

All right, all right. But take it easy on me. I'm plumb wore out.

He swung his legs across the bed, pressed his feet to the floor and pushed himself up, swayed a moment, then stood, barely keeping his balance. The plow mule started up again. He made his way to the sink, grabbed a washcloth and soaked it in cold water, let the coolness splash across his wrists. He squeezed the towel, patted it across his forehead, his aching eyes, the back of his neck. His pain eased; the plow mule slowed. He soaked the towel again, wrung it out a little before dripping cold water onto his head. A soothing shiver went through his body. He squeezed again, gripped the sink, closed his eyes and leaned back, surrendering to the relaxing tingle of water carrying off his pain in tiny splashes that tickled behind his ear and traced a calming path across his face. He took off his clothes and ran hot water in the sink for a sponge bath. A half hour later he checked himself in the mirror on the door and tried to smile. A tired worn out young man stared back at him. He walked slowly down the stairs, tried to keep the plow mule from reaching the turn row. Each time his feet hit a step he felt a jolting, stabbing pain behind his forehead. He rubbed the back of his neck, ran his hands over his face and prayed for an easy day.

The lunch crowd trickled in by twos and threes, never filling all the tables. Even the counter had empty seats. Diana complained and picked up the small change people left behind. Folks just weren't tipping, and they weren't eating. Skip figured he knew what was up. It had been a week since payday. Everybody's pockets were empty, including his, until quitting time, when the boss man would spread around some of that mean green. The mid-afternoon break found him leaning against an empty sink, clutching yet another cup of heavily creamed coffee. It was the only thing besides water he could keep down. The smoky smell of ribs and sweet bar-b-que almost made him sick. When Henry and Diana sat down to supper, he stayed by the sink, where it was quiet and the sunshine couldn't find him. He took another gulp of coffee as Diana wandered in. Her cigarette smoke made his stomach somersault. He choked back the sickness, fanned the air and took shallow breaths. His worn-out lungs still ached from last night.

"Didn't I see you at that baseball game yesterday," Diana said, leaning against the doorway. "Sitting with this nice looking young lady and a little boy."

"Yeah," Skip replied. "You mind putting out that cigarette. Smoke's kind-a bothering me today."

"No problem, honey." Diana crossed over to the sink and turned on the water just enough to kill the fire. She flicked the butt into the trash can. "Don't know why I mess with them damn things anyway," she said, her voice waking up the plow mule and sending it pounding down another row. "That was some game. Satchel Paige is my man. Wouldn't miss him for the world. And he pitched a good game. That old young boy, whoever he was just got lucky. Got himself something to remember. A home run off the great Satchel Paige!" Diana stopped and looked at Skip. "How come you so quiet today?"

"Got me one of them hangovers." Skip tossed out the coffee.

"Was it worth it?"

"Pretty much, but this day after mess is killing me." He squinted against the pain.

"Honey, I knows just how you feel," Diana said, her voice suddenly soft and maternal. "Best thing is sleep, but a working man cain't afford that. I'd suggest you drink some milk. It'll coat your stomach, calm everything down. Whatever you do, don't mess with that dog that bit you, that old Fido Whisky, scotch, or whoever the hell he was. Don't mess with him." She leaned close to study his face. "Must not have been no home brew, and you can thank God for that. Central Avenue bathtub gin won't do nothing 'cept lay you out. Old Diana knows that for a fact." She laughed, loudly, the full sound coming from her gut. "Whoowee! Lord! Lord! Lord! Don't I know, don't I know."

Skip winced. Diana's piercing laughter sliced into his brain. The plow mule was at a full trot now, threatening to break into a run. "Diana," he pleaded., "Could you please keep it down."

"Sho', honey," Diana lowered her voice. "How's that acting business coming along? Don't hear you talking much about that anymore."

"That's only 'cause I was waiting on some good news 'fore I went off shooting my mouth," Skip said, forcing the plow mule to stop.

"Well, you got some news to tell old Diana?"

Skip motioned her close, then spoke low, his voice almost in a whisper as if he was passing on a secret. "I got an acting job."

"You got an acting job! Henry! Come here quick. This boy done gone and got himself an acting job!"

The plow mule broke into a full gallop. Skip closed his eyes and pressed his hands against his head, hearing Henry come from behind the counter.

"Say what?" the boss man said. "An acting job? When? With who?" He was at Skip's side. "Come on, Skip. Quit playing possum. When did all this happen?"

"Yesterday," Skip said, taking his hand down and looking up to see the question in Henry's eyes. "I was gon' tell you sometime today, after we'd cleaned up."

While they stared at each other, Diana carried on as if Skip was her son and his glory was hers. "Lord have mercy! This boy is gon' be in moving pictures!" she said. "And I can say I knew him when he couldn't do nothing 'cept wash dishes and mop floors. I believe we ought to have a toast. You got any liquor stashed behind the counter, Henry?"

"Got a couple of swallows left in a bottle of rum back there, Di. You know where it is." Henry clapped Skip on the back. "So, your career has started, eh? Next stop the marquee lights."

"It ain't nothing big," Skip said, wishing he'd kept his mouth shut until his body could recover. "Ain't even a speaking part. I'm just a face in the crowd."

"Yeah, but whose crowd. That's the question," Henry said. "Zeke get you this job?"

Skip nodded. "Gave me a man to talk to over at Paradise Studios. I talked to him and he told me to report Monday morning. I might be in late."

"Don't worry about that. I'll have one of Di's boys stop by after school. We'll manage. What's this picture about?"

"It's one of them slavery-time things," Skip said, downplaying his success as much as possible. "Bunch of colored folks funning around, scared of living free but ready to die for the Little Missy."

"Hmm," Henry said, walking around the small room, idly arranging boxes on the shelves. "Doesn't sound like the kind of moving picture you came out here for." He turned and faced Skip. "Weren't you the one going on about how Hollywood wasn't putting any real colored folks up on the screen? You were going to change that, right. Or am I confusing you with somebody else?"

Skip shook his head, then buried it in his arms resting on the sink's edge.

"Seems to me like you're just keeping the same old ball rolling."

Before he could answer, Diana returned, with a bottle of rum and three glasses, one filled with milk. She frowned.

"This don't make no sense. Here it is a time for celebrating and y'all in here getting serious." She passed the glasses around. "Now who's gon' give the toast?"

Henry covered his glass and shook his head. Diana frowned again, poured the last corner of rum in her glass and raised it high.

"Skip, I wish you the best of luck. And if one day you come walking a leopard down Central Avenue like old Steppin' done and you see Diana, don't pass me by. Say: 'Hi!'"

Skip smiled weakly and clinked his glass of milk against Diana's glass of rum.

"Over the teeth and across the gums, look out stomach 'cause here it comes!" She tossed down her drink, grimaced a moment, closed her eyes and blew out a long breath. "Lord have mercy! This stuff could grow hair on a bald man's head."

Out front they heard the door swing open and voices asking if anyone was home.

"Be with you in a sec." Henry said, shooing Diana into the cafe. "Let me know if you need anything, Skip. The hard part is just beginning."

IT WAS A PERFECT DAY, THE SKY A THOUSAND MILES HIGH, BLUE AND clear as crystal. Darting sparrows winged through the crisp air as Skip walked Hollywood's streets, a happy, joyous tune carrying his heart up to join the sparrows. An irrepressible smile lit his soul as he approached Paradise Studios' beautiful arched gates. He strolled confidently past the gawkers and autograph hounds waiting for their favorite stars, the hungry dime-store cowboys from Gower Gulch and the eager peroxide blondes who could always be found hanging around the studio gates. Bobby Mumford peeked out from the guardhouse, grimaced and slapped his Undercover Detective on the counter.

"You, again," he said. "You got a pass?"

Skip rolled his eyes. "This good enough?"

"Lemme see that." He snatched the paper, read it once, twice, held it up to the sun and squinted, searching for signs of forgery. He compared the name with the one on his clipboard. Satisfied, he shoved the pass back at Skip. "Sign here," he growled, "and be quick about it. I got work to do."

"Plenty of work," Skip whispered, giving his signature the Ezekiel Washington flourish.

He walked on, chest puffed up like a banty rooster's, soaring heart making him feel like he could reach up and touch the top of the arch. A phalanx of Roman warriors, in polished gold breastplates and burgundy skirts, hurried past, swords and shields clanking. Three chariots hitched to the back of the truck followed. Captain Kidd, with a patch over his left eye, fanned himself with a heavy, tri-cornered cap. Dead-eye Dick stood beside the captain, idly twirling a pearl-handled six-shooter. They whispered amongst themselves, then Dead-eye caught sight of Skip and yelled.

"Watch out there, buddy."

A trailer truck, towing a stack of Georgian columns, rumbled down the street, horn blaring. Skip saw it just in time to jump out of the way. He felt another surge of joy. The truck must be headed for soundstage six, he thought, running over to the driver's side and banging on the door. The driver put the truck in neutral, glared at him, annoyed.

"Say," Skip smiled. "You heading for that slavery-time moving picture?"

The driver frowned. "Sure."

"How do I get there?"

"Jump on the back and I'll give you a ride," the driver said, shifting into first.

He drove slowly, giving Skip a chance to grab hold of one of the slats and swing onto the cargo area as easily as if he was catching a streetcar on Central Avenue. Sitting there, feet dangling over the edge, he felt like a kid heading to his first state fair. The studio buzzed with the vibrant energy of a thousand people as the truck crept along, its engine grinding through the low gears. Finally, it jerked to a stop. The driver leaned from the cab.

"Okay, buddy, here you are."

Skip jumped off and wandered to the edge of the waiting crowd. Cameras, extras, soldiers on horseback filled the back lot. A young man in jodhpurs and polished black boots strutted back and forth with a martinet's self-assurance, slapping a riding crop against the boots, yelling directions. Cameramen and sound technicians wheeled their machines into place. The young man grabbed an attendant's megaphone.

"Quiet on the set," he yelled, then looked around. "And, action!"

A Confederate officer rode up, leaned down from his majestic, dappled gray steed and told a group of southern belles sitting beneath a willow tree that a battle was raging in town. Things didn't look good, he said. The rebel line might not be able to hold. The ladies should pack their things and leave, quickly. The Yankees were burning everything in their path. The lead actress, slender, her hair a mass of flowing black curls, looked around and gazed longingly towards the cameras.

"I'll never leave Pleasant Land," she said. "Even if the Yankees come."

The young man in jodhpurs shot a glance to Kurt Marshall, who frowned and shook his head. "Cut!"

The actors stared, surprised. The assistant marched over to them, whipping his riding crop through the air. They trudged back to their positions and repeated the scene again and again. Skip scratched his head. Why did they keep saying the same things over and over? After several failed takes, the lead actress went down on one knee, grabbed a handful of dirt and, with defiance and anger flashing through her blue eyes, looked up at the Confederate officer.

"This land is sacred," she said. "And, I shall never leave Pleasant Land, never."

Marshall smiled. The young man shouted for the people in scene thirty-two. Skip turned away and spied a rail thin, severe looking brunette holding a clipboard.

"Excuse me, m'am," he said. "Mr. Marshall told me to report to sound stage six. I'm gon' be in the moving picture."

She pursed her thin lips, looked down over her bifocals and asked if he was speaking or just an extra. Skip decided to play it straight. He was just a face in the crowd.

"Get over to wardrobe and change," she said, her words clipped and exact as she pulled a pen from her gray-streaked bun and crossed his name off her list. When she saw him still standing by her, she pointed to a nearby building. "Wardrobe. Over there. And, please hurry. We should be shooting a slave scene in," she shipped through her sheaf of papers, "twenty-seven minutes."

Union and Confederate soldiers in plumed hats, 19th Century dandies in ruffled shirts, women in cascading hoop skirts lounged around the wardrobe room, while a harried little woman with a mouthful of stickpins clenched between her teeth hustled Skip to the back of the room, where black folk traded their street clothes for the torn rags of slavery. He ruffled through the racks, looking for something that didn't fit too badly. Behind him, someone yelled for the troops. Two platoons hurried off, shouldered rifles rattling. Skip watched the others pulling out clothes without a care, and stopped being picky. He grabbed a pair of pants torn at the knees, a shirt missing all but one button, rushed into the crowded dressing area and changed. All around him, people joked about spending their pay on the Avenue. Easy, carefree laughter filled the room. With his good clothes clutched in one hand, he padded barefoot across the floor to a shelf of shoes, some too ripped to wear. He pulled out one pair, then another and another, trying to find something near his size, something comfortable enough to stand in all day. He didn't even hear Harold Q. Osborne step up beside him.

"Stop being so fussy, Skip, and just pick one," Osborne said dryly. "It doesn't matter if they fit or not."

Skip turned around, startled that someone knew his name. "Harry-O!"

"Everything copastetic?" Harry-O said, slapping him on the shoulder.

"Everything's awreet with me." Skip said, slipping on a pair of shoes three sizes too big. "Man, can you believe all this stuff gong on? They got a sure 'nuff mansion out there, and it ain't got but three sides." He stared at his clothes. "Where do I put my good stuff?"

"Over on the other side of the room. They have a couple, three racks. C'mon, we'll drop off your stuff, then take in some of the show until our scene comes."

Outside, a thin layer of gun smoke lay low over the back lot. Fire-spitting rifles sputtered and cracked. The air was heavy with the stinging smell of gunpowder. Skip rubbed his eyes as he, Harry-O and a group of extras watched a skirmish unfold. The Union battled through a narrow, dusty street of storefronts. Rebel soldiers leaped from doorways, went down on one knee, fired quickly, then fell back, leaving their dead. Wounded men from both sides limped to safety, writhed and moaned on the ground or lay still. A bugle sounded the charge. Union cavalry went galloping up the street, pistols firing, sabers slicing through the smoke. Slowly, the rifle fire subsided, and the surviving Yankees whooped in victory.

"Cut!"

The pretend dead and wounded stood, dusted themselves and checked their blood-stained uniforms, before gathering their weapons and hurrying off the set. Skip clapped his hands.

"Man, oh man. Did you see that?" He held up his hands, sighted down his fingers like a kid playing Cowboys and Indians. "Pow, pow, pow. You know there was black soldiers in the Civil War. Pow-pow-pow. How come they ain't got no black soldiers? Pow!"

Harry-O laughed to himself and pulled down the lead finger of Skip's pretend rifle. "Okay, Texas, looks like your chance is coming."

The young man with the riding crop strutted towards the extras, his boots kicking up dust. He ordered them into the cottonfields on the far side of the mansion.

Skip hurried off, then stopped. Where was Harry-O? He turned around and saw him standing by the wardrobe building. "Ain't you coming?"

"Not this time, Texas. This one's on you." He gave Skip the thumbs-up sign.

For the moment, Skip wished Harry-O was with him, but he soon forgot that feeling. He was in Hollywood, and on the right side of the cameras. In the fields, he bent over a row of cotton, remembering a thousand other times when he'd earned his pay beneath a boiling Texas sun. He touched the stalks. They were plastic. The bolls felt like cotton candy. He smiled to himself, thinking, ain't nothing real in Hollywood. All around him, the browns and blacks of Central Avenue, in bandanas and overalls, made ready for a ten-dollar day, while hungry-eyed cameras sat, silently waiting. The directions were easier than Skip could believe: act like you're picking cotton. Shoot, he thought, that ain't acting. He felt at once anonymous and all-important, a face in the crowd, yet, who else here had made his journey? He waved to Kurt Marshall sitting stern behind the cameras. His gesture went unnoticed. Marshall busied himself with the script and the assistants gathered around him. Finally, he nodded to the young man with the riding crop.

"Cameras," the young man said, his urgent voice followed by a slight mechanical whirring. The cameras focused. "And, action!"

The extras bent over the plastic stalks, Skip joining in, going through the motions, feeling a sudden desire to make real his dream of Hollywood. Three rows over, a large barrel-chested brother broke into a field holler that rose deep and beautiful. The familiar sound sent a shiver along Skip's spine. Off to the side, he saw Harry-O running onto the set, waving and shouting.

"Missy Leigh! Missy Leigh! Dem Yankee men is coming up de road and burning everything!"

Skip dropped his cotton sack. Here was his chance. "Freedom's coming!" he yelled.

"Cut! The assistant director slapped the crop against this thigh. "You there!" He pointed at Skip, his eyes narrowed to angry slits. "That's not in the script. And if it's not in the script, that means you keep your mouth shut. We don't have time to waste film on some Central Avenue ham."

Skip heard people laughing and mumbling about the foolish boy hamming it up like he was somebody special. He saw Harry-O shaking his head and felt like a fool, caught doing something he had no business being involved in. "Damn, shit," he muttered, meeting the assistant's cold stare. "I was just trying to make it more real. Seems to me the slaves would be happy to hear the news."

"Yeah, well, when you start making the moving pictures, you can have the slaves say anything you want. For now, though, you're working on my time. So, shut up and do your job." He turned to Marshall, seeking approval. The director simply nodded. His eyes met Skip's for a second, and Skip thought he saw a slight smile on Marshall's lips.

A man with a small chalkboard jumped in front of one of the cameras. "Scene 54, take two."

"Cameras!" The assistant director paused, surveyed the crowd, looking for trouble. He focused an evil glare on Skip, held it long enough to let Skip know; I'm watching you. "And, action!"

Again, the cameras whirred. The big man started singing and Skip bent over the fake cotton, gritting his teeth, choking back the desire to steal the show. He didn't want the man with the riding crop kicking him off the set, sending him home without a penny in his pocket. Still, he stole glances at the cameras, stood up and smiled broadly when Harry-O delivered the news to a frightened Missy Leigh, news that traveled through the toiling slaves, who stopped for a moment, then went back to work, wondering if it could be true. Harry-O raced through the fields shouting.

"De Yankee men is coming. De Yankee men is coming."

"Cut!"

The filming continued, the scenes coming in a sequence that didn't make any sense. One time, Skip thought Yankee cavalry would mount a charge, but instead there was a gay lawn party, people talking about what would happen if the war came, Missy Leigh giving her soldier boy a tearful good-bye, sealed with a Hollywood kiss. The sun was falling from the sky when the slaves returned for the day's last battle scene. The assistant only wanted to shoot it once. Soldiers took their positions, Yanks in the field, Rebels surrounding Pleasant Land, ready to dig in for one final desperate fight. Between the two armies, the slaves waited to run through the Yankee lines. Skip hid amongst them, keeping well to the back. He didn't want any part of the assistant. He looked for Harry-O, but didn't see him anywhere. The crowd of extras pressed around him and he wondered how he was going to stand out, how he could make sure he'd do something memorable so that some day, when he sat in a darkened theater, he'd know when to turn to the person sitting nearest and say, like a Hollywood pro, I'm in the next scene. His mind worked furiously, conjuring up fantastic action. He saw himself leading the Yankee charge, wrestling a rebel rifleman and setting fire to Pleasant Land. Each image whispered to him, insistent and demanding, then vanished when he saw the assistant behind the cameras. Maybe next time, he thought. Next time I'll ask Ezekiel Washington for a speaking role. He searched the black and white faces gathering around the mansion, locked on the smiling face of a white-haired man from the audition.

"Hey," he yelled. "What'd you get?"

"Big Sam," the guy said, his face going weak and submissive.

Big Sam! Skip's heart ached. That was the role he auditioned for. The old man's face went through a series of expressions: anger, calm, the most devoted slavey-time Uncle Tom. Skip thought about himself and figured he was all wrong for the part: too young, too small. He couldn't even pretend to be Missy Leigh's loving, protective old Uncle. Hell, he thought, trying to convince himself. I didn't want that part anyway. The assistant brought the megaphone to his lips. A palpable tension surged through the crowd. One take. The guy with the chalkboard jumped in front of the cameras. An instant later, rifle fire erupted all along the set. Puffs of blue-black smoke filled the air with the stink of sulfur and salt-peter. The assistant moved back and forth, waving the slaves through the advancing line of Yankees. The stern Rebels grimly held their ground. The snap and crack of the spitting rifles, sounding like dry leaves trampled underfoot, grew louder and louder. A charge exploded behind Skip, startling him. Dirt and shattered cotton stalks rained down on his head. Cannons fired. Soldiers fell. Slaves fell. Union cavalry charged into the scene, raised sabers catching the light of flames flickering along a row of burning slave cabins, their horses rearing up and jumping the fallen bodies. Skip stood fascinated, unable to lose himself in the scene swirling around him. Boom cameras swung and dipped, the mechanical eyes zooming in for a close-up of a panic-filled slave running to freedom, a soldier's choreographed pirouette into a false death. People yelled and screamed. Wild-eyed horses stumbled and fell, spilling their riders. The smoke grew dense and thick. Another charge went off nearby, the concussion throwing Skip to the ground. He picked himself up and started to run, first towards the Rebels, then toward the Yankees, his arms swimming though the blinding, choking smoke searing his lungs. Death seemed everywhere, the field strewn with bodies in twisted, unnatural shapes and riderless horses wandering stunned.

A Rebel soldier popped from behind a column, aimed and fired. Now, he thought, clutching his hand to his chest, crumpling to the ground and trying to imagine the terrible pain of being shot. He crawled on his hands and knees towards the Union lines, determined to make his way through the gruesome death swarm, but he knew the bullet had torn his lungs apart, and his chest was filling with blood. He struggled to his feet, looked for a camera and, when he saw one pointing towards him, whispered: Freedom. Then he was gone, falling back in what seemed like slow-motion, falling a thousand miles. His body slammed into the ground and he rolled over, dead, the battle raging all around him.

Soon, he heard victory whoops coming from the Yankees. The wounded groaned and cried out for water. One cried for his mama. Hoofbeats thudded nearer and nearer. Skip rolled over in time to see the Union commander circling Pleasant Land, waving a blazing, spark streaming torch. Missy Leigh chased the officer, screaming, "No, no," but he kicked her away, his boots catching her full in the chest. The torch spun through the night, its flame twirling end over end, arcing high before falling against Pleasant Land. The place exploded in a blinding flash. Instinctively, Skip covered his eyes, then peeked through his fingers. Pleasant Land was burning. Flames raced up the walls and climbed into the night. He wanted to get away from the searing heat, but he was dead. He hugged the ground and waited. Volleys of rifle fire rang out. Then he heard a woman screaming. It was Missy Leigh, standing in front of Pleasant land, screaming and tearing at her blonde hair, looking crazy, like Willie Jean Mason when she saw the train run over her husband. Big Sam tried to hold her back, but she tore herself away and ran into the fire, her desperate cry ripping through the roaring blaze.

"Cut!"

Skip stood and looked around, seeing the world as if in a dream. Though the extras had been dismissed, he lingered behind the cameras, unable to tear himself away. Shadows of flames from the still-raging fire danced across his face. He stepped back a few steps out of range of the heat, but he could not leave. He wanted to stand in this playground, where Hollywood's fanciful dreams became real. The Dancing Bar-B-Que seemed a world away. He wondered if Henry had made out all right, if Diana's boy had mopped the floors, washed the dishes and set the chairs in place without messing up. A roaring crash startled him and he jumped back, his eyes widening. A huge section of Pleasant Land crumbled in a spectacular heap of glowing embers and flying sparks. The film crew captured the mansion's final moments. Off to the side, Marshall and the assistant director bent over the script. Skip started towards them, wanting to find out what Marshall thought of his death scene, but he stopped. The two men were arguing. He turned back to the fire. The flames were burning lower now, dying slowly, flaring briefly over a bit of unburned wood that cracked and hissed, then disappearing, moving on to the last, unseen parts of Pleasant Land. The day was over. And what a fun day it had been! He trudged back to wardrobe, found his clothes and collected his pay.

Riding back downtown, he pulled the pay envelope out of his pocket, held it for a moment, then kissed it. Ten bucks! More than he made in a week of washing dishes and mopping floors. He didn't see why he couldn't get in good with Washington and start making this kind of money regularly, so he could stop pushing that mop, and stop taking those g-damn whore baths. He sniffed his forearm and ran his fingers through his hair. He smelled like an ashtray filled with burned-out butts. A whore bath wouldn't take the stink away. A hot bath at the Y.M.C.A. would, and it would only cost 25 cents. He leaned back in his seat and tapped out a Chesterfield, his mind already luxuriating in the exquisite, remembered sensation of a tubful of hot, sudsy water. Holding the pack in his hand, another thought came to mind. He pictured himself smiling from a magazine ad, a fresh smoke between his lips, the pack's royal design facing out, the ad man's words surrounding him: "Chesterfield. The taste of success!" He rolled the smoke between his fingers, lit it and drew slowly, savoring the taste. He laughed to himself, remembering the frantic morning when he'd run out of the Plaza Arms, knocking over trash cans as he fled down the alley, sticking out his tongue at Mrs. Harrelson, who had cursed him and shook her fists in righteous anger. God knows what would have happened if Phineas hadn't shown up with a piece of tin that bought him a weekend of safety. Murder in Pershing Square. He played with the idea, ran it over and over to see what kind of moving picture it would make. Country boy comes to Hollywood with dreams of making it big, only to end up broke and dead in the city's downtown park. He frowned. Nobody likes a sad story. He replayed the idea, changed the ending and the title. Escape from Pershing Square. This time it was country boy comes to Hollywood, ends up broke and sleeping in Pershing Square, only to be discovered by a producer taking a stroll after a party at the Biltmore Hotel. He smiled. That was more like Hollywood. He finished the cigarette and rode to Sixth and Broadway.

On a penny postcard he scribbled a note to Grandma Sarah. "I'm in the movies. Am fine. Hope you all are too." He wandered along Broadway, saw his name on every movie house marquee. The ten dollars itched to be spent, on drinks with Pee Wee, or maybe a fine time with Sapphire. He headed toward Pershing Square, the movie still running around in his head. Near the fountain in the middle of the park a rumple-suited huckster stood on an orange crate, calling to a small crowd. At first Skip thought nothing of it, his mind busy with country boy-comes-to-Hollywood-and-becomes-a-star, then he recognized Phineas T. Weatherby, hard at work. He attached himself to the rear of the crowd and listened.

"That's right, ladies and gentleman," Phineas said, tapping a bottle of Eternity's Breath. "This marvelous elixir cannot be found in any store, nor can it be purchased from magazines. You know why?" Phineas looked down on the upturned faces and answered his own question. "Stores and magazines only raise the price, and that wouldn't be right, now would it? No sir. The middleman needs his cut. The store owner wants his share. The magazine publisher adds a little bit for his expenses and, before you know it, you're paying two, three times what the thing cost to begin with. And, worst of all, my friends, they'll dress everything up and tell you it's a steal." He looked sad for a moment. "My friends, there is nothing worse on God's green earth than a sharpie in a starched shirt and tie and some fancy San Francisco suit. They'll rob you blind every time. Why, they don't care about you, the good, hard-working people of Los Angeles. But I do." Phineas paused. He seemed so sincere Skip almost believed him. His voice lowered and took on a friendly, caring tone. "My friends, I care deeply about all of you, every man, woman and child. That's why I'm offering this wondrous, one-of-a-kind product to you at a price you can't find anywhere else. Not for a dollar. Lordy me, any magazine'll sell it to you for that. Seventy-five cents?" He shook his head. "That's what the stores would sell it for, and it would be highway robbery at that price. My friends," Phineas stopped again and winked slyly as Skip edged to the front. "What price would you put on this elixir, this nectar of the Gods, this wonder of the ages that has been proven to put hair on a bald man's head and transform many a tired old grandpappy into Stavin' Chain, that hard-loving sixty-minute man? It even relieves women of their monthly pains. Now, what price? Today you can have it for 49 cents. That's right ladies and gentlemen, 49 cents, the lesser part of a dollar. Think of it, health, vim and vigor, a cure for all your ills, and it can be yours for the change in your pocket. Yes, I'll make something on the deal, a dime a bottle to be exact. But don't begrudge me that tiny profit. Think of it as part of the investment you can make today, right now, on your future," He shook the bottle back and forth, tossed it up, caught it behind his back and smiled into the wary crowd. "Now, who'll be the first to step forward and claim this treasure?"

No one moved. An old man standing beside Skip shook a handful of coins in his pocket, but didn't pull out any silver. A gaunt-faced woman snapped open her frayed purse, peered into the darkness and frowned. Disappointment pulled down the corners of Phineas' mouth.

"Surely, y'all ain't gon let opportunity pass you by. Perhaps a demonstration is needed." He searched the crowd, then pointed to Skip. "Young man, forgive me for calling attention to your affliction, but I notice you walk with a limp. Come, try Eternity's Breath. I guarantee you'll walk away a new man."

Skip felt his face burning from the gaze of a dozen pairs of eyes. Two people in front of him stepped aside, leaving a clear aisle. Phineas leaned forward, smiling, one hand beckoning, while the other shook his priceless potion. Skip sucked up some courage and followed Phineas' lead. Remembering the limp from childhood, he stiffened his left leg, grimaced and stepped forward.

"This leg's been bothering me for years," he said. "Doctors cain't seem to do nothing with it."

Phineas nodded his head in solemn agreement. "I understand, son. There are things modern medicine cannot fix. Here." He offered the bottle as if it were the most precious thing in the world. "But only a sip. It's powerful stuff."

Skip unscrewed the cap, feeling the crowd's eyes boring holes through his back. He looked at Phineas, then gulped a mouthful. His stomach convulsed. The stuff tasted like a bad batch of rot gut that should've been tossed into the Brazos. He bent over, coughing and grabbing at his stomach. His eyes started watering. A troubled gasp went through the crowd. A voice behind him whispered: Poison. The word ran from one person to the next. Slowly, the crowd started backing away, hands shielding their faces as if Skip's throat-rattling coughs were spreading influenza, pneumonia, maybe tuberculosis. He tried to catch his breath, his mouth burning, his lungs gasping for air, his stomach flip-flopping inside him. Phineas was at his side, bending low over him, beating him on the back and fiercely whispering.

"God dammit, Skip, I thought you could act!" He turned to the drifting crowd. People waved their hands in disgust. "Wait! Do not be alarmed. It's only the elixir at work. God didn't create the heavens without fire. A child is not born without pain. Wait!"

They were gone. Phineas stood and watched, helpless. Finally, Skip managed to catch his breath.

"Shit," he said. "What the hell is that stuff?"

"A secret concoction. A . . . Dammit, you weren't suppose to drink it." Phineas waited until Skip composed himself. "Well, what do you have to say for yourself?"

"I was only trying to help." Skip worked his tongue around his mouth to clear it of the ugly, lingering taste. "Swear to God, that stuff damn near killed me."

"Killed you! Hah! Killed me, you mean. That crowd was ready to buy. I could feel it." Phineas packed his bottle away and closed his valise. "Perhaps another day, another part of the world," he sighed wearily and straightened his coat. "Well?"

Skip smiled and made a peace offering. "How 'bout a drink? I was looking for somebody to help me celebrate. I was in a moving picture today."

"Ah hah," Phineas said, shaking off his loss. "A libation would ease my despairing soul. A moving picture did you say? This is good news, requiring at least two drinks." He cut Skip a serious, all-business look. "You buying? I would but, finances and all that, besides, I believe some compensation is in order, some measure of generosity for past favors. Hmm?"

"Don't worry," Skip said, tapping his shirt and clapping his friend on the back. "I'm a paid actor."

"Paid, yes. An actor? Not by a long shot."

"You know, Phineas, I might be talking out of turn, but you ever thought of putting a little sugar in that stuff?"

Phineas stopped and rubbed his chin. "You might have something there, Skip. Perhaps an adjustment is needed to rectify the obvious imbalance of ingredients that is inhibiting the potion's medicinal values. But that is work for another day. Let us retire to one who dispenses the true elixir of life. And make my first one a double."

EZEKIEL WASHINGTON BULLIED HIS WAY THROUGH THE THURSDAY night crowd already clogging Central Avenue and stormed into the Dancing Bar-B-Que.

"Where's that boy," he roared, baleful eyes darting around the empty cafe, bald head glistening with sweat.

"Well, well, well," Henry said, looking up from the grill. "If it isn't the blackface king of Hollywood. What brings you down here, Zeke? Looking for some grease paint?"

Washington bristled at the remark. "That was years ago, Henry. Where's that Reynolds boy?" he said, taking a seat at the counter.

Henry nodded towards the kitchen door that had slammed shut seconds after Zeke whipped through the front door. "He should be back there, unless you scared him off."

Skip tensed, hearing Zeke's heavy footsteps approaching. Damn, shit. He'd been ducking Zeke all week. The studio had called him back Tuesday and paid him another ten bucks. He should've handed over Zeke's share Wednesday morning. He was going to, but Sapphire said she'd go out with him tonight and he wanted to be flush to show her a good time. Now Zeke was here. He busied himself with the last greasy plate, then started in on the dirty pots and frying pans he usually let soak overnight. His mind scrambled to come up with an excuse, a lie, anything to keep the Lincolns in his pocket. He wasn't going to miss this chance to have Sapphire on his arm. Bam! The door swung open and banged against the wall.

"Ain't no use hiding, boy," Zeke said, all anger and fury. "Where's my money?"

"I ain't got it, Mister Washington," Skip replied, casually wiping his hands on his apron and turning to face his agent. "But payday's Saturday. I'll have it for you then."

"That's not good enough, Skip," said Zeke, shaking his head. "Now, we made a deal. You signed a contract giving me fifty percent of whatever you make. That means you owe me ten dollars."

"I know, Mister Washington. But I ain't got it. Saturday. I'll have it soon's we close."

Zeke pulled a stogie from inside his coat pocket, savagely bit off the end and spat it on the floor. The veins along his skull writhed like angry snakes. Skip took a deep breath, anticipating the nauseating smoke. Zeke lit the stogie and puffed madly, a bluish cloud covering his face.

"Say, Henry," he yelled over his shoulder. "What kind of help you got here? Boy don't even know how to keep a promise."

"He's alright with me," Henry said from behind the counter. "Whatever is going on back there is between you and Skip. My name's Emmett and I'm not in it."

Zeke turned back to Skip, the stogie jutting out of his mouth. "A man's word is his bond, Skip, and a deal's a deal." A thumbnail's worth of ash dropped off the cigar. "You know, Skip, I was thinking about you before I came over here, and not just about the money. I got a call the other day from a fellow over at National Pictures. He said they were going to be shooting a colored western up in Victorville, wanted to know if I knew anybody who could ride a horse. You being a Texas boy, quite naturally I thought about you. So, I told the fellow I might be able to help him. Now," Washington paused and rolled the stogie between his fat, sausage fingers. "I don't see why I should give you a shot, when you haven't paid me what I'm due for getting you that job at Paradise Studios."

A thin, sinuous line of smoke rose from the stogie's burning ember to splash softly against the ceiling and envelop the room in a thick, sickening cloud. Skip coughed and fanned the air. Was Washington telling the truth or just playing with him? Another picture! So soon? He saw himself riding across the desert, leading a valiant charge of Buffalo Soldier cavalry. Damn, shit. Sapphire was waiting for him. He could see her standing in her doorway, all dressed up and smiling, a happy, luminous light shining in her eyes, her delicate perfume making him think of roses, hundreds and hundreds of roses.

"Can't you wait till Saturday, Mister Washington?'

Zeke shook his head. "Deal's a deal. Besides, I might want to spend it on some Kitchen Mechanic. Of course," he flicked some more ash off his stogie. "I could just call that fellow over at National and tell him I can't help him."

Washington meditated on his cigar, let his final words hang threateningly in the disquieting silence. Skip finished the last pan, pulled the plug in the sink, dried his hands and saw Henry sitting at the counter, counting up the day's take. He shrugged, an idea taking shape in his mind.

"Maybe Henry would give me an advance on my pay," he said, more to himself than to Washington.

"Maybe," Zeke said, smiling now.

"Guess I'll ask him." Skip forced himself into the cafe.

"Come back empty and National Pictures is out," Zeke whispered.

Skip shuffled towards Henry, dragged his feet, feeling Zeke's eyes at his back, forcing him on, ominous words ringing in his ears. Don't come back empty. Henry didn't look up when he took a seat, just kept figuring, humming to himself and occasionally licking his pencil. Skip's fingers drummed a nervous, troubled beat on the counter, but Henry kept on about his business, never once looking away from his money and his ledger. Zeke propped himself in the doorway, thumb and pinky to the side of his face as if he were talking on the telephone. He shook his head, mimicked a sigh of deepest, heartfelt apology, then dropped his hand to his side. Sorry. Maybe next time. No, Skip thought, another Hollywood image taking shape in his mind: Himself as the fastest draw west of the Pecos. He took a deep breath.

"Uh, Henry?" he said, clearing his throat.

"Yes,"

"Uh, I need some money, say, five bucks."

"Payday's Saturday," Henry said, still concentrating on his ledger.

"I know, but, I'm in a bind. Can't you give me five bucks and take it out of my pay?"

"If I do that, you won't have much pay. You weren't here Monday, or Tuesday, remember?"

"So I don't get paid this week. I'll get by, but I need the five bucks now." He let desperation fill his voice. "Zeke's got me over a barrel."

Henry closed the ledger. "I told you about Zeke, didn't I? Told you he was no good, but you didn't listen. Now he's got you in a fix and here you come running to me." He shook his head and counted the day's take. "I know how much they pay over at Paradise."

"Yeah, but," Skip held up his hands. "I spent most of it. Kind-a got carried away, you know, celebrating and all. Had to give some to Mister R.C. I forgot all about the contract Zeke made me sign."

"Contract?" Henry frowned. "Extras don't need contracts. You've been had Skip. If I were you, I'd pay Zeke off and be done with him. But that's just me." He peeled a fiver from his wad. "I guess you earned this. He tossed the bill on the counter. "Don't come around poor-mouthing next week, you hear."

Skip stared at the greenback. He couldn't bring himself to pick it up. He almost wanted to call Sapphire and tell her their date was off, he was sick. Then he could give the five-spot back to Henry, pay Zeke out of his own pocket and make the world right. But the world wouldn't be right without this promised night on the town with Sapphire. They were going dancing at the Lindy. The bill lay on the counter, barely six inches from his fingers.

"Go on take it," Henry said, getting up and walking toward the door. He stopped a moment before leaving. "Zeke," he said. "I'm glad to see you haven't lost your touch."

Then he was gone.

Skip reached in his pocket and put another fiver on the counter. Washington walked towards him, the stogie burned down to a stub.

"Don't mind if I do," he said, reaching for the bills.

Skip's hand was there first. "Henry said you been running a game on me, Zeke. He said I don't need no contract to be an extra."

"Henry doesn't know what he's talking about. We're in for the long haul, Skip. We're partners. Why, I'd be a thief if I took fifty percent and only got you work as an extra. I'm bringing you along slow, letting you work your way up to a speaking role. Don't listen to Henry. He hasn't been in Hollywood in years." Zeke pulled the money from under Skip's fingers. "I'll call my contact at National tomorrow and see what's what. Might even get you some stunt work. But whatever happens, Skip, you pay me first. Understand? Before you do anything else, you pay me." The stern, chastising tone in Zeke's voice changed, became paternal. He patted Skip on the shoulder. "Come on now, partner. Henry paid you what you were due and you paid me what I was due. The circle is complete. Nothing to get all down in the mouth about. Just learn the lesson, boy." He snatched the butt out of his mouth and tossed it on the floor. "Call me tomorrow evening," he said, plucking stray bits of tobacco from his tongue, leaving Skip alone, head hung down, eyes locked on the soggy, chewed butt lying on the linoleum like some horrid slug.

He heaved himself up off the stool and set the chairs on the tables, bore down with the mop, savagely kicked the bucket across the floor, not caring if dirty water spilled where he had just cleaned. He couldn't believe Zeke had been so trifling about ten dollars, that he had come here and made him beg Henry when he could've called him on the phone and told him to bring it downtown. They could've worked things out, kept it quiet. But Zeke had to make a scene. He went over the floor again, saw dirty spots where there were none. By the time he finished, his arms ached, his fingers cramped as if still clutching the mop. He checked the clock over the counter. Seven-thirty. Sapphire was waiting. He hurried up to his room, feet thumping the old stairs. Once inside, his spirits started to lift, slightly at first, then a steady rise, the sight of the three red roses he'd bought downtown at Grand Central Market turning his mind to Sapphire's sweet face smiling in the night to come. The roses were his gift to her. He'd even bought Buster a toy fire truck. Tonight, he was going to be the perfect gentleman.

National Steel sat in a corner, the low E string dropped down to D, ready for a turn at "Big Road Blues," He brushed the strings, knowing if he stopped to play he'd lose himself in the music. Time would dissolve. He'd go from Tommy Johnson to Blind Blake, fiddle around in open G, where Son House and Skip James lived, fall into an exquisite trance brought on by the droning strings and singing octaves. Then he'd go back to standard tuning and practice some scales, or the chord progressions he'd copied out of a jazz guitar book at the library. An hour or more would pass. He'd be late getting to Sapphire, who'd probably be angry and put out about having to wait. If that happened, this night for which he had planned, saved, and lied would be shot all to hell. So he left National Steel alone, scrubbed himself down, splashed himself with Silver Esquire cologne and put on the fine, black double-breasted suit from R.C. He had one foot out the door when the phone rang, but he kept on moving, racing time and the northbound streetcar he caught on the dead run.

Thursday nights thrilled him. Central Avenue, hushed and still every other night of the work week, came alive on Thursday. People jammed the otherwise half-filled nightclubs to bursting. Cars that usually raced up and down the avenue now crept along, but that was okay because the avenue, with its throng of black folk and Kitchen Mechanics set loose for an evening was the only place to be. The girls were everywhere, their gay, happy voices like wonderful music; their brown, yellow, mahogany, black, caramel, café au lait bodies wrapped in eye-catching dresses, their varied, sometimes too-sweet perfumes clashing whenever two or more stood together. They were a glorious, fun-seeking army out on a one-night pass, but not one could beat Sapphire. Skip buried his face in the roses. Sapphire. He was ready to show her a good time, feed her, swing her around the dance floor, show her off to whatever sharp papa might take a look, but that was all anybody had better do, look, and not too long. Sapphire was going to be his!

"Hey, Skipper!"

His daydream shattered. He stiffened as if he'd been splashed with a bucket of ice water. Virginia. Tonight of all nights! He didn't turn around, desperately hoping she'd decide she had made a mistake. It wasn't him sitting in the middle of the streetcar swooning over three roses. Roses! He bent over slowly, cautiously placed the flowers and the fire truck beneath the seat.

"Hey, Skipper. Don't you hear me calling you?"

She was closer now, too close to ignore. He turned around and gave a weak, tentative smile as she grabbed her pleated shirt and settled in beside him, her soft girlish body touching his, pressing him back against the window. Her freshly curled hair glistened, giving her a mature, sophisticated look. She smelled like rain-washed spring.

"Where you been hiding?" she said, playfully squeezing his arm.

"Ain't been hiding," Skip said, trying to control his anxious nerves. "Been working."

Virginia vigorously shook her head from side to side. "You been hiding," she said. "I ain't seen you at none of the tea pads, none of the nightclubs. Nowhere." She stopped her fussing and threw a disappointed tone into her voice. "You said you would call me."

"I was going to but . . ." A vision of beautiful Sapphire opening her arms to him plunged him into another lie. "But I got busy. Besides, if you wanted to find me, why didn't you just come over to the Dancing Bar-B-Que?"

Virginia shook her head again. "I was waiting on you. You said you would call." She paused and sniffed the air. "I smell roses."

"What?' Skip said, startled.

"Roses. Don't you smell 'em?"

He shook his head, thought twice about telling another lie, then nodded. "Uh, yeah. I smell 'em. Must be somebody's perfume."

"Well, I wish I knew who, 'cause somebody should tell her it's too strong. Now, where you been hiding, Skipper?'

"I done already told you. I ain't been hiding. I been working. And don't be calling me Skipper."

"I'm shawy," she said, sounding like Betty Boop, pouting, pushing out a lower lip Skip would have kissed on any night but this. "So, where you going all dressed up?"

"Downtown," he said, forming the lie as he went along.

"Downtown?"

"Yeah, I got to see my agent man about a moving picture. I done already been in one."

"And you didn't call me? Oh, Skipper, that's wonderful. A moving picture!" She turned around and yelled to her friends. "Hey, girls, Skipper's a moving picture star!" She turned back to him and kissed him full on the lips. "Congratulations," she said, all dreamy-eyed. Skip felt her warm kiss burning his lips like a brand. He struggled against the stirring desire to take another kiss and the absolute need to wipe away the last one. No way could he show up at Sapphire's door, roses in hand and another woman's scent on his lips. That would really fix the night. Why Virginia, he thought. Why tonight? At the midnight ramble they had gotten all flushed and excited, grinding away on the dance floor. He could have had her that night. He could have her tonight. Oh, Virginia. Why are you here? Sapphire is waiting. He kept his hands to himself, read the passing street numbers and resolved to ride two stops past the one where Virginia got off.

"I can't believe you're in a moving picture," Virginia sighed.

"It was just a little part," Skip said. "I didn't even get to talk."

"But you made it, Skipper."

He rolled his eyes, the nickname grating against his nerves. Virginia saw the put-upon look and pouted again, her lower lip so tantalizing he had to look away.

"We have to celebrate," she said.

"I done already celebrated," he said, wishing the days had been turned around, the date with Sapphire set for next week instead of tonight, then he could grasp this lovely, willing bird in hand, and make her coo. And it wouldn't be two-timing because Sapphire hadn't claimed him. Damn, shit. "I thought about calling you, but it was Monday. You were working."

"Well, I'm here now, and I'm all yours" she fluttered her eyelids and offered her sweet lips.

Skip steeled himself. "Tonight's a bad night, Virginia, what with this meeting and all."

"I have all night," she said. "Anytime you're ready."

Skip's mind didn't want to hear that, but his body did. He scooted around in his seat, trying to accommodate the bulge growing in his pants. The stop for Sapphire's house passed. Nothing to do but wait, he thought, telling his body to calm down. The streetcar rumbled on.

"Hey, Virginia," yelled one of her girlfriends. "We're getting off at the next stop. You coming?"

"Be with you in a sec," she replied, turning to Skip. "We're going to be at the Lindy, all night. See you there?"

He shrugged. "Depends on this meeting."

"Oh, everything will be fine, Skipper." She leaned close, nuzzled him and whispered. 'I'm gon' save some dance-floor grinding for you."

A code red flashed below his waist. He took a deep breath and sighed, relieved that Virginia was gone. She waved from the avenue, blew him another kiss off her sweet lips as the streetcar pulled away. When she was out of sight, he licked his lips and wiped his cheek, praying she hadn't left her smell on him. He put aside the willing bird in hand, the one he'd let get away, and replaced her with the delicious possibility of finding another. His thoughts took a pornographic turn. But he did not surrender to them. Tonight he was going to be a gentleman, polite, gracious, respectful, the kind of man who could be trusted with Buster's mama.

Two stops later, he took the roses and fire truck from under the seat, stepped onto the crowded avenue and strolled two blocks west, then south, knowing this route would take him behind the Lindy. The quiet streets of Sapphire's neighborhood gave him a chance to relax, think up another plan. The Lindy was out. He couldn't risk running into Virginia with Sapphire on his arm. No amount of fast-talking could fix that mess. The very idea of a chance meeting made him cringe. He could see it already, Virginia catching sight of them, walking over all coy and innocent, placing a branding kiss smack dab on his lips, while Sapphire stood by, fuming, waiting for Virginia to go on her hip-swinging way before telling him she was taking a cab home because she could see he had other plans. Then he'd have to start explaining, pleading, begging, lying. And what if Virginia opened her big mouth and asked if Sapphire was his agent, his downtown agent? Right then he decided to take Sapphire to the Club Alabam, where there was an equally swinging band, and no Virginia.

He walked on, bearing gifts and a pocket full of money. He stopped outside her door, tugged his suit, straightened his tie and knocked three times. Sapphire peeked from behind the curtain, a troubled, worried expression darkening her usually warm, smiling face. Skip waved the red roses, figuring they'd bring back the smile that had stolen his heart.

"Buster's sick," she said, her voice full of fear and concern. "I tried to call you, but no one was home."

Skip's heart sank. He remembered the telephone ringing in the Dancing Bar-B-Que. A shudder of disappointment ran through him. Sapphire wasn't going anywhere tonight. She still had on a drab, yellow housedress. He felt suddenly foolish and awkward, a frustrated suitor standing in this neat cottage staring at the picture perfect studio portrait of Sapphire and Buster in a Madonna and child pose.

"I brought these for you," he said, raising the roses. Words stumbled out of his mouth. "And I bought this fire truck for Buster."

"Oh, Skip, that was so sweet of you." She gave him a peck on the same cheek Virginia had touched with her coquettish passion, took the flowers and rushed off to put them in a white china vase painted with pink rose petals.

He moved to the sofa, feeling like an intruder as he waited for Sapphire, his hands tossing the fire truck back and forth. He looked around for Buster's crib, didn't see it, but heard the little boy's congested cough coming from the bedroom.

"Sounds like he's got himself a little rattle chest," Skip said.

"My landlady said it's nothing to worry about. She even offered to sit with him. But I don't know if I should leave him. I'd be worried sick and no fun at all," Sapphire said, returning from the kitchen and setting the flowers on the coffee table. "There." She plopped down on the sofa, then sat up and crossed her legs at the ankles. "I can't go out tonight, Skip. I hope you understand. He's running a fever." Her eyes pleaded for understanding. "I tried to get in touch with you."

"I heard the phone ringing as I was leaving," Skip said. "I didn't figure it was anything important. Besides, I was running late for our date." He pursed his lips sucked on his teeth. "Guess I should've picked it up." He set the fire truck on the table and gave it a slight push. "I hope Buster likes it, and I hope he feels better. I kind of like that boy."

A strained, disappointed silence filled the room. He looked at Sapphire sitting at the other end of the sofa, almost close enough for him to reach out and touch. He could if he scooted over a foot or two. But where to touch her, and how? The timing was all wrong. He wasn't supposed to be on this sofa with Sapphire until after they'd been out, lost themselves in dancing and celebration, given themselves more time to build a bridge between their souls. Then they'd sit close together on this sofa, or at his place, all of life's worries and concerns pushed aside, leaving only enough room for two. And in that intimate space he would put his arms around her and caress her, his heart searching her beautiful face for the tender look of affection and surrender that would tell him that, yes, he had been a gentleman, their longing and desire would be fulfilled, if not tonight, then soon. That's how he'd dreamed this night. He never thought they'd be sitting here in brittle, oppressive silence with Sapphire distracted and preoccupied. He leaned forward and tapped the truck. A frightened gasp escaped Sapphire's lips when she heard poor

Buster coughing and crying for his mama. She jumped up and hurried into the back room.

"Mommy's coming," she cried.

Skip heard her cooing over Buster, comforting him with soft, loving words. He could almost kick himself for having fallen for a woman who preferred to spend her evenings alone with her kid. Buster was her number one man. Everybody else ran a distant second. But he ignored the signals and tried to break out of the pack. He wanted to be with her. When she returned, cradling a sleepy little boy who nestled in her arms, pudgy hands drowsily pawing her face, he knew why he had fallen for her. She was the prettiest girl he'd ever seen. Her warm smile full of perfect white teeth made his heart leap. She could be his, this kind, gentle woman who was citified without being all high-toned about it. Sapphire picked up the fire truck and waved it back and forth in front of Buster.

"Look, Buster, Mister Skip bought you a fire truck. Vroom! Vroom! Say fire truck, Buster, Fire truck."

"Byer-buck," gurgled Buster, eyes lighting up as his hands reached for the toy.

Sapphire laughed. "Byer-buck," she said, nuzzling her child. "Oooh, you're so hot. Feel him, Skip. I think he still has a fever."

Skip put his hand on Buster's forehead. "Hey, little buddy. You feeling okay?" The boy didn't feel too hot, yet what did it matter. If mama said so, then that's the way it was. "Yeah," he said. "I guess he's a little warm."

"I knew it," Sapphire said, vindicated. "Everybody said it was nothing to worry about, but I knew, didn't I, Buster. Mommy knew."

Skip stood to leave, better that than wait to be shown the door. "Well," he said, smoothing the wrinkles out of his suit coat. "Guess I best be going." He waited a moment, hoping Sapphire would ask him to stay, or change her mind and hand Buster over to her landlady. Instead she walked him to the door.

"You still owe me a date," he said. "The Joe Louis fight is coming up. Maybe we can get together then. And you," he pointed a playful finger at Buster. "You need to get well. Cain't have you messing up my plans."

"You'd better listen to Mister Skip, Buster," Sapphire said, gently rocking her baby boy. "Mommy can't spend every night taking care of you." She turned to Skip. "I'm so sorry about tonight. I was really looking forward to going out. I've practically been a shut-in since Buster came along," she said, a trace of frustration in her voice. "Are you going home?"

"I guess," he said, his body already anticipating the steamy pleasure of slow-dragging Virginia across the Lindy's dance floor. As much as he wanted Sapphire, she still had not claimed him.

"Wait here," she said, turning to take Buster back to his crib. She returned to Skip, walked up him, held his cheeks in her tender hands and brought her lips to his. "Wait for me," she said. "Please."

For a moment he didn't know what to say. Her kiss, so soft and exquisite, had taken him by surprise. He could still feel the press of her, the ambrosial taste of her. For the first time he saw a glimmer of affection in her brown eyes, and saw himself as she must have seen him. He was a good man, a gentleman who brought her roses, and a toy for her son. "Wait where?"

"Here," she replied, and touched his heart.

"Sapphire," he said, pulling her close and kissing her fingertips. He whispered her name again, then embraced her and buried his face in her hair. They kissed twice, lightly the first time, deeply the second time with a growing hunger that made them tremble from the sudden burst of desire. They were two people starved for love. It was as if their lips had known each other for years, but had never tasted the sweet, gratifying tingle of surrender. He felt her hands along his back, his hands sliding firmly along the soft curve of her hips. He wanted to stay, even if Buster was in the next room. They could make coffee and listen to the radio, be together, rather than alone. He wished he lived close enough to run home and get National Steel. There was a song he wanted to play for her. All this he wanted, now. But Buster was sick. Sapphire slowly pulled away from him. Her eyes sparkling and moist, her face flushed.

"You better go," she said, catching her breath.

He nodded, the wonder of the past few moments washing through him. "You sure?" They giggled for a moment, blushing like school kids after a first kiss. Then he opened the door. "See you soon," he said, blowing Sapphire a kiss before stepping into the night.

He walked down the driveway with no idea of where he was going. Sapphire had claimed him. And he had run up the white flag. Goodbye, Virginia. On the streetcar home, he rode apart from the other riders who got off and on, barely heard their laughter, their excited conversations and gossip about who was seen with whom, the swinging band at the Club Alabam, the wild tea pad party starting up after midnight. They were really going to kick the gong around. He was going home. At least the streetcar was heading in that direction. The moments at Sapphire's door had crossed his wires. He felt himself luxuriating in the beautiful after-glow of their last, hot kiss. He had yearned for this, but now that it had come, he was not prepared for where it might lead. She had opened a different door than the one he had expected. He'd been taken by the shape of her, the sway of her hips, her smile. Even Buster played at his heart, one fatherless boy reaching out to another. Now both of them were pulling him into something more than a little rollin' and tumblin'. He stepped off a few blocks from the Dancing Bar-B-Que, strolled into a liquor store and spent a dollar on a pint of Chivas Regal.

Inside his room, he slipped out of the suit and into his comfortable jeans. He took a deep gulp from the bottle, then another, before grabbing National Steel. She was already in Dropped D tuning, ready for him to bring her to life. He ran his fingers lovingly along the dull gray curves of the guitar's steel body. His fingers wrapped around the cool, long neck, shaped easy major chords that played off the low D as he strummed and pressed National Steel close against him. The night's revelation made it hard to think. His mind kept going back to Sapphire and Buster. He laughed to himself, took a swig of Chivas as he lit a cigarette and let another side of himself speak, a side that said be careful, he was too young to be a family man. He should be running with Pee Wee. One of Old Man Williams' favorite sayings from his soldiering days came to mind: *'There's two kinds of women in the world. Them that will, and them that won't. But them that won't, might, if you play your cards right.'*

Happy shouts, the throaty roar of car engines and the tintinnabulation of a streetcar's bell gaily ringing filled the avenue. He felt the room's walls closing in on him, found his mind stealing away to that jubilee going on outside, where every man was dressed to the nines to welcome the Kitchen Mechanics back home. His night did not have to end with National Steel, scotch and cigarettes. He wanted to celebrate this new and wonderful feeling coming over him, lose himself in the bright lights and music, the joyous abandon. He turned away from the window, picked up his guitar and tried a song he'd heard one night on the Negro Music

Hour. It was full of remembrance and desire. He had scoured music shops downtown and on the avenue for a copy. Had Sapphire been here, he would have played it for her and let its words say what he felt. He smiled to himself, counted out the beat and began "Stars Fell On Alabama," his voice lingering over a favorite line: "My heart beat like a hammer. My arms wound around you tight." Satisfied, he took another swig of Chivas and lit a Chesterfield off the one dying in the ashtray. So much for a night on the town.

Across town, Sapphire tucked Buster in for the night and scolded herself for having been so impetuous, kissing Skip, then blushing like she was in the middle of some foolish schoolgirl infatuation. Funny how those feelings never left you, even after life showed you what happens to girls who lead with their hearts. She smiled at her baby boy, nuzzled him and kissed his sleep-heavy eyes.

"Here comes the sandman," she said, walking her fingers along his blanket.

Buster yawned one last time. His eyelids flickered. The sandman had come. Sapphire walked back to her small kitchen, catching sight of Skip's roses along the way. She was going to make herself a cup of tea, but her mind kept wandering back to the roses, to the trembling kiss at the front door, the toy fire truck on the sofa. Who did Skip think he was, bringing her flowers? That only happened in the movies. And a toy for Buster? That was too much. She felt her heart under an assault in which the only weapons were kindness and roses, and that put her off-balance. Skip had to have some dog in him, had to. Every man did. She kept waiting for his to show, kept using Buster as a shield to keep him from getting too close. That worked with most men, but not Skip. He just kept on coming, and his dog was nowhere to be seen. Maybe? She shook her head at the thought. Skip was just a good man, and it felt good to kiss him, to feel his arms around her, to hear her name whispered in her ear, his teeth giving her earlobe a tender, tingling nibble that made her want to throw back her head and say, 'Do it again.' She had gone too long without the intoxicating feeling of those kinds of kisses. It took everything she had to send Skip away. And as soon as he was gone, she wanted him back, wanted to get dressed and step out into the night with him, see herself as she knew she was, young and alive and beautiful, a knockout who just happened to be Buster's mama. She didn't love Skip, yet, but she loved what he had done to her. He had knocked down her defenses with rose petals. And in return she had kissed him, lightly, her heart wavering. Then her lips were moving, telling him to wait, please, wait. She didn't want to lose him or the chance to breathe new life into that alluring and seductive part of herself she had put aside when Buster was born, that part of her that wanted to be caressed, made love to and desired above all else.

Sapphire looked at the roses and thought about dancing. She missed dancing, and the crowds, and the music. She picked up her telephone and dialed the Dancing Bar-B-Que. The phone rang a half-dozen times. She had almost put it down when she heard his voice.

"Skip," she said. "You're still there. I thought you might have gone on out."

"No, no," he said. "Just sitting here playing my guitar. How's Buster?"

"A little better. He's asleep. My landlady's about to kick me out," she said, a smile in her voice. "I told you she said I need to stop acting like an old maid and get some fresh air. Is that offer still good?"

"You know it is," he said. "Can you meet me at the Club Alabam?"

"I'll beat you there," she said, hung up and went to her closet to pick out something to mess up that good man's mind.

Skip ran back upstairs, put his suit back on, slapped on some more Silver Esquire cologne and headed out, taking one last, fortifying sip of Chivas Regal. He left whistling a love song about stars falling and kisses in a field of white. He strolled Central Avenue with a self-assured hipster's stride, waving to people he didn't know, found himself beaming whenever a friendly face turned to his. Outside the Club Alabam, a wary, secretive looking brother with furtive brown eyes stood near the door and whispered. "Rubber man, two bits."

Why not, he thought, remembering Old Man Williams' saying. It could be his good luck charm in case fortune smiled on him in the wee hours of the morning and Sapphire turned to him and said, 'Yes, love. Yes.' He had to be ready and protected. After all, he was too young to be a family man. He fished a quarter from his pocket. The brother smiled conspiratorially and slapped a cellophane wrapped prophylactic in his palm, gave him the thumbs up sign before turning away. Skip handed the suited doorman a dollar and stepped inside.

The Club Alabam was twenty degrees hotter than the avenue. He could feel the heat, thick and heavy. The air smelled of perfume, cologne,

cheap aftershave and sweat. People were everywhere. Lone wolf brothers, looking terminally cool and predatory in their sharpest suits, prowl-
ing the edges of the club with the intense eyes of hunters as they sized
up the girls clustered together in intimidating groups. Couples twirled
and swirled in acrobatic abandon on the dance floor. A swinging, nine-
piece band held the stage. They were all dressed in immaculate black,
except for their leader, who wore sparkling white and bopped across the
bandstand, shaking his head so his glistering, straightened black hair
swung out in wide arcs, Cab Calloway style. Skip scanned the room for
Sapphire, and headed to the bar where an overworked young brother
stood ready whenever someone called out for a drink over ice, straight
up, or mixed with the best money could buy. Then he would turn, grab a
glass off the shelf, flip it over his shoulder and catch it before it hit the
bar. People cheered him, called out fresh orders just to see him toss a
glass high and snatch it from the air. Skip caught his eye and yelled for a
Chivas, on the rocks, daddy-o. Through the din of jazz and shouting
voices he heard Sapphire calling him.

"Skip!"

His heart leapt at the sound of her voice. He turned and saw her
pushing through the crowded nightclub, waving her hand. She looked
stunning in a coral dress that fit her like a tailor's dream, her hair accented by one of his roses.

"Sapphire," he yelled, throwing open his arms to receive her. She
seemed to melt in his embrace, and he in hers. Behind them the band
started in on Duke Ellington's "Take the A-Train."

"Dance with me, Skip," she said. "I want to see if I've lost my step."

He gulped down a mouthful of Chivas and put his drink on the bar.
"C'mon, baby," he said, flushed, high and happy. "Let's catch that train."

They danced nonstop, resting only when the band went on break,
giving them a chance to catch their breath. Skip alternated scotch and ice
water, while Sapphire drank soda. She told him that Buster hated the
smell of alcohol. It made him cry. She thought it was because the smell
reminded him of his father. Skip heard that and pushed his drink aside,
taking one last sip when the band returned. They stayed on the dance
floor until the bartender said it was time to drink 'em. The band played
one last rousing finale. Trumpets, trombones and saxophones traded riffs
with the piano, dueled, clowned. The bandleader swung his glorious

head of hair, waved his hands for more applause, pointed his baton to the drummer who, finally given his chance to cut loose, fired a cannonade from his tom-tom. Machine-gun rolls from the snare snapped ferociously in the dense, sweat-soaked air. A crash on the cymbal brought the band back home for one more swinging chorus. Then the manager flipped on the lights. Skip squinted, shielded his eyes from the harsh white glare exploding overhead. People stood around dazed, stunned by the night's sudden end. Slowly, the exhausted crowd flowed out onto Central Avenue. Some stood in loose knots. Fast friends lingered, exchanged phone numbers, said "Good night." "See you next week?" "Maybe." Others rushed to cabs and cars waiting to carry them to an after-hours spot, an all-night cafe, a dark, smoky viper's den, home, which was where Skip took Sapphire, home to his once lonely room above the Dancing Bar-B-Que.

On the ride down Central Avenue, they snuggled in the back seat of a Black and White cab, playful as puppies, oblivious to the old driver sitting up front stealing peeks in his rearview mirror. Halfway home, Skip threw back his arms and laughed, a giddy, tipsy joy rising up in him, carrying him higher than the moon. The night was better than he ever dreamed it could be.

"What are you laughing at, Skip," said Sapphire, tugging on his coat and pulling him back to earth.

"I feel like the luckiest man on earth," he said.

"We're both a couple of lucky so-and-sos," she said, and leaned her head on his shoulder. She wrapped her arms around his waist, pulling him close.

Skip scooted around his seat, trying to get comfortable, afraid his body was giving him away. Sapphire worked one of her hands under his shirt, just below his ribs. The flick of her fingernails made him giggle. "Girl," he said, putting his hand over hers. "Don't start what you can't finish."

Once inside the Dancing Bar-B-Que, he scrounged around the pantry and the ice box, finding enough for a couple of rib sandwiches. He led Sapphire up to his room, where he poured himself enough Chivas Regal to wet his lips and brought her a glass of water.

"I can't stay the night," she said. "I promised my landlady."

"That's okay," he replied, clicking on the radio. Billie Holiday and her orchestra came on, her smooth, bluesy, elegant voice lilting into the room, shaping the melody like Babe Russin's tenor sax. She was singing "You Go To My Head," singing softly, her fragile heart wondering about her crazy romance.

Skip apologized for the room. It was shabby compared to Sapphire's cottage apartment and bore no hint of a woman's touch. His guitar leaned against the one chair he had. There was no place else to sit, except for the bed. He grabbed National Steel and offered Sapphire the straight-backed chair, but she shook her head.

"I'll just sit here," she said, settling on a corner of his bed and nodding towards his guitar. "Can you play me a song?"

He nodded and smiled. "I've been working on something I pulled off the radio awhile back." He turned down the volume, took a seat in the chair and swung National Steel across his knee. "The Stars Fell On Alabama," he said, and began his love song to her.

He worked through the chords one time to set the mood and pace, winked at Sapphire and started singing, beginning with the bridge because the verse told of a heavenly situation beyond his imagination, just two people together, he and Sapphire. He held her gaze, found himself trying to croon like a big band singer. His fingers, confident and sure, moved through the changes as he shared this intimate part of himself. He repeated the last line, walked through the final chords and ended with an octave on the twelfth fret. He smiled.

"What did you think? Did you like it?"

"I loved it, Skip," she said, her face glowing. "Nobody ever sang to me before." She kicked off her shoes and held her arms out to him. "Dance with me, and sing to me. I want to hear it again."

They swayed gently across the room, holding onto each other, their bodies enfolded. Skip breathed deeply the heady mix of Sapphire's rose water perfume and sweat. He backed her towards his nightstand, leaned down to turn off the light and radio, then, in the settling darkness, sang to her of love and glamour and stars falling on Alabama. He felt her hands up under his shirt, the tingle of her fingernails gliding along his spine, down to his waist around to his stomach then slowly up to his chest. He pulled her close, pressed her up against him so she could feel him bulging and straining inside his pants. His hands reached down and slipped under her dress to feel the soft silk of her stockings. She gasped when she felt his hands touching her thighs, his fingers sliding along her garters, testing them, then around to cup the firm mounds of her buttocks as he leaned down and she offered him her neck, and he bit her, lightly, lingered over her like she was the most delicious thing he had ever tasted. She leaned back from him, her body arched as he gave her a necklace of love bites. His nibbles made her giggle and swoon and say it felt so good, so good, because she had gone too long without this voluptuous feeling of a man she wanted making her wet and hot inside, her nipples already swelling and all he'd done was kiss her and hold her tight.

He pulled her up and she started biting his shirt buttons, one by one, her fingers and tongue working down to his waist until all were undone and his shirt and undershirt had been tossed aside. With her tongue she made long, slow, circles around his navel, kissing him now and then. His body smelled of cologne and sweat and an odor of sex that excited her as she rubbed the bulge in his pants. He struggled to control himself, to settle down and feel his body throbbing, every inch of him tingling, yearning to be touched. Sapphire's luscious kisses made him tremble, but he held on against the wild desire roaring through him, impatient and demanding. He dropped to his knees and felt her hands at his belt, then relief, his body no longer constrained. He brought her hands to his face and kissed each one of her fingers, then held her close. She smiled at him and sighed as she rested her head upon his shoulder and he smelled the perfume in her hair, and rocked her from side to side, his hands undoing her dress, then pulling it from her shoulders so he could feel the silky softness of her camisole against his bare chest. They moaned together when he bent low and sucked her nipples and she dug her fingernails into his back and there was an exquisite mixture of pain and pleasure and they said yes to each other, standing and dropping their clothes to the floor, their chocolate brown bodies naked and glistening in the dark, yes, because it had been a long time since the last time, yes, because this time it seemed like love instead of wham-bam-thank you-m'am, which was better than nothing, but this was so much different, this came after a thousand miles and the terrors of the road and being a stranger trying to find a way, being lonely and hungry for the soft curves of a woman pressed against you, the memory of that and the feel of your stroking hands enough to ease the tension but not enough to satisfy you down deep in your soul, for that you needed another. And so, yes, now, tonight, with the song of moonlight and sweet magnolia running through their heads, yes, to the hot, passionate kisses, the consuming hunger enough to make it seem Skip would devour Sapphire and she him as they rolled back and forth across his narrow bed in this delirium, she on top of him, straddling his waist, her breasts hanging down, just in reach of his flicking tongue and O God the explosion of joy she felt when she let herself go and he filled his mouth with her and sucked on her and imagined sweet honey pouring from her, yes, when they rolled over and he was on top of her, pausing for a moment, remembering the prophylactic tucked away in his wallet, but there was no way to get it now with his head buried between her breasts, his cock probing her, sliding in and out of her, filling her, and she tensing her hips, gripping him, not wanting to let him go and he starting to call her name, Sapphire, Sapphire, and she loved the sound of him calling her as she wrapped her legs around him, raised her hips and pulled him deeper, held him there and said, yes, Skip, yes, because Buster's mama was lonely too and needed a good man to caress her, love her, sing to her like she was a fairy tale princess and he was a troubadour whose song brought her right out of her drawers. They said yes to each other because maybe this night would hook them together, maybe these moments with their bodies afire, arms and legs intertwined, all wrapped up in each other, maybe the memory of this bliss would keep him coming back to her, keep her wanting him to come back, for more, yes, love, for more, and then there was no more control, no more thinking, just their bodies embracing, straining as something powerful and ecstatic poured through them and they locked onto each other, rocked together in joyous abandon and 'O Lord' he felt himself bucking against her and 'O Sweet Jesus' she joined his rhythm and they said yes to each other because nothing on this side of heaven came close to this good fun. Yes, they said, to the emptying release, the peace that follows the exhaustion, the tender cuddling of a brief luxuriant nap that lasts only until the nuzzling begins and fingers resume their sensuous dance along stomachs and thighs and they feel their bodies awakening, rising to start all over again, saying yes, 'O Love' yes, and this time with protection because there was only so much luck in the world.

P HINEAS MOVED THROUGH THE DANCING BAR-B-QUE'S BOISTER-
ous fight-night crowd in stately, regal fashion, holding high a plate of
gnawed rib bones. He squeezed in between a couple of sharp-dressed
dandies at the counter, set his plate down and licked his fingers one by
one, each time tasting a lingering bit of Henry's sweet sauce. Then he
grabbed a mangled bone, cracked it open with his teeth and started sucking, jaws working as if he was drawing on a straw. Seeing Henry behind
the counter, he waved the broken bone.

"Kind sir," he said.

Henry didn't hear him. The babble of laughing, shouting voices
drowned out everything except Diana's insistent, familiar voice demanding more orders of "The Brown Bomber Special"—potato salad, collard
greens, and a heavyweight slab of baby back ribs smothered in the best
batch of sauce Henry had cooked up in a good long while. Phineas
cleared his throat and called out again. He broke open another bone,
sucked at it, his gaze sweeping the counter, then resting on Skip, who
stood elbow-deep in suds and dirty dishes, a little boy in a high chair
behind him. He pointed the mutilated rib at the bruised steel guitar
propped against the supply room's back wall, strummed the air and
raised his eyebrows. Skip nodded. Phineas started to move towards him,
but stopped. Henry was heading his way. The bone dropped from his fingers.

"Again?" Henry said.

"Indubitably, kind sir." Phineas took a final, tasty lick before shoving the plate towards Henry. "I have nearly had my fill and am now going for the knockout, and I don't mean a T.K.O. Sir, I am ready to be floored, knocked down for the count, driven out of my senses by one more serving of the fine victuals that are the sumptuous fare of this splendid evening."

Henry dumped the bones into the trash, jammed the dirty plate into a full tray and pulled a clean one from the stack beside the grill. "What'll it be?"

"Why, "The Brown Bomber Special", of course, with a gut-crunching pile of collard greens, if you please, and," Phineas paused, his tongue rolling dreamily over his lips. "For the coup de grace, a knockout slice of sweet potato pie."

"Coming up," Henry said, ladling the rich, red sauce over the meaty ribs. "But, tell me. Where are you putting all this food? It's none of my business but, I believe this is your fourth plate."

Phineas puffed up his chest and frowned, offended. "The notice said all you could eat for fifty cents. But, to answer your inquiry, I'm stuffing it down this hollow leg of mine." He smiled at Henry's skeptical expression. "Actually, current circumstances have brought about a Darwinian evolution in my metabolism. You see, I try to keep an extra meal in my gut at all times." He loosened his belt a notch and belched. "Ahh," he sighed. "One never knows when the infernal maw will awaken, shake its hoary head and demand to be fed. A ready reserve, such as the plate you are now preparing, keeps the impatient growling to a minimum."

"I see," Henry said, sliding Phineas a full plate. "You're laying in a roll of fat for the winter."

Phineas grinned. "That, kind sir, is a wonderful analogy. And, for this offering, I thank you." He stepped back, bowed graciously, then grabbed his food and went to the first empty seat he could find.

Henry leaned back contentedly, wiped his hands on his apron and watched Phineas go. He looked around the smoky room, checked the crowded tables and the counter, searched for empty plates and satisfied grins, signs that his cooking had filled folks up, set them floating on the good feeling only a plateful of ribs could bring. Fight night was good for business. The place was packed, a pleasant surprise on a night when every two-bit slop house and bar on the avenue offered everything from free drinks and food to a pallet to sleep off the night's celebration, and there was going to be plenty of celebrating, just as soon as Joe Louis took care of Jack Roper. Henry laughed to himself, remembering the fuss his meat supplier made about Roper. The guy said the journeyman heavyweight was too experienced for young Joe, said Roper's hook was going to bring down The Brown Bomber. He'd even slapped a five-dollar bill on the counter and dared Henry to match it, which Henry did, with pleasure. Letting that bet slip by would be like walking past money lying on the ground. He looked at an envelope sitting on the shelf above the counter. Ten dollars waited for the winner. He checked the clock: six-thirty; half an hour till fight time.

"Last call," he yelled. "The rib man's about to shut down."

"Aw, Henry." Pee Wee took his arm from around his girl and yelled across the room. "I was thinking 'bout getting me and Bessie Lee another plate."

"Well, come on," Henry said, turning off his oven. "Last call."

He served Pee Wee and a couple of other folks before carrying a heavy tray of dirty dishes back to Skip. "Boy," he said, straining as he set the tray down. "That all-you-can-eat idea of yours is a real killer diller. I don't know why I never thought of it before. Those folks ate up just about everything."

"Told you." Skip grabbed two handfuls of plates and slid them into the sink. "Good food always brings a crowd, especially when the price is right."

"Ain't that the truth. That friend of yours, Phineas. He ate enough for two men, and I mean two hungry men."

"Yeah, Phineas is one eating fool."

Henry chuckled, "He blames it on Darwin, an evolution in his metabolism. But I don't think so. Darwin said survival of the fittest, and Phineas is about the most unfit man I've seen."

Henry looked over at Skip's guitar. "You still feel like playing?"

"Me and National Steel are ready to go. Just say when."

"Let me give the room one more check. I already said last call, but I don't want anybody going home saying I wasn't true to my word. I'll be back in about fifteen minutes. That'll leave enough time for a song or two." He tapped the high chair. "Hey, Buster. That boy sure has taken to you, Skip."

"Yeah, he's starting to think he's kin to me," Skip said, emptying the tray and working quickly.

"You still saying he ain't," said Diana, poking her head around the door and smiling. "I don't know why you want to deny that child, Skip, cute as he is." She walked over and pinched Buster's cheek. The boy had become such a regular at the restaurant that Diana couldn't help teasing Skip, saying he had been playing possum until he saw fit to bring his wife and child out of Texas. Buster favored him a little too much to blame it on friendly coincidence, she said.

"I ain't denying him," Skip replied, fishing the last few dishes out of the sink. "He just ain't mine."

"Not yet," laughed Diana. "But you just wait." She gave Buster another pinch before heading back to the café, shaking her head sadly, saying in mock seriousness, "It's a darn shame. Denying that little boy your name. Just a darn shame."

Skip dried his hands and gave Buster another spoonful of rib meat. He studied the little boy's eyes and face. Diana was right. Buster was a cute kid, but even a blind man could see they weren't kin. Her teasing him about having a wife and child made him uncomfortable, even scared him. He kept reminding himself that he was too young for such things. Sure, he and Sapphire had been seeing a lot of each other since their night together. They went on picnics in Griffith Park, and Saturday afternoon strolls along the Santa Monica pier, Buster in tow. She had even tried to get him to go to church. But he was not about to give up his Sunday mornings, or his freedom.

He returned to the sink, finished the last dishes and yanked the plug, sending the water swirling down the drain. A soapy, red-rimmed scum clung to the porcelain. He turned on the cold water, flushed out the sink, then wiped his hands and blew on his fingertips, hoping to dry them before Henry returned. An evening's worth of washing dishes had softened his calluses enough to make him wonder if he could get through Tommy Johnson's "Big Road Blues" and a rag he'd been working on ever since Henry talked him into playing for the fight night crowd. He loved the idea. He hadn't played much in front of any crowds since coming to Los Angeles. It was all Henry's idea. The boss man had come up with it one day while they were talking about what to do on fight night. Henry said entertainment would add a special touch. All Skip had to do was play. Henry knew he could do it. He'd heard him playing some nights when he stayed late, heard him upstairs behind a closed door, playing old country blues and rags, singing in a voice that was getting better and better. And, lately, he'd even heard Skip playing songs off the radio. Skip would give the Dancing Bar-B-Que something even the Dunbar Hotel couldn't match: a real live country bluesman, with a touch of jazz.

Skip had been practicing like a demon. He had new songs, new tricks to show off. He picked up his guitar and kicked the kitchen door shut, leaned his head close to the neck, listened to the strings plucked one by one. National Steel was tuned and ready. He looked at his hands. They knew what to do: left hand glide up and down the neck, fingers shaping chords and bluesy, single-note jazz runs picked by his right hand. His body didn't need any coaxing. His voice did. The thought of singing in front of a strange crowd set his pulse racing. He was afraid somebody might laugh. These were city folks, long removed from the dirt roads and down home blues. He wanted tonight to be like the night he played for Sapphire, a night when his nervousness dropped away, his confidence took hold and he caught the melody right on key. He lost himself at such times, closed his eyes and saw a song's story play out like a moving picture: good women lying on the cooling board, lonely broken-hearted men standing at their sides; traveling men going down to the crossroads to wait for the Devil; a midnight train whose smokestack spat lightning and whose bells shined like gold; two lovers holding tight. He dropped National Steel's low E string down a step to D, did the opening, ascending run of Tommy Johnson's tune and wished he could growl like Blind Willie Johnson, or sing the blues smooth and easy like Delta Slim.

"Well, Buster," he said, setting his guitar aside, "the show's about to start." He spoon-fed the boy some more rib meat. "Eat up. You gotta grow up big and strong so you can handle one of these steel guitars." He picked up National Steel and played Buster's favorite nursery rhyme.

"Twinkle, twinkle," the child sang, eyes lighting up as he clapped his hands.

"Yeah, buddy," Skip said. "But it's blues time tonight." He did a tumbling down riff in D. "Nothing but the blues."

He started to sing, then stopped. Someone was coming. Sapphire. He could tell by the tap of her heels along the linoleum. She pushed open the door and walked in. "How are my two favorite gentlemen," she said, giving each of them a friendly kiss.

"He's fed, and I'm ready," Skip said, then frowned playfully. "Gal, what you doing dressing so fine?"

Sapphire smiled and twirled, showing off her powder blue flower-print dress, accented by a white belt that fit snug to her waist and gave her an even more pleasing shape. "I'm just trying to keep you in line," she said. "Like it?"

He nodded and pulled her close. "What do you think," he said, giving her a long kiss.

"I see," said Sapphire. "Are you going to play my song?"

Skip shook his head. "That's ours. Besides, this ain't no love song crowd. They're here for a fight."

Henry poked his head around the door. "Time," he said. "Your public's waiting."

Sapphire scooped Buster out his high chair and followed Henry into the café. At the doorway she stopped, grabbed Buster's right hand and threw an uppercut. "Knock 'em dead, champ."

Skip pretended to duck, then reached out and grabbed National Steel. The familiar touch of his guitar calmed him. He swallowed hard, forced a bit of spit down his drying throat. Out in the cafe, Henry quieted the crowd.

"Ladies and gentlemen. We have something very special tonight. A young man who came out here to be an actor, but after tonight, you all might think he'd be better off as a musician. So, without further ado, let's hear it for Central Avenue's only country bluesman, my dishwasher, Texas Skip Reynolds!"

Shrill whistles and rumbling applause erupted in the cafe. Pee Wee yelled for Skip. Phineas pounded a table and demanded a song from down home. A gold-toothed dandy waved him on.

"Come on, boy. Beat that box!"

The guitar almost slipped from his hands, but he tightened his grip and felt a confident strength surging down his arm. He took a deep breath, stiffened his legs and tightened his stomach muscles. Just play the blues, boy, he told himself. Just play the blues. The applause started up again when he stepped into the cafe. He held his guitar high, waved and winked at Sapphire and Buster. Pee Wee put two fingers in his mouth and blew a high-pitched whistle. Phineas beat a mad, heavy-fisted drum roll on a wooden table, then stood, held his arms wide and told everybody that Skip was the genuine article, bona fide and certified, country as Mississippi mud.

"Now, come on and play," he yelled. "God dammit. Play the blues!"

Henry patted Skip's shoulder, shoved him towards a lonely seat set against one of the cafe's walls. It looked a long way off, small, like a child's seat or a chair seen through the wrong end of a telescope. Diana and her family were near the front, two bright-eyed boys squirming in their Sunday suits while their father, a stern, graying man Diana called The Deacon, sat stiffly beside them, hands resting in his lap. Skip stumbled forward, working hard to keep his nerves in check. The chair seemed to grow bigger and bigger until it became normal size. He touched the worn wood, sat down and swung National Steel across his lap. Everybody waited. A striking match sizzled in the stillness. A chair creaked. Someone leaned back. He tried to look up, but couldn't find the strength to lift his head, tried to speak but a choking fear cut off his words. His hands felt suddenly heavy and awkward as he fumbled through the opening run of "Big Road Blues." Again he opened his mouth. A strained, unsteady voice shaking like a fragile leaf hanging on against a stiff autumn breeze came out. He stopped.

"Uh, I ain't too familiar with this here, but, uh, Henry figured maybe I could play y'all a little blues and get everybody in the mood, 'cause it won't be long 'fore old Jack Roper finds out what the Brown Bomber can do."

"Tell the truth, honey," Diana said. "Now, show me what you can do."

Skip raised his head, found comfort and encouragement in Diana's familiar face. He smiled. "That's Di for you. Always trying to hurry me up." He licked his dry lips, heard his heartbeat thundering in his ears like a trip hammer gone haywire. "I'm gon' play y'all an old Delta favorite. And, I'm gon' sing it for a couple of friends of mine, Miss Sapphire Louise Davis, and my buddy, Little B." He found her in the crowd, her eyes wide with surprise. She smiled shyly, primped her hair and looked around to see who was looking at her. Skip blew her a kiss, took a deep, calming breath and started pounding out the "Big Road Blues."

His body caught the song's rhythm and started rocking from side to side, his foot keeping the time. From somewhere in the room, a pair of clapping hands urged him on. Other hands joined in, all of them hitting every other beat. He squinted down at his fingers. His nervousness drained away as he started crying about how he wasn't going down that big road by himself, 'cause if he couldn't take his best gal, then he was gon' carry somebody else. Midway through the first verse, his voice dropped into the right key, startling him. He almost forgot the words. The music carried him away. He forgot the crowd, saw only his fingers sliding up and down the guitar's neck, sliding up the neck for a little run Delta Slim would have loved. Then he was singing again. Rolling steady, now, sounding better than Tommy Johnson.

"Said the sun's gon' shine, Lord, in my back door someday.

And if that rain don't change, gon' blow my blues away."

He repeated that last line, yodeling like Tommy Johnson, his thumb and forefinger pulling hard on the bass strings, slowing the beat ever so slightly. He flew through the descending run once, twice, hitting the low D at the end of each riff. It rang deep and loud against the high notes. He felt it humming through National Steel's body, shaking with a vibrato he made by putting his left hand just above the guitar's neck and pressing the string up and down, a trick learned from Delta Slim. He finished with a flourish, letting the low D note fade slowly. People started whooping and hollering, whistling and applauding. Phineas jumped out of his seat and yelled.

"Encore! Encore! God dammit, boy, encore me!"

Skip leaned back and caught his breath, tuned the low string back up to E as the applause washed over him. He wished it would never stop, wished he could somehow preserve this good feeling and pour it over himself whenever he felt blue.

"Now tell us about Joe Louis," Diana said.

"Yeah, Skip, " Pee Wee yelled. "Tell us how he' gon' give that ofay bum the old one- two."

"Yeah," people yelled. "Tell us how it's gon' be."

"Play the blues, baby."

"Beat that gitfiddle, boy!"

Skip looked around, saw Henry standing proudly against the counter, arms folded across his chest, nodding; Phineas leaning across his table, talking excitedly, waving his arms and laughing; Pee Wee nudging Bessie Lee, smiling and pointing at him, putting his fingers in his mouth and whistling. He didn't see Sapphire, or Buster. Where were they? Maybe she'd taken him to the bathroom for a diaper change. He'd find her soon enough.

"I guess y'all liked that one," he said, coaxing another round of applause. "Well, I'm gon' give y'all another one, that is if you can stand another one."

"I could stand two!"

Skip searched the crowd for the voice and found a good-looking, brown-skinned gal. He nodded to her. She was pretty enough to give Sapphire a run for the money. Where was that gal, anyway?

"Ragtime Joe," he said, rubbing his tender fingertips across his jeans. "Just a little ditty for the pretty gal in the back of the room."

He found his place on National Steel's neck, shaped a C chord in first position and started playing, but too fast. The sudden sloppiness stole his confidence. His fingers struggled to keep up with the fast-moving chord progression, the demanding rhythm, the intricate syncopated picking pattern and the diminished chords he'd thrown in to give the tune a bit of big-city sophistication. Stray, dissonant notes crashed into the melody. Strings buzzed. A fingernail on his picking hand split and snagged the high E string. He stopped, embarrassed, pressed his right palm against the stings to deaden the ugly sound.

"Uh, y'all gon' have to excuse that mess," he said

"Take your time, honey," Diana said. "Ain't nobody here but us."

Skip dropped his shoulders, took a deep breath. Nothing to it, he thought, running the song through his head, just an old-time rag with new words. He bit off the ragged nail.

"Okay, Ragtime Joe."

This time he worked slowly through a full chorus, gradually picked up speed before settling into his comic prediction of the fight's outcome.

"Look out for the Brown Bomber. He's got dynamite in every blow.
Watch out for his punch, man, or you'll end up on the floor.
He'll hit you with his left and then his right,
And before you know it, it'll be good night."

He heard people laughing, looked up and saw Diana nodding her head, pinching a tight smile from The Deacon. Henry pointed toward the clock. Five minutes to fight time. Aw, hell. The story wasn't finished. He played one more chorus, then brought the rag to an end.

"Time for Joe," he said to another round of applause.

Henry rushed up beside him, beaming like a proud father. "There you have it folks. The blues from down home. Let's hear it one more time for my dishwashing bluesman, Texas Skip Reynolds."

Skip made his way towards Pee Wee's table, shaking hands, saying, "thank you." His body tingled from the heady rush of success. Pee Wee pulled a chair back and held out his hand, palm up.

"Skin me, brother," he said. "Skin me!"

Skip slapped his friend's hand and sat down propping National Steel beside the table. "Whew! I sure was something, wasn't I? That rag almost got me, but . . ."

"Aw, don't nobody care about that slip-up," Pee Wee said. "You care about that, Bessie Lee?"

She shook her head. "But I think Skip's gon' have to carry somebody else down that big road."

He looked around for Sapphire. She was gone. He looked at Bessie Lee.

"She been gone," Bessie Lee said. "Up and left before you finished that first song. Guess she still doing you like she do, do, do."

Skip started to stand up, but Pee Wee pushed him back in his seat. "Forget it," he said, unscrewing the cap on a bottle of Chivas Regal. "She probably just took the kid home. You been seeing too much of her anyway. Drink up, good brother."

Skip poured himself three fingers, took a full, long swallow, his eyes still bouncing from face to face. Where was Sapphire? Why didn't she wait and tell him where she was going? He took another swallow. It warmed him all the way down to his gut. Henry turned on the radio he'd already set to KFI. An announcer's voice cracked through the tiny speaker. The buzz of voices in the Dancing Bar-B-Que died down. Chairs squeaked across the floor. People turned to face the little brown box alive with the shouts and murmuring voices of Wrigley Field's fight crowd.

"Lay-dees and Gentlemen," cried the announcer. "The main event. A scheduled ten rounds of boxing for the heavyweight championship of the world."

"Ten rounds!" Pee Wee shook his head. "Ten seconds is more like it. One punch."

The crowd shushed him. Waves of applause rippled from the radio as the announcer introduced the stars at ringside: Johnny Weismuller, Jimmy Cagney, Steppin' Fetchit.

"And now, for the heavyweight championship of the world. In the red corner, the challenger, Fighting Jack Roper!"

The Dancing Bar-B-Que filled with boos and jeers, stray voices calling out, "Bum," "Overweight Punching Bag."

"And in the black corner, the Motor City Mauler, the Brown Bomber, the heavyweight champion of the world, Joe Louis!" The announcer drew out each syllable, his voice rising to a crescendo as he yelled the champ's last name.

Folks in the Dancing Bar-B-Que started pounding their tables, clapping and cheering, their thunderous approval carrying out into the night, joining the whoops and hollers ringing in every bar on the avenue, in every house where black folks gathered around radios and leaned close, listening, praying, sending their hopes, dreams, wishes to their champion, who calmly stepped through the ropes and onto the white square of canvas at Wrigley Field.

"Joe. Joe. Joe," they chanted, as if the name was an incantation.

The ring announcer waited until the din of the 25,000 at Wrigley Field quieted enough so he could be heard giving the names of the referee, timekeeper and judges. Another voice came over the radio.

"Okay, fight fans. We're just about ready. The fighters are in their corners, getting the last instructions. Now they're in the center of the ring, referee George Blake giving them the particulars. In a moment, the fight will begin, and I hope all of you out there are relaxing and enjoying a cool bottle of Rainer Beer, the beer that won't let you down. Always smooth and easy. Cheers!"

Skip closed his eyes and let his mind carry him across the airwaves to ringside, where the two bare-chested fighters waited, dancing lightly on the balls of their feet, their corner men swabbing their shoulders with sponges of cool water. He clenched his teeth, balled his own fist and brought them close to his body. A collective inhalation went through the Dancing Bar-B-Que, everybody sucking in a breath, holding it, waiting for the opening bell. Ding!

"The fighters are moving out of their corners, circling. Roper looks ready. Not a hint of fear in his eyes. Louis, as always, is deadpan. Roper flicks out a jab. Louis brushes it off, bobs, weaves, feints with the right, counters with a left. Roper is smiling now."

"Come on, Joe," a voice urges. "Hit him one."

"Ooohh! Roper lands a stiff hook, catching Louis square on the jaw. The champ looks surprised."

A gasp went through the Dancing Bar-B-Que. Skip rocked to the side, feeling Roper's hook.

"God dammit, Joe," cried Pee Wee. "Hit him! Hit him!"

"Ooh," the announcer yelled. "There's another left hook by Roper. The champ is backing up, shaking his head. I think that last hook really stung him. He looks a little slow, off balance. Maybe he played Roper too light. There goes a right by Louis, nicking Roper. The challenger shakes it off and comes right back with another hook, catching the champ with his defenses down. It might be a long night for Louis."

Skip heard Pee Wee's whispered pleas. "Come on, Joe. Please. Come on."

"The champ's on the move now. He's backing Roper into his corner. We've seen this happen so many times before. The challenger is trying to dance away, but Louis has him cornered. Oh! A monstrous left upper-cut catches Roper flush on the chin, almost lifting him off his feet."

A hungry animal sound went through the Dancing Bar-B-Que. The crowd smelled victory.

"And there goes a merciless right, snapping the challenger's head sideways. You could feel that one all the way to San Berdoo. Louis is setting him up for the kill. And there it is! A vicious left. Roper is crumpling. He's going down! Blake rushes in as Louis moves to a neutral corner. This could be it fight fans. The count is starting. One! Two! Roper is pawing at the ropes, desperately trying to pull himself up. Five! He looks dazed. I think that uppercut disconnected his brain. Seven! He's still trying to stand, but I don't think it's going to happen. Nine! He's letting go of the ropes. Ten! He's gone. It's a knockout!"

Pee Wee jumped up and howled at the top of his lungs. Skip opened his eyes and saw his friend dancing around the room, jabbing at the air, laughing and slapping strangers on the back. Henry grabbed an envelope on the counter, tore it open and pulled out two five-dollar bills.

"Come to papa," he said, kissing the Lincolns and jamming them into his pants' pocket.

Diana bounced up and down in her seat, hugged her boys, pushed herself back from the table and joined in Pee Wee's victory dance, both of them holding hands, twirling each other, separating and throwing fast right and left uppercuts. The Deacon frowned at her antics, but didn't raise a hand to stop her. Phineas lifted Skip out of his seat, gave him a crushing bear hug, then tossed him aside like yesterday's news, before moving on to Bessie Lee. He pulled her up and grabbed her by the shoulders.

"Kiss me, you beautiful flower of Central Avenue," he said. "Kiss me one time for Joe."

Bessie Lee obliged and kissed Phineas full on the lips. He swooned, backed up and started spinning around and around, doing his own Central Avenue jig. Car horns wailed outside. People ran into the street and yelled at the sky. Through it all, Skip heard the ring announcer coming back on.

"At two minutes and twenty seconds of the first round, a knockout by the winner and still champion of the world, the Brown Bomber, Joe Louis!"

Central Avenue erupted in another delirious roar, followed by rhythmic clapping, stomping and chanting. Pee Wee stopped dancing long enough to grab the bottle of Chivas and raise it high.

"The champion of the world," he yelled before draining off a mouthful and passing the bottle into the crowd.

◦◡◦

SKIP SHOOK HIS HEAD AS PEE WEE TURNED ONTO SAPPHIRE'S QUIET street of shuttered houses. He was still giddy from the alcohol-fueled celebration and the thrill of playing the blues, and he wanted Sapphire to be with him. Bessie Lee knew about a fight-night bash up in the Hollywood Hills that wasn't going to end until dawn, and maybe not even then. Pee Wee didn't want to go, didn't want to be around white folks because somebody might say something stupid, then he'd have to get like Joe Louis and knock the bum stone cold. Why bother with it, he said, when the avenue was jumping. But Skip and Bessie Lee coaxed and pleaded. It was going to be fun. The place even had a swimming pool.

The Plymy eased to a stop. "How long you gon' be?" asked Pee Wee, shutting off the engine. "I got to go back and pick up Bessie Lee."

"Gimme a couple of minutes to find out what's what," Skip said, giving his friend a playfully wicked look. "I may not be going with you. You know what I mean?"

"Hah," Pee Wee replied. "You'll be going. Ain't no way this gal is gon' let a drunk skunk like you in tonight."

"Nix that trash, Pee Wee. Everything's gon' be alright."

Skip opened the door, pushed himself off the seat and stood, then fell back the dull thud of the door slamming shut, breaking the still silence. He peeked through the window at Pee Wee, gave an embarrassed shrug and inspected the Plymy's passenger door. Everything was fine. No dents, no scratches. He gave the okay sign, then sauntered off down the driveway, leaning forward, an aimless whistle spilling out between deep breaths of cool night air.

He laughed to himself at the memory of Phineas' little victory jig. Sapphire should've seen it. Why did she leave anyway? Didn't even say good-bye; didn't even wait to hear the fight. He looked at the dark houses lining the quiet block. What time was it? Couldn't be near midnight. These folks go to bed too early.

"Wake up, my darling," he bellowed drunkenly. "Your bluesman has arrived."

He did his own little jig, skipping his feet back and forth, turning around and around, ending up with a little soft-shoe, like he'd seen Bojangles Robinson do. He started singing and laughing, the words getting all mixed in with his silly giggles and the crazy dialogue carried on between the tipsy fool and the plastered lewd bluesman walking side-by-side within him

"I want you to squeeze my lemon. Hoowee! I wonder what he means by that. Do you hear me, little girl? Said I want you to squeeze my lemon till the juice and I mean de juice. Um, um,um. Lord have mercy, that alcohol is working on me. Here comes the black snake, Sapphire. Juice running all down his leg. Damn, them boys was nasty."

He knocked on her door, then on the window pane. Nothing. He rapped again, harder, breaking into a little tap-tap-tapping rhythm.

"Hey, Sapphire, Come on, now. Open the door."

Again nothing. He turned around, flustered, bleary eyes straining down the driveway, capturing the dim silhouette of Pee Wee in the Plymy, smoking. He rattled the doorknob, jiggled it as if that could somehow slip the lock. "Sapphire. Hey Sapphire. It's me, Skip."

From behind the door she heard him calling her name. She wanted to scream. "Go away." She didn't want Buster to see him sloppy drunk and stinking of alcohol. Buster liked him. Buster. Her baby child, life's reminder of frenzied nights, groping hot hands desiring her body, which she had joyously offered. Buster. Life's gift. Life's responsibility. Now, she wanted, needed, someone kind and dependable, the way Skip seemed. That couldn't be him outside her door. The alcohol had stolen him.

Skip stepped back, brow wrinkling in worry, his mind drowning in a sea of Chivas Regal. The darkened house baffled him. A fleeting thought, barely realized, teased the corners of his brain. Maybe she wasn't home. He shook his head. Hell, where else would she be this time of night. He ran back to the door and banged on the window pane.

"Sapphire! God dammit, open up!"

The fierce, angry tone in his voice startled her. He was going to wake Buster. People would talk. She stepped toward the door, stopped. A porch lamp clicked on. The pale yellow light threw his shadow across her walls. She could hear her heart racing. Outside, he turned, reeling and blinking against the glare, trying to focus on the woman standing on the back porch, wrapped in an old housecoat.

"You there!" she said, her voice hissing and slashing through the quiet. "Get away from that door."

"Go back to bed grandma. I ain't looking for you," he said. "I'm looking for Sapphire."

"Well, she's not receiving any company, especially at this hour of the night."

"Nobody asked you." He turned back to the cottage. "Sapphire. Open up. It's Skip."

He ignored the approaching footsteps until he could feel the intruder at his back. He turned around, ready to tell the woman to mind her own damn business, but he never got to say that. It was Mrs. Harrelson from the Plaza Arms. For a moment they just stared at each other, the shock of recognition firing through their brains, setting off sparks of remembered insults and low-down thievery. Skip leaned back, stifling a gasp. A low growl rose in Mrs. Harrelson's throat. Her lips drew back in a snarl.

"You!" she said, eyes widening, clenched fists slowly rising.

Skip nodded, a stupid, drunken smile coming over his face. "Me. Your long lost tenant."

"You!" she repeated, trembling, fighting to control the sputtering rage building up inside her.

"You ain't still holding that little fourteen-dollar thing against me, are you?" Skip said backing up a couple of steps and checking the distance to the Plymy. "I was gon' pay you. Matter of fact, I got a little bit right here." He fumbled in his pants pocket.

Mrs. Harrelson's steely gaze bore twin holes right through him. Then as if coming out of a trance, she advanced, one hand clutching closed the collar of her housecoat, the other hand a balled fist raised high. Over her shoulder Skip saw a light come on in the cottage. A bit of Sapphire's face, sleepy and troubled, peeked out from behind a curtain. He stepped forward. Mrs. Harrelson blocked his path.

"You stinking, drunken, low-down thieving dog!" She was on the march now, her face fixed and determined, her stare evil and merciless.

"Now, now," Skip said, raising his hands in mock surrender. "No need of blowing your top." He tried to disarm her with a smile.

"Get out of here!" she said. "Get out of here before I call the police." She stopped and screamed. "Police! Somebody call the police!"

Living room lights switched on, then porch lights. Two doors down a screen door creaked on rusty hinges. A man in pajamas bolted onto his front porch, holding what looked like a shotgun.

"What's going on down there," he yelled, as the Plymy roared to life. "Mrs. Harrelson, you all right" He stared at Skip. "Hey you!"

Skip stood on the sidewalk, head moving from side to side. His eyes locked on the long barrel. A rush of adrenalin blasted him out of his alcoholic haze. "I ain't done nothing," he said, reaching behind him for the Plymy. "Just a mistake, that's all. Honest." He found the passenger door, opened it, and jumped in. "Let's get the hell out of here."

Pee Wee shifted into first and stepped on the gas, sending the Plymy fishtailing down the block, tires screaming. "What the hell was that!" Pee Wee said. "I thought you were going to talk to your gal, not try to get us killed."

"Shit, shit, shit!" Skip searched his pocket for a Chesterfield, found one and lit it, the first puff steadying his hands. "God damn that old biddy!"

"Who was she?"

"Don't you know? That was Mrs. Harrelson from that fine place you sent me to, the Plaza Arms. She's still crying 'bout some money I owe her, fourteen dollars."

Skip rubbed his forehead, ran his free hand through his hair and took a few more puffs on his cigarette before flicking it out the window. Damn, shit. Now he'd have to worry about Mrs. Harrelson peeking out her window every time he stopped by, ready to bawl him out about the money he owed her. She'd probably bad-mouth him to Sapphire and do her damndest to snuff out the flame of love burning in Sapphire's heart, a flame he wanted to protect and nurture with flowers, toys, walks in the park. God dammit, he might even go to church.

"Guess you didn't get to talk to Sapphire," Pee Wee said.

"Hell no. That God damn old heifer got in the way. Who the hell does she think she is? Wasn't none of her business."

Pee Wee slowed and turned onto Central Avenue. The street was jammed with cars heading home from celebration or cruising on to unknown destinations where the liquor still flowed and the music played while people laughed and joked about Joe Louis' victory.

"I don't know why you're chasing that gal, Skip, " Pee Wee said. "She ran out on you."

"I know. I know. But she and the kid, they've got my heart. You've seen 'em."

"Skip, you're a damn fool, talking that Hollywood moving picture shit. Got your heart. Hell, that's the one thing you never give a woman. Do that and she'll sure 'nuff try to put a ring in your nose and get a ring on her hand."

"I ain't looking to marry her, Pee Wee. I just want to be with her."

"Well, the way I see it, she sure as hell don't want to be with you. Or don't you see it that way?"

"I don't know, Pee Wee. She's the prettiest gal I ever seen, and she's nice. Not like one of them fast gals. Nice."

"Nice?" Pee Wee spat out the word. "Those gals are the worst kind. I bet she ain't even giving you no pussy."

Skip didn't say anything. That was none of Pee Wee's business.

Pee Wee grunted. "I thought so. She's just stringing you along, and you're following her like some god damn puppy dog."

"Aw, c'mon, Pee Wee. It ain't like that. I done told you. Sapphire ain't one of them fast gals, dropping her drawers for every man she sees. She's got responsibilities. Hell, she's got a baby."

"Humph. Guess somebody got there before you. Me, I'd drop her like a hot potato and never think twice. Here she done gave it to somebody else and now she's holding tight to it. Nix to that. And, she ran out on you." Pee Wee shook his head. "I'm sorry, but I ain't got time for that kind of mess. Don't want no woman trying to put apron strings on me. Free and easy. That's the only way to play it. Otherwise, you'll end up with some nice gal trying to turn you into a family man, keeping you under lock and key, making you stay home Thursday nights when you ought to be stepping out on the avenue, going to some tea pad with a frisky Kitchen Mechanic on our arm. You know that girl, Virginia? She asked after you the other day. You ought to be chasing her tail, instead of some little boy's mama."

Maybe Pee Wee was right. Maybe he was being too nice. Maybe he should tell Sapphire that he wasn't going to keep on hanging around, playing house and being a daddy stand-in. He could try that, but he knew he'd be lying. He loved being around her and Buster, cherished the way his heart seemed to tingle and sing whenever they were together. Sometimes he felt he was fighting against himself, trying to hold back as he waded deeper and deeper into a life with Buster and Sapphire. He kept telling himself he was too young. And he knew that if he tried Pee Wee's way, Sapphire would just tell him to go ahead and leave, no matter how much it hurt. No, Pee Wee was wrong. He wasn't going to leave them.

Pee Wee slapped him across the chest. "Damn, Skip. Ain't no need of losing your head over this gal. There's plenty other fish in the sea."

"Yeah, I guess so," Skip said, knowing he wasn't going fishing anytime soon.

"Guess nothing. I'm telling the truth. Put your line back in the water, boy. You'll catch something soon enough. Maybe even at this Hollywood party. You never know. Miss Ann might be hungry for some chocolate tonight, and you just may be the candy man." Pee Wee winked and gave him a friendly shove.

Skip didn't laugh. He was worried about having to face Sapphire. He hoped Buster had been asleep and had not heard the commotion, or seen him drunk, pawing at his mama's door like a God damn fool who had forgotten everything he'd learned about them in the last month. Damn, shit. He sighed and lit another Chesterfield.

BESSIE LEE JUMPED INTO THE PLYMY, SMILING HER GAP-TOOTHED smile and smelling sweet. Skip got in beside her, all of them squeezing into the front seat.

"Hollywood, here we come!" she said, throwing her arms around Pee Wee, who took his eyes off the road long enough to give her a quick kiss. "What took y'all so long?"

"Business," Pee Wee said, turning onto Central and heading into downtown.

"What kind of business?"

"Just business, Bessie Lee. Hush up, now," Pee Wee flashed her a warning and nodded towards Skip.

"Oh," she said, seeing Skip's hang-dog expression. "Is he gon' be all heartbroke and quiet tonight?"

"He'll be alright, soon's we hit this Hollywood party. Ain't that right, Skip?"

"I sure as hell hope so," Skip replied, trying to shake off his gloom. "I was riding high till we stopped by Sapphire's."

"You should've seen him, Bessie Lee," Pee Wee said, giving in to the urge to tell all, "juiced up and sloppy, crying outside that gal's house like some g-damn alley cat. Damn near got us killed."

"Naw," Bessie Lee said, turning to Skip. "What you doing trying to get my Pee Wee killed?"

He waved her off. "Pee Wee's just playing with you. Didn't nothing happen that was gon' get anybody killed." He leaned forward and looked past Bessie Lee to Pee Wee. "Ain't that right?"

Pee Wee shrugged. "If you say so. Wasn't nothing 'cept a man with a shotgun . . ."

"Shotgun!" said Bessie Lee.

" . . .and a woman hollering for the police."

"Police!"

Pee Wee nodded. "But it wasn't nothing. Wasn't nothing at all." He leaned over his steering wheel and winked at Skip. "Ain't that right?"

Pee Wee made his way to Wilshire Boulevard, turned right on Vermont Avenue and headed north, the Plymy's nose pointing towards Griffith Park. He made a left on Sunset, joined the traffic flowing easily through Hollywood, Beverly Hills, and on out towards Mulholland.

"You know how to get to this place, Bessie Lee?"

"Just keep on driving, Pee Wee. I'll know it when I see it." Bessie Lee strained her eyes to search the dark, tree-lined street. "That one!" She pointed to a row of oaks surrounding a hidden driveway.

"Where?" Pee Wee said, braking.

"There. I mean here. Turn here. This one."

"You sure?"

Bessie Lee cut her eyes at Pee Wee. "I used to work here."

"Okay, sugar. Just making sure." Pee Wee turned and drove slowly up an ascending driveway. He leaned out his window. "I don't hear no party. You sure this is the right one?"

The Plymy's headlights probed the darkness, the twin beams sliding past trees and bushes. Pee Wee downshifted. The car groaned through first gear. Skip cocked his ear and listened. Music, upbeat and jazzy hurried through the night, the sharp blare of horns and beating drums faint at first, then becoming distinct as the Plymy climbed the driveway.

Bessie Lee started popping her fingers and swaying from side to side, bumping Pee Wee, then Skip, then Pee Wee again, holding herself a bit longer against her man before giving Skip another friendly bump. "I just can't sit still when they swing that music," she sang. Pee Wee made a tight turn and slammed on the brakes, jerking everybody forward. A long line of black limousines, luxury sedans, rag-top roadsters with polished chrome pipes wrapping along their sleek sides blocked the rest of the way.

"Damn," he whispered. "Almost kissed me a Caddy."

Parked front to back, the cars pointed the way to a Spanish-style mansion, it's roof covered with expertly laid rows of rounded terra-cotta tile. A wide, manicured lawn spread out before the huge house set proudly atop the hill. Skip jumped out, shook the cramps from his legs, bent over and stretched, while Pee Wee and Bessie Lee slammed the Plymy's doors shut. They followed the line of cars, Bessie Lee running ahead, Pee Wee a little wary, Skip hanging back. He almost wished he'd stayed home, but the idea of spending the rest of the night alone with his shame made him glad for this Hollywood party. There might be someone with connections among the well-dressed white folks lining the second-floor balconies. Skip heard a horn player struggling through a second-rate solo. Three season's worth of Central Avenue jazz and the Negro Music Hour had taught him the difference between a really swinging soloist and one who couldn't survive the first round of an amateur-night cutting contest. Humph, he shrugged. No brother who thought himself half a musician could be up there playing like that, falling off the beat. Had to be a white boy, thinking he was getting hot.

Pee Wee peeked inside each car, his eyes staring longingly at the rich leather interiors, the burnished wood of one-of-a-kind dashboards, his fingers running lightly along the hand-waxed hoods.

"See one you like, baby?" Bessie Lee said.

"All of 'em honey. Every last one of 'em. This here Stutz Bearcat could tear up some empty highway. Got a whole herd of horses under that hood. And look at that Caddy up there."

He started running towards a crystal blue Cadillac, pulling Bessie Lee along.

"I don't think you ought to be looking too close at that one," she said. "Lessen you want to get an eyeful."

Pee Wee stopped. The Caddy was rocking, gently. "Any port in a storm, I guess," he said.

Skip joined Pee Wee and Bessie Lee as they walked up a flight of decorated ceramic tiles leading to a huge, rough-hewn wooden door. Behind it they heard laughter, a crowd of voices. Pee Wee pushed the doorbell. Nobody came. He pushed it again. Nothing.

"Try the doorknob," Bessie Lee whispered.

"Girl, you must be crazy. I ain't breaking into no white folks party," Pee Wee hissed. "I bet we ain't invited."

He leaned on the doorbell, waited, then turned around, convinced. "Told you. Come on." He started back down the steps, pulling a reluctant Bessie Lee along behind him. Skip grabbed his arm.

"Hold on, now Pee Wee. We come all the way across town. Lemme see what them folks up on the balcony have to say." He stepped back a few paces and yelled. "Hey! How do we get up there to join y'all?"

A drunken, redhead, her red lipstick smeared across her face, leaned dangerously over the edge of the balcony, her dress straps falling off her shoulders. Her tuxedoed partner held her by the waist and playfully spanked her wiggling behind. "Ooooh," she cooed over her shoulders. "I'm badder than that." He whacked her again. "Ouch!" she cried, spilling her drink, the drops falling and splashing at Skip's feet. "What ya say?" she yelled down to him, covering herself, tossing back her mane of red curls.

"I said, 'How do we get up there?'"

"Up here?"

He nodded. "Yeah."

"Just come on in. The door's open," she smiled, then a startled frown clouded her face. "Get your hand out of there," she yelled, throwing her drink over her shoulder. Her partner whipped a handkerchief from his breast pocket and mopped his soaked face. The red head pushed herself from the balcony's edge, pulled the strap back onto her shoulder and straightened her dress. "You don't know me that well," she said, jabbing a finger into the tuxedoed man's chest. "And I don't think you ever will."

"The door's open," Skip said, arching his eyebrows and turning to his friends.

"Okay, let's get it over with," Pee Wee grumbled. "But I ain't staying long."

Skip walked down the entry hall and into the main room, his fingers popping to the swing music coming from the balcony, his eyes darting around the refined, patrician faces of white men in cut-away black tuxedos, the sculptured, picture-perfect faces of smoothly made-up white women in floor-length evening gowns cascading down their slim shoulders to trail along the polished wooden floor. Here and there someone brought a long cigarette holder to pursed lips. Volleys of laughter erupted throughout the smoky, high-ceiling room. People reclined on plush velvet sofas and clinked their champagne glasses together. He, Pee Wee and Bessie Lee were the only black folks in the room. He stared, eyes wide, at the huge buffet heaped with piles of ham and roast beef.

"Man, would you lay your peepers on this scene," he said, catching sight of a bar near the door leading to the balcony. "Anybody thirsty?"

"I ain't drinking," Pee Wee growled, looking tense, waiting for one of the white faces to spot him. "And I especially wouldn't if I was you."

Skip waved his hand. "I'm getting my second wind. Now y'all drinking or not?" Pee Wee shook his head. "How 'bout you, Bessie Lee? Can I get you something to wet your whistle?"

She nodded, pulled her hand loose from Pee Wee's tight grip. "Bring me something sweet, and not too strong."

Skip headed for the bar, keeping an eye out for any face he might have seen in *Photoplay*, the picture pages of *The Examiner*, or the *Hollywood Reporter*, not that he wanted to run up to them like some dizzy fan and ask for an autograph, but it would confirm, in some small way that he had really entered Hollywood's moving picture set. He smiled to himself, satisfied when he saw Billy Kidd, dressed in solid black, standing on the balcony, clutching a doe-eyed brunette's slim waist. The papers said Kidd was still fuming over having missed the chance to play the Ringo Kid in *Stagecoach*. John Wayne got that one, and now he was a star, leaving Kidd to content himself with top billing in Victory Pictures' latest B-western, which Skip figured was a lot better than standing around Gower Gulch. He pressed on through the crowd, lit a cigarette when he reached the bar and struck his own, nonchalant pose: back to the bartender, Chesterfield dangling from his fingers.

"Set me up there, bartender," he called over his shoulders. "Your best Scotch and something sweet for my lady friend over there."

"Kind-a far off the avenue, ain't you, mac?" the bartender said, his rough, New York City voice a hoarse whisper.

"Never you mind that," Skip replied, bringing the cigarette to his lips for a slow, studied puff, all the while wishing he had a black ivory cigarette holder. "See," he said, blowing smoke rings. "I was invited. Now, what y'all got to drink?"

"Anything you want," the bartender said, setting two glasses on the counter. "No bathtub gin, though. You're gonna have to go back to the avenue if you want that. Only high-class stuff here, Champagne, French brandy, cognac."

"Looks like I'm in luck," Skip said. "I like the high-class stuff."

"How 'bout your pal? Ain't he drinking?"

"Naw, he's already done had his fill on the avenue, celebrating Joe Louis."

"Fight fans, eh," the bartender dropped a handful of crushed ice into one of the glasses. "Well, let me tell you, mac. Old Jack Roper didn't have a chance tonight. Two minutes. Why, in my better days, I'd have lasted longer. I'm not saying I would've gone the distance, but I believe I'd have made it to the first bell."

Skip turned around and watched the bartender pour four fingers of scotch into one glass, and a thick, licorice-smelling liquid into the other. The guy's face bore the jagged scars of ringside cutmen in a hurry. Thick masses of tissue bulged along his forehead and over his eyes. His nose was crooked, flattened on one side, the bridge lost in some ring, somewhere, sometime long, long ago.

"Looks like you did some fighting in your day," Skip said, sipping the scotch.

"I was a pretty good middleweight. They called me the Bronx Brawler. Had a quick left hook. Got on the undercard once at the Polo Grounds," He pushed the glasses toward Skip. "There you go, mac. Chivas Regal for you, and for the lady, a little anisette. I think she'll like it."

"Do I owe you anything?"

The bartender held up his hands. "Not a thing. It's an open bar. Drink yourself into a stupor if you want. However," he leaned forward, crossed his muscular arms on the bar and nodded towards a bowl brimming with change. "A small tip is always appreciated."

Skip flipped a quarter into the bowl, raised his glass and tipped it towards the ex-fighter. "To Joe Louis."

"The best there is," the old brawler replied, striking a fighting pose.

Walking back across the room, Skip felt a sudden wave of fatigue come over him. The long night and too much alcohol sapped him for a moment. The glasses almost slipped from his hands. Damn, shit, he thought, straightening up, sucking in a deep breath. He ran the icy glass across his face. The jolt cleared a bit of the fog. What time is it, he wondered. He held Bessie Lee's drink under his nose, dipped his tongue into the syrupy liquid, frowned at the sickening sweet taste of licorice. What fool thought of this? Halfway across the room, he stopped, caught in the crush of people backing up to create an aisle for a cocky trumpet player who passed by, twirling his horn like a gunslinger. A drummer followed, lugging a tom-tom and beating out a solid, marching band rhythm. Skip inched along, holding his glasses high, seeing Pee Wee and Bessie Lee where he had left them, a few steps inside the room. Pee Wee looked evil and angry, while Bessie Lee stood by, looking like she wanted to have some fun, but couldn't because Pee Wee wouldn't let her. She gave Skip a weary smile when Pee Wee said something fierce, his hands waving as if to say he was through.

"Here you are," Skip said, handing Bessie Lee her glass of liquid licorice. "What you so down in the mouth for, Pee Wee?"

"We're leaving," he said, the words terse and final. "Soon's Bessie Lee gets done with that drink, maybe sooner if she don't hurry up."

"C'mon, Pee Wee. We just got here," Skip said, sipping slowly on his scotch. "Why look-it over there. Here comes a colored brother with some free food."

An older butler, stoop-shouldered with a crop of snow-white curls ringing his head, moved through the room, balancing a silver tray filled with finger sandwiches, crackers covered with cheese, or dollops of what looked like tiny red marbles. Every now and then his eyes locked on the three young black folk. He made his way toward them, stopping whenever a white hand summoned him, but always returning to his course. No smile disturbed his face, which was at times held an obsequious expression, then impassive. Finally he stood in front of Skip, Pee Wee and Bessie Lee, bowed deeply and, with a flourish of his free hand, offered the tray of delicacies.

"Hors d' oeuvre?" he intoned, the strange word flowing effortlessly off his tongue. He smiled knowingly at the trio's blank expressions. "Snacks. Cheese and crackers. And here," he pointed to the marbles. "Caviar." Again the dumb expressions and, from the butler, the wry, understanding smile. "Fish eggs, salty as the dickens, but rich white folks love 'em."

"Ummm, caviar," Bessie Lee said, virtually singing the word as her hand hovered above the tray. "I've heard about this."

Pee Wee slapped her wrist. "Ixnay to that, baby cakes. Drink up and let's get moving."

"But Pee Wee," she cried. "I'm hungry."

"There's plenty of food on the avenue," he said. "Don't need none of this fancy white folks' food. Fish eggs. Who ever heard of such a thing?"

The butler stood by, silent, an eyebrow raised just a bit. He turned to Skip. "Caviar, sir?"

Skip popped one of the marble covered crackers into his mouth, then gagged. It tasted awful. He took a quick gulp of scotch to clear his throat as he choked down the cracker. "These aren't too bad, Pee Wee," he said, offering one and struggling to look pleased.

"You're a damn lie." Pee Wee slapped the offered cracker out of Skip's hand and sent it sailing across the room.

The butler stepped back. "Perhaps I should let you gentlemen resolve the matter?"

"Do that," snapped Pee Wee.

"Yes, please," Skip said, embarrassed, putting an apologetic tone in his voice that made him sound like a down-home Barrymore. "My friend," he paused, staring hard at Pee Wee, "is a little out of sorts."

"Very good, sir," the butler said, bowing and continuing his rounds.

"Dammit, Pee Wee," Skip hissed under his breath, looking around to see if anyone had noticed the little scene. "What you have to do that for?"

"Cause I don't have to put on no airs for nobody, understand. Nobody." He pointed around the room. "Look at this place. White folks everywhere, walking around with their noses in the air, acting like they shit don't stink. Naw, this scene ain't for me. And it ain't for you neither. Hell, we stick around here long enough, one of them might come up and ask us to fetch some of them damn fish eggs."

"Not with that suit you're wearing," Bessie Lee sneered.

"Hush up, gal," Pee Wee said. "Ain't nothing wrong with what I'm wearing, and I ain't about to get all trussed up in one of them penguin suits just so's I can be around white folks." He turned to Skip. "You coming or not?"

"Pee Wee," Skip pleaded. "We just got here. Why don't you let me get you a drink? It's free."

Pee Wee shook his head. "I ain't taking nothing from these folks." He grabbed Bessie Lee's hand and pulled her toward the stairs. "Come on."

Skip stepped in front of Pee Wee. "What're you getting your back up for?"

"Listen, Skip. I told you I didn't want to come here. That was y'all's idea." His angry eyes flashed from Skip to Bessie Lee. "Y'all said it was gonna be such a high time. Well, I think it stinks. I don't know what you're going to do, but I'm taking my gal back to the avenue."

Skip took Bessie Lee's drink and stepped aside. "Do what you will," he said, draining off the last of his scotch. "I'm gon' get me another glass of this good, free liquor."

Pee Wee glared at him for a moment, started to say something, then shook it off as he headed down the stairs, snatched the door open and stepped into the cool, spring night. Bessie Lee stumbled along behind him, waving bye-bye and calling out.

"Eat some caviar for me!"

Skip walked back to the bar, his mind on Pee Wee, who could take a broken-down Detroit engine and make it purr like a well-fed kitten; Pee Wee, who could strut down Central Avenue confident as a king; Pee Wee who, caught off the avenue, fumed and snarled, slapped people's hands and stood by the door, nervous and unsure. He was like Old Man Williams' catfish, beached and gasping for air. Skip pressed on through the white crowd, feeling a bit uneasy now that he was alone here, stranded beyond the streetcar line. He remembered Peola's pitiful cry in *Imitation of Life:* "Mama, I want the same thing in life other people enjoy." White people, she should've said. This was their world, and they moved easily through it. Did he even belong here? Maybe he should've gone home with Pee Wee and Bessie Lee. But the avenue was only half the world. He was here to make the whole world his. It didn't make sense to leave Tunis and not change. He had to stay here, test himself, find out if he could walk in their world. He strained for a glimpse of the butler, another black face with which he could connect and nod to as if to say: Yeah, here we are. Glad to see you're still around. He thought about Zeke's arrogance, took strength from the man's ability to plow through both worlds, chomping stinking cigars and wearing cheap suits, barking into a telephone as he sat, enthroned upon a raised platform in his downtown office. That was the way to be, not like some dumb-eyed catfish, hauled out on dry land, gills working desperately, drawing nothing.

No, not like that. Zeke had the answer. You had to live in both worlds: The black one on Central Avenue and the white one along the outer reaches of Sunset Boulevard. He stepped up to the bar and set his glass down.

"Chivas Regal, right," the bartender said.

Skip nodded. "High-class stuff. Only the high-class stuff."

"Where are your friends?" The bartender dropped another handful of crushed ice into the glass.

"Gone to the avenue," Skip said, a bit wistful and self-concious.

"They left too soon," said the old brawler. "The show's about to start."

"Show?"

"Yeah, the strip show. She's a real knock-out, too. I seen her a couple of times." He made hour-glass shapes with his hands, winked and did a wolf whistle. "A body to make the most sanctified preacher lay his Bible down. Should be starting up about now."

From somewhere in the house a muted, sensuous trumpet snaked in and around a tom-tom's insistent beat. Men moved slowly through the room, called by the beckoning music. Skip turned to the bartender, who made the hour-glass shape and nodded toward the dark hallway.

"Go on," he said. "I'm thinking about getting an eyeful myself."

Skip stayed at the bar. Was the man joking? Black men had been murdered just for looking crossways at a full-dressed white woman. He couldn't imagine joining a roomful of white men, watching one of their women strip down to God knows what, then live to tell the tale. What kind of white men would let him do that? He swished a sip of scotch around his mouth. The bartender stepped from behind the bar, lightly tapped a cigarette from his pack, lit it and puffed contentedly.

"Anything goes in Hollywood, bud," he said, heading for the hallway. "Anything."

Skip's eyes followed him until he turned into an open doorway. He took another sip, felt his drunk coming on again. The trumpet called. The tom-tom boomed. He wavered, wondered if he could break the taboo, vanquish the old fears and step into the dark room where Jezebel displayed her butt-naked self? If he did, then it would mean he had truly stepped into their world. A brief war raged inside him. The boy who had grown up achingly aware of Tunis' harsh doctrines, battled the young man trying to free himself from the ancient, blood-soaked strictures.

Curiosity and desire pulled him through the hallway. At first he moved cautiously, half-expecting someone to tell him the show was off limits. But no one stopped him. His pace quickened at the sound of rough, male voices and heavy fists pounding tabletops. He smelled the stink of burning cigars as he grabbed the cold doorknob in his sweaty palm, sucked up some courage and entered. A sight he could not have imagine minutes ago stopped him. There, on a table in the middle of the room, danced the redhead he'd seen on the balcony, wearing a Roman warrior's armored breastplate and a skirt that barely covered her hips. She rolled a slender black riding crop along her legs and stroked her inner thighs, her movements matching the music's rhythmic, sensual insinuations. She stared blankly towards a far wall, never meeting the hungry eyes devouring her, raping her as if she were a nubile virgin offered as sacrifice in a Dionysian orgy. Skip shielded his eyes and looked away, feeling nasty, ashamed, totally removed from the decent young man who had spoon-fed Buster a few hours earlier. Slowly, his gaze returned. He tried to look without giving in to the irresistible call of woman to man.

The redhead's high heels made her hips firm and tense. The supple muscles in her legs flexed slightly as she dipped low, her sexual grinding following the trumpet's surprisingly graceful slide down a bluesy scale. She swayed from side to side, spanked herself in time to the insistent tom-tom, rode the riding crop and flipped up her skirt, revealing delicate folds of pink skin shaved clean and smooth as a newborn's. A low, sex-hungry moan came from her throat. Skip's fingers tightened on his glass. He tingled all over, felt his own erection pushing against his pants. He looked around, wanting to hide the evidence of his attraction. No one noticed him. The Bronx Brawler stood enthralled, licking his thin lips. A couple leaned in one corner, the woman facing the wall, rubbing herself against her man, whose eyes were fixed on the redhead. The music kept an unrelenting pace, built to a climax. The redhead flicked a latch and the breastplate fell to the floor. She pushed up her small breasts, as if offering them to the crowd. She licked her fingers, moved them in teasing circles around her nipples. Skip felt himself weakening, the dance of sex making him hot. A hard-faced, bleary-eyed drunk whipped a five-dollar bill from his wallet, folded it lengthwise and slapped it on the table. The guy looked like Kurt Marshall.

"Pick it up," he yelled, leering up at the female body dancing without shame. "Pick it up, God dammit!"

A startled expression broke through the redhead's calm, distant mask. She looked down at the bill waving enticingly in the drunk's hands, then towards the musicians. The trumpet started a long, slow descending run of blue notes, accented by the tom-tom's boom, boom, boom-boom. The drunk stepped back arms folded across his chest. The redhead stood over the bill and wantonly shook her body. Her skirt fell away and she stood naked. Approving yells filled the room. She dipped once, twice. Every eye fixed on her squatting over the bill, her body tense. Her vagina opened, close along the fold. She strained, slowly pushed herself up, brought her legs together, holding tight the bill that stuck out from between the wet, petal-like folds of flesh. She arched her back in brazen display before bending over, snatching the bill with her teeth, and standing triumphant. The music stopped. Crumpled bills, like flowers at some ancient celebration of Eros, sailed through the air. Someone yelled that he'd give her twenty dollars just to see her pick it up. She laughed, and the music started up again. Skip turned away, barely able to contain himself.

The music faded as he walked down the dark hallway, but the image of the redhead remained, disturbing him, taunting him with wild thoughts of unbridled sex. He wanted her like a dog in heat. He looked over his shoulder at the closed door. Had he really seen a white girl dancing naked on top of a table, her slender body offered to the crowd of greedy, staring eyes? It seemed unreal. How could she do it? Dancing in a room with only her lover, that he could understand. He remembered Sapphire undressing, her brown body moving to the sensual rhythm of Billie Holiday's voice. They had been alone. The seductive dance was their secret. But the redhead had danced in front of strangers, teased them with lewd acrobatics, performed for money. And he had been drawn to her, had heard the call of flesh to flesh and stood ready. He stared at the door, heard the music and voices, then turned and walked on.

Another door opened, spilling the strip show's crowd into the hallway. Back-slapping men, faces heavy with broad, drunken smiles, banged on the walls, rolled their hips in grotesque imitation, yelled.

"Get ready, girls, 'cause here we come."

"I need a drink, but I don't want to cool off."

"Outta the way, nigger-boy. Outta the way."

Nigger-boy? The remark jolted Skip like a backhand to the jaw. Dry-mouthed fear pinned him to the wall as the raucous crowd passed. A desperate, choking uneasiness took hold of him. No one here looked like him. They could turn on him any moment, become surly and mean, accuse him of enjoying the dance of their woman, of intruding on their fun. And then? He held his breath. He wanted to disappear. When the crowd had thinned, he fell in behind the stragglers. All he wanted now was a glass of ice water to clear his head, then he was getting the hell out of here, walking all the way back to Central Avenue if he had to. In the main room, he made sure to keep his eyes straight ahead and focus on no one. He wondered what they thought of him. Nigger-boy long ways off the avenue. Nigger-boy trying to walk in the white world. Outta the way, nigger-boy. His nerves tightened to a keen, hair-trigger point that needed only the slightest pressure to set him off. Just let somebody say something, he thought. Just let somebody call me out my name and . . . He slammed his empty glass down on the bar.

"Easy there, buddy," the old fighter pried the glass loose from his grip. "Chivas Regal right? That was some show, eh?"

Skip lit a Chesterfield and looked away. "What show?"

"The strip show. Don't try to deny you were there. I saw you, eating it up like every other man in the room. And she was something, wasn't she? Just like I said." He made the hour-glass shape and kissed his fingers as if tasting something indescribably sweet. "How much you think she'll go for?"

"I wouldn't know. And nix that scotch. Just gimme a glass of ice water."

"Sure, buddy, coming right up. Man, oh man. I'd love to have her pull that dollar bill trick on me. Suck you right up." The bartender made a loud, obscene slurping sound. "Right up the spout. Here you go and, as always, tips are appreciated."

Skip emptied the loose change in his pocket, almost a dollar.

"Say, buddy. Thanks. I'll put that in my fund. See if I can buy that hot little redhead." He winked slyly and made the hour-glass shape again. "Hell, I'd even step back in the ring, if that's what it took."

Skip turned away. He felt the room pressing in on him, the hard eyes of the stern-faced portraits lining the walls following him as he steered

a careful path through the obstacle course of white people, his eyes looking at no one, his body avoiding even the slightest touch, the hair-trigger anxiety of being here alone building. A yearning for a face the color
of his seized him. He looked for the old butler. The servant was nowhere
to be seen. Had he, like Pee Wee and Bessie Lee, fled this foreign world
for the avenue's comfort, the battle of the bands at the Savoy, probably
going full blast now, horn players swinging through tremendous solos,
folks doing the Lindy, jumping and sliding across the dance floor, black
folks everywhere. He crunched on an ice cube and walked onto the balcony. Cool evening air washed over him. He closed his eyes, flicked the
burning Chesterfield into the dew-wet grass and coughed out the last
puff of smoke, thinking as he breathed deep and slow: Out with the bad
air, in with the good. Alone, his heart locked in secure solitude, his mind
settled down. The cocked trigger rested.

The band started a slow, melancholy ballad, filled with longing. Skip
smiled bitterly. The music took his mind back to the redhead. He saw her
dancing in slow motion, holding her hands out to him, bidding him to
come, come and lose himself in the pleasure of her forbidden body. He
shook the vision out of his head. Enough, he said to himself. Enough.
Behind him, the party gained momentum. The ballad gave way to a dance
number. Laughter carried on a passing breeze. He tried to escape the
happy sounds, found an empty bench by the swimming pool and sat
down. His eyes cast fitfully over the still water as he sat swirling his
glass, listening to the ice cubes clinking against each other.

He downed the last bit of cold water and sucked on an ice cube, his
jaws working in and out like a bellows. He didn't hear the sharp, staccato click-clack of approaching high heels on the Spanish tiles until the
final step stopped beside him. He looked up. It was the redhead. He
shrugged and stared at the pool.

"Oh, don't be like that," she slurred, her breath rank with alcohol and
cigarettes. She teetered on her heels and dropped down beside him.
"Whew! I gotta get out of these. They're killing me." She swung a leg
across Skip's lap and fluffed her hair. "Here, help me out."

He recoiled from her stinging touch and pushed her leg away. "Get
away from me," he said, standing and looking around, scared someone
would see them together. He felt her hands clawing at his pants, pulling
him back down.

"Gosh, you don't have to make a scene," she said. "I'll take 'em off myself."

Skip edged toward the end of the bench, sat brooding, watching her out of the corner of his eyes. "You got a roomful of white men back there, how come you're bothering me."

"You looked lonely," she smiled.

"Well, I ain't," he lit a Chesterfield he didn't really want.

"Did you like my dance? I saw you looking."

"I wasn't looking."

"Stop lying," she said. "You couldn't take your eyes off of me." She put a finger in her mouth, then drew it out slowly, flicked her tongue around its tip and moaned in a tone he thought indecent, yet full of play. "Sweet as candy. Try some."

"Jesus! Are you crazy?" He tapped ash off his cigarette and turned his back to her.

"I'm sorry," she said, her voice quiet and lost sounding. "Sometimes I can't turn off my act." Another ballad flowed from the main room. The trumpet player reached down deep for a muted, lyrical intro that was still second-rate but good enough for Hollywood. "Say, you got another cigarette?"

Skip tossed the pack over his shoulder.

"Hey, that's no way to treat a lady."

"A lady?' He whipped around, shaking his head. "Ain't like no lady I ever seen." His eyes dared her to say otherwise.

A moment passed, and she nodded. "You're right, I ain't no lady. But that don't mean I can't expect a little kindness. You don't have to throw the cigarettes at me, like I had some disease and you were scared to touch me."

She struck a match, slowly brought the flame to the cigarette trembling between her lips. She seemed transformed now, no longer the forbidden ivory goddess, just a woman, plain-faced and tired, smelling of cigarettes and sweat. Her red lipstick was smudged from some man's rough kiss. The makeup beneath her high cheekbones had already cracked. Her green eyes, unflinching, settled on him, looked down a long, crooked nose bent slightly to the left. He grinned to himself. Her body had fooled him, caught him up in desire that made him and every other man overlook the imperfections of her face.

"How can you dance like that?" he said, meeting her gaze.

"Like what?" she replied, a sigh of smoke escaping her lips. "Didn't you like it?"

He did not answer. Wary, anxious fear gripped him, made him nervous, afraid to admit that, yes, God yes, he had loved the sight of her, had been unhinged by the provocative, taunting tease that left him sweating with lust, body aflame. He had thought she would excite nothing in him, that a lifetime of being told never to look upon her kind meant that if the chance ever came, he would look with a cold, superior indifference. Instead, he had yielded to her like all the others. Yes, he liked it, and felt himself betrayed by a part of himself beyond his control.

"How can you dance like that?" he persisted. "With no clothes on. Why?"

"Because they pay me. Why else? I sure in hell wouldn't do it for free. And," she flicked an ash off her cigarette. "And I thought it might help me get into moving pictures. My agent man said it would."

"Shoot," Skip said. "Ain't no moving picture gon' show you dancing like that."

"I know," she said, staring into the water, sounding resigned and frustrated. "But my agent man said maybe I'd get an invite, a screen test. Maybe somebody would take a liking to me. Lots of girls make it that way. You heard of the casting couch, ain't you?"

Skip shook his head. Poor girl. She was fooling herself. Hollywood wasn't going to take her, not with that face, not in a million years.

"What're you shaking your head for?" She said. "Don't you think I'm pretty enough?"

"Sure, sure," Skip said. Why not tell her a lie. It was what she wanted to hear, maybe even needed to her so she could go on with her hopeless dream. "You're a knock-out."

She smiled, pleased. "Since you're busy asking me questions, what are you doing here?"

Skip dropped his cigarette, crushed it out with the heel of his shoe. "I'm an actor, and I wanted to see what one of these Hollywood parties was all about."

"Hah," she laughed. "You sure picked a good one. Hollywood makes you do things you'd never do back home. I changed my name to Savannah Starling." The ever so slight southern drawl she added to the pronunciation made it sound like Suvanuh Stahlin. "It sounds better than Sarah Kotlowitz. Savannah, like the glorious South." She pressed her hand to her bosom imitating some faint of heart southern belle. "And Starling, like moving star, and singing birds. Savannah Starling. Do you like it?"

Skip shrugged. "Sounds alright, I guess."

"You got a Hollywood name?"

"Naw, just Skip Reynolds."

"Pleased to meet you, Skip." She held out her hand. "Come on shake. You don't have to kiss it. Like you said, I ain't no lady."

Skip touched her hand, then quickly drew it away, hearing heavy footsteps sliding drunkenly across the tiles. The white man who had put the five dollars on the table stumbled toward them, leaning forward as if fighting a strong headwind. It was Kurt Marshall.

"There you are," he said to Savannah. "What're you doing, trying to get a little chocolate dessert?" He leered at Skip. "Is that it, boy, a little something to crow about back in darktown?"

Skip jumped up and backed away. "No sir, Mister Marshall, sir. I wasn't doing nothing."

Marshall swayed from side to side, blinking and trying to focus. "Do I know you?"

Skip nodded, half smiling. "It's me. Skip Reynolds. I was in that picture you directed for Paradise Studios. The Civil War one. Remember? Ezekiel Washington sent me over." His mind scrambled for one Big Sam's lines. "I'se ain't gon' leave you, Missy Lee," he said, his voice deep and full like Paul Robeson's. "Remember?"

"Hollywood bullshit," Marshall grabbed him by the shoulder and pulled him close.

He could see beads of sweat collecting on Marshall's forehead. He smelled the man's stink through fading cologne. He tried to slip out of Marshall's grasp, but Marshall only tightened his grip, then pointed his drink toward Savannah.

"Just look at her," he said. "She'll dance naked as the day she was born and jump damn near anything in pants. Won't you, Savannah?"

She glared fiercely, turned her back to them.

"Aw don't be shy now. Wasn't so shy awhile back, was she, boy," Marshall said, his voice taking on a collegial tone. "No, not shy at all."

He clapped Skip on the shoulder and pushed him away. "Now, boy, why don't you run along and leave us white folks alone, and while you're at it, fetch me a drink."

Skip felt the tension rising up in him, the trigger pulling back. Marshall didn't remember him. All he saw was a colored boy to carry his liquor. He recalled trying to catch Marshall's eye on the set at Paradise Studios. What a fool he'd been, thinking Marshall was his friend. Now he wondered if Marshall was the one who called him Nigger-boy.

"Get it your damn self," he said. "I ain't no butler."

"Then what the hell are you doing here." Marshall said.

"I'm an act . . ." Skip stopped, started walking away, but Marshall slapped a hand on his shoulder.

"Hold on now, boy. I told you to fetch me a drink."

Their eyes met, Skip's narrowed to angry slits, Marshall's bloodshot and flushed. The trigger cocked. "And I said . . ."

Marshall cut him off. "Nigger, I don't care what you said. Fetch me a drink."

There it was again. That word. Nigger. Skip heard it slicing into him, screaming into his mind, ripping open a thousand sealed shut doors. A lifetime of insults, some remembered, some long buried and forgotten, flashed across his eyes. He looked at Marshall and saw Sam Willard, the yard bull in Fort Worth, a group of white boys chasing him down Highway 53, all of them yelling the hateful word, saw them and countless others who had spat the epithet in his face and walked on without a care, leaving him bruised, each instance another stab wound taken and accepted as a part of life, the price for living in this world. But not this time. The trigger slammed against the firing pin. His fist caught Marshall full on the jaw. The blow felt good. He could feel its power rippling through his right arm. The surprise on Marshall's face excited him. He swung again and again, doubled Marshall over, snapped the slack-jawed head back. His punches were methodical, exact, precise. Each one drained off a little more of his pent-up anger. He heard Savannah screaming, begging him to stop, but he could not. His fists searched out Marshall's white face. His knuckles scraped against Marshall's teeth. For an instant, he felt pain. But it vanished beneath his withering rage. Marshall stumbled backwards, flailing wildly, trying to shield himself from the onslaught. Skip caught him again in the gut and smiled, thinking. This must be how it feels for Joe Louis when the punches are flying and the white boy is going down. Marshall dropped his hands, clutched his stomach. Skip claimed the opening with a rapid combination that sent Marshall reeling back. He charged, a guttural snarl rattling in his throat as he grabbed Marshall by the collar, stared into the dazed, bloody face, then hit him again. Marshall collapsed into the pool. Skip stood at the water's edge, and yelled down at the floundering body.

"Don't you ever call me that again! Don't you ever call none of my people that again!"

Then a heavy hand spun him around, and the Bronx Brawler's storied left knocked him stone cold.

D AYS LATER, EVEN AS HE LEANED AGAINST THE DANCING BAR-B-Que's empty porcelain sink, reading *The Examiner* final and waiting to mop the floor, Skip could still see Kurt Marshall splashing in the swimming pool. Pee Wee didn't believe the story the first time he heard it, minus the part about the Bronx Brawler. The ugly purple bruise and busted blood vessels in Skip's right eye told him all he needed.

"You don't have the guts to hit a white man," he'd said one afternoon in Skip's room. "You probably just stood there and took your licks like a good colored boy."

But Skip swore it was all true. He'd knocked the man out. The shiner came from hitting his head on a door. "The guy never laid a hand on me," he'd said, crossed his heart and hoped to die, asked God to strike him down if he was telling a lie. Then, as if on cue, heavy thunder had rumbled ominously through the threatening, iron-gray clouds hanging low in the sky. Pee Wee heard the thunder, rolled his eyes and waited. But nothing happened. Skip smiled and the rain came hissing down, doing a paradiddle against the window, and they laughed, tapped their sweat-beaded bottles of cold beer together in a victory toast. Pee Wee slapped him on the thigh and nodded in agreement as Skip drained his bottle and said: "I don't care if the guy was a Hollywood director. The bum had it coming. Sure `nuff had it coming. Calling me a nigger. Shoot, Pee Wee. I stopped being a good colored boy a long time ago."

He skimmed the newspaper's front-page. Mayor Bowron and the City Council had sent the vice-squad sweeping through the B-Girl bars around Fifth and San Pedro. Some rich westsider probably got taken one too many times, Skip thought, turning the page. The new train depot was almost finished. A fleet of German battleships, cruisers and submarines maneuvered in the waters off Spain, practicing for a war the editorial page said was coming if Europe didn't watch out, and Uncle Sam wasn't going over there to save the day. Not this time. One European war was enough. He peeked into the cafe. Henry and Helen talked in low voices across a table. He couldn't hear what they were saying, but he could tell Helen was hot about whatever it was. Her proud eyes flashed intently behind her glasses. Every now and then she slapped the table, stood up, paced a few steps before sitting back down to argue her point. Henry listened quietly, occasionally added a few words or put a calming hand on Helen's tense arm. Skip checked the clock. Ten minutes, that's all he was going to give them, then he had to start mopping. Zeke wanted to see him tonight, said it was important. He wondered if it was about Marshall. Maybe Zeke was fixing to cut him loose, do like old Willie and say, `Sorry, Skip, but I can't help somebody who goes around hitting white folks.' The possibility bothered him, but not enough to make him change his mind about what had happened. He'd seen enough of Hollywood to know a long road lay ahead to realize his dream, and even then there was no guarantee of success. He rustled the pages loud enough for Henry and Helen to hear, and was about to turn to the sports section when a small headline stopped him.

WOULD BE ACTRESS FOUND DEAD
Coroner Says Suicide

He folded the page, pulled it close, eyes locking on the accompanying picture of a smiling young woman standing on the Santa Monica Pier. It was Sarah Kotlowitz. A shallow breath caught in his throat. Images of her came back to him: Savannah Starling dancing lewdly and picking up a five-dollar bill; Sarah Kotlowitz pretending to be a southern belle as she sang the sibilant sounds of her Hollywood name; Sarah and the Bronx Brawler packing him into a Yellow cab headed for Central Avenue.

He turned to the story:

> Police summoned to a third-floor apartment in the 3700 block of Sunset Boulevard near Western this morning found the body of a 26-year-old woman.
>
> A neighbor identified the body as that of Savannah Starling, though papers found in the apartment were in the name of Sarah Kotlowitz. The neighbor said the young woman had lived in the apartment for about a year and had come from Chicago to be an actress.
>
> The neighbor said she and Miss Starling shared coffee almost every morning and that Miss Starling often told her wild stories about the Hollywood life. She also said Miss Starling came home distraught late Thursday night and cried for hours. The neighbor called police when Miss Starling did not show up for coffee.
>
> Police found Miss Starling lying on her bed, an empty bottle of strychnine beside her, and a crumpled note in her hand. They would not reveal the note s contents.
>
> The coroner has ruled her death a suicide.

Skip read the story again. The news came to him in bits and pieces he collected until the mosaic was complete. Sarah had poisoned herself. He clutched his stomach. A deathly shudder, cold and unnerving as an icy finger tracing his spine made him shiver. He tried to imagine her crying alone in her apartment, her insides burning. Why did she do it? What was in the note? Something about Hollywood? Damn, shit. She took her own life. Her own life! He couldn't believe it. Life was too precious. He put the story face down on the counter, as if hiding it would make it go away. Then he grabbed the mop bucket, hoping the water sloshing against the tin would drown out the disturbing, troubling thoughts screaming inside his head. He'd seen her not more than two weeks ago, naked as a jaybird. He'd even lit her cigarette. The stinging touch of her shapely calf thrown boldly across his lap came back to him, bringing with it the memory of her tired voice asking him to take off her high heels. Now, she was dead. He kicked the bucket into the cafe, ignored the cold water lapping over the edge and soaking his shoes.

"Hold off on that, Skip," Henry said. "We're not finished."

"Cain't do that, Henry," he growled. "I got a meeting."

He swung the chairs in wide arcs, slammed them down on tabletops. Helen glared at him.

"Say, Skip," Henry said, annoyed. "Keep it down, huh?"

"All right, all right. Jesus, a man cain't even do his own job around here."

"What's that?"

"Nothing. Just talking to myself."

He kept on working, his mind struggling to grasp runaway thoughts about the sanctity of life, the cruel uncertainty of death, Hollywood, Sarah's beautiful body laid out on the coroner's cooling board, ready to be wrapped up and shipped home, a grim offering from the City of the Angels. What was she thinking about last night? Last night! He shuddered again. He'd slept good last night, turned in early, eased into comforting slumber and awakened to this day. Memories of Tunis sermons, came back to him like precious stones glimpsed beneath the surface of a clearing stream. The Christian soldiers called waking up a miracle. They said it was God breathing so lightly on your eyelids, you barely felt it. He didn't have to do that, they said. It was His will, His inscrutable, divine, blessed will to hold you close until your appointed time. *Like fishes in a net, or birds caught in a snare, so are the sons and daughters of man taken in an evil time, when Death falleth suddenly upon them in a time not of their knowing.* That was His will ever unfolding in the days of man. He let Death take the steering wheel from a soldier daddy's hand. He sent Death slipping into Sarah's room to steal her away in the quiet hours before dawn. That's why you had to be prepared, had to have somebody ready to go your bond with God, and that somebody was Jesus, His only begotten son, who died on the cross, shed his blood to wash away the sins of the world.

Skip felt a sudden urge to stop back-sliding and go to church. He would answer the altar call and ask the congregation to pray for him, a wayward sinner who had looked upon Jezebel and found her appealing. Would God take him back? The Christian soldiers said He was ever merciful. His door was always open. Maybe he would go, call Sapphire and apologize, for his drunken display outside her door, ask her and Buster and God to forgive his trespasses.

What was he doing here? He'd gone to a Hollywood party, and left with a black eye. His own Hollywood dreams, a crazy-quilt of country-boy fantasies lit in bright, glowing neon and impossibly vivid Technicolor, remained unrealized. Sure, he'd been in two moving pictures, one of them a colored western that left him sore from two days of stunt work, but he had punched a white director, and was no closer to playing a Buffalo Soldier than when he had first set out from home. He dipped the mop into the bucket's catch basin, pressed the handle to drain off the excess water. What was he doing here, scuffling around, getting in debt, tasting freedoms unknown to him in Tunis. He had come to tell a story, and his efforts had led him into a new life.

"It's unbelievable," Helen said, outrage rising in her voice. "In this day and age. After all we've said and done. We make one do right, then, just like that," she snapped her fingers, "another one wants to do us wrong."

"Sometimes life is like that, Helen," Henry said. "You can't fight every battle."

"Oh, yes I can, and I will. Anybody who takes this role is going to have to walk right past me, because I'm going to be standing in front of that studio gate, alone if I have to."

"Why bother yourself, Helen. You got Selznick to change his tune. Miss Scarlett is going to say `freedmen.'"

"That's not enough, Henry, and you know it. I'm going to keep hitting those studios. I'm going to do just like General Sherman. Selznick was my Atlanta! Now, I'm marching to the sea, and I'm going to keep marching until Hollywood starts treating us right." She smiled confidently. "Are you with me?"

Henry nodded. "How can I not be with you? This thing doesn't have two sides."

Skip worked his mop around a nearby table. "Y'all sound like you're getting ready to go to war."

"We're already at war," Helen said, and turned to Skip. "Are you with us or against us?"

Skip stopped and leaned against his mop. Helen always seemed to be riding him, taunting him with ultimatums. He met her stern, unflinching stare. "Depends on who you're fighting," he said, dipping the mop in the bucket. "Your enemy might not be mine."

"Humph." Helen huffed, eyed him as if he was a traitor to her cause. "They're your enemies, all right. Yours and every other Negro actor."

"And just who are they?" Skip said over his shoulder. He tensed, hearing Helen's chair slide back across the floor. She was coming for him.

"They, young man, are the producers, directors and scriptwriters. They are the ones who, even in 1939, insist on keeping us down on the levee, singing and eating chicken, rolling our eyes at the first sign of fear. They are the ones who tell Louise Beavers to fatten up so she can play another mammy, who sign Nina Mae McKinney to a five-year contract then offer her nothing, nothing worth putting on film." Helen was on him now, her fervent voice riding a wave of righteous anger. "They are the ones who distort us and parade us in front of America, who make us the butt of their jokes. And, they expect us to grin and be happy."

Skip turned around. Helen had him cornered. "I'll not stand for it," she continued. "And you shouldn't either."

Skip looked past her fierce eyes. "Excuse me," he said, holding the damp, dirty mop. "But I got to clean this floor."

She whirled around and stormed back to her chair, one hand to her forehead. "This young man is not listening, Henry. He is just not listening."

"Sure he is," Henry said. "Everybody can't be as hot-headed as you." He looked at Skip, busy wringing out the mop. "Helen's found out a movie coming up has a colored character who's supposed to be in blackface." He let the last word hang in the silence broken by the mop bucket squeaking across the floor. "What do you think of that?"

"Hollywood's always doing some mess," he said. "Hell, I'd be surprised if they could find somebody to do it."

Henry turned to Helen, a hint of satisfied pride in his voice. "See, he's listening."

"Yes, but is he a man of action?" Helen replied, daring Skip to tell her otherwise.

"A man of action," Skip said, buying time.

"That's right." She leaned back, a haughty, superior look in her eyes. She had him in her cross-hairs and fired away. "Are you a man," she paused, putting her emphasis dead on target, "of action?"

Skip heard the challenge, but didn't answer. Of course he was a man of action. He was out here, wasn't he?

Henry cleared his throat. "Helen's organizing a picket line in front of," he turned to Helen. "What's the name of that studio?"

"American Pictures. I want to let them know how we feel, and I want to see the low-down, good-for-nothing dog who goes in there to put on blackface for white folks. So, young man, are you with us?"

Skip tried to ignore her crazy talk about walking a picket line. Only fools walk picket lines. That's what Zeke said. Carry a picket sign, and you'll never work in Hollywood again. Zeke didn't say what would happen if you knocked out a Hollywood director. He shook his head. Blackface was out, and he didn't have to walk a picket line to prove it.

"Well, young man." Helen's voice teased him. "Which side are you on?"

"My side," he said. "I do what I want to do. Don't need nobody, black or white, telling me right from wrong."

"That's right," Helen laughed. "You know the difference between, say, freedmen and free niggers. And there is no difference, right?"

"Sure, there's a difference, but one word ain't gon' change white folkses minds. They're pretty thick-headed when it comes to us. Hell, half the time they don't even see us."

He started to tell her about the Hollywood director he'd knocked silly for calling him a nigger, but she turned away. He worked quietly, strained to catch the words whispered between Helen and Henry. He caught her looking furtively at him, heard her say his name and, a moment later, heard her say "coward." His fingers choked the mop. He felt like throwing it down, marching over to Helen and telling her she didn't know a damn thing about him, but Henry's presence kept him back. He wished they were alone, then he could make her eat that insult. Coward. Who was she anyway? Wasn't even in moving pictures. Just came around acting like Miss Do Right, making him feel small and wrong because he didn't jump on her bandwagon. Now she was calling him names. He steered the mop bucket into the kitchen. Picketing ain't the only way to fix things, he thought, stopping at the doorway and turning around to see Helen on her high horse, pointing a polished fingernail at Henry's face.

He tried to put her words out of his mind, but they intruded upon his thoughts, needled him. Helen was carrying the battle to the studio gates, wheedling producers and directors into changing a single word, then looking for the next wrong to be righted. He didn't want to fight the studios. He wanted to join them, help tell the stories of his people. It had seemed so simple when it was only a country boy's dream. Now he knew Hollywood didn't want any new style of colored actor. That was just a huckster's line to pick the pockets of daydreaming fools. Harry-O knew the score and had left for the Harlem stage. Why stay and fight, bruise yourself in a war where you won skirmishes that barely changed the landscape? Freedman or free nigger, did it really matter? The colored western, where the light-skinned cowboy got the girl and the dark-skinned one played the clown, was just a standard B-picture shoot-`em-up, with a Negro twist.

What was he doing here, Sarah had asked. Now, with the giddy, high-pitched joy of his early success faded to merely a story to be passed on, he asked himself the same question and couldn't come up with a satisfying answer. He only knew the dream was fading.

He reread the newspaper story, found his eyes drifting from the words to the picture of Sarah standing beneath the arching sign, while behind her the blue waters of the Pacific splashed along the sand and the sun shone bright and warm on a clear day. She seemed caught in the springtide of life, when all was glorious hope, promise, possibility. There was no hint of despair, of death's sudden coming. There was only the gay, untroubled face of a young woman in full flower, smiling into the future. What had she left? What to mark her time here? What that you could pick up and hold, run your fingers over and say: `Yes, this was Sarah's'? He walked up to his room, looked at the radio sitting on the windowsill, the clothes he'd bought. They meant nothing, really, just fine vines to strut on the avenue, turn the girls' heads and have the boys say, "Where'd you get that crazy drape, 'gate?"

Only National Steel, its dull gray body pockmarked with dents and dings, was worth remarking on. That guitar and his music had taken him to the deepest places of his heart, and he had brought forth all the world's joy and pain to share with anyone who would listen, and for that he had to thank Old Man Williams, who first saw his gift and showed him how to use it. National Steel was his anchor and his savior. He could lose himself with that guitar, become a rattlesnakin' daddy with a ragtime git-box, or a bottleneck slidin' Delta boy making those steel strings ring, and lately he had taken on the persona of a swinging jazzman who could croon a tune or two and charm a young woman into his arms. Skip picked up the guitar, tested its weight and sighted down the neck, which, thankfully, was still straight. He stared at the strings, marveling over how they could tell the whole story of life. All they needed was someone with enough skill to discover the magic hidden within them, and enough heart to make them sing a song that could lift the heaviest burden, salve the deepest wound, or make you kick up your heels and dance with joy because you were alive and the Lord had smiled on you. The charcoal gray, double-breasted suit he'd bought at R.C.'s with money from his last acting job was a sharp looking number, even better than the one that made him look as good as George Raft, but a thousand of them couldn't match his beat-up guitar.

National Steel was paid for. That couldn't be said about the suit, the ties, shirts. R.C.'s credit line had turned him into the sharp dressed dandy of his dreams. Sometimes he missed payments, came in a week late, or short. One day Erline stopped him on Central Avenue and told him he was looking good, so good that she'd hate to take R.C.'s clothes off his back. After all, he was a walking advertisement. But credit didn't mean free.

Henry had frowned when Skip asked for a raise, told him he was making good money, living rent-free on Central Avenue, eating whenever he pleased. Skip said he had other considerations, movies, clothes, nightclubs, Sapphire and Buster. A man couldn't live on ribs alone, even if they were damned good ribs. He needed more than the seven bucks Henry gave him every Saturday afternoon, needed it to fill up the credit hole he couldn't stop digging. Two acting jobs didn't provide nearly enough, especially when Zeke took half right off the top. He laid the gray suit across his cot. A raise, or a better paying job meant he could move out, get a decent apartment, one with a real bathroom. He was tired of taking whore baths, or paying the Y.M.C.A. a quarter every time he wanted a hot bath. Everything cost money in the city. Used to be he'd think nothing of walking five miles. Now, he could barely imagine walking five blocks. Why walk when seven cents bought a seat on a streetcar? Why try to scrape a harvest from a backyard garden, or risk losing a finger to chop off a chicken's head, when the nearest Safeway had all the food a man could ever want?

He walked over to the sink, resigning himself to another whore bath. Afterwards, he dressed slowly, the fine clothes making him feel better. He rolled up his starched white shirt sleeves, lazily rubbed black polish across his Wellington wingtips, remembering the newspaper sales ad that had sent him hurrying downtown to the Broadway: "Wellington shoes for the elegant man-about-town. Wellington. The five-dollar shoe with the ten-dollar feel." He didn't know how a ten-dollar shoe felt, but the Wellingtons almost felt like slippers. He slipped them on, wriggled his toes a bit before tying the laces and giving the shoes a final brushing to bring up the shine. Standing in front of the mirror, carefully knotting his tie, he had to admit Erline was right. He was a walking advertisement. If only Delta Slim could see him now.

Henry and Helen were still talking as he headed out the door. She'd calmed down. The rich smell of fresh brewed coffee filled the Dancing Bar-B-Que. Henry looked up from his cup and smiled.

"There goes the sharpest dishwasher on Central Avenue. Look at him, Helen. Clean as the Board of Health, and I only pay him seven dollars a week. Why, I remember when he used to wear overalls and broken down brogans."

Skip tugged at his suit and gave Henry a wink. "Cain't have your employee looking like a country bumpkin, Henry. Folks might think you don't pay a living wage." He slammed the door and walked into the night, glad to be free of Helen's tirade, his doubts about Hollywood, and the sad, sad story of Sarah Kotlowitz.

Outside the Bradbury Building, Shoeshine Billy played heads or tails, bony fingers flipping a nickle up in the air and slapping it down on the top of his left hand. Now and again he stopped to fumble through his box for a watch with the right time. He saw Skip walking with an easy stride, showing off another fine suit, and polished shoes.

"Say," he said, streaking a smudge of black polish across his cheek. "Is somebody else working this block? That looks like a fresh shine."

"You know you own this stretch of Broadway," Skip replied. "I'm just trying to save a little money. Pretty good, huh?"

Billy squatted down, inspected the shoes like a craftsman checking the work of an apprentice. "Not bad. Not bad at all. But you really ought to let a professional take care of shoes good as these. See here?" He pointed to the dull insteps. "And here?" He pointed to the heels. "A sharp papa like you can't afford to miss spots." He stood, gave Skip his endearing, baby-face smile. "Whadda-ya say I fix `em up. I'll do it for a nickel."

"Maybe next time." He pulled a pack of Chesterfields from his coat pocket, tapped out one for himself and one for Billy, who took two. "Out kind of late, aren't you," Skip said, leaning over to light his cigarette off Billy's match. "School's tomorrow."

"School, schmool," Billy said, enjoying the smoke. "What's a working man need with school. Besides, Jimmy the Midge's got me running errands, paying good money, too. A buck every time."

"Ain't there some kind of law against that?"

"Against what? Working?" Billy looked up at Skip with wary, suspicious eyes. "You ain't finking for the cops are you?"

"Shoot." Skip flicked some ash off his cigarette. "Ain't no colored cops in this town."

"Well, you never know. Them vice boys'll do anything, and I mean anything. They been swarming all over the district around San Pedro. That's why Jimmy hired me on. Nobody'd suspect a shoeshine boy."

Just then, the Bradbury's door opened and out stepped Jimmy the Midge, resplendent in spats and a sporty, yellow and black checkerboard, double-breasted suit. The bright yellow carnation poking out of his lapel looked overly large and out of place, its delicate scent overwhelmed by Jimmy's strong cologne and perfumed hair oil. Still, he dreamily sniffed the flower, twirled his small, gold-tipped cane with the ease of an impresario and nodded at Skip.

"How-ya doing, Texas?"

"I'm alright. You?"

"Couldn't be better." Jimmy smiled, taking deep breaths and slapping his chest. "Excuse me."

He snapped his fingers. Billy ran over to him and they stepped. They stepped out of Skip's earshot, leaned together, co-conspirators passing on secrets, Jimmy standing on his tiptoes, cupping his hand to Billy's ear, while the kid's eyes, constantly on the lookout, checked the passing cars and passersby. When they finished, Jimmy slapped a fat envelope into Billy's hands, reached up and patted him on the shoulder. Billy, eyes still tracking the street, bent over his shoebox, hid the envelope in the bottom then stood, waiting for the cash-end of the deal, which Jimmy produced with a flourish, pulling out a shiny gold-plated money clip choked with greenbacks. He casually peeled one off, folded it around his middle finger and stuffed it in Billy's shirt pocket. The kid swung the box across his shoulder and started off, whistling a carefree tune, his body swaying from side to side, his hip giving the box a saucy bump right on the beat.

"Neither rain, nor sleet, nor snow, and especially the Los Angeles Police Department must keep the merry messenger from his appointed rounds," Jimmy said, clipping the end off a six-inch cigar. He brushed his manicured nails across his coat, struck a match and puffed contentedly. The cigar flared red-hot. "What brings you around this time of night?"

"Business, Jimmy. Hollywood business."

"Bah," Jimmy said, approaching, his thin voice taking a serious turn. "You'll never get ahead in the acting game. That's sometime work. A colored man will never make enough to enjoy the finer things in life which, if you'll excuse me, is just what I intend to do." He stepped to the curb, waved his cane to hail a cab, then turned around as if remembering something he'd forgotten. "You a betting man?"

"Depends."

"Well, let me give you some free advice. Destiny's Mare in the third tomorrow at Santa Anita. Two bucks'll get you ten, guaranteed."

A Yellow cab pulled up and Jimmy scooted inside, his head resting against the back seat. "Here," he said, flipping Skip an embossed business card. "Look me up sometime, if you ever get tired of the acting game. I got plenty of customers on the avenue."

The cab eased into the evening traffic as Skip read the card: James R. Royster, Esq. Speculations Analyst. He flicked his cigarette into the gutter and walked into the Bradbury, thinking about what a sight they must have made, the midget, the shoeshine boy and himself, all three of them standing together for a few minutes in a world that was neither black, nor white. Above, he heard a lone typewriter clattering away in a corner office, the muffled tap-tap-tapping breaking the thick, heavy silence. He hoped it was Sapphire. He hadn't seen her since his drunken night, and she was always absent whenever he stopped by the office. His footsteps echoed across the marble tiles, the sharp sound rising up, growing softer as it reached the skylight. He rode the cage elevator to the third floor, thought about Zeke and the fight with Marshall. The familiar stink of cheap cigars made him cough as he stood outside the office door. He fanned his face, already figuring the cost of another trip to the dry cleaners: fifty cents. Damn, shit. The cost of doing business. The typing stopped the moment he entered. His heart trembled. There she was, looking haggard, overworked, the bags under her eyes ruining her soft face.

"Hi," he said, lowering his eyes, catching the scent of roses amid the cigar smoke.

"Hello, Skip." Her voice was distant, cool. "I'll tell Mister Washington you're here."

"How have you been," he said, sitting down, working himself up to an apology. "How's Buster?"

"We are fine," she said, her words clipped and precise.

That was all. Fine. No elaboration, no small talk. She busied herself with a stack of papers beside her typewriter, spoke into the intercom box and told Zeke that a Mister Skip Reynolds was here to see him. Skip wrung his hands, twiddled his thumbs, fought the tight anxiety gripping him. He thumbed through an old Collier's, heard Zeke's gruff voice grumbling through a telephone call: "Yes. No. What the hell do I care." Sapphire cranked a fresh sheet through the typewriter, sat up, her back perfectly straight, and started banging furiously on the keys. She flung the carriage back with a vengeance the second she heard the bell. Two lines into the page, she stopped, fussed over a mistake and ripped the sheet from the typewriter. She cranked through another. A brittle, strained silence filled the spaces between the rapid tapping of the typewriter's keys. A weary draft crept up from Broadway to push lazily against the curtains. Skip tried to concentrate on the magazine, but the memory of the last time he'd seen Sapphire distracted him, shamed him. He could tell she was waiting for him to make amends. He watched her work, her long fingers playing the keys as easy as Earl Hines at the piano. She did not look up. He cleared his throat, hoping an apology would break the unsettling tension and repair the damage. If she didn't take him back, then at least her lasting image of him wound not be that of a drunken fool.

"Uh, Sapphire. About the other night. I'm sorry. I . . ." He shrugged. Was that enough?

Sapphire answered with a smoldering, unforgiving glare. "Excuse me?"

"I said, I'm sorry. You know, about the other night, coming to your house all drunk. Guess I kind of lost myself celebrating Joe Louis."

"Sorry?" She raced through a line of type, her muttering lost in the machine-gun clatter of the keys. "Sorry?" She looked at him again. "Is that all you can say? 'I'm sorry.' As if that's going to make everything all right." She pushed her chair back and marched over to him. "You come to my house in the middle of the night, drunk as a skunk, calling out my name, waking up my neighbors, shaming me, and all you can say is, I'm sorry!" She whipped around so fast her dress billowed out and wrapped around her legs. "And that song about going down the big road with somebody else. Mrs. Harrelson told me all about you." She smiled now, glad to see Skip flinch. "Um hum, told me all about you running out on her, leaving two weeks' rent unpaid. She helped me see the real you, Mister William Henry Reynolds."

Skip held up his hands. "Now, wait a minute, Sapphire. I can explain all about that. I was down on my luck, broke. I did what I had to do. I offered Mrs. Harrelson some money the other night, but she wouldn't take it. Sapphire . . ."

She cut him off. "Don't call me Sapphire. From now on I'm Miss Davis to you." She stopped long enough for Skip to see the hurt in her eyes. "I thought you were different, Skip. I thought, oh, I don't know. I thought we were making something special."

"We are," he said, reaching out to her. He wanted to hold her and take the hurt from her eyes, but just then Zeke poked his head out the office door, eyes twinkling with amusement, a stogie bouncing in the corner of his mouth.

"What's all that racket? Y'all having some kind of lover's spat?"

"Lover's spat!" Sapphire stepped away from Skip. "This man is not my lover. We were just friends."

"That's not what I heard," Zeke said, smiling. "Now, I don't care what y'all call this conversation, but whatever it is, could you keep it down. I'm trying to conduct some business in here."

The door closed, leaving Skip and Sapphire to stare at each other in the awkward silence. Her fury spent, Sapphire quietly went back to work. She cranked a fresh sheet of paper into her typewriter as Skip walked in front of her desk and crouched down to look in her eyes.

"Cain't we get together again, maybe go to church come Sunday?" he said.

"You'll have to do better than that," she replied, making sure not to meet his eyes.

"Well, what do you want me to do, Sapphire? I done already said 'I'm sorry.'"

"You could try being a little more considerate. Buster's been asking after you. Keeps saying he wants to go to the bar-b-que, when's Mister Skip going to come and take me to the bar-b-que. Think about him. He needs a man, but a responsible one. Drunks and vipers need not apply."

"Well, I ain't none of that," he said. "I get out of my head once every once in awhile, but so does damn near everybody else." He searched her eyes, hoping for understanding. "Come on now, Sapphire. Why don't y'all stop around one afternoon? I miss seeing you, and the kitchen ain't the same without Little B. Whadda-ya say?"

"I'll think about it," she replied, no hint of surrender in her voice.

Zeke opened his door. "Now, that's what I like to see, two young people having a friendly conversation, instead of all that carrying on." He nodded to Skip. "Come on in."

Skip hurried into Zeke's office, glancing at Sapphire as he passed by, whispering, "I'll call you." She stared right past him. Once inside the office, he collapsed in the nearest chair, slumped back and blew out a long, unwinding breath that drained off his frustration like a valve opened on a tire filled to bursting. Zeke relaxed on his throne, kicked off his shoes, brushed aside the papers, sandwich wrappers, half-filled coffee cups and ledgers littering his desk before putting his feet up.

"What you do to that gal, boy? I ain't seen Sapphire that hot in a good long while." He reached over to scratch the big toe poking out of his torn sock. "Don't tell me you're two-timing her?"

Skip shook his head. "I stopped by her house after that Joe Louis fight, little drunk, said some stuff." He rubbed his eyes and forehead.

"Whew! I was hoping she might have gotten over it by now."

"Boy," Zeke said, looking at the ceiling as he thoughtfully rolled the stogie between his fingers. "A woman is like an elephant. They never forget, but they can forgive. Um hum." He nodded as if he had spoken the Gospel truth. "Never forget. I had me a woman once, remembered every little wrong thing I did. Swear to God. She was like a crazy pit bull terrier, wouldn't let go of nothing. But Sapphire? She'll get over it. Just had to let off some steam. Why don't you take her some candy, and something for the boy. She'll come around." He swung his feet off the desk, stood and leaned towards Skip. "Now, what's this I hear about you taking up boxing?"

Skip rubbed a balled fist into his open palm. "I guess you could call it that."

"You guess," Zeke roared in mock anger. "Don't play with me, boy. You're training to be a middleweight, right? Acting's not good enough. After all I've done to get you a toe-hold in moving pictures, now I find out you want to try your hand at the fight game. And who of all people do you pick to practice on but a Hollywood director."

"He had it coming," Skip said, looking up. "He called me a nigger."

"That's a hell of a reason. No white man ever called you nigger before?"

"Plenty times, and if I hadn't been scared of dying, I'd have hit every one of `em. But I was. So I let `em do it, let `em call me out my name and didn't do nothing. Even smiled sometimes. But them days is gone. Next one does it is gon' get just what I gave Marshall, a mouthful of fist."

"I see." Zeke said, sitting back down and folding his arms across his chest. "Boy, I'm proud of you. That took some guts. I wish I could've seen it."

"Yeah, I gave him the old Tunis one-two," Skip said, and tapped out a Chesterfield. "How'd you hear `bout it?"

"I make it a point to know what my people are up to," Zeke said, flicking his lighter and holding it for Skip, who drew deep on the cigarette, slowly working himself up to asking if this was the set up to good-bye.

"Why's everybody working so late?"

"Well," Zeke said, getting up and coming around the desk to put his hand on Skip's shoulder. "Boy," he said, the two of them strolling shoulder-to-shoulder across the room. "Mankind is like a cow's udder. All you have to do is squeeze the tit to get that sweet milk, money. And, you can't take out too much time to rest. If you do, somebody'll take your place. So, I'm up here tonight, squeezing them tits. Got Sapphire counting checks and filling orders. But that's not what I wanted to talk to you about."

Skip steeled himself. Here it comes.

Zeke turned Skip around and looked into his eyes as if sizing him up for a job. "Are you ready for the big time?"

"Big time?"

"That's right. The big time. A speaking role."

"You mean you ain't fixing to cut me loose?"

"What, for hitting some white man who probably had it coming? Hell naw. I'm fixing to take you to the next level, if you're up to it."

The dying flame of his Hollywood dream flickered, brightened.

Zeke leaned into his intercom. "Sapphire. Bring me that script from American Pictures." He turned and leaned back against his desk. "Skip, in every life there comes a time when you find yourself standing in front of opportunity's door and you have to decide if you're going to open it. You know, step up to the plate and take your turn at bat. You following me?"

"I think so."

"Good. It's like in the old days when Julius Caesar had to cross that Rubicon river. Now, he could've stayed on his side and slinked back to camp, and just think what the world would be if he had. But, and I emphasize this, he didn't. He crossed that river, opened opportunity's door and marched on into something new. You did the same when you came out here."

"Only the door was locked," Skip said.

"Yes, yes. Well, sometimes that happens too. But you didn't let it stop you, and now look at you, dressing like one of them society boys from Sugar Hill. Ought to have your picture in *The Eagle*." Zeke nodded at Skip's embarrassed smile. "Feels good, don't it?" He waved his hand at the pictures lining his wall. "These people, every last one of them, was just like you, scuffling, trying to get a break in moving pictures, and they did." He stopped as Sapphire stepped into the room.

"Here's that script, Mister Washington."

"Give it to Skip."

She hesitated, her head shaking ever so slightly.

"Go on, gal," Zeke said. "He don't bite, least not that I know of."

Sapphire slapped the bound script against her thigh, then threw it across the room. It hit Skip full in the chest, surprising him. The cigarette flew out his hand.

"Say," he said, standing up. But she was already gone. "Jesus." He picked up the burning cigarette. "Women." He sat down and read the script's title page. "Ain't We Got Fun?" He flipped through the script.

"You'll have plenty of time to read that," Zeke said. "It's a boy-meets-girl story, nothing special, except for the role I'm talking about." He walked over to Skip, put one hand on back of the chair and the other on Skip's leg. "You remember what I said about old Steppin' and Sleep `N Eats," he said, leaning close. "How they play the role but don't live it? Well, that's what this role requires. There's a scene, a big one, mind you, and it's done in blackface."

The word exploded inside Skip's head. Blackface. This was the role Helen had talked about, the one she was going to picket, the one she had used to test his loyalty. This was Zeke's big time role? He shuddered. Tommy Murchinson's troubled ghost stepped into the room and looked at him, cork-blackened face grinning at the end of a rope. He tried to get up, but Zeke pushed him back down, the firm hand heavy on his shoulder.

"Now, now. Hold on a minute."

Skip slapped Zeke's hand away. "No, no, no, Mister Washington. I cain't do nothing like that. I didn't come out here to do nothing like that."

"Now, hear me out, son." Zeke put his hand back on Skip's shoulder, held it there until he was sure Skip wasn't going to bolt and run. "Now, I can tell by the look on your face that you think this ain't for you. Well, a lot of folks, some better than you, have done it. I've done it. But there's more than just a little grease paint involved here. There's money, lots of it."

"I don't care how much money there is, Mister Washington. I won't do it. Helen Lipscomb's talking `bout getting folks to picket American Pictures over this, and I don't want to be caught in the middle." He handed Zeke the script. "You better find someone else."

Zeke faked disappointment. "Here I thought I had a man on my hands. A tough guy. Knocked out a white man. Turns out I just got a boy scared of some loud-mouth woman. And a fool to boot. That's right. They say a fool and his money are soon parted. Truth is, a fool never comes across the money in the first place. Walk away from this, Skip, and you not only walk away from a speaking role, but you'll be missing out on a hundred bucks, maybe more, and that's your cut."

"Mister Washington. I didn't come out here to put on Rastus. I want to do us right, play a Buffalo Soldier like my grandfather and Old Man Williams. And I ain't scared of nobody, you hear. Nobody." He fought the urge to knock the stogie out of Zeke's mouth. "Why the hell you asking me anyway?"

"Why not you? You came out here to be an actor, didn't you? Well, here's an acting job."

"Yeah, but."

"But nothing. This ain't no ten-dollars-a-day extra work. This is a real job. Sooner or later everybody does things they ain't proud of, but they do it. And sometimes it pays off later. Hattie McDaniel's probably done a few roles she ain't proud of, but look at her now. That role she's got in *Gone With the Wind* is big.

"Now, I'd be lying if I told you Hollywood was going to make a Buffalo Soldier picture this year, or next year, or even in five years. But they will, one day. You could be in it, and by then this role would be a forgotten stepping stone." He picked up the script, pressed it in Skip's hands, then put his arms around him again, his voice now taking on a fatherly tone. "I know this is a lot to chew on all of a sudden, but give it time, son."

"But what about them pickets?"

"The hell with them. In a week or two, it'll all be forgotten."

A hundred dollars. The idea of that much money teased him with visions of moving out of the Dancing Bar-B-Que, paying off R.C., finally getting ahead, buying something nice for Sapphire.

"I ain't forcing you to take this role, Skip. And don't be blinded by the money. Think about your future, and maybe one day getting big enough to do that Buffalo Soldier story." He tapped the script, pointed Skip towards the door. "Why don't you sleep on it, then give me a call."

"Tomorrow," Skip croaked, feet shuffling across the dirty rug.

"Now, that might be asking too much, don't you think? Just call me when you've made up your mind, but don't wait too long. They want to start shooting within the month." Zeke patted Skip's shoulder and opened the door. "Call me. Soon."

The door clicked shut. The thin curtain hung limp. The rushing, metallic sound of Broadway's thinning traffic barely made it up to the third floor. Skip felt woozy from the conversation, the offer, the botched attempt to make things right with Sapphire. He looked around the spare office, seeing mocking reminders of how Zeke milked the world's tits. The guy in the framed Photoplay ad laughed at him. "If it wasn't for Ezekiel Washington's school, I'd be just another cotton picking fool . . . I'll see you in Hollywood." Skip frowned. Probably never was an acting school. But this offer was real. He pressed his ear to the door, hearing the phone ring.

"Yeah, yeah. I got someone for you," Zeke said. "Is he any good? I wouldn't send you somebody who wasn't."

Skip smiled at the compliment.

"Ha! Ha! Ha! Don't you worry about it. If he backs out, I'll find some-body else. Plenty boys down my way hungry for that kind of money. Huh? What's that? Destiny's Mare in the third? Sure, sure. I'll tell Jimmy. Ten bucks? Ok, I'll cover you. Bye."

Skip let himself out of the office, the script held under his coat. Half-empty streetcars rumbled along, carrying tired riders whose heads leaned against the windows, ears closed to the grinding sound of iron wheels rolling across the rails. Skip laughed to himself, thinking about the script's title. "Ain't We Got Fun?" Was that some sort of Hollywood joke? What fun could there be for the man who signed on to wear black-face? The answer eluded him as he walked along, head and heart worn out by the evening's roller coaster of emotions. The news about Sarah had pitched him into a brooding gloom that deepened with Helen's taunts, became numbing frustration and anger, despair over the mess with Sapphire, a problem he'd brought on himself. He missed seeing Buster. Then there was Zeke talking about opportunity, the bigtime. Step up to the plate and take your swing. But a homerun only meant a tiny step on a road leading God knows where. What had once seemed possi-ble, now seemed absurd, hopeless. He felt like he was waking up from a delusion that had held him in its thrall. Could that have been him eagerly cutting out a magazine ad by the fading light of a Tunis sundown, secreting five dollars in an envelope he sent forth like bread upon the waters, him waiting in fields of high cotton for a reply he mistook for a life rope? Was that him dancing in Murphy's Emporium, waving bye-bye from the open door of a northbound Katy carrying him away, his heart racing up, up, up, like a Fourth of July skyrocket, only to crash in Forth Worth, a nameless stretch of desert, the Plaza Arms.

He moved on down Broadway, battling doubt and uncertainty. Nothing in the darkened windows caught his eye until he saw an electric Gibson ES-150, like the one Charlie Christian played. The streetlights reflected off the guitar's polished rosewood body and silver tuning pegs. A black cord ran from the guitar to a small amplifier. The sign in the window said the set was on sale for ninety-five dollars. His fingers started working through a bluesy jazz run. What would it sound like electrified? He had never thought of buying another guitar, because there was never a chance of having enough money, until now.

~

PHINEAS, WEARING A LONG BLACK COAT WITH THE COLLAR TURNED up, stepped out of a side street as Skip passed by, head down, looking blue. He fell in behind him, pulled a slender piece of pipe from his pocket and jammed it into the middle of Skip's back.

"Stand and deliver," he said, like some nineteenth century European highwayman.

Skip stiffened, his blood turning to ice water. "I ain't got nothing, mister," he said, raising his hands. The script dropped from under his coat and slapped against the sidewalk. "No money. Nothing. I'm just a poor boy long ways from home."

"Well, I'll just see about that," Phineas growled, masking his voice. He rummaged through Skip's pockets, patted him down. "C'mon, now," he snarled, voice full of evil. "Where's the money?"

"I . . . I . . . I told you. I ain't got nothing. I swear I ain't." Nervous sweat broke out under his arms, on his forehead, his chest. "Honest, mister. I ain't got nothing."

"Well," Phineas swung him around and smiled. "You should always carry a little something, in case you run into a friend."

Skip slumped, relieved, then he couldn't decide whether to throw his arms around Phineas or knock the living daylights out of him. "God dammit, Phineas!"

Phineas chuckled and twirled the piece of pipe between his fingers. "Scared you, didn't I?"

Skip grabbed the pipe and threw it into the street. "God dammit! You trying to give me a heart attack?"

Phineas put on a hurt, hang-dog look. "I was only trying to have some fun. You looked like you could use a smile." He shrugged.

"Yeah, well try that game on somebody else." Skip turned and headed down the avenue.

"Wait a minute," Phineas said, bending over. "You're forgetting something." He picked up the script, moved beneath a streetlamp, his eyes squinting in the pale light. 'Ain't We Got Fun?' What's this?"

"Something I picked up downtown."

"Ah, downtown." Phineas thumbed through the script. "Looks like Hollywood to me. How you making out with moving pictures?"

"Doing alright, I guess."

"Hmmm. Is that despair I hear? Surely the bronze Errol Flynn isn't singing the blues, or is he." Phineas leaned close and looked Skip in the eye, cocked his head from side to side like a carnival bear. "Why, I believe that noble visage is hiding the grief of the ages. Por que? Why?"

Skip sighed. "Jesus, Phineas." A streetcar's ringing bell brought a little music into the troubled night. Two lovers, arm in arm, walked by. Skip envied their easy togetherness, the little world he knew they'd built to keep out life's worries, the world he'd almost built with Sapphire. "Jesus H. Christ."

"Out with it, Skip," Phineas implored. "Loose yourself of the poison. Lance the damnable pustule on your soul. Speak!"

Skip rolled his eyes. Why did Phineas always take so long to get to the point? He gritted his teeth against the burdensome flood of confusion and questions. Maybe Phineas had an answer. He turned to his friend. "Would you put on blackface? I mean, if somebody came to you and said, Do this and something good'll come of it, would you do it?"

"Me?"

"No, the goddamn streetlight. Yes, you. Would you?"

Phineas grunted. "So that's what this is all about. Well, it depends on the circumstances, the promised prize which, in this case, is what?"

"God only knows. Maybe a bigger role next time. But I'd have to do this first." Skip tapped a Chesterfield from his pack, started to offer one, then remembered Phineas didn't smoke cigarettes.

Phineas looked up at the stars. "Great is the price of stardom, and heavy the burden those who seek it." He rubbed his chin. "Is there more? I must know everything before I can give you an honest answer. I have a preliminary opinion, which tends towards the negative, but I need more information, and a warm place to collect my thoughts. What say we tip a glass or two at the nearest dispensary and there I shall impart to you my thoughts on this subject that has so clouded your usually sunny disposition?"

"I say, 'yes'."

"Excellent! We'll chase your blues away," Phineas said, turning around and dancing along Central Avenue.

"You buying?" Skip said, running to catch up. "I only got a couple of bucks."

Phineas stopped. "I thought you said you didn't have any money." He held up his hands and whined. "I ain't got nothing, mister. Honest."

Skip dragged on his cigarette. "I didn't have nothing for a robber."

"Good show! Sure, I can spot you a drink or two. The fish were really biting, Skip. Folks couldn't buy fast enough. Even now selected members of the citizenry are drinking the blessed sustenance of Eternity's Breath. But we shall slake our thirsts with more secular and common fare, and we shall discourse. Blackface, you say. Maybe I would, and maybe I wouldn't."

Phineas steered them away from the high-toned places where the drinks were expensive and the well-dressed crowds too busy looking around to see who else had made it past the doorman. He wanted a serious drinking place, where no one cared who you were and folks left you alone. Three blocks past the Dunbar Hotel, he stopped in front of a no-name bar with a handwritten sign over the door that read: Cold Beer. "Good enough," he said.

A clock with a red and white Lucky Strike pack on its round face hung above the bar, cigarette hands reading 12:15. Phineas ordered two glasses of scotch with beer chasers. Skip waved off the beer.

"Hmm," Phineas said, leading Skip to an empty table in back. "This must be serious." He contemplated his scotch, took a sip, then a swallow of beer. "You know, whites were the first to put on blackface. That's right," he nodded, seeing a flash of surprise in Skip's eyes. "You don't think we'd be crazy enough to come up with something as foolish as that, do you? They started it, trying to ape us. 'Wheel about, turn about, do just so. And every time I wheel about, I jump Jim Crow.' You ever heard that song?"

Skip shook his head.

"Figures," Phineas said. "You can't expect them to teach history. They'd have God sending them down with orders to redeem the poor, misguided heathens. But about your dilemma. Imagine, if you will, our nineteenth century brethern performing for whites who expected the blackface minstrel, Zip Coon and the Gold Dust Twins. It was what the people wanted, so we gave it to them. We aped the white man who was aping us. It's incredible, when you stop to think about it, like a hall of mirrors. Look on one side and you see white folks in blackface. Look on the other side and you see black folks in blackface. And who, what, is this perpetually grinning thing in burnt cork? Is it you? Is it me?" Phineas didn't wait for an answer. "Of course not! It's a mask, like one of Barnum's clowns. But there is a difference. No one mistakes the clown's sad visage and funny antics for The White Man. All they see is a clown. We put on blackface and, suddenly, as if by magic, we are transformed. You could be around white folks all your life and they'd never give you a second thought. But put on blackface and something in their collective mind goes `click', a switch turns on and you are recognized — Old Black Joe come home with a happy tale of dear old dixie." Phineas knocked back deep swallows of scotch, cleared his throat and started talking like Al Jolson. "Mammy, oh mammy. Look what they done to me, mammy." He laughed to himself. "Would I do it? Should you do it? You're an actor, aren't you? At least you're trying to be. Well, what is acting but putting on a mask? You leave yourself and become whoever it is you're paid to be. Once you strip it of all that historical mishmash, blackface is really nothing, just another mask, a harmless clown's face. But there's all that history, all that pain. Matter of fact, I can hardly believe it's still around, that someone actually wants you to do it. Who is this agent of yours anyway, a white man?"

"No," Skip said. "He's colored."

Phineas grunted and drained his beer. "We are our own worst enemy. Denmark Vecsey would tell you that." He turned around. "Bartender! Another round to wash away the memory of betrayal." He continued after the drinks arrived. "We've talked about Dunbar's 'We Wear The Mask,' haven't we? Old Paul knew the score. He knew we were shamming every-time we faced our ofay brothers and sisters. We grinned and lied to hide our tears, our suffering. It was our way of easing our passage through this vile and often unfriendly new world to which we were brought in chains." Phineas looked across the table. "The poem is beautiful, perfect. Yes, yes, let the world dream otherwise. We wear the mask! Why should-n't you wear it?"

Skip drained his first scotch, then started in on the second one, feel-ing that alcohol dullness creeping over him. "`Bout a year before I left home this colored brother in the next town crossed that line white folks have. You know the one?"

"Indeed I do," Phineas said.

"He had a right to do what he did. A white man raped his wife. So he hunted the guy down and shot him. Phineas, he didn't live to see the sunrise. They beat him up, shot him, strung him from a tree. But that ain't all. They painted him up in blackface. I never saw him, and I thank God for that, but I could close my eyes and see him right in here." He tapped his forehead. "See him big as life. Tommy Murchinson hanging from that damn tree, grinning that coon smile."

"Diabolical and instructive," Phineas said, leaning back and studying the ice cubes slowly melting in his glass. "You've got to hand it to white folks. They can be damn inventive when it comes to terror. Yes, Lord, you've got to give the devil his due."

Skip called out for a glass of water. "You see, it's because of Tommy Murchinson that I can't do this. At least that's one reason. I'd be think-ing about him all the time, what they did to him. It just wouldn't sit right with me. Besides, I didn't come out here to put on blackface."

"Then you've got your answer. Don't do it."

"Yeah, but my agent man said some good could come of it, if I wait-ed long enough."

"Hell, Skip, that man's promise probably isn't worth a Confederate dollar. Anyway, doesn't sound to me like you want what he's offering."

"I know, but . . ."

"But? You talk of bringing shame upon yourself, tell this story of a good brother who was murdered, whose corpse was defiled, and you hesitate. But? Is there something else?"

"Money."

"Oh. Money. The great corruptor. Many is the man who has sold his soul for a handful of legal tender, banknotes negotiable the world over. Humph." Phineas gulped his scotch. "What measly sum is he offering?"

Skip whispered, almost embarrassed to mention the amount. "One hundred dollars, maybe more."

Phineas choked on his scotch. "A hundred dollars!" He pushed his chair back, walked around the table, muttering to himself and waving his arms, pressing his hands to his head as if he was trying to keep it from exploding. He dropped back into his chair, pulled it forward and leaned across the table, his hand on Skip's forehead. "Hmm. You feel normal. No sign of fever. Are you all right, or have you clean lost your mind?"

Skip shrugged. "I'm a little tired, but I feel fine."

"Like hell. Here we are, running around in these mental circles, talking about history, clowns, Dunbar, and there's money, big money, at stake. A hundred dollars!" Phineas knocked off his scotch and drained half his beer. "You know the problem with you, Skip? You think too damn much. Hell, for a hundred dollars, I'd sleep with my mother-in-law, if I had one, call the old gal `honey' and give her a goodbye kiss on the lips."

"What happened to all that talk about selling your soul, being corrupted?"

Phineas dismissed the question. "That was before. Someone's offering you a king's ransom to put on a little burnt cork and jump around in front of the cameras." He nodded gravely. "That's right, a king's ransom, and here you sit, plagued by an American nightmare and thoughts of honor." Phineas rubbed his forehead and sighed. "Do you have any idea how much money that is?"

"'Bout half of what a 'cropper makes in a year."

"At least that! People work months for that kind of money, and I mean work. Coal miners, guys in steel mills, factories, they get it doled out a little bit at a time and here you can make it in, what, a couple, three days. Where's your mother wit? Put all this worrisome mess behind you. Chalk it up to experience, or whatever, but take the money, baby. Take the money."

"My grandma used to say that."

"What?"

"Take the money. She told me that before I left home, but I don't think she meant this."

"Well, she spoke the truth," Phineas said. "The true wisdom of the ages. Take the money, and let the devil deal with the rest. Hell, only a fool would hold it against you."

"Think so?"

"You start flashing a handful of Jacksons, and the only thing folks'll want to know is how they can get hold of some." Phineas winked and smile. "To your grandma," he said, holding his scotch high. "In hopes that you will take her words to heart." He drained the liquor, grabbed the beer, finished it. Then he slammed the empties on the table and belched. "'Nuff said."

LOS ANGELES WAS GIDDY. NEVER MIND THAT HALF A WORLD AWAY Adolph Hitler proclaimed Germany's right to plow a 15-mile wide road through the Polish Corridor, or that the $150 million New York World's Fair had opened with a dazzling display of fireworks. Those stories were just fodder for the newspaper. Even the municipal elections and in-fighting in City Hall received only the slightest mention. The multitudes in the great sprawling basin beneath the San Gabriel Mountains were hopped up on something far more important. Just north of downtown, on forty acres right across from where the Spanish missionaries met the Gabrielino Indians and founded a village named for an angel, preparations were underway for the grand opening of Union Station. Half-page and quarter-page ads bought by the big department stores and specialty shops filled *The Times, The Examiner, The Sentinel,* each touting the advertiser's role in the city's history, the contributions and support given to the magnificent, exalting project. They called it a landmark of progress, a lodestone for travelers the world over, the gateway to the east. Three great western railroads – the Southern Pacific, the Union Pacific and the Santa Fe – had, after years of wrangling and bickering and plain old stubbornness joined with the city's stewards to build an $11 million testament to Los Angeles' place as the crown jewel of California. Supporters had grown old, stooped and gray fighting the decades-long battle of civic pride. But success had come. Move over San Francisco!

Along the avenue folks read the newspapers and dreamed of Pullman porter, Red Cap and custodial jobs. Even Henry had caught the fever. All day long he'd been singing, "Dinah won't you blow. Dinah won't you blow," or "I've been working on the railroad." An old train lantern, rescued from a Central Avenue junk shop, sat cleaned and polished above the Dancing Bar-B-Que's stove, its kerosene-fed flame flickering behind thick, red glass. Diana had brought in her boys' Lionel train set and put it on a corner table with a newspaper cut-out of the stunning, Spanish-mission styled train station in the middle. As Henry peered into his oven, grimacing against the heat like a fireman checking the coals, he sang another song from the storied rails.

"Will Fox said to the fireman, bring me a little more gin." He closed the door and yelled to Skip. "You know that one?"

"Henry, that song is as old as dust," Skip yelled back. "I learned it when I was still in short pants."

Henry mopped his face with a red and white handkerchief he'd bought off a brakeman. "I didn't know you were a railroad man."

"Shoot. I was raised on the rhythm of the five-o-nine running through Tunis. Casey Jones ain't got nothing on me."

"Guess you're going to the parade then," Henry said, clearing the counter and carrying an armload of plates back to the kitchen. "Mayor's declared tomorrow a holiday. I'm going. You?"

"Don't know," Skip replied, taking the plates.

"How 'bout you, Di? I bet your boys would love it."

"I wouldn't miss it for the world," Diana said, working a hunk of rib meat into the side of her jaw, "and not because of my boys. No sir, they ain't got a thing to do with it." She propped her elbows on the table and smiled like a schoolgirl remembering her first kiss. "I got a soft spot for trains. A Pullman porter did that to me. Gave me this big old soft spot right here." She patted her bosom and stared off into her past. "Horace Anderson was his name, and Henry, laying with that man was like riding the Santa Fe, smooth, smooth, smooth. I'm going to be there, just to stir up a sweet memory."

Skip spanked a plate dry and checked the last few customers lingering over their rib dinners. Closing time was coming, and not soon enough. He wanted to get back upstairs and study the script. Zeke told

him to report to the Palm Hotel at Olympic Boulevard and Central
Avenue, early. The studio wanted him in the parade. For days he wrestled
with the idea of doing the scene. He'd worried over it like a rotten tooth
his tongue couldn't leave alone. At first he said 'No', unwilling to betray
the dream that had brought him to Los Angeles. But that dream was
dead. Life killed it. And in its place came a newly-discovered mercenary
spirit that kept coaxing and nudging him, telling him to forget those
country boy dreams and whatever Zeke said about opportunity, the big
time. That was just talk. Here was money, enough to make a new start,
or buy the Gibson and an amplifier. Only a fool would walk away from so
much money, and he knew Grandma Sarah didn't raise no fool. He'd
convinced himself that blackface wasn't nothing but a mask. Put it on,
take it off, and go on 'bout your business. But take the money.

Zeke was the only one who knew. Skip made him promise not to tell
anyone else, especially Henry, who was going to spend part of tomorrow
morning carrying a picket sign with Helen Lipscomb's group. One team
was going to march in front of American Pictures; the other would take
the Palm Hotel. Skip hoped Henry and Helen wouldn't be downtown.

Out in the café, the front door's bell sent tinkling music ringing
through the room. Another customer; another casual dinner to wait
through; another table to clear. Skip cursed to himself and yelled to
Henry. "Say, boss man, ain't it time to lock them doors?"

"Clock on the wall says we got ten minutes. What's your hurry anyway? Nothing happens on Tuesday night. And there's no way any of those
Kitchen Mechanics are going to be sneaking down here. Too many affairs
going on. Now, why don't you set up a table for the nice couple that just
walked in?"

Skip grabbed pairs of knives, forks, spoons and napkins, then
stepped into the café. He stopped immediately. Sapphire, looking fine as
ever, took a table by the window with her date. He hadn't seen her since
the night Zeke gave him the script. She'd quit shortly after that, taken a
job at U.C.L.A. She wouldn't take his calls, and had sent back a box of
candy. Now, she was here, waiting for her impeccably dressed gentleman
to pull out her seat. She settled in like a mother hen, turned and saw Skip
standing, utensils in hand, a soaking, bar-b-que stained apron wrapped
around his waist. She looked away, busied herself with her compact. Skip
sized up her date, a handsome, dark-skinned brother in a natty, navy

blue suit, starched white shirt and red-striped tie. Gold cuff links peaked out of his coat sleeves and caught the café's light. At least the boy knew how to dress, Skip thought, marching across the café, barely holding the service-with-a-smile look, steeling himself against the seductive, memory-filled rush of Sapphire's rose-scented perfume. She watched him work and, in a tone that made it seem like they'd been nothing more than casual friends, said: "Hello, Skip."

"Hi," he said, straightening the silverware, struggling to match her calm. He turned to leave, but her voice stopped him.

"Skip? I'd like you to meet Richard Lawson. He's at U.C.L.A."

Lawson popped out of his seat, tugged at his coat and held out his hand. "Call me Dick," he said in a deep baritone.

For a moment that stretched towards infinity, Skip stared at the extended hand with the polished cuff links gleaming at the wrist. He was surprised to find he was nearly a head taller than Lawson, who nervously cleared his throat and brought him back to real time, reminded him that he was being rude by not returning the polite gesture.

"Yeah," he said, quickly wiping his hands on his apron. Their eyes met. Lawson tightened his grip. Skip stood tall to get every bit of his height advantage. Slowly, he pried his hand from Lawson's grasp and turned to Sapphire. "Y'all stepping out?"

"Why, yes we are," she said, her voice gay and excited. "Richard is taking me to the Dunbar Hotel. They're having a chamber music concert!"

Lawson nodded. "I find Bach to be most comforting. Are you familiar with the classics, mister? I'm afraid I didn't catch your last name."

"Reynolds," Skip said, dropping all effort at politeness. "And, no, I ain't familiar with the classics. "Have a nice time, Miss Davis." He turned to Lawson. "You, too, college boy." He headed for the kitchen, passing Diana on her way to take the order. She whispered under her breath.

"Now, now, Skip. I do believe I see smoke coming out of your ears."

He grunted and kept on walking, fuming inside. What was Sapphire doing here anyway, parading around with her college boy, showing him she was getting along just fine, thank you. He gritted his teeth, the happy sound of Sapphire and Lawson burning his ears. Are you familiar with the classics? Yeah, buddy, he thought. Real familiar. That's all they play in Tunis. Sharecroppers love the stuff. What the hell was chamber music anyway?

Pee Wee slipped in just before Henry locked the front door. He headed straight for Skip, pulled a blue and white striped engineer's cap off his head, drummed his fingers along the empty counter and whistled his own syncopated jazz version of "I've been working on the railroad." He blew Diana a kiss, took a cigarette from behind his ear and lit it, his head turning from Skip to the café, then back to Skip.

"Ain't that your gal?" he asked, an impish smile on his face.

Skip shook his head and frowned. "Not anymore."

"So I see," he said. "Looks like there's another mule kicking in your stall."

"Shut up, Pee Wee," Skip said. "We was just friends, that's all." He pulled the sink plug. "Don't matter now anyway. She's got herself a college boy. U.C.L.A."

"Naw!" Pee Wee peeked around the corner. "Did you check his fingernails? That's how you can tell if he's lying or telling the truth. College boy's gon' have clean nails. No sign of a hard day's work on a college boy's hands." Pee Wee studied his own beat-up fingers and chipped away some caked on oil and axle grease. "Yeah, clean nails is the sure 'nuff giveaway. Working man don't have time to worry 'bout such things." He dragged on his cigarette and shook his head. "College. That's a line I never tried. So, did you check his nails?"

"No," Skip sighed. "I did not check his fingernails. What the hell I care if he's lying or taking her for a ride? She's got who she wants. Ain't no skin off my back."

"That so," Pee Wee said, leaning over to dip the burning end of his cigarette in the last bit of dishwater. Skip slapped his arm away.

"Yeah, that's so. You wanna make something of it?"

Pee Wee stepped back, hands held up. "Well, up jumped the Devil. I believe I done hit a sore spot. But I ain't the one you want to be fighting, good brother."

Skip blew out a long breath and waited for his heart to slow down. He had lost Sapphire and didn't know how to get her back. He thought time would soften her heart, but how much time did she need. He looked for a dirty plate to occupy his mind, but everything in the kitchen was clean. The only dirty dishes were out in the café, where Sapphire sat smiling at her college boy. He grabbed a skillet, inspected it and found what looked like a spot of grease. "Sorry," he whispered.

"Forget it, Skip. I know how it is. Chase a gal. She gives you the brush, then comes around with some chump to throw it in your face. Happens to the best of us. Anyway, you going to the parade?"

"Yeah, you?"

Pee Wee nodded. "I gotta see them new diesel engines the Union Pacific done bought. Newspaper said they had four-thousand horse power. Man, oh man. Drop one of them in the Plymy, get a couple of wings and I'd be flying. Breaking records every damn day. Them Germans would never catch me. I read last week where one of them got a plane going 468.94 miles an hour." He picked up a clean knife and twirled it between his fingers. "You feel like riding around tonight? I could call Bessie Lee, see if she has a lonely friend to take your mind off that gal in there. Whadda-ya say?"

"I would if it was just me and you, but I don't feel like messing around with some party girl. I'll just stick around here."

"You know, that gal has done messed up your mind," Pee Wee said. "How about tomorrow night? The avenue is gon' be jumping."

"It's a date. Maybe we can catch a midnight ramble like we used to."

"Well, alright then." They slapped palms and Pee Wee put on his engineer's cap, tugged at the bill so it sat at just the right angle. "I'll look for you tomorrow. You know where I'll be."

"Drooling over them damn diesel engines."

"Four thousand horsepower," Pee Wee said, and headed out the door.

A few minutes later, Sapphire and her perfect gentleman finished their meal and left in a hurry. She didn't even stop or look over her shoulder to see Skip standing in the kitchen doorway, a frown on his face and an empty dish tray in his hand. He cleaned their table with one sweep, his heart smarting from the sight of Sapphire's red lipstick mottled around the rim of a white porcelain coffee cup. Was she going to let Lawson kiss her soft, full lips? Was she going to let him hold her? He buried the coffee cup beneath scraps of gnawed, half-eaten ribs, dirty plates, saucers, water glasses and utensils. To hell with those fancy college boys, he thought, as he hoisted the heavy tray and headed for the kitchen. He was going to make a lot of money, flash Jacksons and Lincolns all up and down the avenue. He might even buy Sapphire two dozen roses and see what she had to say about that. He wasn't about to let U.C.L.A. have her.

Out in the dining room, Henry hummed his old railroad songs and scrubbed down the grill before blowing out the kerosene lamp and turning off the Lionel train. His day done, he stood in the kitchen doorway, watching Skip finish up.

"You joining us tomorrow?"

"You know I ain't, Henry. Carrying pickets ain't my way. Remember Gilpin and Lowe? They acted up and got booted out. Remember? You told me that story. Well, I can see the writing on the wall, Henry. Hollywood ain't about to change. Not now, not tomorrow, not in five years. So, I'm just gon' take whatever I can and not worry about it."

Henry grunted. "You've been talking to Zeke too much."

"Zeke ain't got nothing to do with it. I'm just looking out for me."

A wave of relief washed over him when he heard Henry slam the front door. Alone now, he walked into the café, put on a pot of coffee and collapsed on a stool. He couldn't get his mind to stop worrying and fretting about whether he was doing the right thing. He looked up at Bert Williams, staring cooling down from the picture frame. Williams had done blackface and made out alright. Did he carry any soul scars to his grave? Skip poured himself a cup, remembering Henry had once told him Williams said there was nothing wrong with being a Negro in America, except that it could be so damn inconvenient. Williams could give a command performance for the Queen of England, but he couldn't walk into the Biltmore Hotel downtown if he had a million dollars. Inconvenient? That wasn't the half of it. White folks laid out rules and anybody looking to make his way had to find his place, which was the hardest thing, finding your place, shutting out all the voices saying Do This, Don't Do That. You had to ignore those voices until the only one you heard was your own, and you learned to walk in your own way. He gulped the warm, sweet coffee and looked up at Williams. If the great actor could do blackface and still stand proud, then maybe he could do it and not fall apart inside. He finished his cup, folded his arms across the counter and rested his head for a moment, then trudged upstairs and fell into bed.

THAT NIGHT, WHILE HE TOSSED AND TURNED, TOMMY MURCHINSON jumped down from the live oak and, in the white circle of a spotlight, did an old soft-shoe with Shirley Temple. Their shuffling feet sounded like sheets of sandpaper being rubbed together. Delta Slim sat stone-faced on a nearby stool, playing a banjo. Everybody sang.

"Way down upon the Swanee River, far, far away. That's where my heart is turning ever, that's where the old folks stay . . ."

But they couldn't finish the verse, not with Skip standing beyond the spotlight, elbow-deep in suds and dirty dishes, looking on and shaking his head: No. No. No. Delta Slim nodded towards a beautiful, rosewood Gibson ES-150 gleaming with polish, translucent Mother of Pearl inlay marking the frets, its fat neck resting against a tiny amplifier that buzzed softly. The bluesman stopped playing.

"Come on, young daddy. Help me out. That there's one of them new-fangled electric guitars. I don't mess with it none, but I hear tell you'd like to. Why don't you give it a try?"

The banjo started up again, the trio bending their voices to the old lament. Tommy twirled Shirley. The everlasting grin made him look like he was having fun, even though his eyes were as cold as death. Slowly, the spotlight dimmed, but Skip could still hear the shoes shuffling and Delta Slim plinking on a banjo. Then he heard Zeke's voice, saying:

"Five, ten, fifteen, twenty, twenty-five, thirty. Look at all them dead presidents," he smiled and fanned the bills, licked his thumb and count-ed them out again. "Don't stop me, boy. I ain't near finished. "Ninety, ninety-five."

"That's more'n you'll see washing them damn bar-b-que stained dishes," Phineas said. "Get on in that spotlight, Skip. It's what you want, isn't it?"

"Yeah, but I got to finish these dishes," Skip said, working fast on an endless pile.

Zeke pulled a half-smoked stogie out of his mouth and stuffed the wad of bills into his hip pocket. "Don't be a fool now, boy. You remember what I said? A fool and his money don't get parted because a fool never comes across the money in the first place."

"Hah! Hah! Hah!" It was a woman's voice, laughing so hard she seemed on the verge of tears. "Hah! Hah! Hah!"

Skip covered his ears with his hands to shut out the crazy laughter, but it was already down deep, ricocheting around in his brain. High in the air another light went on. He looked up and saw Mrs. Harrelson, Sapphire and Richard Lawson, all sitting in a balcony box, dressed in their best Sunday go-to-meeting clothes. The rent lady pointed to him and nudged Sapphire.

"Look at that fool, girl. Didn't I tell you he was a common, good-for-nothing thief?"

Sapphire winked at him, then pulled Lawson close for a long, slow kiss.

"Um, um, um," Lawson said, suddenly standing beside Skip, shucking and jiving and wiping his mouth. "That Sapphire's lips sure am sweet. Sweet as cherry pie." He held out his hand for some skin.

Skip threw a punch, but Lawson disappeared, then reappeared back in the box seat, kissing Sapphire, libertine hands working down low where he couldn't see. Sapphire moaned a deep, pleasured sigh.

"That Sapphire is on fire!" Lawson said, standing beside him again and looking flushed. "She's gon' wear me out."

Skip threw another punch, connected with nothing. The blow's momentum sent him falling through the floor, falling into darkness. He thought he was screaming, but couldn't hear a sound. Not until. Bam! He landed flat on his back, the wind knocked out of him. A blinding spotlight bored into his eyes. Phineas' face, disembodied and looking worried, floated above him.

"I declare, Skip. I just don't know what I'm going to do with a country boy that ain't got no mother wit."

A hand pulled him to his feet, turned him towards the stage where Tommy danced with Shirley, while Delta Slim played the banjo. Grandma Sarah, Henry and Helen Lipscomb marched silently in front of the stage, carrying picket signs. Phineas patted him on the shoulder.

"Forget those signs," he said, and started clapping and singing: "Zeke and Skip playing blacken up. Skip win the money, scared to pick it up." He pulled a tin of black shoe polish from his coat pocket. "Here, let me help you out."

He heard a startled gasp. It was Old Man Williams, but as a child, standing beside his father, pointing to a big old catfish flopping around at his feet.

"That there's a lesson, Georgie-boy. That catfish done gone and got hisself caught outside his mudhole. Look at him now. He's in a world of trouble, heading straight for the frying pan."

The little boy bent over and tried to grab the fish, but it slipped out of his hands and flew across the room. It plopped at Skip's feet. Tommy and Shirley stopped their dancing to gaze at the catfish, whose wide, mustachioed mouth gulped the killing air. Then it stood, produced a cane and walked off, humming a hokum rag. Delta Slim grunted. An announcer's voice boomed.

"Introducing Hollywood's newest colored sensation, Skip Reynolds."

Shirley did a curtsy and took his hand. With the other she took Tommy's. The shuffling, sandpaper sound of their feet started up again. Skip's feet felt as if they were made of clay. Delta Slim cracked a wry smile.

"Relax, young daddy. You got to ease into it," he said. "There you go. Now, didn't I tell you I'd see you dancing with little Shirley? Okay, let's sing the song."

"All the world is sad and dreary everywhere I roam. Oh, darkies how my heart grows weary, far from the old folks at home."

❧

SKIP BOLTED UP IN HIS BED, SHIVERING AND GASPING, HIS BREATHS coming in short, hurried bursts. Stephen Foster's wistful melody drifted through his sleep-fogged brain. He threw off the covers, stumbled towards the bathroom, afraid he might see a shoe-blackened face staring back from the mirror he'd hung over the sink. All he saw was himself, groggy and sleepy-eyed. Relieved, he splashed his face with cold water, each splash hitting him like a stiff slap upside the head. He shook away the disturbing dream. From the far wall a picture of Paul Robeson that Henry had given him stared with accusing eyes. He turned away from Robeson, and slumped on his bed. An image born of the nightmare made him sick with disgust: Himself on one knee, all done up in blackface, a half-eaten watermelon in his hands. That could be the next speaking role. Damn, shit. He wanted out, but felt trapped by his own decision. He'd been fooling himself. This was not just another role.

He pulled out a Chesterfield. The morning was slipping away, and with it the chance to call this off. A ray of sunlight broke through morning haze and into his room. It was going to be a perfect day for a parade. He crushed out one cigarette, then lit another, his soul struggling towards action. He reached for National Steel, more out of a nervous habit than a real desire to play. He stopped before he could grasp the familiar neck of wood. There wasn't time. He slapped his thighs, stood and pulled on yesterday's jeans. No use getting dressed up. Today wasn't a day for putting on one of R.C.'s suits and being the fine-vined boy of the avenue. Today was a day to remember who he was and why he'd come to Los Angeles. He grabbed a shirt, winked at Robeson and headed downstairs to the phone.

In the still silence between the telephone's sequential rings, he heard ghostly conversations murmuring inside the cold receiver pressed tightly to his ear, spectral dialogues interrupted only by the soft burbling of a solitary phone ringing in a third-floor office on Broadway, a phone no one answered. Damn, shit, he whispered. Today was a holiday. He dropped the receiver back into its cradle. A moment later, it rang.

"Henry's Dancing Bar-B-Que," he said.

A woman's voice drawled between pops of chewing gum. "This is Western Union calling. Is there a Mister Reynolds?"

"That's me."

"Mister Reynolds, we have a telegram for you. It's from a Misses Sarah Reynolds in Tunis, Texas."

"From Grandma Sarah? That's my grandma! What did she say?"

"I'm sorry Mister Reynolds, but we're not allowed to read telegrams over the telephone. You'll have to come in and pick it up. Please bring some identification with you."

"Bring it where?"

"Well," the voice drawled out the word. "There is a downtown location at the Palm Hotel near Olympic and Central. They're open until nine, and thank you for using Western Union."

The line clicked dead. A telegram from Grandma Sarah? What could she want? Her last letter said everything was okay. The only bad news was that Old Man Williams had a stroke. But the old man was as strong as a plow mule. He'd pull through. Something was wrong, something too important for the mail. Was she sick? Did she need him? His mind scrambled for answers. Maybe, he thought, frightened by an idea that made him shudder. Maybe she was dying. Maybe someone else sent the telegram. He shook his head, but the idea took hold of him. He saw her lying on her death bed, surrounded by her dearest friends, but not one of them family, not one who shared her history of blood and remembered names. He leaned heavily on the counter. God dammit! Why couldn't the Western Union lady just tell him what the telegram said, instead of leaving him to the wild wanderings of his imagination. All worries about Zeke, blackface and pickets disappeared under the pressing need to find out what the telegram said. He hurried outside, dodged the passing traffic and threw himself onto a streetcar heading downtown. He found himself praying for the first time in years.

The streetcar veered off its normal course at Olympic, turned left and skirted the parade's stepping off point. Skip forced his way to the nearest door. The crowd moved in a steady, flowing stream, with him caught in its current. It seemed all of Los Angeles, young and old, black, white, brown and yellow, was here, laughing, shouting, walking side-by-side beneath the brilliant sun. Souvenir hawkers, some balancing a dozen sun hats piled on their heads, worked their way through the confusion, their sing-song voices carrying above the constant hub-bub: "Programs! Get your authentic, certified Union Station programs. Santy Fee, Union Pacific, Southern Pacific. Programs! Only a nickel."

A dozen pickets blocked the front door of the Plaza Hotel. Damn, shit. Helen Lipscomb, like a warrior queen who knows down to the marrow of her bones that her cause is right, walked proudly, eyes ablaze with conviction. Henry was behind her, his face set in the same hard, unforgiving expression Skip had seen a thousand times. The sign in his hand read, "Sambo is Dead." Skip smiled to himself, relieved. He didn't have to worry about a confrontation. He moved on. Henry's eyes flashed between joy, surprise and worry as he broke from the line and ran towards Skip.

"You joining us?"

"Not hardly, Henry. I got business to tend to."

"In there!" Henry pointed to the hotel. "You can't go in there." He put his hand on Skip's shoulder and lowered his voice. "You aren't the one, are you?"

"No," Skip replied, taking Henry's hand off his shoulder. "I ain't the one. I gotta pick up a telegram from my grandma."

"Is everything alright?"

"I'm-a find out."

Henry started to step aside, but stopped. "Is this on the level? Zeke didn't tell you to say that, did he?"

"God dammit, Henry! I done told you why I'm here. I'm picking up a telegram. I ain't studying Zeke, or you, or them damn pickets. Now, get out of my way." He pushed past Henry and headed towards the hotel, plowing through the crowd. Helen caught him near the front door.

"Ah hah!" she cried. "Sambo is not dead.

"Lady," Skip said, voice low and determined. "You'd better get the hell out of my way." She didn't move. Skip opened and clenched his fists. Troubled whisperings ran through the line of pickets. "Get out of my way," he said, fierce now, the measured words matching the glower in his eyes.

"Helen," Henry yelled from down the street. "He's okay. He's going to get a telegram."

"Better be." She stepped aside and let him pass.

He flung the door open, walked inside and stopped, momentarily blinded by the sudden change from bright, sun-splashed street to dimly lit lobby. He could smell last night's Chinese dinner rotting in a corner trash can. The room had a musty, big-city smell of desolation. A bare light bulb dangled from the ceiling and struggled to fill the forlorn room with its pale light. Zeke stepped out of the shadows, a fat, unlit stogie rolling around in his mouth.

"Where you been?" he snarled. "This ain't no C.P. time deal. This is money time."

"Not now, Zeke," Skip said, nervously waving him off and looking around, distracted.

"What do you mean, not now? Make-up's upstairs, waiting on you." Zeke struck a match and puffed on his cigar.

"In a minute," Skip said, turning to the front desk, where a short, balding man sat squinting through bifocals that kept slipping down his nose as he read a newspaper, lips silently tracking the words, bony fingers playing absently with wisps of gray hair combed across his head. A yellow and black sign hung above him. "You the Western Union man," Skip said.

The clerk nodded, eyes still on the newspaper.

"I got a telegram."

"Got any identification," the clerk replied, putting his glasses aside and folding his newspaper. "Driver's license, library card. Something with a picture on it?"

"All I got is my name," Skip said, leaning on the counter, forearms settling into the grooves worn smooth by countless other arms.

The clerk squinted at him, doubt furrowing his brow. "Just a name, huh." He wheeled his chair around and stared at a wall of chipped cubbyholes, some empty, others filled with slips of paper or numbered keys. "Reynolds, you say?" His fingers tapped the slots like a blind man reading Braille. "Reynolds. Reynolds. No identification." He scooted over to the last row, reached inside one of the cubby-holes and pulled out a yellow envelope. "Here it is. Must be a code question in here. You got to answer the question before I give you this. Can't just walk up and say my name is Skip Reynolds, gimme my telegram. No, sir. Anybody could do that. So, we take precautions. You can appreciate that, can't you Mister Reynolds?"

"Yeah, yeah. Come on. What's the question?"

A lazy sigh slipped from the clerk's pursed lips as he fixed his glasses back on his thin nose. "Who," he said, lips quietly shaping the words. "Who discovered Tunis? Yeah, that's it." He held the slip of paper behind his back and gave Skip a challenging stare. "Who discovered Tunis?"

Skip laughed. "Colonel Artemis Willard."

The clerk turned away and peeked at the slip of paper, every now and then looking over his shoulder. "What was that name again?"

"Colonel Artemis Willard. He was a Confederate officer. Come on, now. I know that's the answer."

The clerk turned around, smiling now. "Guess this is for you. My granddaddy was a reb. Fought with Bobby Lee all the way to Appomatox Court House. Here."

Skip tore the envelope open and moved beneath the bare bulb. He read the message once, then again. "Come if you want to see the last of Old Man Williams. He asked for you. Grandma Sarah." Asked for me? That didn't sound like the old man. He sought out the empty couch, the telegram's words repeating in his head as he absently pulled a Chesterfield from his shirt pocket. He lit the cigarette, saw his fingers twitching around the slender smoke. The old man was dying. Zeke stood over him. He heard the fat man's gut rumbling, smelled the stink of cheap cigars . But he didn't look up, just stared at the words printed on the paper shaking in his hand. It didn't seem real. The old man was eternal. He'd dodged Spanish bullets on San Juan Hill and lived to tell the tale of rescuing Teddy Roosevelt's Rough Riders, done that and returned to the terrible days when a black man could disappear and everybody know what happened and who dumped the body and where, but it didn't matter 'cause nothing could be done to make it right. He'd pulled Skip's shattered spirit out of the silence it had fallen into after the accident, reached down into the little boy's aching world and, with a guitar and a song, brought him back to the land of the living. He was stronger than death. Skip's heart stumbled, lost its rhythm, seemed to stop in the mid-exhalation of blood. Then he felt it pounding against his ribs. The last of Old Man Williams. He remembered the last time he saw the old man. It was the day before he left, and the old man had told him the story of the nigger and the catfish. Old Man Williams had been too interested in protecting him that day, and so the fearless old soldier had let another part of himself speak. Skip still had the pouch of specially cured tobacco. And there was enough for one last smoke. One day they were going to sit together beneath the warm, southeast Texas sun and pass the smoke. The old man would listen to his story about a catfish who strayed outside his mudhole and ended up in a world of trouble. But that didn't stop the old catfish. He just learned to live in the world. That's what was supposed to happen.

He saw the old man standing in the doorway that distant day, one hand shielding his eyes against the sun, the other waving good-bye before he turned back to the dark cabin where framed jig-saw puzzles shared the walls with layers of unfolded Cream of Wheat boxes. The image faded, replaced by another: The old man sitting before him, smiling patiently, nodding, leaning forward, strong, callused hands lightly touching his five-year-old fingers, pushing them into the right places on the frets of a cigar-box guitar that was still too big; strong, life-toughened hands nudging his little boy fingers into unfamiliar shapes on the strings, the old man passing on the supple skills needed to draw from steel strings and wood wondrous sounds that when properly ordered and arranged became music, giving voice to his deepest longings, sorrows, fears and joys. The memory was not one of mastery, but of an earnest child trying to learn a simple railroad song about a firemen shoving coal into some Moore Girl engine bound for the end of the line. To his young ears the song had sounded like a funny animal story about a gin-drinking fox named Will and his friend Varmint.

"Go slow now," the old man had said. "Get it down right before you try to be fancy. Here, let me show you."

And he had watched, amazed, as the old man picked up a big 12-string guitar he had then and played the simple old song. Old Man Williams had taken him from a cigar-box, to a tenor guitar, all the way up to National Steel. And when Skip had bested him, the old man kept on teaching, showing him songs that had been around for years but were just being recorded. The telegram's words came back into focus. "Come if you want to see the last of Old Man Williams. He asked for you. Grandma Sarah."

He looked at Zeke. "Old Man Williams is dying."

Zeke grunted. "Everybody's got to die sometime. Is he your kin?"

No, Skip thought. Not kin. Not blood. More than that. Something deep and timeless, strong like the love between father and son, teacher and beloved pupil. The old man had guided him, nurtured him, let him wander, but never into danger. Old Man Williams calmed him when the first fires of manhood burst forth. It was the old man who had convinced Grandma Sarah to let him go to Willie's juke joint. Go, the old man had said, but remember, the juke joint wasn't no playhouse. Mess with the wrong man and you could end up cut and bleeding. So, be careful. No, the old man was not kin or blood. He was more than those words could ever hold.

A thumbnail's length of ash fell off the cigarette. Skip felt the burning ember creeping toward his fingers. He crushed out the butt, fired up another cigarette. Come. That's what Grandma Sarah said. But how? The Union Pacific's Challenger to Chicago took three days and cost $41.55. Houston might be quicker, maybe cheaper, but he didn't have that kind of money. And how much time did he have before Old Man Williams passed? A week? A month? Time enough to save, beg or borrow train fare? He dragged on the cigarette, wishing he could walk outside, spread his arms and fly away home. How far to Tunis, as the crow flies, he thought.

Zeke grunted again. "You coming or not?"

Skip ignored the question. He had to get to Old Man Williams. Next to Grandma Sarah, no one else was as important. He couldn't go on washing dishes and chasing a fading Hollywood dream knowing he had not done everything in his power to go home, tell his story, smoke that last cigarette, say "Thank You" to Old Man Williams for giving his soul a way to speak. He thought about asking Pee Wee or Henry for a loan, money he would pay back when he returned. Returned? To what? More of Zeke's bit parts. Helen Lipscomb's crew battling studios over words, freedman or free nigger. Return to the Dancing Bar-B-Que's dirty dishes and the struggle of life here in this city of concrete and asphalt where thousands upon thousands lived and died amid the palm trees and tropical flowers fed by winter rain and summer sun. And if he didn't return, then what would he do? Stay in Tunis? Never. The memory of flushing toilets and hot running water, the rumble of streetcars carrying him anywhere he wanted to go, even to the Pacific Ocean, would push him out of his hometown. Here the air was alive with jazz and swing. Kitchen Mechanics filled the avenue on Thursday nights. And there was Sapphire and Buster with their hooks still in him, no matter what he told Pee Wee. The little boy needed a man the way he had needed Old Man Williams. If only he could turn Sapphire around and bring her back to the way they used to be. He rubbed his eyes. He'd decide about Tunis and Los Angeles later. Now he had to get back to Old Man Williams. Maybe Jimmy the Midge had a sure thing at Santa Anita. He heard Zeke clearing his throat, looked down at the fat man's scuffed shoes scratching the frayed rug. Zeke had money. A hundred dollars was waiting for him. All he had to do was join the parade. The old man would understand. "Boy," Zeke growled. "I'm tired of waiting. Are you coming or not?"

"Yeah," Skip said, stuffing the telegram in his pocket, standing and praying he would get to Tunis in time. "I'm coming."

〰

"I DIDN'T BELIEVE IT WHEN THEY TOLD ME," SAID THE MAKEUP artist, a dumpy white woman whose soft, pudgy hands smeared black greasepaint on Skip's smooth, brown face. 'A colored person in black-face?' I said. 'In nineteen and thirty-nine?' I said. But, here we are. This kind of work doesn't come around too often, I tell you. Oh, there might be some funning on the set. Once in awhile they do it on camera. Mickey Rooney does that a lot, you know. That Andy Hardy is always putting on a show."

Skip said nothing, sitting there in the hotel room, shirtless in denim overalls, feeling as if he were outside himself, looking on as he silently suffered the hateful mask. The coarse, black paint clogged his face in a suffocating layer.

"Close your eyes, now, and let me get this last little bit of paint on your eyelids," said the artist. "Stop squinting. Relax. There, that's better. Now for the smile."

Skip stuck out his tongue, tasting the bitter white paint.

"Sorry about that," the artist said, wiping the excess off the inside of his lips. "Just a little more. There." She handed him a mirror, stepped back and smiled proudly. "Al Jolson never looked better."

Skip put the mirror face down on his lap, counted calmly to himself, five, ten, fifteen, twenty, counted by fives until he reached one hundred. But he could not turn the mirror over.

"Go on," urged the artist, tapping his shoulder. "Take a look and tell me what you think."

Again he took up the count. What did it matter that no one really knew or cared why he was here. It was enough that he knew. He had to see the last of Old Man Williams. When he reached fifty, he closed his eyes, turned the mirror face up, then looked down. A grotesque clown smiled up at him, mimicked his expressions, raised a curious eyebrow when he did, wriggled its irritated nose when he did. But when he frowned, it smiled. He touched his face, then the reflection in the mirror, the face that was, yet was not his. He had vanished beneath the grease-paint, his spirit trapped by the mask. No matter what he did, no one would see him. Instead, they would see Rastus, ready for a rollicking ride; Shine, who forgot the Golden Rule; Eight-Ball and Burr-head Billy. They would see Sunshine Sammy's blackfaced, chicken-stealing cousin; Uncle Tom's dim-witted nephew; Old Black Joe's grandson, the slap-happy nigger in the woodpile; Zip Coon dressed up for a Saturday night strut through darktown; Steppin' Fetchit degraded. He had become all that, and it made him sick.

Minstrel show images danced across the glass in a comic chorus line. Black boys smiled through mouthfuls of watermelon. Pickaninny babies played in high cotton, bits of torn tissue paper tied in their kinky hair. I'se been wurread all de time 'bout you. How comes you don' right me?" Tommy Murchinson's face, distorted by death and the strangling rope, flashed across the mirror, scaring him. A solitary tear rolled down his cheek and his lips trembled. Inside, he felt his soul crumbling from the weight of memory and all those coons. He wiped the tear away, knowing his dream of Hollywood was gone forever.

"You look great!" Zeke said from the doorway. "Now, let's go make some money."

Skip pushed himself off the chair, followed Zeke into the long, dark hallway, then down the back stairs. Cool shadows shaded the narrow alley, keeping down the stink of rot and decay. Every few steps, Zeke stopped, waited for Skip to catch up.

"What's your trouble, boy," he said. "This is going to be the easiest hundred dollars you'll ever make."

"When do I get my hundred dollars?"

"When do you want it?"

"Now," Skip said, his voice firm, yet weary. "Now."

"Hell, you ain't done the job yet. I give it to you now and you might run off. I'll be waiting at the end of the line with your money. How's that sound?"

"Fine, long's you keep your word."

"Hah," Zeke laughed. "We're partners, Skip." He stopped at the end of the alley, peeked around the corner. "Guess we gave 'em the slip. Last thing I wanted was to parade you past them damn pickets." He lit another cigar as they crossed the street. "Did alright by you, didn't I? Got you a break. All you have to do is pretend to sing and play the guitar. The studio'll do the rest."

He stopped beside an old buckboard hitched to a pair of skittish horses. The team stomped nervously, flicked their manes in agitation. Beside the buckboard, a cameraman fiddled with his machine mounted in the back of a pick-up truck. He nodded at Zeke and the blackface clown who grabbed hold of the buckboard's front wheels and pulled himself up. A battered old guitar, its body cracked and scarred, leaned against the worm-eaten seat. Skip strummed the instrument, winced. It was horribly out of tune.

"A guitar's got to be in tune," he said, repeating the old man's first lesson.

"You ain't supposed to play it," Zeke said. "Studio's got that all worked out."

"Don't matter," Skip replied, listening to the low E. "I might want to play something."

"Suit yourself, Skip. Just remember the song." Zeke turned and headed off the lot.

Skip had worked his way down to the high E string when, from the far side of the parade staging area, a shrill whistle cut through the low buzz of idle conversation. The excitement and tension that had built all morning among the parade's legions exploded in a roar of cheers. The grand marshal, immaculate in a white suit draped in silver and gold, gave a loud whoop, then wheeled his prancing Palomino toward Alameda Street. Skip waited until the camera truck pulled away, then released the buckboard's handbrake, flicked the reins and fell in line.

The parade route was barely passable. Thousands of Angelenoes, natives and newcomers, dreamers, believers in Sister Aimee's Foursquare Gospel and Father Divine's promise of wealth through prayer, lined the street, stood five and six deep, those at the rear on tiptoes, necks craned to view the fantastic caravan. They had squeezed into every inch of space on the sidewalk, and when all the room there was taken, they spilled onto the street from both sides, leaving a narrow path where the streetcar tracks lay. Shoeshine Billy and a gang of boys from Pershing Square, every one of them wearing New York Yankees caps, perched on lamp posts. Jimmy the Midge sat on the windowsill of an office crammed with people, one hand waving a whisky bottle, the other clutching a hefty blonde. Smiling faces leaned from every window, called to friends packed in the dense crowd below. Ticker-tape fluttered crazily in the air. People waved, laughed, pointed at celebrities, stuffed hot dogs, sandwiches and mustard-covered pretzels in the mouths until the jaws bulged. Then they washed it all down with lemonade, soda or beer.

The buckboard crept along, each block a seemingly interminable journey of stops and starts. Skip stared wearily at the mechanical, cyclopean eye staring back at him. He strummed the guitar and pretended to sing Hollywood's song. Zeke's lines came back to him. This was his big chance. The big time. Sheeit. He tried to force a smile. But couldn't. It didn't matter. The mask smiled. His eyes searched the crowd for a familiar face, but found none. That was good. He didn't want anyone to see him. He felt numb, as if his soul had pulled back to someplace deep inside where it could hide, safe from the humiliation.

"Pick it up there," the cameraman yelled. "You can't deadpan this."

Skip returned his gaze to the camera's hungry, indifferent eye, and started a ragtime rhythm to match the darky's song: "Dey all calls me Shine, 'cause I'se happy all de time. Don't sing no blues. Don't believe in school. I done even forgot de Golden Rule. Dey all calls me shine, 'cause I'se happy all de time."

Over and over he sang the tune, each time blocking out the nagging voice that said no matter what happened to Old Man Williams, he had lost his self-respect and become a blackface clown. The voiced followed wherever his mind went, insinuated itself into every thought, even as he came up with words about a ragtime millionaire strolling Central Avenue with a hundred dollars in his pocket. The voice grew louder each time he sang, "Dey all calls me Shine, 'cause I'se happy all de time."

Deep in the crowd, Henry followed the line of Helen's hand pointing to a passing buckboard. Zeke had found someone to wear the mask. He shrugged. There was always someone who could be bought. He shook the bag of salted peanuts in his hands, fingers searching for an uncracked shell. Helen kept pointing, nudging him, telling him to look, look hard.

"Isn't that your dishwasher riding that buckboard?" she said.

Henry squinted against the noonday sun. "Naw. That's not him. He's off somewhere, watching the parade. I don't see why you always think the worst of Skip, Helen. He's alright, just young. I told you he wasn't going into the Palm Hotel to put on blackface. He was going to pick up a telegram."

"That's what he said." Helen grabbed him and pointed him towards the creaking buckboard. "Now, tell me I'm wrong. Take a good look, then tell me I'm wrong."

Henry shaded his eyes. "Damn," he whispered. "God damn."

Skip had lied. Skip, whom he'd taken off the street, given a job and a place to stay, had played him for a fool, looked him in the eye and said one thing, then turned around and did another. He remembered the naïve country boy who'd come in out of the rain last fall, the boy who'd worked like a dog his first day, but had been almost too scared to ask if he'd won the job. What had happened to him? Was he the same one who rode by now, guitar in hand, face covered in black greasepaint?

"Didn't I tell you," said Helen. "I knew he'd go with Zeke."

At Fourth and Alameda, Phineas celebrated his final sale of Eternity's Breath. "Hail this blessed day," he whispered, "this glorious, wonderful . . ." He stopped. There was a buckboard being driven by a man in blackface. He leaned forward, curious. Skip had talked about a blackface role. But not in a parade. Still . . .He narrowed his eyes, focused his gaze. Could it be? He stepped away from the crowd for a closer look. Was it? His eyes lit up. Yes! It was Skip! The boy had some sense after all. Phineas started chuckling to himself, softly at first, then giving in to a full belly laugh. It was too good to be true. He clapped his hands, bounced on the balls of his feet, turned to those behind him and yelled: "Three cheers for the capitalist imperative! Hurrah! Hurrah! Hurrah! Come on, now, you great gathering of the unwashed hoi polloi. Three cheers and a toast to good, old-fashioned mother wit." He whipped a half-empty flask from his hip pocket and raised it toward the passing buckboard. "Skip, I salute you." Then he drained off a quarter of the scotch, took another sip for good measure and left just enough to wet his throat later on.

Skip saw rolly-polly, speechifying Phineas waving from the edge of the crowd, saw him but couldn't hear him through the constant din of cheers, yells, shouts, scattered bursts of wild laughter, saw him but didn't wave back, saw him and looked away. The crowd along the route had become a roiling, uneasy mass of strangers and friends. Entire sections seethed back and forth, probing for a weak spot in the line of police officers and boy scouts who tried to keep them beyond the streetcar tracks. A morning's worth of alcohol and the sun's heat was beginning to work on some, making once care-free drinkers agitated and mean. Fights broke out, over a foot stepped on, an apology not said, an accidental elbow in the face. The unruly mob pressed closer and closer as the parade neared the viewing stands around Olvera Street. A volley of rifle fire announced the 63rd Coast Artillery's arrival at Union Station. The sharp, snapping report of the gunshots startled Skip's horses. They trembled nervously in their traces, the lead horse bucking and pulling the buckboard out of line. Skip dropped the beat-up guitar and slipped the reins around his wrists.

"Easy now," he said, calming his team. "Easy."

Families sneaked through the cordon of scouts and cops, the children stopping to reach up and run their soft, tiny fingers cautiously along the shiny brown coats of Skip's team. Then they moved on, cutting him off from the pick-up. The cameraman tried to shoo them away, but no one listened to him. Another wave of rifle fire, this time accompanied by the boom of cannon, erupted from the plaza. Hats twirled up into the air. The horses leapt forward. Skip pulled tighter on the reins, leaned back and jammed his foot against the floorboard. Twice more the cannon roared, the explosions loud enough to send pain shooting through the ears of anyone close by. Eye-stinging smoke and the bitter smell of gunpowder floated on the breeze. The parade slowed. The crowd found its weak spots. People surged forth from both sides, exploited the gaps, pushed the officers and scouts back against the tracks. The route became a chaotic mass of people and horses, trucks and cars done up as locomotives. Phineas ran for a stagecoach pulled by six white horses. He had taken a foolish fancy to a woman who had leaned from the coach, smiling and waving a black Bolero hat. He darted around those in front of him, pushed his way forward and leaped up on its step.

"Room for one more?" he asked, gripping the door and leaning in through the window.

Three other men who had been sharing a bottle raised a cheer and charged the stagecoach. They rocked it back and forth. The woman inside recoiled from the sudden motion, the startling sight of a happy black face less than an arm's length away.

"Don't be alarmed," he said. "These ruffians are only having a bit of fun." The woman was as he had envisioned, dressed in silk and lace, beautiful, though a bit pale for his tastes. Still, he gave her a sly wink and said, "Don't worry, my coy mistress. We'll make the sun run a'fore day is done."

He was on the verge of trying to climb through the window when a scowling, thin-mustachioed man whom he had dismissed as a dime-store rogue reached around the woman and, arms swinging wildly, threw a punch. Phineas leaned back. The three others gleefully persisted in their new-found game. Two officers hurried over from their posts, creating yet another opening for the crowd. They jumped a pair of the men, grabbed them harshly by the shirt collars and dragged them through the crowd. More people joined in the row. They yanked on the coach's doors, clawed their way toward the driver's seat. All the while Phineas held on, waving and laughing, drinking the last bit of his scotch. Skip saw his head bobbing above the crazed, delirious crowd that had gotten fed up with standing aside and watching, while the lucky few rode by. This was Los Angeles' great day, and they were Los Angeles, all of them, the gray-haired pensioners who'd straggled in from the heartland and stopped when they hit the ocean, the star-struck Hollywood extras, the blacks, whites, Mexicans, Japanese and Chinese who usually kept to their own sections. They were Los Angeles. This wasn't some Hollywood premiere with klieg lights and red carpets and movie stars who strolled by like royalty. This was a Los Angeles affair, and they wanted to be in it.

The coach's bearded driver reached for his whip. The hard-faced guy riding shotgun tore his Winchester rifle from its holster and fired in the air once, then again and again. The gunfire stopped the riotous crowd. Some fell back from the coach. Others halted their advance and looked around, surprised at how close they'd come to joining in the mad merriment. An unspoken question ran between them.

"He's just shooting blanks," yelled Phineas, still holding on, balancing himself on the running board and urging on those who had lost their courage. "Just blanks. Come on. Let's go for a ride."

A fist shot out from the coach, this time catching Phineas on the jaw, pitching him back into the arms of two more police officers, who quickly handcuffed him and wrestled him through the crowd. One of the officers clubbed him on the head with a nightstick.

"Help," he cried. "Someone call Earl Warren. The local constabulary is attacking a tax-paying citizen!"

A wave of shouted curses followed Phineas and the arresting officers. An empty soda pop bottle sailed from deep in the crowd and crashed against the coach. People roared and raised their fists. The rifleman cranked another round into his Winchester. This time he aimed lower.

The second-story window of a warehouse shattered. He cocked the rifle and stared, daring anyone to move.

"I ain't shooting blanks," he growled. "Now, get back."

The driver saw his chance and cried to his team. "Ya!" A long black whip snaked and cracked through the air.

Two more bottles tumbled through the air, end over end like off-center gyroscopes. One sailed harmlessly over the coach. The rifleman caught the other with the butt of his Winchester an instant before it hit his face. Broken glass slashed into the crowd, cutting some. A hand reached up behind the rifleman and grabbed him by the ankle, pulling him off-balance. He turned and butted a young man. The rifle's stock opened a bloody, two-inch gash in the man's head. Still, he wouldn't let go. A couple of burly men, built like stevedores up from San Pedro, took hold of him, one wrapping muscular arms around his shoulder, while the other took his waist. Then all three pulled, sending the rifleman tumbling into a mass of angry arms.

Skip saw the rifleman struggling to stand, but the crowd, fueled by the beatings and the sight of innocent blood, would not let him up. He collapsed under their fists. The rifle raised up, barrel pointed toward the sky, disappeared into the crowd and rose again. Skip winced, hearing a dull thud and an awful groan each time the rifle descended. A current of brutality had consumed the crowd. He wondered if they would turn on him. He started to get out of the buckboard. But people were everywhere, pressing ever nearer. Their hands seemed to be reaching for him, straining to pull him down into their midst. The cameraman motioned for him to stay put.

"This is great," he yelled, wheeling around and filming the crowd. "The studio'll love it."

Great? A man had just been beaten senseless. And God only knew who had the Winchester. Skip searched the crowd, tried to measure the distance to Union Station. Was he close enough to say his job was done, close enough to get the hell out of here before somebody decided Sambo would make a fine punching bag? Up ahead, a flying wedge of police officers turned the corner at First Street, creating a path for an ambulance that followed, its siren wailing an emergency.

Pee Wee edged away from the roiling commotion swarming around the stagecoach. He'd been on his way to Union Station for a look at the Union Pacific's mighty diesels when he saw the crazed throng pummeling the rifleman. He couldn't get close enough to get in any licks, but he cheered every blow, grunted and threw short jabs, yelled for those up front to give it to the guy. Now his blood was up. The diesels could wait.

He wanted the guy in blackface. It was just like white folks to drag out something like that, he thought. Here they went through all this trouble to put on a parade, a damn good one, with trains, fire engines, trolleys, camels, mule-skinners, prospectors, marching bands, but they couldn't leave well enough alone. They had to put in a nigger, with a moving picture camera right in front of him. He threw four more punches. Pow! Bap! Pow! Bam! Just like Joe Louis dropping bombs on Jack Roper. That's what the white guy in blackface was going to get. It had to be a white guy. Nobody on the avenue would go around looking like some old-timey coon. He walked against the thinning crowd strolling up Alameda, grim and determined, head down, one eye out for the police. He kept near the sidewalk, passed the buckboard, circled back to move in for the kill.

Skip jumped up, hearing a heavy thud behind him. A rush of fear shot through him. Somebody was trying to sneak up on him, catch him off-guard and do him like the rifleman. He turned, fists up, ready for a fight. It was Pee Wee. He started to smile. His hands dropped. Pee Wee recognized him too late to keep his bare knuckles from smashing into Skip's nose.

"God dammit, Pee Wee," Skip yelled, falling back, tasting hot blood pouring from his nostrils.

"Damn me," Pee Wee screamed. "Damn you! What the hell are you doing with that shit on your face?" He was shaking now, opening and closing his fists, the fighting muscles in his arms tensing. "Damn me?" He grabbed Skip by the straps of his overalls, pulled him close. "Damn me?"

Skip felt himself go weak in Pee Wee's grasp. He hung his head. He couldn't look Pee Wee in the eye. The horses tramped forward. Pee Wee pushed him away, as if he were week-old garbage.

"You really had me going," he said. "Here I was getting proud of you, telling folks I knew a guy in moving pictures who was going to be somebody. People see you now, they'll think I'm crazy."

"I had to do it," he whispered. "I needed the money."

"Shit. That ain't no reason," he said. "How come you didn't ask me? I bet white folks put you up to this."

"Say, mac," the cameraman yelled. "Get a move on. I'm filming."

"Fuck you!" Pee Wee fired back, then turned to Skip. "White folks. See, this is why I don't mess with them. They're always trying to make a

M. DION THOMPSON

fool out of the colored man. Next thing you know . . . Hell, they got you running around with shoe polish on your face." He shrugged and sat on the buckboard's side. "How much they paying you?"

"A hundred dollars," Skip said, wiping some of the black paint off his face. "That's a lot of money."

"Like hell. They got you cheap, Skip. Me? They couldn't pay me enough. John D. Rockefeller don't have enough."

"Maybe not for you. But it was enough for me." Skip tugged at his nose, still feeling the throbbing pain from Pee Wee's fist. "You throw a mean punch," he said, holding out his hand.

"Yeah," Pee Wee replied, staring at Skip's hand a moment before grabbing it and pulling himself up. "I do."

Stragglers filled the street. The ambulance passed by, parked in the next block near the dazed, bleeding rifleman. Police officers and a few reporters kneeled beside him. A newspaper photographer took his picture. The cameraman propped an arm across his machine. Another volley of rifle fire erupted from Union Station. Pee Wee ducked and covered his head. A string of popping, smoking firecrackers, dropped from an office window high above, twisted through the air, bounced on the street in a mad dance. The horses bolted. The sudden jolt threw Pee Wee off balance. Skip fell back against the seat, saw his friend's feet fly up, parallel to the street, heard him fall.

"Shit," Pee Wee said.

The frightened horses started to stampede, jerking the buckboard left and right, around the pickup, into the crowd. People ran screaming to get out of the way. Some stumbled, scrambled on all fours. A sharp pain sliced into the middle of Skip's back as he tried to reach the reins. A woman fell in the horses' path, crawled frantically, the asphalt tearing her dress, bloodying her knees. The horses, driven wild by the rippling report of more firecrackers, reared up and pawed the air. The woman collapsed, face down, rolled over to shield her eyes from the oncoming terror. Her shrill screams ripped through the air.

"No! No! Noooooo! Oh God!"

Skip stretched out full, fingers desperately straining to catch the reins flopping up and down inches beyond his reach. He heard Pee Wee rolling around behind him like a pinball. The horses charged toward the helpless woman. Their strides seemed to come in slow motion. The reins slapped against Skip's fingertips, fell away before he could close his fist. Damn, shit! He had to save her. He heard her begging, pleading, calling on sweet Jesus. She took her hands from her face, then covered her eyes again. In that instant he saw it was Mrs. Harrelson. Save her? He pulled his hands back, remembering her insults, the mocking tone in her voice, the way she helped turn Sapphire against him. Who would know it wasn't an accident? She'd fallen. He'd lost control of the horses. They'd been skittish all day. The gunfire and the firecrackers made them run. No one could blame him. The loop of the reins bounced around the seat. Mrs. Harrelson shoved herself back, but she didn't get up. She just kept on screaming.

"Somebody help me!"

A lifetime of memories raced through his mind: Grandma Sarah reading Bible stories by the firelight and telling him to always do right; Willie Jean Mason keening every time a train went by; Hetta Mae McFarland falling from a Katy stock car in Fort Worth. He'd risked his life to save her, a white girl who'd turned around and saved him when she could have let the yard bull have his way. He stretched out, timed the movements of the reins and grabbed them, wrapped the leather loop around his wrist and tugged hard, driving the bits into the horses' mouths. Again the lead horse reared up, tossing its head and fighting against the cold, biting steel. He held on, praying he'd acted in time. The lead stallion stamped the street. Sparks flew up from its hooves, but it moved no further. Mrs. Harrelson's wild, blood curdling shrieks continued. She tore at her straightened hair and pounded the street. People rushed to her, tried to calm her.

"There, there," they said. "You're alright."

A policeman who had come upon the scene looked up and stared quizzically at the blackface clown. "You saved her, Rastus. You're a sure-fired hero."

The cameraman whooped in celebration. "Praise the Lord and pass me the Oscar. I got the whole thing, the whole damn thing!"

A reporter and a photographer broke away from the onlookers standing around the ambulance. The reporter, his eager, young face serious and intent, waved Skip down.

"You're gonna make the front page," he said, smacking on a stick of chewing gum. "Guaranteed." He turned to the photographer. "Get a picture of them."

Skip jumped out of the buckboard. The photographer leaned in front of him. The reporter fired questions. "Where you from? What's your name? Who's paying for the get-up? Hollywood? City Hall?"

Skip mumbled replies as another crowd formed. The reporter pushed him next to Mrs. Harrelson. "Go on," he said. "Get close to her. A hug would be perfect."

Skip didn't move. He tried to hide his face.

"Go on, Skip," Pee Wee said, sitting up and rubbing his head. "Get your picture in the newspaper."

He inched closer, raised his arm and placed it lightly around her shoulders. She sniffled and daubed at her eyes.

"Raw emotion," the reporter said, glancing around and smiling. "Nothing like it. Get a picture of them together. Savior and saved. How's that for a cut-line?"

Two more reporters ran over, Zeke too, a stogie rolling around in his mouth.

"Outta the way," he said. "Outta the way. Anything this boy says has got to come through me."

"And who the hell are you," asked the first reporter, looking up from his notebook and frowning.

"I'm his agent," Zeke replied, putting an arm around Skip and pulling him away from Mrs. Harrelson. "This boy's gonna be in American Studios' next picture. He's gonna be big!"

"His agent, huh," said the first reporter, still suspicious. "What's your name?"

"Ezekiel Washington." Zeke leaned close and spoke slowly. "That's E-Z-E . . ."

The reporter waved him off. "I know how to spell Ezekiel. It's in the Bible."

Mrs. Harrelson stared at Skip, a glimmer of recognition in her eyes. "You?"

Skip nodded. "Yeah. Me. Guess this low-down dog is good for something after all."

"Look this way," yelled the photographer, camera pressed against his face. "That's good. Now, smile."

Zeke jumped into the picture and wrapped his arms around them as if they were his long lost friends. The camera's shutter clicked open, capturing the image of a grinning, fat black man with a half-chewed, half-smoked cigar sticking out of his mouth; a woman who, suddenly self-conscious, patted her disheveled hair and reached down to straighten her torn, soiled dress; and a young man in blackface, who didn`t need to smile. That evening's editions carried the picture, along with a short story headlined:

RASTUS TO THE RESCUE
Blackface Clown Saves Negro Woman From Certain Death

"TUNIS! NEXT STOP IS TUNIS."

Skip groaned, slowly opened his groggy, sleep-heavy eyes and wearily scanned the rows of empty seats. Through the dust and grime streaking the train window he saw the familiar landscape of his homeland, the lush, green, rolling hills, the stands of live oaks along the muddy Brazos. He raised his arms to stretch the kinks out of his stiff, aching back. They'd been there going on two days now, ever since he tried to find a comfortable way to sleep scrunched up on the hard bench seat of a Santa Fe Texas Chief making its way eastward from Los Angeles to Fort Worth, where he switched to a Mo-Pac local bound for the gulf. It had been a hard ride, but better than hoboing. He never slipped into a deep sleep, just snatched catnaps whenever the whirlwind of anxiety eased enough to let him relax and surrender to the overwhelming fatigue. Then it didn't matter whether he balled up on the seat like a baby, or sat with his back against the window, knees pulled up to his chest. Sleep found him. But only for a while. Sooner or later, the shrieking scream of the train whistle stabbed his ears and he awakened, startled by the sudden, piercing sound, unsure of where he was. If it was night, he'd smoke a cigarette, stare into the bejewelled black sky and let his mind wander back to Los Angeles.

He'd left the city in a daze, his nerves frayed, his soul bruised and beat up by the chaos and confusion of that last day. He could still hear Phineas calling out for the State Attorney General and struggling against the cops with their handcuffs and billy clubs. Where was his friend now? He remembered the sight of Mrs. Harrelson pounding the pavement and tearing her hair until the newspapermen showed up, then she became all prim and proper, smiling and trying to look nice for the cameras. He saw himself in blackface, singing Shine's happy song, and it galled him. He winced everytime he unfolded the copy of *The Examiner* he had bought at the train station. No wonder Pee Wee had punched him. He had betrayed the dream that had brought him to Hollywood, and no one really knew why. All they knew was the half-truth they read in the damned newspaper, or the rumor Zeke set loose on Central Avenue. Thank God he had left before people recognized him and started calling him Rastus. That would have surely chased him out of the Dancing Bar-B-Que, if Henry didn't fire him first. No one knew the whole story and Skip hadn't stayed to tell his side. Had there been time, he might have asked Phineas to write a letter explaining everything, fill it full of big words and send it to all the newspapers. Then everybody would know the truth. Or maybe they'd just say it was some press agent's ploy to keep his name in the papers. It would make for great headlines: "Rastus' Defense"; "Rastus Heads Home For Dying Friend"; "Rastus Back In H'Wood To Ride Again." That would be life's supreme joke; his shame the source of his fame.

Sometimes, when the T.C. pulled slowly into a small town, he'd pull his mind away from Los Angeles and imagine the lives of the people who stood on the platforms, welcoming a returned love, or gazing with tenderness and sorrow on the face of their departing other. The sight of children waving from the rain-bent porches of lonely houses set down in the middle of nowhere sent his thoughts back to his own childhood. He'd been like them once, a barefoot boy looking up in wonder from a sun-beaten cottonfield, inventing stories for every hobo who waved from the doorway of a passing stock car. He'd caught one of those trains, ran it down and let it carry him away into the wild and wonderful world, where he followed his dream onto the back lots and neon-splashed streets of Hollywood, the desert around Victorville and the big houses along Sunset Boulevard. That was all behind him now. The dream had died a slow death, starting the moment his fist slammed into Kurt Marshall's gut and ending in the instant the newspaper cameras captured Rastus' moment of triumph. He felt exhausted, scoured clean of all the illusions he had brought to the City of the Angels. The emptiness was bewildering, yet strangely comforting. The conductor stopped by his seat.

"This one's you, buddy."

He nodded, his thoughts returning to Los Angeles. He'd left in a hurry. The hundred dollars was nearly gone. The train ticket took almost half; R.C. most of the rest. He'd made peace with Pee Wee, counted out the bills, handed them over and told his friend to pay off the debt. To Henry he scribbled a quick note: "Thank you for helping me. Maybe one day I'll get to explain." He left the Dancing Bar-B-Que, wishing he could have heard Diana's sassy voice one last time, shared a final drink with Phineas in some no-name Central Avenue bar, gone on one more midnight ramble, or called on Sapphire one more time to see if she'd let him take her and Buster picnicking by the Santa Monica Pier and in the evening, with the boy asleep, he'd see if she would let him hold her close, dance her across the room and sing "Stars Fell On Alabama." She was still there. Would her heart soften if he showed up on her doorstep, a wiser man? He still had a picture of the three of them a traveling photographer took one day in Griffith Park. If only there had been more time. The last day flew past him, the hours slipping through his fingers like running water. He didn't even get to walk inside Union Station. There was only time to pack, pay his bills and send Grandma Sarah a telegram: "I am coming."

Hurry back, Zeke said. They could cash in on the newspaper story, grab the world's tits with both hands and squeeze until the udder ran dry. Skip promised nothing. The dream was over. No use trying to put a good face on it. He'd rolled the dice and prayed to Lady Luck. She came up with heartbreak, told him: Peddle your story somewhere else. Hollywood ain't buying. And there were no angels waiting in the wings to fly in at the last minute and save the day. That only happened in the movies. It was time to pack up, catch the evening train and move on down the line, for a life precious to him would soon be over. That's what he thought about as the T.C.'s leaving whistle blew and the engine started huffing and there was a slight jerk before the train began its slow, gentle rocking out of the Santa Fe's old La Grande Station at First Street. Old Man Williams was calling him home. Half of his heart crumbled when the train rounded a bend and City Hall disappeared.

Now he was back in Tunis, feeling a twinge of regret, of sadness over the sight of forlorn, tar-paper shacks housing desperate, beaten down sharecroppers like Billie Dee Josephs, the out-houses leaning beneath the bleaching sun in this, his land of memory. But there were more memories now: Los Angeles' teeming streets, the big red streetcars rumbling along Central Avenue on a Thursday night. Those memories made Tunis seem utterly impoverished and deprived, a backwater lit by flickering kerosene lamps carried to dark, stinking privies. How had he lived here? How could he stay here now, his spirit even less at ease than when he had fled, his mind wracked at every turn by reminders of a fuller life, of freedoms forbidden in the land of Jim Crow. He grabbed his cardboard suitcase, picked up National Steel and walked to where the conductor slouched by an open door. The train slowed, its wheels grinding across the rails, clouds of smoke and steam spilling from the locomotive.

It was spring, the morning air fresh and surprisingly cool as he stepped onto the packed dirt beside the tracks and looked around for Grandma Sarah. She was not here. No one was here to comment on his return, or carry him to the old man's side. Tunis lay somnolent in the quiet before the arrival of Saturday's shoppers, its narrow streets empty. The Mo-Pac's whistle blew once, a long, high-pitched report carrying across the countryside like the wild call of a shrieking bird. Then the train pulled away, steel couplers wrenching and jerking, the engine laboring, getting up enough steam for the next stop down the line, Somerville, and after that, a slow ride to Houston.

When the last car had passed, Skip crossed the tracks and walked toward Main Street, eyes taking in the memorial of Colonel Artemis Willard astride a warrior steed, mind cycling back to the day Delta Slim and Scrapper had played beneath the still-hot sun of late summer, their blues carrying away that morning's brooding despair. Had that really happened only a few months ago? Had less than a year passed since he danced in Murphy's Emporium? It seemed a lifetime ago. He'd become someone else. Yet Tunis had not changed. It was still a drowsy little town, barely a speck on the map. He had thought it was bigger, not quite a city, or even a major crossroads like Somerville, but somehow larger. It had been his universe, his home. He walked the dusty, unpaved streets, looking as awkward and out of place as somebody's big-city, suit-wearing cousin. He felt at odds with everything he saw. The buildings were made of wood, covered with chipped and peeling whitewash. None stood taller than two stories. The heels of his polished Wellingtons scrapped across the nail heads sticking up out of the rough, wood-plank sidewalks.

He stopped when he saw an old childhood friend. Tommy Ray Jones, lean and raw-boned as ever, only now sporting a young man's thin moustache, approached, idling away the morning. Their eyes locked on each other for a moment, like gunfighters waiting to see who would make the first move. They could not smile or greet each other as long ago friends, could not pay some small homage to childhood comraderie. Tommy Ray kept on coming, looking through him, expecting him to step aside. Skip tensed, caught himself in mid-step turning away, because that's what he was supposed to do in Tunis. The act, so subtle and instinctive, had crept up on him, catching him off-guard, pushing aside the months that had passed. The ease with which he had almost slipped back into the old ways startled him. He put his foot down, turned and faced Tommy Ray. No use pretending he was the same Skip who had picked cotton and bent his will to the unnatural ways of Tunis. He'd changed, and wasn't about to step in the dirt for anyone. Tommy Ray drew near, looked him up and down, knowing he would move. They bumped shoulders. Tommy Ray stopped a step beyond him, turned:

"Say, boy," he said. "You supposed to step off and let me pass."

"Says who," Skip replied, setting his gear down on the wood planks. "Who said I got to step off?"

Tommy Ray stepped up to him, flinty blue eyes cold and mean, harsh breaths blowing around the bulge of tobacco in his jaw. "I said." They were almost touching, neither flinching, both waiting. The world seemed to hold its breath. Then Tommy Ray spoke again. "Just 'cause you been away don't mean you can come back and start acting uppity." He reached for Skip's lapel, but Skip stepped back, hands held up, ready.

"Watch yourself, now," he said. "You don't know me."

Tommy Ray hocked a reddish glob of spit and juice into the dirt. "I tell you one thing I do know, boy." He wiped his mouth with the back of his hand. "Them city clothes don't mean shit down here. You home now." He backed up, pointing his finger, saying, "Don't forget your place, boy. You home now."

Then he was gone, looking over his shoulder, mumbling. Skip walked on, worried. Tommy Ray had been easy. The next guy might want to fight.

He stopped outside the Rialto, tried to imagine going back to the "colored only" balcony, but could not. He'd acquired a new attitude and a cocky, hipster's walk. He grown big and strong on city food, city living and city ways. To stay here would be like trying to wear a suit he'd outgrown. A simple flexing of the shoulders, a bend at the knees, and the suit would rip apart. He'd forget where he was and sit next to one of the fans downstairs at the Rialto, forget to hang his head and call some halfwit ofay "sir." He could die here. His only hope was to hold on until the cotton was in, suck up his pride and make enough paydays to catch a leaving train to take him the hell out before he forgot he wasn't living on Central Avenue. He turned away from the Rialto, tapped out a Chesterfield and headed for Willie's layover spot. Somebody would be along soon enough to carry him back down Highway 53.

An hour passed before the old black '32 flatbed Ford came rocking and swaying up the road with Grandma Sarah riding shotgun, sticking her head out the window, waving and smiling. The Ford's horn squawked in celebration. He dropped his gear and ran. The truck swerved off the highway, skidded to a stop in a cloud of swirling dust. Grandma Sarah was out of the cab in an instant, running with open arms. She hugged him close, shook slightly as she smothered his face with wet kisses, half-crying, half-laughing.

"Thank you, Jesus. You brought him home, Lord. You brought him home." She held him at arm's length, long enough to get a good look at him, then pulled him close again. "Thank you, Lord. Thank you."

"Grandma Sarah," he said, surprised to find himself on the verge of happy tears. "You knew I was coming, didn't you? I sent the telegram. You knew I'd find a way."

"Yes, son," she said, sniffling. "I knew, but it's so good to see you, to have you back home."

Willie stood off to the side, tapping his pipe against his palm, looking on, waiting to join the reunion.

"Hey Willie!" Skip said, holding out one hand and slapping him on the back with the other. "How you been?"

"Mighty fine, Skip. Mighty fine, indeed. Glad to see you're still kicking."

"I heard that picking machine didn't work out."

"Yeah," Willie said, packing his pipe with Bull Durham. "Sometimes it be's like that. Looks like we'll need some extra hands this season. You still pick cotton?" He stepped back to admire Skip's charcoal gray double-breasted suit. "You looking pretty high-toned, like you fixing to promenade. Don't he look good, Aunt Sarah?"

"All the Reynolds men like to look sharp, Willie," Grandma Sarah said. "And I believe he done put on some weight too."

"Y'all leave me be," Skip said, embarrassed, but loving the sound of his home folk. "I bet I don't weigh a pound more than when I left, and I still got a pair of overalls."

"Sure you do," Willie said, puffing on his pipe. "And I bet you ain't worn them since the day you left." He turned to Grandma Sarah. "I believe Skip done gone and got citified on us."

"That may be, but his heart ain't changed. He came when I called."

"Did I come in time?" Skip said.

The smile left Grandma Sarah's face. "He's hanging on, but Lord knows his time ain't long. And I don't know what Miss Hattie is gon' do when he's gone. After all these years." Her voice trailed off. She shrugged and shook her head. "All those years, and the Lord never blessed her with any children to stand by her. She helped bring many a child into this world. Guess that's why she was put here. Well, let's get going. Old Man Williams is waiting."

On the way, Grandma Sarah filled him in on the latest news. John Lee's girl-baby was barely nine months old, and walking, saying something that sounded a lot like "mama." State folks came and took Willie Jean after Billie Dee found her lying on the railroad tracks, crying.

"What about the children?" Skip asked as they passed the empty, boarded-up house where Willie Jean had wailed her lamentation.

"Scattered to the four winds," Grandma Sarah said. "Just gone. Family took the younger ones. Those that could just struck out on their own, disappeared."

"Yeah," Willie broke in. "No more Masons around here."

"Poor kids," Skip said, his heart stinging from the acute loss he knew they felt.

"I wouldn't worry 'bout it too much," Grandma Sarah said. "They'll be alright, I reckon. The people that came and took them seemed like nice folks."

Willie stopped outside the old man's house, told Skip to drop by the juke if he had time. He'd seen Delta Slim and Scrapper over in Somerville. They said they might pass through to play a blues or two and see how he'd made out in Hollywood.

"Depends on Old Man Williams," Skip said. "I came to see him."

Willie nodded. "Well, I'll be seeing you. I got some folks to carry home from Sam Willard's."

Then he was gone, leaving Skip and Grandma Sarah staring into the darkness beyond the cabin's door. Miss Hattie stepped onto the porch, her tired red eyes showing she'd been crying. She tried to speak, but no words came, only the frail, choked breaths of an old woman struggling to understand the heartbreaking loss that was suddenly upon her. Her small body seemed to crumple beneath Skip's light embrace. She seemed incredibly fragile, birdlike, as if the slightest pressure would crush all that held her together. Skip cursed his inability to do more than hold her. He had no words of comfort, had not prepared for this assault of sorrow. He let her go. She staggered toward Grandma Sarah, thin arms reaching out. A whimpering sob escaped from her lips. Skip turned to the cabin's dim, quiet front room. It was as he'd remembered, only now a musty, stale smell of decay and death's slow approach hung thick in the air. A funereal gloom filled the space where once there had been joy. He tiptoed into the bedroom. The old man lay stretched out on a pallet, head propped on a feather pillow, eyes closed against the pale, yellow streams of sunlight filtering into the room. Leaning over the pallet, Skip gazed sadly upon the dying man who had delivered him from the dark terrors of his boyhood.

"Old Man Williams," he whispered.

"Skip," the old man's rheumy eyes fluttered. His lips formed a faint smile, pulled down on the right side by the stroke's paralysis. "Is that you?"

"Yeah, it's me."

He grabbed a chair, turned it around and straddled it, did all this as quietly as possible, as if too much sound would break the tenuous thread by which the old man clung to life. He reached out and stroked, softly, the head of white curls. It all seemed unreal. This was not the strong old man he'd remembered, or even the fearless soldier he'd imagined. A tired old man lay before him, wasted and worn out, helpless against the brutal, merciless ravages of the body turning upon itself. An empty bedpan, stained brown and yellow, rested next to the pallet. Was this what life came to? The vigorous body becomes a skeleton sheathed in aged, wrinkled skin whose reddish brown tone has turned ashen; the cheeks become hollow; the eyes, draining mucous and grayed by cataracts, are no longer luminous, but sink deep into their sockets. The tyranny of time had taken hold, turning the once-proud warrior into a near baby, incontinent, privates swaddled in a diaper. The hard lines of the old man's skull showed beneath the slack skin and dying muscle.

Skip looked away and saw a faded blue uniform, freshly starched and pressed hanging in the wardrobe. Three chevrons were stitched on the shoulder. Below them, a handmade buffalo patch told all that the man who wore this uniform was a Buffalo Soldier, a smoked Yankee of the 10th Colored Cavalry. He thought about his grandfather and his father, soldiers long gone, one taken in war, the other driven mad by war and the bitter irony of risking death for Europe's freedom, only to return from the bloody trenches and be denied the freedom to walk the streets in peace. Skip pushed words out of his mouth to break the painful silence.

"I . . . I came as soon as I could."

"I know you did, son," the old man whispered. "Your grandma told me you were coming. I wanted to hear what happened to that old catfish." He tried to laugh and raise up on his left elbow.

Skip shook his head, pressed him back against the pallet. "No, no. You rest now."

"Rest?" the old man laughed. "Plenty rest where I'm going." He slumped back and sighed. "Did I ever tell you 'bout that day on San Juan Hill, the day your granddaddy died?"

Skip nodded, picturing the Cuban battlefield.

"I thought that was my dying day," said Old Man Williams. "Bullets were flying everywhere. I could hear `em, zipping and buzzing like bees. One nicked my ear. `Georgie-boy,' your grandpa said. `You won't hear the next one.' Sam never heard the one that got him. It hit him in the head, spun him around like you spin a nickel on a table. I ran to him, but I could see it was bad and that there wasn't no use yelling for a surgeon. I just held him in my arms. I cried that day, son. Looking down on your granddaddy, his blood running all over my fingers. I cried like a baby. `Sam, I said. Oh Sam. I promised Miss Sarah I'd look after you.' He turned his head. Their eyes met. "Look after Miss Hattie."

"I will," Skip said, knowing he was lying. Looking after Miss Hattie meant staying in Tunis, which he was not going to do. Yet the lie did not seem like a lie at all, but a bit of consolation offered to a dying friend.

He heard Miss Hattie crying on the porch, heard her and heard Grandma Sarah's comforting voice sounding just above a whisper, saying: "Hush now, Miss Hattie. Hush now."

Let her cry, he thought. Now was not the time for strength, for the trembling lip holding back sorrow's flood. Now was the time for her to feel keenly the cold pain and hurt of her man's passing, feel it down into her marrow, feel it and the secret desire to join him, for without him life would be an empty succession of days spent with constant reminders of his having passed—the odd sag of the feather mattress they had shared; the smell of him on the sheets; the heart-rending absence of his touch, his hands that though wrinkled and palsied still stroked her cheeks with heavenly tenderness; the vanished beating of a heart she'd felt through his nightshirt as they lay coupled in sleep. Now was the time for tears, for the mourning of two score and ten years spent together, for the loss of love. Let her tears flow. Let her wail, for this was the last of Old Man Williams. There would be time enough in the grim days to come, time for the final accounting, time for remembering, time to hush. But not now. Lord, God, not now. Let her cry.

The old man spoke again, bravely, without fear. "Guess they getting the cooling board ready." A death-rattle cough overcame his bitter laugh. "Oh, Lord." Spittle formed at the corners of his mouth and bubbled between his lips.

Skip wiped the stuff away with his fingers, turned his chair around and leaned forward. The old man's time was short. He knew it. That last cough scared him. He'd almost yelled for Miss Hattie. But the old man was still holding on. He pulled the soiled tobacco pouch from the inside pocket of his suit coat. With trembling hand he tapped the last few cuts of leaf into a rolling paper, carefully twisted a slender cigarette, then struck a match.

The old man smiled, sniffed the air, turned his head to catch the familiar scent of tobacco cured the way he knew how. His feeble hands lifted an inch or two off the pallet, then fell back. Skip placed the cigarette between the old man's dry lips, held it there. Old Man Williams puffed, his rasping breaths quick, short, shallow.

"Thank you, Skip," he said, hacking and trying to clear his throat. "I ain't smoked in quite while. Figured you'd have smoked all of my stuff by now."

"I was saving the last bit for us."

Again the immense, frightening silence, Skip tried to smile and shake off the gloom, but it was no good. An oppressive sense of foreboding gripped him. Death was in this room. He had come half-way across the country to be here because he knew he could not stay in Los Angeles knowing the old man was dying. But now that he was here, he wanted to be somewhere else. He barely had the strength to see the old man like this, body half-limp. It scared him to think that one day he too would come to this miserable end. Better to go when you're still standing, he thought, taking a long pull on the cigarette. Better that than this slow decline, this awful knowing that death was standing by, ready to walk you down that lonesome road. He held the smoke to the old man's lips, let it rest a moment in the left corner.

"Why'd you come?" asked Old Man Williams.

"Grandma Sarah told me your time was coming. She said you asked for me."

"I never expected to see you," he said, and turned his face away for a moment. Then he turned back to Skip. "It's good to see you, son."

Skip stood and swung the chair around, sat down and leaned forward. He grabbed Old Man Williams' hands. "It's good to see you, too. And I wanted to thank you."

"Thank me? For what?"

"For saving me back when I was kid, knocking some sense into me when I needed it."

The old man shook his head. "I was only doing what any man with half a heart would do for a hurting child. Besides, that promise I made your granddaddy included you."

"That don't mean I cain't thank you. Besides, you taught me to play guitar."

The old man's trembling lips sagged into the faintest smile. "I sure 'nuff taught you how to play the blues, didn't I?" He pointed his good hand toward the cigarette.

Skip gave him the final puff, then snuffed out the smoke. The old man turned his head to him. "What all did you do out there? Did you learn anything?"

"Hah," Skip said. "I had me a time." He sat pensive, thinking, rubbing his hands together, wondering where to start. "Almost got myself killed in Fort Worth. Wasn't nothing but fool's luck that saved me. Boy, I sure thought I was hot stuff when I set out, but I was about as shaky as a new-born colt."

"Or a catfish that didn't know no better," said Old Man Williams.

"Touche," Skip said, laughing. "You ever heard that word before? Touche. Frenchmen use it, least that's what Phineas T. Weatherby told me, and he'd know about such things. He graduated from college." Skip paused to light a Chesterfield. "I'll tell you, folks'll get you all turned around inside, Old Man Williams. They'll have you believing any damn thing because you're all hopped up on a dream and don't want to let it go. So you start lying to yourself, thinking that might help things come your way. What is it that circus man said? There's a sucker born every minute. Well, I been a sucker, done stuff I ain't proud of. Got dressed up like a blackface clown and sang, 'Dey all calls me Shine.' Made a hundred dollars." He nodded, seeing Old Man Williams' raised eyebrows. "That's how I got here. You can make good money being a fool. Remember that acting school I was all hot about? Damn thing wasn't even real. It was just another tit for old Zeke Washington to squeeze out a little bit of money from suckers like me. Found me a good girl. Got her picture right here." He reached into his coat pocket. "There she is. Sapphire. And that's her boy, Buster."

Old Man Williams raised his head and squinted. "Oooh, Lord, she's a pretty one."

"Yeah, but she ain't mine no more. I lost her on account of my own damn foolishness."

"Cain't you get her back?"

Skip shook his head. "I done tried. Last time I seen her she had a college boy on her arm. She wasn't studying me."

"A woman's funny that way. She probably came around to see if you still want to be in the running. And since you're carrying around that picture, I reckon you do. Well," the old man paused and raised up again. "Do you?"

"Hell, yeah, if she'd have me back. But my life out there is all gone. I gave up my job. What would I do if I went back to Los Angeles?"

"Same stuff you did the first time, only better." He nodded toward the picture. "You ought to buy her a sapphire. It's a shiny little stone, almost like a diamond. Put it on a ring or a necklace. And what about that little boy? You ain't gon' leave him to a college man are you? Those book learners don't have enough mother wit to raise a child right."

"I don't know, Old Man Williams. She'll probably be done moved on by the time I get back, if I get back. Sure would be nice, though. That boy took to me like I was his kin. I kind-a had a soft spot for him." He sat back and puffed on his Chesterfield. "Yeah, I made out alright, I reckon. Still got some learning to do." He leaned forward, his voice excited. "I heard a guy name of Charlie Christian play an electric guitar, jazz style, full of blues. Turned me all around."

The old man mumbled. "'Lectric gee-tar?"

Skip nodded. "He said that's the way guitar playing is going. Only us country folk'll be doing the old-time stuff. I was thinking `bout buying me one of them guitars, see if I can turn some of these old blues around. I ain't no actor. I'm a guitar player. You should hear me now, even got me a little singing voice." He paused. "I bet I could make a go at being a guitar player. I had people cheering back at the Dancing Bar-B-Que."

"Listen to you," said Old Man Williams. "Talking 'bout jazz and 'lectric gee-tars." The fingers of his right hand twitched uncontrolled, the nerve lines shot, while his left hand moved slowly through a picking pattern only he could hear.

"You know something else?" Skip said. "Now I know you know this, but I'm gon' tell you, just so's you can see I learned a few other things out there. The world is a mean place, too tough for some folks. Gal out there killed herself. And nobody batted an eye. You got to keep your wits about you. I learned that too. Got to keep your wits." He slumped back in the chair, feeling tired enough to sleep for days.

"Skip." Old Man Williams turned to face him. "I want you to do something for me."

"Anything," Skip replied. "You just name it."

"Go back."

"To Los Angeles? But you done already asked me to look after Miss Hattie."

"I know, I know. But your grandma'll take care of her. Son, you got to leave. You're too big for this mudhole. I know how hard it is to try to fit back in after you done seen some of the world."

Skip nodded, thinking about his run-in with Tommy Ray Jones. "I was figuring on staying 'round till the cotton was in. I'd have enough money by then to head out."

The old man shook his head. "I don't want you going back in them fields, Skip. That's behind you. Listen," he raised a feeble hand and beckoned Skip to lean closer. He touched Skip's face, stared into his eyes. It seemed all their years passed between them. "There's some money in the bank in Somerville. Take what you need." Skip started to say, 'No,' but the old man grabbed one of his hands, gripped it with a strength Skip thought the stroke had stolen. "Do as I say, son. There's nothing here for you. Go back to Los Angeles. Help that gal raise that boy. Pass along some of what I gave you." He slumped back against the pillow. "Pass some of me along," he said, his voice fading to a whisper. "Can you play me a song? Not a sad one. Something with a smile to it, and tell me `bout that catfish."

Skip walked outside, death's shadow beside him. The sun's bright glare blinded him, and he staggered against the door, weak, as much from the sudden explosion of light as from the aching pain that made it seem his heart was about to implode. Spears of sunlight shot off pieces of broken glass by the roadside. Song birds perched and sang in a chinaberry tree, their gay chirping sounding odd, bewildering. They were carrying on like this was the finest day God ever made. And it was an exquisite creation, glorious blue sky streaked with high clouds, the air unbelievably clean, the freshly turned earth smelling of renewal. He breathed deep, filling his lungs. The old man was right. He could not stay here, but did that mean he should go back to Los Angeles? What if he did and things were worse than when he left? What then?

Grandma Sarah looked up from where she sat on the porch, arms wrapped around Miss Hattie, her hands patting the older woman's shoulders in the gentle, soothing manner of a mother whose child has come in screaming and undone by the careless ways of the world. For a moment she seemed Christ-like, sitting there, opening her heart without complaint to take on the grief of another, to make the pain her own, but the pleading gaze in her eyes said: "Help me. I cannot bear this alone." Skip went to her, bent down on one knee to embrace her and Miss Hattie. Sitting inside the dark room had been torture. More than once he had wanted to escape. Yet now he knew those were merely childish thoughts. He must stay here and bear witness to the last of Old Man Williams. He started crying from all the sorrow that had built up inside him.

"He was a good man, Miss Hattie," whispered Grandma Sarah. "A good man."

"Was?" Skip pulled away and stood up. "Was? He is a good man, Grandma Sarah. Is, and he's not going to die. He's not . . ."

He knew he was talking crazy. Old Man Williams was dying. Everybody knew it. Just as surely as the sun would set and the moon would rise, Old Man Williams would die, maybe today, and in His own appointed time, so too would Miss Hattie, Grandma Sarah, himself. All would pass away because death don't have no mercy.

He grabbed National Steel. The old man wanted a song, something with a little fun to it, laughter to chase away these time of dying blues. And that's what Skip was going to give him, the best song he could think of, played the best way he could. But this wasn't how it was supposed to be, Old Man Williams an invalid, barely holding on, while he assumed the role of the strong one who would live on, carrying the legacy of this life – country blues, and Buffalo Soldiers fighting for Uncle Sam. They were supposed to be sitting on the porch, watching the big old red ball sun go down slow as they passed a smoke between themselves and drank sugared tea, the old man listening to his big city stories about Hollywood and Central Avenue, Phineas T. Weatherby selling homemade potions from a soap box in Pershing Square. Then they would get down to the business of picking some blues, Skip following the old man's lead, putting in single-note flourishes, showing off jazzy riffs he'd stolen from Charlie Christian. That's how it was supposed to be.

Why was life always throwing changes at you, the curveball high and outside when you expected the fastball right over the plate? Just when you thought you had it licked and a home run was coming your way, life jumped up and all you hit was air. You struck out. Or you got hit from the blind side, knocked silly and left groggy, wondering, What the hell? You helped somebody without really thinking about it and got beat up for your good deed, saved somebody who'd bad-mouthed you without fail, and for that you got your picture in the newspaper, you standing there in makeup you swore you'd never wear, standing there with a woman who'd called you out and a hustler who thought the whole world was a milk-heavy tit, all of you together, them smiling, you frowning through a clown's smile, staring into a news photographer's camera. **RASTUS TO THE RESCUE**. Rastus? Was that you, who had wanted to exalt your people, but instead left them scratching their heads, looking at a newspaper picture and wondering, 'Who is that Negro'? That was the kind of trick life played on you. It seemed living was like a shell game with life doing the shuffling, calling out the sing-song chant—*The hand is quicker than the eye. Listen to me, now. I tell you no lie. You got to watch close, 'cause I sure ain't slow. Come on, now, give it a try*—and you steady watching until it was your turn and you knew, just knew which shell hid the pea. But you really didn't know. You'd blinked, and that was long enough for life. The shell you picked held nothing, was empty as a forgotten, deserted office on Central Avenue. That's how life was, sometimes. But it wasn't all bad. You lost your parents and gained an old man and a grandmother who together lifted you back into the world; you walked a God forsaken stretch of desert highway and got picked up by a stranger who took you to the City of the Angels, which was where you needed to be after all, and this stranger became a friend who taught you about fine vines and midnight rambles, taught you the hipster's walk and the hipster's talk until you could say, "Awreet-awroonie. Slip that tea-stick to me," and mean it. A merciless biddy kicked you out of your apartment and into the arms of a fast-talking, sometime salesman with a quick smile and a head full of words arranged in ways you'd never heard before. That's what life did. So, maybe this was how it was supposed to be, you sitting beside the deathbed, waiting for the old man's ghost to rise up and enter you so you could carry on all that he had been and all that those before him had been. Maybe this was just life working through its eternal, mysterious rhythm, teaching you, if you had sense enough to learn.

"What you gon' play?" Old Man Williams said, raspy voice barely a whisper.

"Something I been messing with." He strummed the guitar.

Old Man Williams winced. "The G string. It's sharp. Cain't you hear it?"

Skip strummed again, leaned his head toward the neck as he plucked the G and B strings. They were close, but the old man was right. "Always did have trouble with that one." He loosened the G.

"Little more," said Old Man Williams, listening, sounding the note with his dying voice.

Skip nudged the G string down once more, then hit the harmonic. They smiled, and together said: "It's got to sound right to play right."

"Now, play me a song," Old Man Williams said.

And he started, his thumb bouncing against the bass strings to get the rhythm going, fingers joining in, adding the melody, then a fancy break with a diminished chord. He emptied his head of everything, except the good old ragtime blues played and sang the way Old Man Williams had taught him.

"Well the catfish, he was swimming, lazy in the deep blue sea.

Got hooked one day and cried, Lord what's gon' become of me.

Now the Lord, he looked down, at that catfish on dry land.

Said, stand up son, and walk like a natural man."

Epilogue

B USTER SAW HIM THE MOMENT HE STEPPED OUT OF THE PLYMOUTH coupe that had pulled up to the driveway. The little boy pushed open the screen door and started singing, his brown eyes lighting up at the sight of his old friend, "Mister Skip! Mister Skip! I want bar-que," he said, toddling towards him.

"Hey, Little B." Skip said, running to scoop up the child. He held him close for a moment, tickled him and made him laugh. "Where's your mama?"

Barely two weeks had passed since he had left Los Angeles. Old Man Williams was gone, but Skip had kept his promise and done as he was told. He took one hundred dollars from the old man's account, hopped a freight train to Houston, then a bus to the coast. Grandma Sarah said it was the right thing to do and made him promise to bring Sapphire and Buster back home to Tunis, if that was the Lord's will. Pee Wee almost dropped a carburetor when he saw him walking up to the filling station, guitar in hand, casual as ever. He told Skip that Central Avenue had gone nuts about him after the parade. Everybody was asking, "Where's Rastus?" Folks said he was a hero. Skip laughed when he heard that. Hero? Hell, he wasn't none of that. He was just trying to live up to what he'd been taught, trying to be a good man without making too much of a mess. And right now he had one that needed cleaning up. He set Buster

M. DION THOMPSON

down and slowly walked him toward the cottage, where Sapphire stood just outside the doorway, arms folded. She watched them come up the driveway side by side, like they belonged together. Skip took a deep breath to calm himself and accept whatever happened. He stopped at the edge of the porch and gave Buster a tap on the behind to send him back to Sapphire.

"How you been?" he said, wishing he didn't feel so damn awkward, hoping she'd say something warm and kind, something to let him know their war was over, that there was a chance to reclaim the peace they had known.

"Look, mommy," Buster said. "Mister Skip. Can we have bar-que with Mister Skip?"

"Well, baby." She kneeled down and straightened his shirt. "We'll just have to ask him." Sapphire stood and held Skip's gaze for a few moments, long enough to let him know she wasn't going to fall as easy as Buster. "Mister Skip," she said, then let go, her voice relaxing into a smile. "It's nice to see you. Would you like to take this little man for some bar-b-que?"

"I'd love to," he said. "And I know just the place. Best ribs in town." He reached for her hand. "Hungry?"

Sapphire nodded, and in that moment, Skip knew they could start again, a bit wiser this time, but with hearts still open. He turned and waved to Pee Wee, who shifted the Plymy into first and pulled away, giving his horn three playful toots as he headed toward Central Avenue, leaving the three of them together to share in the wonder of life.